DESERT FIRE

"M'lady, a Muslim wife never walks beside her husband. She stays several paces behind him, with her head bowed."

"Wife?" Lorna asked in a shocked voice. "Are you saying that we're posing as husband and wife?"

"We certainly are. Muslim women don't travel unless they are accompanied by their husbands, or perhaps their fathers, and I certainly don't look like your father, do I?" Nathan smiled mischievously. "Now, bow your head and follow me."

"The devil I'll bow my head!"

"I know you're unaccustomed to showing humility of any kind," Nathan said dryly, "but I'm afraid you're going to have to follow the Muslim customs."

"Well, I'm not a Muslim! I won't bow my head, and I won't walk behind you. I'm not your slave!"

Nathan's hard gaze roved over her body and landed on her heaving breasts. "Oh, yes, you are, for as long as we remain in the desert."

Also by Joanne Redd

TO LOVE AN EAGLE
CHASING A DREAM

DESERT BRIDE

Joanne Redd

A DELL BOOK

Published by
Dell Publishing
a division of
Bantam Doubleday Dell Publishing Group, Inc.
666 Fifth Avenue
New York, New York 10103

ISBN: 0-440-20224-8

Printed in the United States of America
Published simultaneously in Canada

June 1989

10 9 8 7 6 5 4 3 2 1

KRI

*For my sister, Mary Ann, whose
strength of character, steadfastness,
and warmth endear her to all and make
her so richly deserving.*

Prologue

Lorna Winters walked to the ship's railing and looked out at the vast ocean, saying a silent prayer of thanks that she was still alive. Last night she hadn't thought she would live to see another day's dawning. The sudden, violent storm that had hit slightly after dusk had terrified her as she had lain in the dark in her small cabin, the sound of the wind shrieking like a demented woman, thunder rolling and lightning crashing, the ship thrashing wildly about, and the timbers groaning and creaking ominously from the tremendous beating the small vessel was taking from the monstrous waves. At that time she had been certain the ship would break apart and she would meet a watery death in the cold, dark depths of the Atlantic, a seemingly cruel twist of fate—that she would die at the tender age of nineteen, just when she had barely escaped imprisonment and dared to hope that her anxiously awaited new life was finally beginning.

Somewhere during the long, agonizing night she had fallen into an exhausted sleep, and she had awaked this morning to discover that the storm had passed and the ship had not sunk after all. She had rushed topside, as if only by seeing with her own eyes could she confirm this miracle. Now, standing there at the rail with the brisk wind ruffling her auburn curls and the ocean sparkling beneath the bright sunlight, her spirits rose and burst from her in a laugh of immense relief.

Lorna took a minute to enjoy the beauty around her: the crystal clarity of the air; the tangy, salty smell of the sea; the silence. All were new to her. London, where she had spent her entire lifetime, was a gloomy, dirty city where the stale smells hovered in the air and the noises of the teeming metropolis infringed upon the quietness of even the most well-built homes.

Despite the beauty of the sea and her relief at finding herself alive after her close brush with death, nagging doubts still preyed at the back of her mind. Maybe she wasn't safe after all. Maybe she'd still be arrested and imprisoned and never have the life she had looked forward to for so long. Jamaica was a British possession. Would the authorities search for her there? Even though she had given an assumed name when she boarded the ship and had passed herself off to the others as a merchant's daughter going to the island to visit her married sister, this was the only convoy that had left London that day. Would they seek her out, using only her description to find her? And even if they didn't, when she reached Jamaica, what was she going to use to live on until she could find employment—providing she could find a job without references. She'd had to spend every shilling she had for her first-class cabin. Damn, if she couldn't find a ship sailing for the United States, then why couldn't she at least have found one with steerage passage? Not only was she a fugitive from the law, but she was destitute too.

Lorna's gloomy thoughts were interrupted by a high, female voice whose shrillness made her cringe. "Captain Morris! Where is our naval escort? And where is the rest of the convoy?"

Lorna glanced quickly about her. Where were the other ships in the convoy? She turned from the railing to see the captain, looking weary and harassed, rushing down the deck to the woman who had summoned him. Lady Hampton stood in front of the companionway from which she had just emerged, flanked on one side by the only other passengers on board: a portly West Indies planter and his middle-aged wife.

The captain swept his cap from his graying head, saying to Lady Hampton, "I'm afraid we were blown away from the rest of the convoy last night, m'lady."

"Blown away?" the planter asked in alarm. "Are you saying we're out here all alone? With no protection?"

"Only for the time being," the captain reassured them. "My men are on the lookout for the rest of the convoy right now."

Lorna followed the upward sweep of the captain's hand, seeing the two sailors hanging from the yards of the mainmast as they craned their necks to look about them. A third, high on the eagle's nest above them, was peering out at the ocean with a long spyglass.

"Where are we, Captain? Or do you even know?" Lady Hampton asked in a scathing voice.

"Yes, m'lady," the captain answered in a clipped voice, "I do know where we are. We're off the coast of Africa."

"Africa?" Lady Hampton asked in surprise. "We were blown that far off our course?"

"Yes, m'lady," the captain answered tightly.

"But we were supposed to dock at Cadiz tonight," Lady Hampton objected.

"I'm beating my way north as fast as I can, m'lady. Using every inch of canvas at my disposal. We may . . . or may not reach Cadiz by nightfall. We're sailing into a brisk wind and—"

"I don't want to hear any of your excuses, Captain!" Lady Hampton snapped, cutting across his words. "My ship sails from Cadiz for Naples tomorrow morning and I expect to be on it. If I miss that sailing, you can be sure the Lord Admiral will hear about your incompetence. Getting us separated from the convoy is inexcusable!"

Lorna saw the captain's eyes flash at Lady Hampton's insult. She didn't blame him for being angry. The rude, haughty woman infuriated her, too. She was the typical aristocrat, spoiled, self-centered, demanding, expecting everyone to bow and scrape to her. Oh, yes, Lorna knew the nobility only too well, and she'd had a bellyful of them. She may have had to tolerate their domineering and snobbish ways in the past, but she didn't have to here. Nor would she ever again! Lorna stepped forward and said angrily, "You have no right to blame Captain Morris for what has happened, Lady Hampton. The storm was an act of God, and I for one am thankful that I'm still alive. For all you know the entire convoy—save us—may be at the bottom of the ocean right now. We may owe our lives to the very man you are accusing so unjustly."

Lady Hampton glared at Lorna while Captain Morris shot Lorna a quick smile, wondering how two women could look so much alike and yet be so totally different in temperament. Standing across from each other, the two looked almost identical—tall, slimly built, stately, their eyes and hair the exact same color. Everyone on the ship had noticed the remarkable resemblance and commented on it, something that obviously displeased Lady Hampton, who felt herself much above the merchant's daughter. As the days passed, Captain Morris had seen the subtle differences in the two women's appearance. Besides being a few years older, Lady Hampton had a cruel glint in her violet eyes that Lorna's lacked, although the younger woman's eyes were now flashing just as angrily. And there was a petulant droop to the noblewoman's mouth that told of her spoiled, pampered existence. No, even though the two looked enough alike to be twins, they were as different as night and day.

At that moment everyone's attention was drawn by the call "Sail, ho!" from the eagle's nest.

Captain Morris slammed his cap back on his head, stepped to the railing, and looked up, calling, "Where?"

"Two points off starboard, Cap'n!"

Taking the spyglass that his first mate handed him, the captain walked rapidly to the front of the ship, while Lorna, the passengers, and the first mate followed anxiously behind him.

"Perhaps it's the escort come to search for us," Lorna suggested hopefully.

Looking through the spyglass at the speck in the distance, the captain knew such was not the case. Naval escorts didn't go searching for ships that had gotten lost by lagging behind or had been separated from the other ships by a storm. Their job was to protect the convoy, the group of ships, and it was left up to the individual captain to see that his vessel stayed with the others. But the captain didn't want to tell his passengers that. He didn't want to frighten them any more than they already were. Realizing he couldn't distinguish the ship's lines from this distance, and thereby, he hoped, identify its nationality, the captain snapped the spyglass closed and called up to the sailor in the eagle's nest, "What colors is she flying?"

"Can't see any colors yet, Cap'n. But she looks like a sloop."

Lorna sensed the apprehension in the captain and the entire crew as they all stared out at the speck in the distance. If it wasn't the escort coming for them —for the captain had almost pointedly ignored her suggestion—then what country did the ship belong to? Could it be a French vessel? But they were at war with France! The entire Atlantic was swarming with their privateers. That was the reason for the naval escort, to protect the merchant ships. Not knowing if the sloop was friend or foe, her nerves began to crawl.

"She's flying the Union Jack, Cap'n!" the sailor aloft cried in obvious relief. "And she's carrying cannon. Must be one of our privateers."

Lorna felt a wave of relief wash over her. She watched as the ship sailed closer and closer, then frowned when she noticed that the sloop was bearing down on them hard. What in the world was wrong with that captain, she wondered with alarm. Why, it looked as if he was going to ram them!

Then suddenly the sloop coming down on them veered and presented its broadside. Lorna saw a puff of smoke and heard the roar of a cannon. She watched, dumbfounded, as the ball sailed across the water and splashed into the ocean by the bow of their ship.

"Those damn fools are firing at us!" the first mate cried out in shock.

"They're lowering their colors, Cap'n!" the sailor in the eagle's nest called in alarm.

Lorna watched in stunned disbelief as the Union Jack fluttered down on the sloop and a strange striped flag was raised in its place.

"My God!" Captain Morris exclaimed, sucking in his breath sharply. "They're Barbary pirates!"

At the captain's words every muscle in Lorna's body tensed and her heart raced. She knew that of all the pirates who roamed the seas, those who operated from the protected ports of Morocco, Algeria, Tunisia, and Tripoli—the Barbary States on the northern coast of Africa—were the most feared, notorious for their cruelty and brutality and their barbarous slave trade.

"But why are they attacking us?" the first mate asked when he recovered from his shock. "Our government has paid its tribute to their bloody deys."

"Yes, it must be a mistake," the planter joined in. "Surely when you show them your pass, Captain, they'll let us go."

"The hell they will!" Captain Morris spat. "Those heathen devils mean to take us as a prize—and passes and tribute be damned!"

At that moment a second ball flew across the water and hit the bowsprit with a loud, cracking noise, sending mast, sails, and rigging splashing into the water as the small ship shook from the impact of the blow. If there had been any doubt in anyone's mind, the shot made the pirates' intent perfectly clear.

"Bring down the colors and reef the sails!" the captain yelled urgently to his crew.

As the sailors scrambled frantically up the masts to obey, Lady Hampton asked in a shocked voice, "You're surrendering?"

"That's exactly what I intend to do, m'lady," the

captain answered, looking her straight in the eye. "And the sooner, the better."

Lady Hampton went rigid with fury. "Why you coward! You should stand and fight!"

"With what?" Captain Morris snapped back. "There're ten men in my crew, and there are at least two hundred on that ship. They're armed with muskets and pikes and swords, to say nothing of their cannons. What would I fight them with, m'lady? The little swivel gun I carry on my deck and the old rusty sword I keep in my cabin? This is a merchantman, not a naval ship."

Lorna glanced over at the sloop. The ship was close enough now that she could see the muzzles of the squatty cannons poking through the gunports. But it was the sight above deck that brought terror to her heart. The pirates were swarming up the masts and hanging from the yards, their long, flowing robes billowing in the wind as they aimed their long muskets down at the British ship. Below them in the waist of the ship, over a hundred bearded, turbaned corsairs waited to board with pikes, swords, and grappling hooks held ready in their hands. "Isn't there anything you can do?" she asked the captain, her voice made sharp by her fear. "Can't we at least make a run for it?"

"I'm afraid not. That sloop is three times as fast as this ship. Besides, they've already got us in cannon range. If we tried that, they'd blow us clean out of the water."

The captain glanced back over his shoulder at the pirate ship, then looked at the frightened passengers and said in an urgent rush of words, "Go below to your cabins. When the pirates come, don't show them your fear. And whatever you do, don't resist them.

They'll strip you of your valuables and your clothing—"

The planter's wife and Lorna gasped in shock, while Lady Hampton possessively clutched the necklace at her throat, her jewels apparently much more valuable to her than her virtue. "No, ladies. They won't ravish you," the captain said quickly. "They won't harm you unless you fight them. The personal possessions of those aboard the prize are all the pirates themselves can lay claim to. The ship, everything in the hold, even the captives themselves belong to their dey. After they have stripped you, if there is any way you think your relatives and friends can possibly raise the ransom they'll demand, tell them so. It might save you from the slave block."

The planter and his wife exchanged horrified looks, both knowing that their relatives and friends could never raise the ransom for the two of them. The woman burst into sudden tears, and her ashen-faced husband took her in his arms, trying desperately to comfort her with anguished, meaningless mutterings.

Lorna was no less terrified. She knew what happened to the pirates' captives if the ransom they demanded wasn't paid, and there was no one, absolutely no one, to pay her ransom. The color drained from her face.

Realizing that the pirates were almost upon them, the captain said in a firm voice, "Now go below. Quickly! They'll be boarding any minute now, and I don't want anyone inadvertently injured."

Again Lorna glanced over at the pirate ship, seeing that her sails were now reefed and the men rowing in her galley were bringing the ship closer and closer, the rhythmic splashing of the oars marking the last moments of her freedom. Tears sprang to her eyes as a bitterness surged in her. For the second time in twenty-four hours it seemed that fate was dealing her a cruel blow. Then, as the middle-aged couple turned and stumbled away, still locked in their anguished embrace, Lorna turned with grim resignation and numbly followed them to the companionway.

"This is an outrage, Captain!" Lady Hampton shrieked. "I demand that you stop them!"

The captain shot the woman a look of mixed disgust and pity, then turned to his first mate, saying, "Take Lady Hampton below. Then bring me my manifest."

The mate hesitated, reluctant to touch the angry woman glaring at him and still feeling a little stunned by the sudden turn of events. "Hurry, man!" the captain barked. "They're almost upon us!"

In her small cabin belowdecks Lorna sat on her bunk stiffly and wondered desperately if there wasn't some way she could escape, someplace she could hide. But where? If she had seen the pirates, they must have seen her. They knew she was on board someplace, and undoubtedly they would search every inch of the ship to find her. No, there would be no escaping this time. She wished she had jumped overboard while she'd had the opportunity. She'd rather drown than go to a harem or a brothel to satisfy some filthy man's lust or face a lifetime of slavery under some cruel Arab master. Even imprisonment in England looked better than the fate she was facing.

Lorna heard the first mate struggling to force Lady Hampton down the hallway outside her door, the irate noblewoman's angry, shrill curses grating on Lorna's already jangled nerves. Lorna longed to scream for her to shut up. She had no right to be that upset. Her ransom would be paid. Damn, Lorna thought, why couldn't she have been born rich like that hateful woman? Why was it the poor who always had to suffer?

The slam of the door as the first mate shoved the noblewoman into her cabin before he ran back down the hall was followed by the sudden lurch of the ship as the pirate sloop bumped against the British vessel. Lorna strained her ears, hearing the metallic clatter of the grappling hooks, the victorious Arabian cries as the pirates swarmed over the rails, the drumming of feet on the deck above her and then in the hallway outside her door. What if the captain's wrong? Lorna thought wildly. What if they rape me? Or what if they just kill me? Icy fear clawed at her vitals and her throat turned dry. She sat with her eyes glued to the door, every nerve in her body strung taut with intense dread.

She heard the door in the next cabin bang open and Lady Hampton screaming furious curses. A split second later the door to Lorna's cabin was suddenly flung wide. A dark-skinned, bearded pirate stood before her, naked except for the full white pantaloons that covered his lower body, the jewel in his turban and his raised, razor-sharp scimitar glittering in the sunlight from the open portal. Terrified, Lorna jumped to her feet and backed to the wall behind her, pinned there by the pirate's gleaming black eyes and his cruel leer.

Oh, God, Lorna thought, her legs quaking and her heart drumming wildly in her chest. What will happen to me now?

Chapter 1

The United States consul, Gilbert Graves, closed the door to his private office behind him and stood, allowing his eyes to adjust to the dim light of the room before he walked to the desk across from him and set his papers down on it. Gazing out the arched window that overlooked the walled courtyard, he longed to be out there under the cool shade of the fig and citrus trees, for the heat inside was still oppressive, even though the beastly sun was setting and the temperature was finally dropping.

The sound of the evening call to prayer being shouted by the muezzin from the minaret of the mosque a few streets away drifted in the air. *"Lalahaula-'elah. Mohammandun rasculu-'elah."* There is no God but Allah. Muhammad is the messenger of Allah.

A hush fell over Tunis as the Muslims fell to their knees to pray, and the consul relished the sudden quiet. Then he stiffened, sensing that there was someone in the room with him. The hair on the nape of his neck rose and his blood ran cold, for assassinations were a daily occurrence in this part of the world, where a man eliminated his political foes by having them murdered. Deciding that he would rather face death than have a knife slipped into his back, the consul whirled around. Then, seeing the man lounging negligently in the high-backed chair, he went weak with relief.

"For God's sake, Nathan!" the consul said testily. "Must you sneak around like some thief in the night? You scared me half out of my wits."

"When I received word that you wanted to see me, I assumed President Jefferson had another mission for me and that you would prefer I not use your front door," Captain Nathan Sloan answered calmly. He shrugged his broad shoulders and stretched his long, muscular legs out before him, crossing them at his booted ankles before continuing. "So I came in through your window, since your back door was locked."

The consul admitted to the wisdom of the captain's cautious entry. Undoubtedly both the pasha and the dey had spies watching the consulate, as they did every foreign consulate in Tunis—and probably half the homes of the influential Tunisian citizens, too, for the Arabs trusted each other even less. But his fright had left him feeling shaky, to say nothing of the uneasy feeling he always experienced in the enigmatic captain's company. With his exceptional height, his superb athlete's body, and his cool, commanding air, Nathan Sloan was a man who intimidated other men with his presence alone. And then there was that tightly controlled savagery that the consul sensed lurked just below the surface of the man. Not even

the fierce-fighting Janissaries with their wicked, razor-sharp scimitars and their cruel eyes made him
feel as nervous, for he knew that Nathan was infinitely
more dangerous.

While he was thinking these thoughts, the consul
lit the lamp on his desk. He turned to see Nathan's lips
curved in amusement and had the unsettling feeling
that the captain had guessed his thoughts, leaving the
consul even more disconcerted.

Nathan arched one dark eyebrow quizzically.
"Well?" he asked. "Am I correct in my assumption?
Does Jefferson have another mission for me?"

"Yes, he does." The consul sat in the chair behind
his desk. "One of the utmost importance to our war
effort. It's in Tripoli."

"Tripoli?" Nathan asked in surprise. "What does
Jefferson want me to do in Tripoli?"

"The President wants you to escort someone
from the capital and out of the country. Of course,
you will have to do this secretly, and naturally, since
the Tripolitan coast is blockaded by sea, you will have
to travel overland."

"Overland? Hell, it's our country that's doing the
blockading. Why don't you just ask our navy to let me
pass through? I could sail in at night under the pretense that I'm a gunrunner, pick up this person, and
be back out of the harbor by daylight."

"I'm afraid that would arouse suspicion. Since
Commodore Preble has taken command of the blockade, he's allowed no ship to enter or leave the harbor
—except for that Russian ship, that is. And thank God,
Preble had the presence of mind not to stop them
from leaving. What with the czar's unpredictable
temperament and his large navy in the Mediterranean, that could have been disastrous for our country.
No, we can't risk the possibility of making the pasha

or the dey in Tripoli suspicious, and they're both so adept at intrigue they can smell a plot a mile off."

Nathan's green eyes narrowed. He cocked his dark head, asking, "Why all this secrecy? Who is this captive?"

"A British citizen taken from a British merchantman the pirates attacked and took as a prize."

"British?" Nathan asked in surprise. "The pirates attacked a British ship?"

"You know how these Barbary nations are," the consul answered tightly, his anger coming to the rise. "Even if a country bows to their extortion and pays their outrageous yearly tribute, it's no guarantee that its ships won't be attacked, particularly if the pirates think they can get away with it. And that is exactly the case here. With Great Britain and France at war with one another, the pirates know both countries are much too busy to spare either the ships or the time to punish them. God! Ever since those two red-bearded Barbarossa brothers made a deal with the king of Tunis to pay him a fifth of their plunder for a safe harbor, the shipping in the Mediterranean and a good part of the Atlantic has been terrorized by these blasted pirates. And the countries that give them protection are no better. It's ridiculous that a bunch of sandbox bandits have kept Europe on its knees for almost three centuries. These damned Barbary nations are long overdue for a sound thrashing, and if the European powers can't do it—then we will!"

Nathan wholeheartedly agreed that the Barbary States needed to be taught a lesson, as did President Jefferson and Congress. It was for this purpose that Congress commissioned the building of six heavy frigates back in 1794, giving birth to the United States navy. Then, when Tripoli demanded an increase in its yearly tribute in 1801, the United States refused to comply. Tripoli declared war, and the United States sent what it could spare of its small navy to put the extortionists in their place. But the war had been going on for three years now, much longer than anyone had expected, and Tripoli had still not sued for peace. Nathan was beginning to wonder if his country was going to be any more successful in bringing the Barbary States to their knees than the European nations, who had in the past sent their navies against them, navies much more powerful than that of the United States.

Seeing the deep frown on Nathan's face, the consul said, "I'm sorry. I didn't mean to get off on that tirade."

"That's okay. You know how strongly I feel about the subject. What I don't understand is why our government is getting involved in this. Great Britain isn't at war with Tripoli, and they have a consulate in the capital. Can't their representative there make the arrangements for the release of this captive? And why is it so important to get the captive out of the country?"

"The British consul *is* handling the arrangements. He's been negotiating with the dey over the ransom price for over nine months now. As usual the dey started out with a ridiculously exorbitant demand, but he's finally agreed to accept ten thousand pounds. And naturally, Lord Hampton is most anxious for his wife to get out of Tripoli, what with our navy bombarding it and all."

"Wife?" Nathan asked in a shocked voice, sitting bolt upright in his chair. "Are you telling me the person I'm supposed to escort out of Tripoli is a woman?"

The consul winced at the captain's hard tone of voice. He had suspected what the man's reaction would be and had deliberately delayed telling Nathan the captive's sex for that reason. But now, with the captain's green eyes boring into him, he was forced to admit to the truth. "Yes. Lady Hampton."

Groves's revelation that the captive was female was only a part of what was upsetting Nathan. That Jefferson was asking him to take a woman over some of the most dangerous country in the world was impossible enough, but Nathan had no great love for the British as a whole and even less for their aristocracy. The rugged seaman was an American to the core, a firm believer in the equality of man. That the nobility should place themselves above others simply by virtue of their birth infuriated him. Birth had nothing to do with the value of a person. That was something that each individual had to establish for himself, and in his opinion the nobility had never proven their worth. For the most part they were weak-minded, gutless, useless people. And Jefferson was asking him to risk his life to save one? Like hell he would!

Nathan stood, towering over the much shorter consul. "This entire scheme is ridiculous! In the first place the woman isn't in that much danger in Tripoli. The harbor's too shallow for our navy to penetrate far enough to bombard the city successfully. The best they can do is shell the fringes, beneath the walls along the harbor. And since when does Jefferson worry about the safety of some damn British noble-woman? I happen to know for a fact that he has as much disdain for aristocrats as I do."

"None of us have any use for nobility, Nathan. We fought the British for that very reason. But that's not the issue here. Jefferson isn't rescuing this captive because she's nobility. No, there are reasons why we must get Lady Hampton out of Tripoli, other than her immediate danger. You see, what the pasha doesn't know is that she's Neapolitan royalty, the favorite cousin of the king of Naples no less, and he, too, is concerned for her safety, so much so that he's putting up the ransom. Thank God the woman had the presence of mind not to tell her captors of her relationship to the king. All the Tripolitans know is that she is the wife of a lesser English nobleman, a man reputed to be politically insignificant and without great wealth." The consul leaned forward over his desk, his look intense, saying, "My God, Nathan! Can't you just imagine what the pasha will do if he discovers what a valuable hostage he has in his possession?"

Raise the ransom to whatever price he thought the King of Naples could bear was Nathan's first thought. Then he remembered the part the kingdom of Naples was playing in his country's war with Tripoli and knew why Jefferson wanted the captive out of the country as soon as possible. Lady Hampton was valuable to his country, but not because of her birth or her unearned high station in life. "The pasha will use her as a pawn to force the king of Naples to withdraw his support in our war against Tripoli."

"Yes, and undoubtedly make himself a tidy little sum in the process," the consul answered with rancor. "Now you can see what Jefferson's interest in this case is. The government in Naples may be the most corrupt in Europe, but they're the only nation that has given us any help. And we need the king's support, both the use of his harbors in Sicily and the loan of his gunboats."

"I can well understand our government's predicament," Nathan conceded. "But why did Jefferson pick me for the job? Hell, I'm not a diplomatic courier. Nor am I a bodyguard and nursemaid. I'm a merchant captain! Now I don't mind slipping couriers and dispatches—or even a few guns—through a blockade for Jefferson. Running blockades is part of my business. But not this. Besides, he knows how strongly I feel about nobles. I can't stand them, in any shape, form, or manner. I seriously doubt that I could remain civil to the woman, much less courteous. In view of that, it would be much more prudent to send someone else."

"I'm afraid there isn't anyone else to send. Because of your past experiences you know North Africa better than any other American. You know the language, the people, the customs, the lay of the land."

"So do you," Nathan pointed out.

"Yes, but not the interior of North Africa. Like the European consuls, I've never been past the Maghrib, the coastal fringes. And in order to bring the Lady Hampton back to Tunis, you will have to travel over part of the Sahara. For that reason Jefferson wants someone who's not only familiar with the territory but proficient with both pistol and sword—in case of an attack—and quite frankly, there's not a man in the diplomatic corps who has your expertise with those weapons. So you see, this is not so much a diplomatic mission as one of expediency. Besides, I'm sure Jefferson would never have chosen you if he didn't think you could exercise some control over your feelings about nobility."

"Well, I'm not so sure. I told you I'm not a diplomat. I'm a sea captain. I don't take orders from anyone, and I don't bow and scrape to anyone."

"Jefferson doesn't expect you to bow and scrape to the woman, and he certainly doesn't expect you to take orders from her. All he expects is for you to act reasonably mannerly, and surely that's not asking too much for your country. Besides, there is another reason why Jefferson selected you. He wants you to take Lady Hampton to Naples on your ship and deliver her personally to the king. He's hoping our aid in seeing her safely returned will influence the king in any further requests we may present to him."

"My ship? Why can't the navy take her to Naples?"

"What with blockading Tripoli and escorting our merchant fleet in the Mediterranean, the navy can't spare a ship. Besides, your schooner is the swiftest vessel in the Mediterranean and almost as well armed as any of the navy's lighter craft. There should be no problem on that end."

Of course there was no problem, Nathan thought. On the *Seabird,* he could outsail any ship on any sea or ocean and outfight any pirate who dared to attack him. But he still didn't like what the consul was proposing. Not only was the prospect of being in the company a pampered, self-centered, spoiled noblewoman totally repugnant to him—to say nothing of risking his neck to protect the hated aristocrat while they traveled over some of the most rugged and dangerous country in the world—but his ship would be idle for weeks, what with traveling time from Tripoli to Tunis and then transporting the woman to Naples. Nathan didn't want to miss out on the trade that was open to the neutral countries at this time, trade that could be very lucrative if one was willing to take the risk of running blockades. But he knew he couldn't refuse Jefferson. Besides being his President and his godfather, the man was a personal friend, and Nathan was not a man to refuse a friend a favor.

Resenting being put into his present position, Nathan snapped, "How in the hell did Lady Hampton's ship get captured? Didn't the captain wait for a naval escort?"

"He *was* with a convoy. But his ship was separated from the others by a severe storm. According to the captain there were other passengers on board, a

West Indies planter, his wife, and another young woman who was killed during the boarding. Poor thing. She must have thought she was going to be raped when the pirate stripped her. She resisted, even though the captain swears he had warned all the passengers not to do so. The enraged pirate killed her with his scimitar. Of course, the pirate responsible was punished. He paid with his own life. You know how strongly the dey feels about his plunder being damaged. But I'm sure that was no consolation to the poor girl's family," the consul ended bitterly.

Nathan frowned deeply then asked, "And the planter and his wife?"

"According to the British consul their families couldn't raise the ransom and they were sold on the block as slaves, as were the crew. Naturally, the British consul objected strenuously, but the Tripolitans ignored him. The bastards!"

The old rage rose in Nathan. He knew only too well the indignities, the backbreaking labor, the brutalities those poor people would be forced to endure. They would have been better off dead. God, how he wished he could play a more active role in this war, but his desire to punish the extortionists wasn't enough to make him join the navy. He'd been a captain too long, accustomed to giving orders and making his own decisions. He would grant a favor to a friend in his nation's behalf, but he wouldn't take orders from anyone. It was a promise he'd made himself long ago. No one dictated to Nathan Sloan. He was his own man.

The consul sensed his thoughts and said, "I know you're not happy with this request, Nathan, but look at it this way. You would be helping the war effort. Getting your licks in, so to speak."

When Nathan made no comment, the consul

asked, "You will do it, won't you, Nathan? The President is depending heavily upon you."

Nathan made a noise that sounded like a mixture of a snort and a snarl, then answered, "Yes, I'll do it."

The consul sighed deeply in relief and unlocked the desk drawer to his right. Lifting the oilskin pouch from the drawer, he handed it to Nathan. "Would you mind delivering this to the British consul in Tripoli? It's the rest of the ransom money. He was a little short on cash since our navy is blockading the country, and he can't get money or supplies from his government."

Nathan accepted the pouch. "I assume the British government is in accord with our plans."

"They certainly are," the consul answered, rising to his feet. "They're just as anxious as we are to get Lady Hampton out of the country. To some degree they feel responsible, since she was on a British ship, and they don't want to lose the good faith of the king of Naples either. As soon as the ransom has been paid and the lady released from the pasha's *iyal,* she'll be turned over to your safekeeping."

"The pasha's *iyal?*" Nathan asked in surprise. "What's she doing there?"

"Since she's a noblewoman, the dey had her interned in the pasha's women's quarters in the palace, where all the important female hostages are kept. The palace is practically a fortress, you know. I guess the dey was afraid someone might try to sneak her out of his *iyal.*"

"Anyone who would try to sneak a woman out of any of those Arabs' *iyals* would be a damned fool. And a dead one. They're all heavily guarded."

The two men walked from the room and down the hall to the back door of the consulate. Slipping the heavy bolt from the lock, the consul opened the door. As they stepped into the darkened courtyard, the sweet smell of night-blooming jasmine surrounded them.

When they reached the heavy gate at the back of the walled courtyard, the consul asked, "When will you leave?"

"I'll sail with the next tide. I'll have my first mate drop me off about thirty miles up the coast from Tripoli and take the *Seabird* to Malta. He can meet me back here in Tunis in about ten days. I should be back by then."

"Malta? Why not have him bring the *Seabird* back here to Tunis? That way, as soon as you and Lady Hampton reach Tunis, you can board your ship and be on your way to Naples."

Nathan stopped in midstride, saying, "You're crazy if you think I'll leave my ship riding at anchor in any Barbary harbor. I won't take the risk of having it confiscated and my men thrown into prison."

"But Tunisia is at peace with our country."

"For how long? A day? Two days? Hell, you never know from one day to the next when these bastards will take the notion they want more tribute and declare war. For all you know the Janissaries could be out there chopping down your flagpole right now."

The consul paled at the thought. "Perhaps you're right," he admitted. "The pasha here in Tunis has been complaining bitterly about our blockade interfering with his trade with Tripoli. All the Barbary States are up in arms about it."

"Trade, hell!" Nathan spat. "They just don't like seeing their Muslim brothers being held at bay."

With that Nathan opened the gate and slipped into the darkened streets of Tunis, as agile and quiet as a cat.

Chapter 2

Lorna pushed aside the sheer curtain of her cubicle and peered out at the *iyal*, her violet eyes searching the huge room for Zarifah, her only friend in the pasha's women's quarters, where she had been interned since her arrival in Tripoli. Not seeing Zarifah anywhere, she felt a keen disappointment. There would be no lessons in Arabic today, nor even someone to talk to. Another long, boring day loomed before her.

She leaned back on her pallet, absently stroking one of the bright silken pillows that lay there, wondering once again how the women who lived here stood years of this idleness without going out of their minds. A few had books to read, while others played chess, but the majority of the women passed their time in lazy indulgence, spending a great deal of it in self-adornment and allowing themselves to be bathed, perfumed, massaged, and generally petted by the female slaves. No wonder most of the women were on the plump side, with their inactivity and the rich food they ate. But then, Zarifah had told her that Arab men preferred their women fleshy. When Lorna learned this bit of information, she became very careful about what she ate in order to retain her slim figure. Above all she didn't want to attract the attention of the pasha, even though the British consul had assured her she had been placed here for her protection until the ransom was paid, and not because of any designs the pasha had to get her into his bed.

Lorna wrinkled her nose, thinking the Muslim institution of keeping a harem was utterly disgusting. Zarifah—an Englishwoman who many years ago had been taken captive, sold as a concubine to the pasha, and given a new Arabic name—had explained that the term originally came from the Arabic word *harim*, signifying that which is forbidden or sacred. Over the years it had evolved to "harem" in Turkey and to *iyal* in the Arabic countries. Lorna didn't give a tinker's dam what they called it. It was disgusting and degrading to the women. The idea of one man having so many wives and concubines was ridiculous. Why, there must be at least two hundred women here in the pasha's women's quarters, the sexual gratification of the pasha seemingly their only purpose, and certainly no man was that potent. Being used to satisfy a man's lust was bad enough, but what the women had to go through to make themselves attractive was almost as bad. Lorna had been horrified when she learned the women were denuded of all body hair by pouring hot wax over their bodies and then peeling it off when it had cooled, painfully taking the hair with it. And then they had to wear that grotesque kohl over their eyes and paint the palms of their hands and feet with henna. Why even their nipples were rouged! And all for the satisfaction of one greedy man.

Lorna was torn from her thoughts by an eerie, birdlike sound, a noise that sounded rather like a rapid falsetto gargling. She looked out to see a group of women in one corner of the harem watching a dance being performed by the slave girls, and she knew the women were applauding the dancers in the Arabic manner. As the women began chattering to each other, a shiver ran through Lorna. The guttural Arabic language wore on her nerves, for it had a distinctive sound called the glottal stop, accomplished by momentarily closing the vocal cords in the larynx, making the women sound as if they had a dry, hacking cough that interrupted every word. Lorna had had a difficult time trying to learn the language. Swallowing letters didn't come easily to her, but it had given her something to do to relieve the monotony.

God, Lorna thought in despair, would she ever get out of here? The *iyal* was a beautiful place, she admitted, her eyes drifting over the pools and splashing fountains, the rich, colorful tapestries that hung from the walls, the plush carpets that covered the gleaming mosaic floors, the exotic potted shrubs, the high-domed ceiling where the light passed through the shards of colored glass, casting dancing multicolored lights over everything—but it was still a prison. The British consul, on the one and only visit he had been allowed, had warned her that negotiations took time, but that had been over nine months ago. Had they forgotten she was here, or—God forbid—had they discovered her true identity, that she was nothing but an impostor?

Lorna chewed her full bottom lip nervously. When she told the pirates she was Lady Hampton, she had congratulated herself on her quick thinking.

Knowing there was no possibility of her being ransomed, her only thought had been to save herself from the slave block. Since Lady Hampton had been killed while resisting the taking of her precious necklace, Lorna saw no harm in impersonating her. Surely her rich nobleman husband would be able to come up with the ransom. It wasn't until later that she realized she had gotten herself into a tricky situation.

Her first fright came when she was thrown into a small cabin on the pirate ship with the planter's wife. She was terrified that the woman would recognize her and give her true identity away. At first Lorna thought the woman didn't realize who she really was because they had both been stripped of their clothing and wore only the filthy burnooses the pirates had given them. But as the days passed, Lorna realized that she could have been wearing the clothes she had worn on deck and the poor woman would have not recognized her. The planter's wife was much too distraught over being separated from her husband.

When they arrived at Tripoli and the planter's wife was taken away to the slave pens, Lorna thought herself safe. There was no one in Tripoli who could identify her. It wasn't until the British consul came to visit her shortly thereafter that Lorna fully realized what a mess she had gotten herself into. Oh, yes, she'd be ransomed, but she'd also have to go back to England, the very place she had fled. And as soon as her true identity was discovered, she would surely be imprisoned, if not for impersonating the noblewoman, then for her alleged crime. The news that she would be taken back to England came as a shock to Lorna. She had assumed that the British noblewoman was going to her summer home in Naples and that she would join her husband there. Lorna had mistakenly thought that would be her destination. In her desperation to save herself from slavery, it seemed all she had accomplished by pretending to be the noble-woman was to get herself out of one dire predicament and into another. But the fear of her deception's being exposed to the Arabs overrode the fear of what might happen to her back in England. The Arabs were exceedingly cruel. There was no telling what kind of fiendish, brutal punishment they might dream up for her for deceiving them. She decided she would rather face punishment at her own countrymen's hands. So Lorna held her tongue about her true identity when the consul came to visit, promising herself that she'd manage to escape somehow on the trip back to England. But first she had to escape *this* prison.

Damn Phillip Leighton! Lorna thought angrily. If it hadn't been for him, she wouldn't have had to flee England in the first place and she wouldn't be in this desperate fix. That was why she felt no guilt in letting Lord Hampton ransom her. It seemed fitting justice that one aristocrat should have to pay the price for what another had unfairly done to her. God, how she hated nobles. They were nothing but snobbish, demanding, hateful people who looked down on every-one else. She was just as good as they were, even if she was a commoner, a penniless orphan.

At the reminder that she was an orphan, Lorna again wondered who her family had been. It was a puzzle that had teased her for as long as she could remember. She had absolutely no recollection of them—and no wonder. She had been brought to the orphanage as a baby. All she knew of her family was that her parents had been killed in one of those terri-ble fires that periodically swept over London and that she had been miraculously saved.

She recalled her years in the orphanage. They

hadn't been easy. Other than feeding her just enough to survive and giving her some tattered clothing, the people who ran the orphanage left her to fend for herself. She had learned early in life to protect her few meager possessions, even if it meant fighting larger and older children to do so, and she had grown up to be very self-reliant, so much so that she was just a little too independent for her own good when she left the orphanage at thirteen. The director of the orphanage had placed her in a position as a parlor maid in the home of a nobleman, and Lorna resented taking orders from her snobbish employers. Had it not been for Maddie, the cook who took the orphan under her wing and cautioned her to watch her tongue, Lorna would probably have been fired. It was under Maddie's tutelage that Lorna learned to appear meek and subservient, but it galled the girl no end to have to bow and scrape to the impossible and never-ending demands of the nobility. Lorna was hard put to keep her feelings to herself, which earned her a reputation among the other servants as somewhat of a rebel. She seemed to have some inbred fierce hatred for the class distinction that was so much a part of her country.

That was why when one of the grooms told of her his plans to save his money to go America, the idea appealed to her so much. She decided that she would go to that golden land of opportunity, too, where she wouldn't be a victim of class distinction, where there would be no hated nobles to hold her down, where people could better their lot in life by their own determination and industry. She started saving every shilling she earned and hoarding it away until she had enough to buy passage.

But she hadn't gotten away from England soon enough. Her flight had been precipitous—and all be-

cause Phillip Leighton had taken the notion that he
desired her. Damn, she wished she could have stayed
skinny, the way she had been when she came from
the orphanage. Then maybe he wouldn't have found
her attractive. But the food in the nobles' house was
much more nutritious and abundant, and over the
years Lorna had blossomed into a very pretty woman.
The spoiled son of the nobleman wasn't the only one
who noticed how desirable she was. So had the other
male servants. But Lorna had learned to defend her
possessions in the orphanage, and her virtue was one
of the most prized possessions she had. It was something she was determined she would give only to that
very special man whom she dreamed about—when
and if he ever came into her life.

She had no trouble fending off the male servants'
unwanted attentions. A well-aimed gouge with her
elbow or knee did wonders to cool their ardor. But
Phillip was of a different breed. He was accustomed to
getting everything he wanted, and Lorna's spurning
his advances made him all the more determined to
get her into his bed. It became a fierce contest of wills,
and Phillip stalked her the way a cat stalked a mouse,
so much so that Lorna had to keep her wits about her
at all times. She never knew when he was going to
jump her and she would have to tussle with him to get
free. And she knew it would do no good to complain
to his father. The nobility seemed to think that parlor
maids were fair game and should be honored to share
a bed with one of the elite of the land, the conceited,
arrogant bastards!

Finally, things came to a head. Frustrated beyond
his endurance, Phillip threatened Lorna that if she
didn't submit to him he would see her sent to prison.
Lorna didn't take his threat seriously. She soon found
out she had underestimated his vindictiveness.

She was cleaning one of the upstairs bedrooms when Maddie rushed in and informed her that Phillip had called the constables and that she had overheard him telling them his mother's priceless diamond jewels had been stolen by Lorna. According to the nobleman's story, he had seen Lorna take them from his mother's jewel box and slip them into her pocket, and his mother confirmed the fact that they were indeed missing. Lorna was shocked. She had never dreamed Phillip would go to such lengths to get revenge on her for refusing him. But she knew it would do no good for her to deny it. The constables would never take her word against a nobleman's. She had been tried and convicted before she had even been arrested. While Maddie diverted the constables to another part of the house, Lorna rushed to her room, packed her belongings, and fled for the harbor. Yes, it was all Phillip's fault that she was in this predicament, and if she could get her hands on him right now, she'd gladly murder the man.

For a moment Lorna seethed silently. Then she realized that her anger wasn't going to get her out of this mess. She had no recourse but to follow through with her impersonation of Lady Hampton. She'd saved herself from the slave block and no telling what kind of horrors by using her wits. She'd just have to continue to rely on her resourcefulness. She'd be damned if she'd get out of one prison and then go to another. Her internment here had made her even more determined to attain her freedom. No, she was never going to let anyone take her freedom away again!

Hoping to clear her mind of these distressing thoughts, Lorna rose from her pallet and walked across the pavilion, ignoring the squeals of the naked women splashing each other in one of the pools and stepping around others lying beside the pool being massaged with perfume oil by the slave girls. Her thin silk pantaloons made a whispering sound at each step she took. When she reached the billowing curtains at the high-arched window, she peered out through the sheer material and looked down on the harbor of Tripoli, thankful that the pasha had put his *iyal* at the top of his palace instead of the back. At least here she could look out and see something.

Squinting her eyes, she searched the horizon past the harbor, then, seeing the ship that was hardly more than a speck on the blue Mediterranean, she smiled. Yes, the American ships were still out there, patrolling the inlet to the harbor. Just knowing they were there raised her spirits.

Her eyes dropped to the pavilion before the palace far below her. It was teeming with Arabs in their long, flowing robes, some black, some striped, some brightly colored. One Arab, dressed in a gleaming white robe and a striped headdress, caught her attention. Towering over the others, he walked with a swift, sure stride that marked him as a man of action and a man accustomed to command. Then he stopped and looked up, seemingly staring straight at her. Lorna couldn't distinguish his features from where she stood, but she could tell that his skin was deeply tanned and that he was beardless. As the man continued to gaze up, Lorna felt a peculiar tingle run up her spine. She knew that he couldn't possibly see her, not while she was standing in the dim shade of the room with the curtain before her, and yet she felt as if he had reached out and touched her. When he turned and walked away, Lorna felt a strange disappointment.

Two hours later Lorna was standing at another window that was screened from the rest of the room by a large potted plant when Zarifah rushed up to her and said in an excited voice, "Here you are! I've been looking everywhere for you and so has the head eunuch."

Lorna frowned and asked, "What does he want with me?"

"He wants you to dress in your own clothing. You've finally been ransomed and they've come for you. This is the big day you've been waiting for."

Lorna was filled with sudden doubts. "I'm afraid, Zarifah. What if they find out who I really am?"

"Are you still worrying about that?" the older Englishwoman asked in exasperation. "I thought we had decided that you really don't have any choice. You've got to follow through with your impersonation. Now hurry. The head eunuch isn't noted for his patience, you know."

Zarifah rushed Lorna across the large room to her cubicle. Seeing the head eunuch standing in front of it with a deep scowl on his black face, Lorna didn't need any further urging. As Zarifah had said, he didn't look at all pleased with her disappearance. When the two women reached the cubicle, Zarifah pushed aside the curtain and they stepped into the small room. The first thing Lorna noticed was the trunk sitting on the floor. She had never seen it before in her life. "That's not my trunk."

"Of course not, silly. It's Lady Hampton's. Now hurry and undress while I find you something to wear."

As Lorna started to undress, Zarifah opened the trunk and started pulling out frothy dresses, tossing them to the side after giving each a quick, critical look. Then pulling out a muslin dress with just a tinge of lavender and a violet velvet sash beneath the high bodice, she said, "This will be perfect. It will bring out the color of your eyes."

Lorna looked at the dress. "But I can't wear that," she objected. "It's so thin you can see right through it."

"Yes, it is a little revealing," Zarifah admitted. "Is this the style now?"

"Well, the high bodice and straight skirt and short puffed sleeves are, but no one wears anything that sheer in England. Why's, it's scandalous. Even more so than what I'm wearing. Why, I might as well be naked!" Lorna glanced at the dresses strewn all around her, pastel shades of every color in the rainbow, then asked, "Isn't there something more appropriate here?"

"No, they're all made of that same thin material," Zarifah answered. "Are you sure the nobility aren't wearing this?"

"Of course I'm sure. I lived with them for years. They may be haughty and arrogant, but the women would never dream of going out in public in something so revealing. They do have some morals."

"Then there must be something you wear beneath it," Zarifah concluded, searching the bottom of the trunk. Then, pulling out a strange looking, flesh-colored garment, she said, "Ah, this must be it." She held it up, then said in astonishment, "What a peculiar-looking garment. It looks like a big silk stocking."

"That's what it is," Lorna answered with sudden insight, "a body stocking. I've heard they're the rage in Paris."

"But you can see right through it, too."

"I know. It's designed that way on purpose, to give the impression that the woman is totally naked beneath her dress."

"And the women actually wear them?"

"In France they may, but not in England. Why, it's disgusting!"

"Didn't you tell me Lady Hampton said something about going to Naples?"

"Yes."

"Then that explains it. From what I've heard, the Neapolitans are even more risqué and immoral than the French. Lady Hampton must have bought these clothes to wear while she was visiting in Naples." Zarifah handed the sheer stocking to Lorna and said, "Here, put it and the dress on."

"I won't go out in that scandalous outfit!"

"Then what are you going to wear?" Zarifah countered. "Besides, have you already forgotten who you're supposed to be? Lady Hampton! If she wears this, then you'll have to."

Lorna realized she had no choice. She took the flimsy garments and donned them, feeling as if she had absolutely nothing on. She looked down and gasped, seeing that a lot of cleavage was showing. Even more shocking, she could see the outline of her nipples clearly through the layers of thin material. After slipping on the silk lavender slippers that Zarifah handed her, she glanced down at the piles of clothing on the floor and spied a soft, white cashmere shawl. She pulled it out and wrapped it around herself.

"You're not going to wear that wool shawl in this heat?" Zarifah asked in disbelief.

"I certainly am!"

Seeing the disgusted look on the older woman's face, Lorna said, "Oh, Zarifah, I know it looks ridiculous. But I can't walk around so exposed. I told you I didn't think I could pull if off."

"Of course you can," Zarifah assured her in a firm voice. "Have you forgotten what's at stake? Your freedom! And you've been around aristocrats long enough to know how they act. All you have to do is pretend you're one of them. Why, not even your speech will give you away."

No, it wouldn't, Lorna admitted, and she had the director at the orphanage to thank for that. He abhorred the way the commoners in London massacred the English language and insisted that all of his wards learn to speak proper English. Lorna hated him at the time for being so rigorous about it. She didn't see what difference it made if she dropped letters or spoke with a nasal twang, but now she knew that it might well be her saving grace.

Seeing that she was dressed, the head eunuch and another burly guard stepped into the cubicle. Lorna barely had time to bid her friend a hasty farewell before they rushed her away across the women's pavilion. When they stepped through the arched door that was protected by two other eunuchs and into the wide hallway, Lorna didn't feel at all elated finally to be leaving her prison. She was filled with icy dread at what she was facing. Was her "husband" waiting for her downstairs? The thought brought terror to her heart, for surely, he would know she was an impostor. For a moment she had the ridiculous urge to turn and run back to the *iyal*.

Stop it! she told herself firmly. Get a hold of yourself. Zarifah was right. You've gone too far to back out now. You'll just have to bluff your way through from now on. Now hold up your head. You're Lady Hampton, remember?

It seemed an eternity of stairs to Lorna until she saw the British consul standing at the bottom in a huge foyer and smiling up at her. The immense relief she felt when she saw he was alone made her falter in her step, and she would have tumbled down the stairs had not the eunuch quickly grabbed her arm and supported her.

Seeing the near disaster, the consul rushed up the stairs, saying in an anxious voice, "Are you all right, m'lady?"

"Yes. I . . . I just tripped on the hem of my dress."

"Here, allow me to assist you," the consul said, offering his arm and shooting the eunuch a resentful glance.

Lorna laid her hand on the consul's proffered arm, hoping he wouldn't notice her trembling.

As they walked through the foyer flanked by fierce-looking Janissaries holding their wicked, bared scimitars before their chests, the consul said, "As soon as we reach the consulate, you'll be able to lie down and rest, m'lady. I'm sure this has been a terrible ordeal for you. But it's over now. Within a matter of weeks you'll be safely in Naples."

Again Lorna's step faltered. "Naples?" she blurted. "But I thought you said I would be sent back to England?"

"No, your husband is waiting for you in Naples, at the king's insistence. They're both most anxious for your safe return."

Lorna was vastly relieved to hear that she wouldn't be sent back to England, but she couldn't understand why the king of England was concerned about her. She had been under the impression that Lady Hampton's husband was of lesser nobility.

They stepped from the palace into the glaring sunlight. It was as if she had stepped into an oven, the sudden, oppressive heat enveloping her.

Walking down another long flight of marble stairs, the consul led her to a large sedan chair then assisted her into the enclosed, boxlike vehicle. Com-

ing from the outside bright glare into the dim light of
the sedan chair, Lorna was temporarily blinded, and
she fumbled to find the seat.

"Allow me, m'lady," a deep masculine voice said
as a strong hand closed over her elbow to guide her
down to her seat.

Lorna stared at the dim outline of the man seated
across from her, thinking the white robe and striped
headdress looked familiar. Then it dawned on her
that the man seated across from her was the same
Arab she had seen from the window earlier that day.
She had the strangest feeling that her meeting with
this stranger was not just some casual happening, but
very fateful and important to her. The premonition
that she had somehow met her destiny was so strong it
left her shaken.

Chapter 3

"Are you all right, m'lady?" the consul asked in an alarmed voice. "Why, you're as white as a sheet."

"It's probably the heat," the stranger sitting across from Lorna said. "It's stifling in here with these curtains drawn."

As the man jerked the curtain between them open, Lorna felt a blast of hot air on her face. Then she stared at the Arab, who was leaning forward and gazing at her intently. She was shocked to see that his eyes were not black, but a vibrant green, a color that was startling against his deeply tanned face.

Lorna was not the only one shocked by what she saw. When she entered the dimly lit chair, all Nathan had been able to ascertain was that Lady Hampton was tall and slenderly built, but now he could see that she was much younger and much more beautiful than he had expected. Her violet eyes looked like two exquisite jewels against her dark, sooty lashes and her flawless complexion. His eyes drifted over her narrow nose to her mouth, pausing at the full lower lip. Then, noticing that she was clutching her wool shawl tightly around her, he frowned.

"Permit me, m'lady," Nathan said, prying Lorna's hands from the shawl and pushing it back off her shoulders, "but I think you would be much cooler without this."

As Lorna felt Nathan's fingertips brushing across the bare skin on her shoulders, she gasped.

The consul said quickly, "Captain Sloan meant no offense, m'lady. He was just concerned for your comfort."

Lorna was so surprised by the consul's words that she momentarily forgot the man's strange effect on her or that Lady Hampton would never have tolerated a commoner's touching her. Nor did she remember that her breasts were almost completely bared to him in her thin garment. "Captain?"

"Forgive me, m'lady," the consul said. "May I introduce Captain Nathan Sloan."

"Then you're not an Arab?" Lorna asked in astonishment.

Seeing her eyeing his Arab dress, Nathan smiled. "No, m'lady. I'm not an Arab. Because of the blockade my ship was forced to drop me off about thirty miles up the coast, and I found it more prudent to dress as a Muslim since I would have to travel the remainder of the distance overland."

Of course the man isn't an Arab, Lorna thought. His English is much too flawless. But she still didn't understand why he was here. Was he a personal friend of the consul who had just come along for the ride?

As if guessing her thoughts, the consul said, "Captain Sloan just delivered the remainder of the ransom money to me, m'lady. I was a little short on ready cash because of the blockade, and the British consul in Tunis had to send me the remainder. I suppose it would have been wiser to wait until it was a little cooler to pick you up, but we were anxious to see you released."

"Then you're a British naval captain?" Lorna surmised.

"No, I'm an American," Nathan answered stiffly, as if she'd insulted him. "An American merchant captain."

An American? Lorna thought. She had never met an American before. A little tingle of excitement ran through her. She wished she could ask the captain about his country, but she didn't dare. Lady Hampton would undoubtedly scorn the American, thinking him one of those horrible rebels who'd had the audacity to challenge the authority of Britain. But what was the captain doing here in Tripoli? she wondered. Had he been sent to spy on the enemy? Then what was he doing with the British consul?

Seeing the puzzled expression on Lorna's face, the consul said, "If you will permit me, m'lady, I believe I can explain. Since the kingdom of Naples has been helping the United States in its war against Tripoli, the American government has decided to return the favor by seeing you safely escorted to Tunis and then to Naples. Captain Sloan has been chosen by his government as your escort because of his unique knowledge of North Africa and his possession of one of the swiftest ships in the Mediterranean. Both your husband and cousin know of these plans and are in full accord. I'll be placing you in very capable hands with the captain here."

Lorna was even more baffled. Who the devil was her cousin? And why did the American government give a fig if he approved or not? And what did the kingdom of Naples have to do with her? My God! What had she gotten herself into?

"Why didn't you tell me about your cousin when I visited you, m'lady?" the consul asked in a mildly reproving tone of voice. "I can understand your not telling the Tripolitans. As a matter of fact I applaud your astuteness. But you could have trusted me."

I didn't tell you because I don't know who the devil you're talking about! Lorna thought wildly. Then she suddenly realized how addled she was behaving. She wasn't acting like Lady Hampton, but like Lorna. Why, Lady Hampton would never tolerate having a commoner take her to task, not even mildly. Her mind flashed back to the consul's visit. Then, remembering something, she said in a haughty voice, "I was afraid the eunuch would overhear."

"Ah, yes, the eunuch. I completely forgot about him. And undoubtedly that was why the pasha insisted the man remain during our interview, to spy on us. Forgive me, m'lady. Again, I applaud your keen judgment."

Lorna decided that it was time to play her role to the hilt. "You certainly should apologize! I should think you would have realized the eunuch was listening. Thank God one of us kept our wits about us. But you're supposed to be the expert in dealing with these Arabs, not I. No wonder it took so long for you ransom me if you're no more competent than that."

The consul's face turned beet red with anger. With supreme will he forced his feelings down and replied in a tight voice, "I'm sorry you're displeased, m'lady. But I did warn you in the very beginning that it would take some time."

"Some time?" Lorna asked in a scathing voice.

"My God, it's been almost nine months! I could have died from boredom in that prison in that time."

"The dey was asking a ridiculously exorbitant sum for your ransom, m'lady, a sum your cousin didn't feel he could afford," the consul explained, hoping the irate woman would realize that it was not his fault. "Negotiating with the dey to lower his ransom took time. These Arabs are incredibly greedy and they don't give in easily."

Lorna wondered why the Lady Hampton's mysterious cousin was paying the ransom and not her husband. "And just how much did my cousin finally pay for my release?"

"Ten thousand pounds, m'lady."

Lorna gasped in shock at the sum. Why, it sounded like a fortune to her. Then realizing that both men were staring at her curiously and that she had almost given herself away, she quickly assumed an outraged expression and said, "Why, that's an insult! I'm worth four times that much. You can certainly believe my cousin is going to hear about this!"

Rebuked, the consul kept silent and stared morosely out the window.

Nathan had watched the entire exchange with utter disgust. Yes, it was just as he had suspected. Lady Hampton was nothing but a spoiled, haughty bitch. She had better not try talking to him like that. He'd quickly put her in her place. To make matters worse she was totally immoral. Imagine wearing a dress like that in public and flaunting her body for everyone to see. But then the flimsy, outrageous garment shouldn't have surprised him. Lady Hampton was Neapolitan by birth, and the Neapolitans were even more hot-blooded than the French, their court the most amoral of all the decadent European courts.

Realizing that his body was responding to the

sight of Lady Hampton's high, full breasts, Nathan leaned back on the cushions and crossed his arms over his broad chest, forcing himself to look at Lady Hampton's profile as she pouted and gazed out the window beside her. He frowned. Directing his attention away from her luscious body hadn't helped at all. She had the most graceful throat, and that seductive mouth of hers was driving him crazy. Damn, her being so beautiful and desirable was going to complicate matters. He wasn't made of stone, as his body had so blatantly reminded him, and they were going to be thrown together for weeks. This mission was going to be even more difficult than he had thought. He should have followed his instincts and refused it. Damn Jefferson! Then, despite his resolve not to look at her body, Nathan's eyes drifted to Lady's Hampton's beautiful breasts again.

Lorna turned from gazing out the window and found herself looking directly at Nathan. For the first time she saw his rugged good looks, having been too stunned earlier by the remarkable color of his eyes to notice features that perfectly matched the rest of a man who fairly reeked of power and strength and masculinity. And that little white scar on his darkly tanned cheek only added a dash of mystery.

Fascinated by what she was seeing, Lorna glanced up at the striped kaffiyeh on the captain's head, wishing he wasn't wearing the headdress. She would like to know the color of his hair. But then, with such black eyebrows, it was bound to be the same color. Yes, he was undoubtedly the most handsome man she had ever met. Suddenly, remembering that the consul had said the captain would be her escort for the next several weeks, a thrill ran through Lorna.

Then Lorna became aware of Nathan staring just as avidly at her, except his gaze was locked on her breasts. A little glow deep inside her flared, suffusing her entire body, and once again that strange tingle ran up her spine before Lorna's innate modesty came to the fore. Horrified, she almost grabbed the shawl to cover her near nakedness when she remembered who she was supposed to be. No, Lady Hampton wouldn't cover herself. She wouldn't have bought the revealing garment if she hadn't wanted to flaunt her body. Damn Lady Hampton for putting her in this mortifying situation! She would just have to bear the captain's staring at her so boldly.

Nathan was aware that Lady Hampton knew he was staring at her breasts. Suddenly her revealing herself to him so brazenly infuriated him. How dare she sit there and deliberately tease him, for undoubtedly she wouldn't allow a common seaman like him to lay a hand on her. No, she considered herself much too above him. Well, he'd show the teasing bitch what he thought of her. He wouldn't take her body if she offered it to him on a silver platter. Aware that she was watching him, Nathan deliberately sneered, then looked her straight in the eye.

Lorna felt Nathan's sneer like a slap in the face. Then, when he looked her straight in the eye, Lorna sensed that he was issuing her a silent challenge of some sort. Was he telling the despicable Lady Hampton that no matter what she did she couldn't seduce him, something that Lorna took as a personal insult to her femininity. But there seemed to be something more than that in his look. She sensed that he was pitting his will against hers in all ways. Did he think he could dominate her? He was a sea captain, accustomed to giving orders and having them obeyed without question. Well, she'd be damned if she'd let him dominate her. She'd already put up with a bellyful of domineering people back in England. She'd show

him. She was going to gain the upper hand right now
and keep it. And she'd start with throwing herself at
him until she had him begging for mercy. Deliberately she pushed out her breasts, taking immense satisfaction when she heard Nathan suck in his breath
sharply. Then, seeing the angry look come over his
face, she thought, Good. She wanted to goad him.
And he didn't dare lay a hand on her. Not on Lady
Hampton!

But despite the fact that Lorna had picked up the
challenge Nathan had issued, she couldn't help but
feel a little nervous with his green eyes boring into
her. The very masculinity she had admired just a few
moments before now seemed overpowering, so stifling that she found it difficult to breathe. Combined
with the oppressive heat and the rocking motion of
the chair, it was beginning to make her feel a little ill.
She could have cried out in relief when the chair
stopped and was lowered to the ground.

The consul helped Lorna from the chair and she
stood relishing the breeze. Even though it was hot, it
had the fresh, tangy smell of the sea about it, a blessed
relief after the musty chair. Curious to know where
she was, Lorna looked about her, seeing that the consulate lay on the fringes of the city on a small rise that
overlooked the bay. Following the coastline, she saw
the massive walls that lined the harbor in the distance
and the flat-roofed houses above them, the monotony
of the sand-colored buildings relieved only by the
feathery leaves of an unusually tall palm and the
spires and domes of the mosques and the huge palace
that towered over all. Glancing back at sea, she could
see the big American frigate patrolling the inlet to the
bay much clearer than she could from the window of
the palace, noting that there were several smaller
ships with her. For a moment, Lorna drank in the

scene, oblivious to the sun beating down on her head, thinking the ships with their sails filled with wind and gliding across the blue water a beautiful sight.

"M'lady?" the consul urged, exerting a gentle pressure on her arm. "Don't you want to step into the house where it's cooler?"

Feeling a little twinge of resentment at being torn away from the lovely sight, Lorna turned and allowed the consul to lead her up the small rise. Looking about her, she was surprised to see the landscape looked so barren. What grass and shrubs there were, were all brown and withered, and there was hardly a tree in sight, except for the tops of those in the consulate courtyard that she could see over the flat roof of the building.

Then, hearing a flapping noise, Lorna glanced up, seeing the British flag at the top of the flagpole in front of the consulate whipping about in the breeze from the bay. Her lagging spirits suddenly soared as the full impact of her being set free hit her. She wanted to dance, to sing, to shout at the top of her lungs. But of course she couldn't. Lady Hampton would never sink to that.

But Lorna wasn't totally successful in hiding her elation. A spontaneous smile crossed her lips and her eyes sparkled. Watching her, Nathan realized what she was thinking. It came as rather a surprise to him, but then he supposed even a spoiled, worldly woman like her could feel happiness at being set free. He could well understand the feeling, but as she stood there, with the breeze ruffling the auburn curls that had escaped her chignon at her temples and the nape of her slender neck, the lights in her jewellike eyes dancing with joy, the thin, almost transparent material of the gown molding her beautiful breasts and long, well-shaped legs, she was undoubtedly the love-

liest sight he had ever seen. Again he felt himself
responding to her beauty and cursed beneath his
breath.

The consul once more urged Lorna toward the
house, and when she stepped into the coolness of the
shade, she stood relishing it, then looked about her.

"I'm sorry my wife isn't here to greet you," the
consul said politely, "but I had her sent out of the city
because of the bombardments. She'll be most disappointed when she learns that she missed meeting
you."

Lorna was on the verge of saying she was sorry
she had missed meeting the consul's wife when she
realized Lady Hampton would never say something
so gracious. Instead she stuck her nose up in the air,
showing her disdain for the commoner's wife.

The consul was aware of her insult and again
fought down his anger. "Would you like to step into
the parlor, m'lady, or would you prefer to go to your
room?"

"I'd like to lie down for a while. I'm feeling a little
weary," Lorna answered, not feeling in the least
tired, but anxious to be by herself where she could
think.

The consul clapped his hands sharply three
times, causing Lorna to jump at the unexpected noise.
An Arab servant suddenly appeared, bowing at the
waist.

"This is Ahman, m'lady. He'll show you to your
room and bring you something cool to drink. If you
need anything, just ask. He speaks English and he'll
be waiting right outside your door to be of service."

Lorna turned and followed the servant up the
stairs.

"I hope you will be rested enough to join us for
dinner," the consul said.

"Oh, I'm sure I will," Lorna answered absently over her shoulder, her mind already occupied with trying to sort out all the new developments.

"Fine. I'll have Ahman knock on your door a few minutes before it's served."

Something suddenly occurred to Lorna. She turned on the stairs. "How soon can I expect my trunks to be delivered?" she asked, thinking that Lady Hampton was bound to have more than one trunk and certainly there would be something more respectable to wear in one of them. The noblewoman hadn't worn such risqué clothing on board ship.

A flush rose on the consul's face. "I'm afraid you won't be seeing your trunks, m'lady. The North Africans have a particular fondness for European clothing. You were only allowed to choose the one ensemble for you to leave in."

"Why that's an outrage!" Lorna said. "I won't stand for it. I demand that you get them back."

"I'm afraid that's impossible, m'lady. This is Tripoli, and the dey does not bow to our demands. As much as I regret it, I'm afraid there is absolutely nothing I can do."

"And I'm supposed to travel all the way to Naples in this dress?" Lorna asked with genuine horror.

"Of course not, m'lady. You'll have other clothes for your trip as soon as Captain Sloan can buy you something."

"Captain Sloan?" Lorna asked in astonishment. "Why, that's the most ridiculous thing I've ever heard. I'll buy my own clothing."

"I doubt very seriously that you would know the first thing about buying clothing for a Muslim woman," Nathan said, entering the conversation. "And since we'll be traveling in Muslim disguises, that's the kind of clothing I will be buying for you."

"Traveling in disguises?" Lorna asked in surprise. "For what reason?"

"The North Africans also have a fondness for white slaves, m'lady," the consul explained, "and the sea isn't the only place these bandits are apt to attack. It isn't safe for a European to travel into the interior. You'll be much safer traveling as Muslims."

"What are you talking about, traveling into the interior?" Lorna asked in bewilderment. "I thought you said the captain was going to take me to Naples on his ship."

"Yes, from Tunis."

"But why Tunis?"

"I can hardly sail an American ship into this harbor," Nathan answered in a hard voice. "Have you forgotten that there's a war going on?"

His sarcastic answer irritated Lorna no end. With unexpected things coming at her so fast, she *had* forgotten. "Of course, I haven't forgotten! But why do we have to travel all the way to Tunis to board your ship. I should think there would be a closer bay or inlet than that."

"No, m'lady, there are very few bays or inlets on the North African coast deep enough to bring an oceangoing vessel into," Nathan answered, highly resenting the arrogant noblewoman for questioning his plans. "And the Tripolitan coastline is particularly treacherous, filled with rocks and uncharted reefs, to say nothing of the unpredictable winds at this time of the year. I don't intend to risk sinking my ship by attempting to do something so foolish." Nathan looked Lorna directly in the eye and said in a firm voice, "We sail from Tunis."

With that Nathan turned and walked away, telling Lorna in no uncertain terms that the issue was closed. It was more his attitude than his words that angered Lorna. She stared at his broad back as he walked to the door, silently fuming. Yes, it was just as she had suspected. He intended to try to dominate her. As the door closed behind him, Lorna thought, Well, we'll just see about that! She turned and walked angrily up the stairs, looking every inch the irate noblewoman she was pretending to be.

Chapter 4

When Lorna entered the dining room that night, Nathan and the consul where already there. Without volition her eyes went to the rugged American, noting that he had shed his Arab dress and was now wearing a white shirt with long, flowing sleeves, dark, skintight breeches, and a pair of knee-high black boots, the lower apparel molding his long, muscular legs to perfection. Her eyes flew to his hair, seeing that it was black and thick and lustrous as she had known it would be and that it curled around the back of his ears. Then she became aware of the captain's bold gaze sweeping her from tip to toe in her revealing dress. She bristled at his silent insult and glared back at him.

"M'lady, please allow me to introduce my naval attaché, Lieutenant Harris," the consul said.

Lorna glanced at the man standing next to Nathan. Dressed in his colorful, impressive uniform, the naval officer was fairly preening, and Lorna realized that the man must have thought she was staring at him. Why the arrogant fool! He was crazy if he thought clothes made the man. Even in his simple garments, Nathan outshone the Englishman, dwarfing the man with his superb physique, his magnificent height, and his powerful masculinity.

Smiling broadly, the officer crossed the room, made a sweeping bow before Lorna, and picked up her hand, muttering, "My pleasure, m'lady."

Besides feeling ridiculous at having her hand kissed, Lorna was appalled, for the idiot was slobbering all over it. Deciding that not even Lady Hampton would welcome this disgusting show of attention, she jerked her hand away, nodded curtly, and said in an icy voice, "Lieutenant."

Stepping forward, the consul took her elbow and led her to the table, saying, "I hope you're feeling rested this evening, m'lady."

"Oh, yes. I had a very nice nap," Lorna lied smoothly. She hadn't been able to relax at all, so great was her anxiety over the strange situation in which she found herself. After hours of pondering, the only conclusion she'd come to was that her life depended on her playing the role of Lady Hampton convincingly. Then she added, "even though the mattress was much too hard and lumpy."

Lorna saw the consul stiffen and, from the corner of her eye, Nathan's look of disgust. She hated behaving so rudely but she knew she had keep up her pose. Her freedom depended upon it.

As soon as they were seated at the table, with the consul and Lorna at the ends and the two men on either side, the servants began serving the meal. Lorna was glad for the distance that separated her from the naval officer, for despite her rebuff the man was still sending her broad smiles and admiring glances, and more that once she saw him casting sly glances at her almost exposed breasts, fugitive looks that made her long to throw her bowl of soup at him. She decided to ignore him and concentrate on her food, wishing that it was Nathan smiling and admiring her instead. Sneaking him a quick glance as she sipped her soup, she saw that the captain was absorbed with his food, apparently not even aware of her presence.

From then on Lorna barely picked at her food, her appetite suddenly deserting her. When the dessert was served, the long silence at the table was broken by the lieutenant, who said, "I understand that you're from Naples, m'lady. I've heard it's a beautiful country."

Lorna almost dropped her fork at this surprising bit of information. She had thought Lady Hampton was British. And now would the lieutenant ask her questions about the country that she couldn't answer? Suddenly she felt ill. She gave the lieutenant a weak smile and answered, "Yes, it is a beautiful country, but the court there is terribly boring."

Nathan winced. Boring? he thought. As risqué as it was? My God, she *was* decadent!

Deciding to ignore her insulting comment about her cousin's court, the consul said, "Well, you'll soon be home and back with your loved ones, m'lady." Looking directly at Nathan, he said, "And I'm sure the king of Naples will be most appreciative to the American government for its help in getting his favorite cousin back to him."

The king of Naples was her cousin? Lorna thought in astonishment. Or rather, Lady Hampton's cousin. Suddenly all the pieces of the puzzle fit together. Oh, my God! The king of Naples was the man

who had put up her ransom, and she had heard that
he was even more of an ogre than any of the British
nobility. Whatever she did, she thought in fear, she
couldn't reveal her true identity. Why, there was no
telling what that man might do to her if he found out
she had tricked him.

Seeing Lorna pale, Nathan wondered if the
woman realized that she was being used as a pawn by
the United States to secure the continuing aid of the
king of Naples. No one—not the British, the Americans, or him for that matter—had ever stopped to
think of the woman herself, just her political importance. Would she think them all callous, including
him?

Suddenly Lorna became aware that every eye at
the table was on her. She felt conspicuous. Could they
see her fear? She had to turn their attention away
from her.

Looking directly at Nathan, she said, "Speaking
of the war, Captain, I happened to see the burning of
the *Philadelphia* from the palace window. May I
commend your countrymen on their brave and daring deed."

One dark eyebrow arched in surprise before Nathan answered, "Thank you, m'lady. It just so happens
that the officer who led the boarding party is an ac-
quaintance of mine. The next time I see him I'll relay
your compliment."

"You know Stephen Decatur?" the consul asked.

"Yes, I know all of Preble's Boys, as the rest of our
navy and merchant fleet have come to call the commodore's junior officers because of their youth. Several are personal friends. They're all bold, daring
young men, eager for action and glory."

"Strutting bantam fighting cocks would be a
more appropriate description, with their arrogant

swagger and their fondness for dueling," the lieutenant said nastily.

Nathan's green eyes swiveled to the naval officer. "True, they're proud and high-spirited, but they only need some discipline and firm guidance. And they're getting that under Commodore Preble. He's making them naval officers of the finest caliber."

"If they're such fine officers, then why didn't Decatur sail the *Philadelphia* out of the harbor that night, instead of burning her?" the British officer countered. "He could have, you know. His boarding party had completely overpowered the guards. Instead, he destroyed a valuable ship."

"Commodore Preble didn't tell Decatur to use his own discretion. He was ordered to burn the ship, and a good officer always obeys orders," Nathan pointed out.

"And Captain Bainbridge? What is your excuse for his actions? He *was* told to act at his own discretion. And what did the fool try to do? Sail a frigate into a harbor he knew was too shallow. And as if grounding her wasn't bad enough, then he tried to sink her. He should have blown up the ship right then and there!"

"Bainbridge didn't rush in that day," Nathan replied, the small muscle twitching in his jaw the sign of the anger he was holding tightly in check. "He had his men sounding the depths. The reef he hit was uncharted. It could have happened to anyone, even the best of captains. And I'm sure he didn't feel at liberty to put to death the three hundred and six men he had on board by blowing her up. Unlike the British, the American navy values its men more than its ships."

Lieutenant Harris stiffened in his chair. "And what do you mean by that remark, Captain Sloan?" he asked in an icy voice.

"I mean if the officers in the Royal navy treated

their seamen with any decency at all, their men would live to serve longer, and your navy wouldn't have the rampant desertion that it now has. If you could learn to control your senseless brutality, then maybe you could maintain a navy to fight your war with France without impressing the free seamen of the other nations of the world, notably those of the United States."

The Englishman thrust out his chin, saying hotly, "Sir! I resent that statement."

"I didn't expect you to like it," Nathan answered in a carefully measured voice.

When Lieutenant Harris attacked first the American officers, then their tactics, Lorna at first thought he was trying to impress her, since every remark was made with a smug smile in her direction. But when Nathan hit back and the naval officer became so angry, she sensed that there was a deep animosity between the two that surpassed their dislike of one another as individuals. She watched breathlessly as the two men stared across the table at each other, the room charged with tension. Glancing at the Englishman, she saw that his face was mottled with rage and that he seemed to be having trouble breathing. Nathan, however, gave the outward appearance of being totally unaffected, except for the dangerous metallic glitter in his eyes, a look that made Lorna's heart race in fear.

Lieutenant Harris slammed to his feet so suddenly that Lorna jumped. "Sir! I demand—"

"Lieutenant Harris!"

The consul's sharp bark cut across the officer's words. The lieutenant's head jerked around to face his superior at the head of the table.

"May I remind you that there is a lady present,

Lieutenant," the consul said in a hard voice, "and that Captain Sloan is a guest in this house—at *my* request."

The officer glared at his superior as he struggled to suppress his anger, his body trembling with effort. The damn fool! the consul thought, thinking to challenge Nathan Sloan—of all men—to a duel. If he hadn't stopped him, the lieutenant would have met the same fate as the personal secretary of the governor of Malta, who had made the lethal mistake of deliberately goading one of the American navy's young, hot-tempered officers into challenging him to a duel. And if he remembered the incident correctly, British naval officers had been encouraging the secretary by taunting the American with insults. Yes, there was bad blood between the British and American seamen, and the consul feared that the Admiralty's high-handed methods on the high seas and the arrogant manner of her officers would some day force a war between the two countries. In the meanwhile he had to contend with this pompous fool standing before him.

The consul rose, saying, "I suggest that we retire to the drawing room, where we can enjoy the evening breeze from the bay. I hope it will be much cooler there," he ended with a pointed look at the naval officer.

As the four walked into the drawing room, the lieutenant lagging behind resentfully, the consul led Lorna to the open doors at one side of the room, saying, "There's a small balcony out here that overlooks the bay, m'lady. While you won't be able to see much, the breeze is refreshing."

Almost as soon as Lorna and the consul had stepped onto the balcony, they heard the sound of cannons being fired, the thundering noise drawing the attention of Nathan and the lieutenant and bringing them from the drawing room to join them.

"The Americans must be attacking again," the consul said.

"No, those aren't American cannons," Nathan informed him, stepping up to the balcony railing.

Nathan looked out to sea, barely able to distinguish the dim outline of the big American frigate in the thin veil of low-lying fog that was drifting in from the Mediterranean. Turning his head in the direction of the harbor, he saw the small ship that the Tripolitan gun batteries were firing at. "What ship is that?" he asked the consul.

"I can't tell for sure from this distance. Let me get my spyglass."

The consul rushed away and returned with his spyglass shortly thereafter. Peering through the glass, he said, "It looks like the *Intrepid* to me."

"Isn't that the Tripolitan ketch that the navy captured about a year ago and renamed?" Nathan asked the consul.

"Yes. The *Intrepid* is the only ship your navy has at its disposal with a draft shallow enough to penetrate the harbor fully. Decatur used her the night he burned the *Philadelphia*. But why are they sending her into the harbor all alone at night?"

"May I look?" Nathan asked, holding out his hand.

The consul handed him the spyglass. As Nathan peered into it, he said, "They're sailing the *Intrepid* toward the Tripolitan pirate fleet anchored in the middle of the harbor."

"But one ship can't attack their entire fleet," the consul objected in alarm.

"They aren't going to bombard the fleet. Unless I

miss my guess, they've turned the *Intrepid* into a fireboat."

"A fireboat?" Lorna asked. "What's that?"

"A floating mine," Nathan answered in a grim voice. "They've filled her hold with gunpowder and exploding shells. When they get as close as they possibly can to that fleet, they'll light the fuses, dive overboard, and swim back to the longboats that must be waiting in that fogbank."

"Why that's suicide!" the lieutenant said in a shocked voice. "No. It's murder! Preble has sent those men to certain death. When that fireboat explodes, they'll be blown right out of the water."

"No, it's not certain death," Nathan countered. "Not if they use long fuses. It's dangerous, yes. Fuses can be unpredictable at times. For that reason I'm sure Preble asked for volunteers. And knowing how high the navy's élan is right now, I'd be willing to bet almost every man in the squadron volunteered."

Lorna strained her eyes to see in the darkness and could barely make out the two triangular sails of the ketch. As the small ship sailed slowly into the harbor, the gun batteries on the shore let go with a steady fire that sounded like one long continuous roll of thunder, and the Tripolitan gunboats rushed from their moorings to head off the *Intrepid* before she reached the anchored ships.

Suddenly there was a blinding flash of light that lit up the heavens and the entire bay, followed a split second later by a deafening explosion that shook the earth. Sheets of red and orange flames leaped into the sky, hurling blazing planking and spars through the air and sending shells arching across the dark firmament, leaving sputtering trails of red stars in their wake before they burst like giant skyrockets.

"What happened?" the consul asked in a shocked voice. "It was too soon for the fireboat to be set off."

"I don't know," Nathan answered, feeling stunned and handing the spyglass back to the consul. "They must have suffered a direct hit from a red-hot ball."

The consul peered through the spyglass. Where the *Intrepid* had floated just moments before, there was nothing in the water, not even a piece of burning planking. He lowered the glass, muttering, "My God! Those poor devils."

Everyone on the balcony knew that none of the men on the *Intrepid* could possibly have survived the explosion. As a long, stunned silence followed, tears swam in Lorna's eyes and a lump came to her throat. She glanced across at the lieutenant, afraid he would say I told you so, but saw that the man was just as shocked and shaken as everyone else.

Finally, the consul turned from the railing and saw Lorna's ashen face. Walking to her, he took her arm in his hand and said gently, "I'll escort you to your room, m'lady."

Numbly, Lorna allowed the consul to lead her from the balcony and through the drawing room. At the doorway she turned and looked back, seeing Nathan standing at the railing, his hands tightly grasping the cold metal as he stared out at the harbor. He had just seen a group of his countrymen blown up, and she remembered his saying that he had many friends among the American officers. Was he wondering if one of them had been on the *Intrepid* and had just met a violent, flaming death? Her heart went out to him and she fervently wished she could drop her hated pose and behave as herself. She wanted so badly to comfort him.

Chapter 5

Lorna had just arisen early the next morning and donned the robe the consul had loaned her the night before when a knock sounded at the door. Thinking it was Ahman coming to tell her breakfast would soon be served, she walked to the door and opened it.

Nathan stood in the hallway, his broad shoulders filling the doorway, once again wearing Arab dress. Lorna's heart did a strange little flip-flap as her gaze quickly swept over his tall form, wondering how a man clothed in a simple white gown could look so utterly masculine. Then, becoming acutely aware of her bare feet and her legs exposed almost to her calves—for the robe belonged to the consul's much shorter wife—a spontaneous flush of embarrassment crept up her cheeks.

But Nathan wasn't looking at Lorna's bare feet and legs. His eyes were locked on the rosy glow of her face, her violet eyes, still heavy-lidded from sleep,

and her long, thick hair that framed her face and
shoulders, the sunlight from the window picking up
its rich reddish highlights. Realizing that he was staring like some country yokel who had never seen a
beautiful woman before, Nathan was irritated with
himself, and his words were more clipped than he
meant them to be. "I'm delivering your new wardrobe."

No good morning, no nothing, Lorna thought,
feeling disappointed and a little hurt. Why, even if he
disdained Lady Hampton, there was such a thing as
common courtesy. Well, if he was going to be rude to
her, she'd be just as rude. She motioned to the chest at
her feet and said sharply, "Well, if my new clothing's
in that, Captain, bring it in. Surely you don't expect
me to carry it."

Lorna turned and walked back into the room,
actually enjoying her role as Lady Hampton and being able to put the rude American in his place. Then,
realizing that he hadn't followed, she turned and saw
him still standing in the doorway. "Well, what are you
waiting for?" she snapped.

"I'm waiting for you to say please," Nathan answered in a tightly controlled voice. "I'm *not* your
servant."

There was a look in Nathan's eyes that made
Lorna beware. Apparently her demands had made
him very angry. A tingle of fear ran through her.
Maybe she *had* come across a little too strong, but it
still galled her to have to back down. "Please," she
said, a bit sarcastically.

Nathan was tempted to tell Lady Hampton to go
to hell and carry her own chest. Even though she had
bowed to his wishes, she didn't sound at all like she
meant it. But he knew she could never carry the
heavy chest. Why, he seriously doubted if she could

even push it, considering she had never done a lick of work in her life. He picked up the chest, walked across the room, and dumped it on her bed.

Lorna expected Nathan to leave the room immediately, particularly as angry as he was, but to her surprise he flung open the lid and began pulling out garments, saying, "Since you are unfamiliar with Muslim clothing, I'll explain how some of these are worn." Picking up a pale blue silk garment, he said, "These are called *chalwar*."

Lorna recognized the full pantaloons. "Yes, I'm familiar with them. I wore them in the palace."

Nathan was a little surprised that Lady Hampton hadn't said something sarcastic. Why, she had actually sounded civil. Had his showing her he wouldn't tolerate her making demands on him taught her a lesson? He certainly hoped so. He tossed the *chalwar* aside, and picked up a long chemiselike garment with wide, long sleeves that was made of a thinner silk in the same pale blue. "This *entarie* is worn over the *chalwar*."

When Nathan pulled out the pantaloons, Lorna was afraid the next garment he showed her would be the brief bolero that she had worn in the *iyal* and that she would be going around with half her belly showing again. The modest *entarie* was a pleasant surprise, but it was the caftan that Nathan next brought from the chest that caught her eye. Open at the front like a coat, the royal blue outer gown was elaborately scalloped with silver and light blue embroidery along both sides, the hem, and the bottom of the wide, long sleeves. When Nathan pulled out a *kusak*, a wide silver sash that he explained was tied over the caftan at the hip, and a pair of silver *babouches*—soft leather slippers with turned-up toes—Lorna thought the ensemble the most beautiful she had ever seen. She

could hardly wait for Nathan to leave the room so she
could put it on.

Taking a piece of folded silk the same color as the
caftan from the trunk and laying it on the bed, Nathan said, "This is a *haik,* the outer covering that all
Muslim women are required to wear when they go
outside. Since there's an art to wrapping it around
you, I'll show you how it's donned when we leave
later this morning. That and this *yashmak,*" he
ended, placing a long, semitransparent veil on top of
the folded material.

"We're leaving this morning?" Lorna asked in
surprise.

"Yes. As soon as you've dressed and eaten breakfast."

Lorna felt a twinge of fear. She realized that she
knew nothing of this man. True, the rugged captain
was exciting, but he was also a stranger, a very dangerous stranger, and she would be all alone with him.
If only she had time to get to know him before em-
barking on a long journey with him. "Why so soon?
Can't it wait until tomorrow?"

There she goes again, acting like the spoiled prin-
cess she was and questioning his plans, Nathan
thought, his anger on the rise again. The captain
wasn't in the best of moods to begin with. When he
was in the city earlier that morning to pick up Lady
Hampton's wardrobe, ordered the day before, the
Tripolitans were gloating over their victory the night
before. Then, when he heard one Janissary telling
another that the pasha had forced William Bainbridge, the imprisoned captain of the ill-fated *Philadelphia,* to view the mutilated remains of the twelve
Americans whose bodies had been washed ashore,
Nathan became enraged. It had been all he could do
to keep from smashing his fist into the smug Turk's

face. No, he was in no mood to put up with any interference from the haughty Lady Hampton.

"My instructions were to get you out of Tripoli as soon as possible," Nathan answered in a terse voice. "No, m'lady, we can't wait until tomorrow to leave, particularly not after what happened to the *Intrepid* last night. As soon as the wind shifts later this morning, Commodore Preble will have his fleet in the harbor bombarding the city with a vengeance. Besides, caravans don't leave the city every day. It might be a week before another departs for Tunis." Nathan turned and walked to the door, saying in a firm voice over his shoulder, "We leave in an hour, m'lady."

Lorna was taken aback by Nathan's abrupt manner after she had tried to soothe his anger by being more civil, but it was his announcement that they would leave in an hour that galvanized her. Quickly, she stripped off the robe, washed with the pitcher of water and basin she found sitting on the dresser, and donned her new clothing, noting that it was made of the finest silk. After arranging her long hair in a simple chignon at the back of her neck, she couldn't resist quickly rummaging through a few layers of clothing in the chest before closing it. Everything was as luxurious and beautiful as the ensemble she wore, a rainbow of vibrant colors and soft pastels, many shot with silver and gold threads that gave the material an iridescent appearance.

Closing the lid, she ran her fingers over the chest, admiring the wood and bone inlays on it and thinking that Lord Hampton must be a very wealthy man to afford such expensive clothing for his wife just to travel in. Why, he had spent a small fortune on clothes that Lady Hampton would probably never wear again after she returned to Europe. If her husband was so wealthy, then why did Lady Hampton's cousin pay her ransom? she wondered. She pushed the puzzling thought aside, picked up the *haik* and veil, and rushed from the room.

When Lorna entered the dining room, the vision she presented took Nathan's breath away. He had cursed himself for a fool to pay so much for clothing for the noblewoman. Since no one else seemed to have taken into consideration that the woman would have to be completely outfitted, it was coming out of his own pocket. But for some strange reason, he had wanted to clothe her in the finest, rejecting the cottons and linens in favor of the rich silks, satins, and brocades. Now, seeing her standing before him, Nathan had no regrets. A beautiful woman deserved beautiful clothing—and what the hell! After the profits he had made the past several years with his blockade running, he could well afford it. Why not clothe her to be pleasing to his eyes? He was the one who was going to have to look at her for the next several weeks.

When they were standing in the foyer after their hasty breakfast, Nathan took the *haik* from Lorna and shook it out. Lorna was astonished, for the piece of material was a good six feet wide and seemed to go on and on and on. Draping it over her head, Nathan began wrapping it around her. On his third circle around her, Lorna frowned and asked, "How long is this thing, anyway?"

"About six yards."

She was to be wrapped in up in six yards of material? Like a mummy? Lorna thought in horror. "Is this really necessary, Captain?" she asked in an irritated voice. "Why, I already have on two layers of clothing. I'll burn up!"

"The natives of Africa contend with the heat in two ways, m'lady. In the north they swaddle themselves in layers of clothing to protect themselves from the sun. Farther south they go virtually naked. Would you prefer the latter?"

Lorna remembered that she had been all but naked in the sheer garments she had worn the day before and knew without a doubt that the captain was referring to that. She wished he hadn't brought up the indecent garment. "Of course not!" she snapped.

"Oh?" Nathan asked, the word dripping with sarcasm. "Well, I couldn't be sure, considering you were almost naked in that flimsy thing you were wearing yesterday."

He just isn't going to leave it alone, Lorna thought angrily. He was determined to insult her. Her violet eyes flashed. "Watch your tongue, Captain! I won't tolerate such insolence from anyone. What I wear is none of your concern."

Nathan took satisfaction in seeing that he had riled her. He smiled smugly and answered, "You're right, m'lady. What you wear is none of my concern. I was just making an observation."

Picking up the *yashmak*, he started to attach the bosom-length veil at the Lady Hampton's temples, but when his fingers brushed the soft skin of her cheeks, Lorna snatched the veil away from him and said, "No! I'll do it!"

Nathan stepped back, his eyes glittering. "Very well, m'lady."

Lorna guessed what Nathan was thinking. That he thought his touch repulsed her. To the contrary. Just the brush of his fingers had sent tingles racing through her, arousing feelings that *were* beginning to frighten her with their intensity. She wondered what he would think if he knew how much his touch, just his presence, affected her. Why, he would probably be even more disgusted with her, a married woman being attracted to another man, particularly one who was practically a stranger. It would only confirm his suspicions that she was a wanton.

She looked down at the veil in her hand and asked, "How does it attach?"

Nathan was tempted to tell her to figure it out for herself, but he was anxious to get started. He didn't want to take any chances of missing the caravan. "It hooks into your hair at the temples."

After Lorna had put on the veil Nathan opened the door and she walked outside, very aware of the tall, disturbing captain following her down the stairs and over to where the consul stood waiting by the open sedan chair. Seeing her chest sitting at the back of the chair beside one that she assumed to be Nathan's gave her a strange feeling in the pit of her stomach—somehow it seemed rather intimate—and she almost missed the step when the consul helped her in.

After she was seated the consul said graciously, "Good-bye, m'lady. It was a pleasure to serve you."

Lorna wanted to thank the man for all he had done on her behalf, but she knew Lady Hampton wouldn't. She acknowledged his words with a curt nod of the head, as if she expected his serving her as her due.

Thank God she's leaving, the consul thought. He didn't envy the captain his job. One day in the hateful woman's company had been more than he could bear. He turned to Nathan and said, "I place her in your capable hands, Captain Sloan, and wish you a safe and speedy trip."

Nathan, too, only nodded in acknowledgment, the consul's words somehow disturbing him. He shook hands with the Englishman and climbed into the chair, pondering over this new oddity. He was accustomed to the awesome responsibility of seeing to the protection of valuable cargoes and the lives of his crew. Then why did responsibility for seeing to the safe transportation of this woman suddenly disturb him? Yes, what lay before them was a dangerous trip, as well as grueling, but danger was no stranger to him. And certainly no woman could be more valuable to him than the lives of his own crew, most of whom were friends as well as trusted employees, particularly not a woman he disliked as much as he did Lady Hampton. And yet, Nathan felt an uneasiness that he might have attributed to fear had the emotion not been foreign to him.

Lorna was glad for Nathan's preoccupation with his thoughts as the four bearers picked up the sedan and trotted through the countryside. It gave her an opportunity to enjoy all the new and exciting sights around her, something that she was sure the worldly Lady Hampton wouldn't do. But then, maybe the noblewoman might show some interest. This was an exotic land, so different from Europe, a land that few Europeans had ever seen.

They rode by fields of ripening barley and groves of citrus and olive trees, then, entering the city itself, passing through narrow, dark streets that twisted and turned between two-storied houses that lined each side, the air heavy with the smell of mold and the lingering odors of the Muslims' spicy cooking.

When they entered a large, sun-splashed plaza where the *souk*, an open marketplace, sat, Lorna was amazed at the goods she saw for sale as they passed the long, narrow rows of cubicles. There was every imaginable kind of leather goods, luxurious carpets, gold and silver jewelry, colorful pottery, gleaming copper goods, to say nothing of the stalls where clothing, fresh produce, and herbs and spices were sold.

The going was slow since the plaza was crowded with people coming and going, and Lorna noted that the majority of the shoppers were dressed in black, the color of the poor, many of the women not even wearing veils, but holding their *haiks* over their lower faces, while they balanced their shopping baskets on their heads. The marketplace was also incredibly noisy, for it seemed the Muslims traded by bargaining, and many of the shoppers were loudly and heatedly arguing with the merchants over the prices they were asking, some even shaking their fists in others' faces.

They left the plaza and entered another maze of streets, these even darker and narrower. Lorna sensed something sinister here that she hadn't felt before. The hair rose on the nape of her neck. Apparently the bearers felt it, too, for they were glancing apprehensively about them. Seeing Nathan make a small movement, she glanced across to see that he had pushed his caftan aside and placed his hand on the hilt of the long dirk he had tucked into the wide leather belt he wore over his gown. Then, seeing the pistol that he had tucked on the other side, she looked about her nervously, thinking the place dangerous. Probably a lair for cutthroats and thieves. Her heart raced with fear.

A moment later they left the dark, dank streets and Lorna sighed in relief, not even realizing she had been holding her breath. As they left the city behind them and once again traveled through the countryside, Lorna noted the landscape was perfectly flat and broken only by an occasional date palm. They passed a tannery and the rank, acrid smell coming from it made Lorna's nostrils burn and her eyes water. Then, noticing a thick cloud of dust hovering over the ground in the distance before her, Lorna strained her eyes and saw where the caravan was forming. As they came closer, she stared at the muddled mass of men and beasts, but it was the animals that caught her attention, for she had never dreamed there were that many camels on earth, nor had she ever known that they came in so many colors. There were pure whites, creams, grays, and all shades of brown. Some of the animals were kneeling on the ground to be loaded, while others were already being led away by their drivers to assume the position they would take in the caravan.

Lorna looked about her as the bearers weaved their way through the crowd of milling Arabs and beasts. Piles of goods lay scattered about on the ground: boxes, crates, baskets, rolled-up carpets, hides, and textiles. The camels grunted and squealed; Arabic shouts and curses hung in the air as the drivers forced the obstinate animals to their knees by pulling on the ropes attached to their front legs and beating them on the nose with a stick. Lorna wrinkled her nose at the strong smell of man sweat, animal sweat, and camel dung, the choking dust kicked up by the activity rolling around her, stinging her eyes and making her cough.

The bearers carried the chair to the fringes of the area where the caravan was forming and stopped, lowering it to the ground. As Nathan helped Lorna alight, a wiry Arab dressed in a striped gown and grimy turban rushed up to them. Touching his forehead, then his breast, he bowed low in the traditional Arabic greeting. As Nathan talked to the man, Lorna looked at the captain in surprise, not at his fluency in the foreign language, for she had expected that, but rather at the sound. With his deep, rich voice, the Arabic didn't sound in the least guttural or grating. It came from his lips in a pleasant, rolling lilt.

As the Arab hurried away, Nathan turned to Lorna, saying, "That was Hamid. I've hired him and his brother, Jabir, to act as our drivers and servants on this trip. He tells me that everything is loaded and ready to leave. If you will just follow me."

As Nathan turned to walk away, Lorna hurried to catch up with his long strides. Seeing her by his side, Nathan stopped, saying, "No, m'lady. A Muslim wife never walks beside her husband. She stays several paces behind with her head bowed."

There was one word that caught Lorna's attention. "Wife?" she asked in a shocked voice. "Are you saying that we're posing as husband and wife?"

Dammit, Nathan thought, here she goes again. Trying to interfere with his plans. And undoubtedly she found the idea of even posing as a commoner's wife repugnant. "We certainly are, m'lady," he answered in a hard voice. "Muslim women don't travel unless they are accompanied by their husbands, or perhaps their fathers, and I'm certainly not old enough to be your father. Now bow your head and follow me."

"The devil I'll bow my head!"

Nathan struggled to control his patience. "I know that you're nobility and unaccustomed to showing humility of any kind," he said in a scornful voice, "but I'm afraid you're going to have to follow the Muslim customs."

Posing as Lady Hampton had nothing to do with Lorna's strong objection. No, it was personal. She highly resented the way the Muslim male lorded it over the female. "Well, I'm not a Muslim! I won't bow my head and I won't walk behind you. I'm not your slave!"

"I didn't say you were," Nathan answered. "But

behaving as a Muslim is as important as dressing like one to maintain our disguises."

Lorna was aware of all the Arabs around them, many within hearing distance. Suddenly something occurred to her. She looked around her nervously, then hissed in lowered voice, "How dare you accuse me of giving away our disguises! No, you're the one who's giving us away. You should have spoken to me in Arabic instead of English."

"They don't know we're speaking English. All they know is we're speaking in a strange tongue. We're posing as Berbers, who have their own language. Since Berbers are well known to isolate themselves from the Arabs, these people won't think it at all strange that we're speaking in our own language."

"But you said we were pretending to be Arabs," Lorna objected.

"No, I didn't say we were pretending to be Arabs," Nathan answered in exasperation. "I said we were pretending to be Muslims."

"Arab or Muslim, what difference does it make?" Lorna tossed back in agitation. "They're all the same!"

Nathan took a deep breath to control himself and answered, "No, they aren't. A Muslim is anyone who practices the religion of Islam. It has nothing to do with race, ethnic origin, or nationality." He looked Lorna in the eye and said in a firm voice, "Now stop arguing with me. I know what I'm doing. Besides, you're drawing entirely too much attention to us. A Muslim wife would never dare to challenge her husband in anything."

Lorna glanced around her and saw that many of the Arabs were staring at them curiously. Then, as Nathan turned and walked away, she bowed her head and followed, looking like the meek Muslim wife, but fuming silently. She should have known Nathan wouldn't make a slip of the tongue in front of the Arabs, she thought. He was too much in control of everything, including her. And undoubtedly he was enjoying lording it over her. Damn him! Then she thought of something that puzzled her. Where in the world had he, an American, become so knowledgeable about North Africa?

Nathan was enjoying lording it over Lady Hampton, although that was not why he had insisted she follow the Muslim customs. The shrew had never taken orders from anyone in her life, and he thought it fitting justice that she should be on the other end for a change. Besides, even if she had been a pleasanter person, he wouldn't tolerate any interference if it would endanger them.

When they reached the place where Hamid stood beside a kneeling camel, Nathan turned and assisted Lorna up the wooden stairs of the enclosed sedan on top of the animal. Looking inside, Lorna turned on the stairs and said, "Certainly we're not both going to ride in this little thing. Why, there's hardly room for one, and there aren't even any seats."

Christ! Nathan thought. He should have known he hadn't put her in her place. He had seen the resentful glance she'd shot him as he helped her up the stairs. Again he fought down his anger and replied in a tightly controlled voice, "No, m'lady. I'll be riding a camel. As for the sedan's size and lack of seats, it's large enough for you to stretch out your legs and there are cushions for you to sit on."

"But I'll burn up in there," Lorna objected. "Why can't I ride a camel too?"

"It will be much cooler in there in the shade than out here in the hot sun," Nathan pointed out. "Besides, Muslim women traveling in caravans keep themselves hidden."

That stupid Muslim rule again, Lorna thought, her eyes flashing with anger. Domineering bastards!

Nathan saw the expression on Lorna's face. He'd had all he could tolerate of her spoiled temper tantrums. "Let's get something straight right now, m'lady," Nathan said in a hard voice, his eyes boring into her. "I give the orders on this trip, and you'll obey them whether you like it or not. This plot to rescue you wasn't my idea, and if I had my way about it, I wouldn't be here right now. You may be willing to risk your life by giving us away, but I'll be damned if I'll let you risk mine. So don't push me too far." Taking her arm in a firm grip, Nathan guided her up to the box, saying in stern voice that brooked no argument, "Now, get in. You're holding us up."

Lorna found herself forced into the dark box. She had hardly sat down before the door was closed. Still seething with resentment at Nathan's domineering attitude, she peered through the sheer curtain on the window and saw Nathan striding to a kneeling camel, then the billowing of his long robes as he gracefully swung into the high-backed wooden saddle that was padded with blankets.

Suddenly Lorna was thrown backward as the camel beneath her rose partially on its front legs, then thrown forward as it rose completely on its hind legs, then backward again as the animal came to a full stand. Frantically she groped for something to hang onto, sliding from one end of the sedan to the other, terrified that she would be thrown out or that the sedan would topple off the camel. Then, when the violent rocking stopped, she looked down and felt a twinge of fear, for the ground looked a long way off.

When the camel began to move, Lorna clung to

the windowsills on both sides, still terrified that the strange contraption would fall off, for with every step the animal took, the sedan swayed precariously from side to side. It wasn't until they had traveled a good mile that she finally felt secure enough to let go her tenacious hold.

"If you like, you can take off your *haik* and veil now."

Lorna was startled by Nathan's deep voice. She had been so occupied with hanging on that she had forgotten about him. She looked out the window and saw him riding beside her. For a moment she admired the ease with which he sat in the saddle, not looking at all out of place. If she hadn't known better, she would have thought him an Arab instead of an American sea captain. He seemed to be perfectly attuned to his surroundings, as if he had been born to them. Then realizing what he had said, she bristled and answered sarcastically, "Thank you, master."

Ignoring the sharp glance Nathan shot her, she took off the veil and set it aside. But removing the *haik* in her close confines proved to be difficult with it wrapped around her so many times. She squirmed and twisted and rolled, tugging at the hot garment and muttering curses under her breath, thinking it would take a contortionist to disrobe in this little box. By the time she had finished removing it, she had worked up a good sweat and an absolute loathing for the garment.

Two hours later Lorna had slipped off her caftan also—and was still burning up. The box seemed to hold the heat like an oven, the temperature so hot that her perspiration evaporated before it even dampened her skin. Her lips were parched and her throat dry. When the caravan stopped, she let out a little cry of relief, thinking they were stopping for their noonday break and she could finally get a drink of water.

When the camel didn't kneel as she had expected, Lorna pushed aside the curtain and looked out, seeing the Arabs were throwing down small carpets on the sand. As they fell to their knees and prostrated themselves in the hot sand, all facing east toward Mecca, Lorna felt a keen sense of disappointment. They hadn't stopped to eat and quench their thirst but to pray.

Glancing down, Lorna's eyes widened, surprised to see that Nathan was kneeling with the others, his broad back bent to the ground. Then she reminded herself that they were traveling under the guise of being Muslims, and naturally, he would have to pretend to pray to keep the others from becoming suspicious. Then, as the opening words of the Koran drifted up to her, she realized with a little shock that he wasn't pretending. He *was* saying the prayer. She strained her ears, hearing, *"Bismillah ar-Rahman ar-Rahum."* In the name of God, the most merciful, the most compassionate. A shiver ran through Lorna at the sound of the words. With Nathan's deep voice and rolling lilt, the Arabic words had a poetic beauty about them.

Lorna was still staring when Nathan rose and turned. Seeing the thundering look that came over his face, another shiver ran through her, this one of fear. In three long strides, he was beneath her, saying, "Shut the curtain! You're exposing your face."

Even though Lorna realized he was concerned about her arousing the Arabs' suspicions, she felt his words like a slap in the face. He doesn't have to be so ugly about it, she thought in self-defense. Anyone can make a mistake. She dropped the curtain and snapped back, "I just wanted to ask when we'll be stopping to eat."

"Not for another hour. And from now on if you push the curtain aside, wear your veil. You're supposed to be a Muslim, remember?"

"Of course I remember! You won't give me a minute to forget it!"

Lorna saw the flare of anger in Nathan's green eyes, and a little twinge of fear ran through her. He had warned her not to push him too far. Then as he whirled and walked rapidly away, her courage returned, and she glared at his back. Oh, yes, she thought, he's enjoying lording it over me immensely.

But in the next hour that passed, Lorna forgot her anger at Nathan's domineering manner. Her acute thirst took precedence over everything. When the caravan stopped and he told her she must don her *haik* and veil before emerging from the sedan, she hurried and haphazardly wrapped the covering around her, her only thought to get to the small tent the servants were setting up and get a drink of water.

As soon as she entered the dim tent, she looked around her. Seeing nothing that resembled a water container, she asked, "Where's the water?"

"There won't be any water to drink until we stop tonight. We'll eat, but not drink."

"I'm not hungry," Lorna snapped. "I'm thirsty!"

"I know. So is everyone else. But drinking at midday in this heat is the worst thing you can do. If you drink now, your thirst will be ten times worse this afternoon, so intense you can feel it clawing at your vitals."

"I don't care! I *must* have a drink of water. Now!"

"No," Nathan answered in a firm voice, "I won't let you have any water. You must trust my judgment in this. I'm only doing what's best for you."

With that Nathan turned and walked from the tent. Lorna stared at his back in disbelief. What was wrong with him? Couldn't he understand? She'd *die* if she didn't get a drink of water. Why, she'd been a silly fool to have felt attracted to this cruel American. He was a brute! No one with any decency at all would refuse someone a drink of water.

When Hamid brought Lorna her meal, she discovered she couldn't eat. There was no saliva in her mouth, and the bread and meat tasted like leather. She shoved it aside, feeling hot and miserable and unbearably thirsty.

The afternoon was one long agonizing passage of time for Lorna. The blazing sun beat down on the sedan, sucking the moisture from her skin, the hot air searing her lungs. Looking out the window at the landscape did nothing to take her mind from her excruciating thirst and the unbearable heat, for the land looked as miserable and dried out as she felt. Totally barren, except for the browned, withered shrubs that dotted it, it was nothing but hot rock and sand beneath the blinding white glare of the sun, heat waves radiating from everything.

By the time the sun was setting, Lorna was so weak from dehydration that she couldn't even sit up. She lay limply sprawled on the cushions, her lips cracked, her tongue thickened, her throat feeling as if someone had stuffed a wad of cotton into it, the sway of the sedan making her seasick on her empty stomach. She'd die here in this miserable, hot box, she thought, and no one would even care, certainly not that heartless bastard out there. A painful sob escaped her parched throat, and a single tear fell from her eye, to evaporate before it even reached her cheek.

Lorna was unaware when the caravan finally stopped. The door to the sedan was opened, and

strong arms lifted her from it and carried her to the
tent that had been hastily thrown up. Gentle hands
laid her on soft cushions, then stripped her of her
caftan and bathed her face and arms with tepid water. It wasn't until Nathan placed a cup at her lips and
commanded softly, "Drink, m'lady," that she became
aware of her surroundings.

At the feel of the liquid against her cracked lips,
Lorna grabbed the cup and would have drunk its
entire contents had Nathan not stopped her, holding
the cup firmly to keep her from turning it on end and
saying, "No, just sip it at first. Otherwise, it will make
you sick."

Lorna glanced up in surprise. Had she only imagined it, or had there been concern in his deep voice?
She looked into a pair of shimmering green eyes, once
again dazed by their startling contrast to his tanned
skin. Then, becoming aware that he was sitting beside
her and supporting her back with one arm, her head
resting on his broad shoulder, she relished the feel of
him cradling her, drinking in his strength and atten-
tiveness as thirstily as she did the cup of liquid he held
at her lips.

When Lorna had emptied the cup, Nathan released her and turned to the low brazier beside him,
pouring another cup of tea from the pot sitting on it.
Lorna missed the comforting presence of his strong
arm around her and was disappointed when he
handed the cup back to her instead of resuming his
former position. As an orphan, she had never had
anyone show concern for her, treat her with any particular kindness. Even though she knew it wasn't herself he was concerned about, but Lady Hampton, it
had been a wonderful feeling.

As she placed the cup to her lips, she realized for
the first time that the liquid was hot. "Can't I have

something cool to drink?" she asked. "I'm already burning up."

"No, putting something cool in your stomach at this point would be too much of a shock to your over-heated system. You start with hot liquids, then graduate to tepid, then cool. And you'll find the mint tea much more refreshing than a drink of plain water."

After her fourth cup of tea, Lorna found Nathan's words true. She did feel remarkably refreshed. Why, she almost felt human again. Remembering how she had behaved at the noon break, she was ashamed of herself, for her pose as Lady Hampton had had nothing to do with her anger. Surely Nathan knew better than she how to survive in this heat, and surely he must have been just as hot and thirsty as she. And yet, he had denied himself water, too. No, he wasn't cruel. His gentle, almost tender ministrations to her had proven that. No, not to her, she brutally reminded herself. To Lady Hampton, his charge, as obviously he was a man who took his responsibilities very seriously. The reminder that his attentions had been directed at another woman brought her an acute pang of disappointment. But still, she didn't want him to think ill of her, regardless of who he thought she was. Why, she had acted like a spoiled child. Besides, playing the role of the arrogant woman was beginning to get wearisome. Surely even Lady Hampton could be civil at times.

"I'm sorry I was so unreasonable about the water earlier."

Nathan looked down at Lorna with surprise before answering, "There's no need to apologize. Intense thirst, such as you were experiencing, has been known to drive men insane."

The flap on the tent was pushed back, and Hamid entered, carrying a tray laden with food. Keeping his eyes averted so as not to gaze at Lorna's unveiled face, he placed the tray on a low table, salaamed, and withdrew.

As the spicy aroma of the food filled the tent, Lorna suddenly realized she was famished. She could hardly wait while Nathan moved the table before her and then sank down on the carpet across from her. As he removed the lid from the crockery bowl, Lorna looked down at the thick stew, her mouth watering. When Nathan broke in half the sheet of thin, crusty bread that accompanied the stew, there was no hesitation on Lorna's part in accepting it and tearing off a small piece. She knew from living in the *iyal* how the Arabs ate. Since they had no eating utensils, they used bread to scoop up the food if it was of a loose consistency, or the first two fingers on their right hand if it was of a firmer consistency. Nor did she object to Nathan's eating from the common dish, as was Arab custom, something that Lady Hampton would probably never have done but which Lorna didn't even think of in her intense hunger.

Placing a piece of bread soaked with gravy in her mouth, Lorna savored the delicious flavor of lamb stewed with dried vegetables and spices before she chewed and swallowed. Breaking off another piece of bread, she scooped up another bite, careful to capture a small piece of meat this time. Over and over she repeated the procedure, unaware that she was matching Nathan bite for bite. When the gravy had been removed from the top, she scooped up the thick residue in the bottom of the bowl with her two fingers, placed the food in her mouth, washed her fingers in the small dish of water provided for that purpose, and dried them on her napkin before reaching into the pot again.

Suddenly, just as she was licking her fingertips

after putting a bite in her mouth, she became aware of Nathan watching her. Was licking one's fingers a breech of Arab etiquette? she wondered. No, she distinctly remembered the women in the *iyal* doing it, and she had done it much more delicately than they had. Then why was he staring at her so strangely? Surely he must know it's acceptable. Deciding that he was shocked at her appetite, for there had been nothing delicate about the way she had dug in, she flushed and said, "I was famished."

"I'm not surprised," Nathan answered, tearing his eyes away from Lorna's mouth, for the sight of her small pink tongue licking her fingers had been highly erotic to him. "I understand from Hamid that you didn't eat anything today at noon."

Lorna was acutely aware of Nathan's gaze drifting slowly over her face. Then, abruptly, he rose and clapped his hands three times, causing Lorna almost to jump out of her skin from the unexpected noise.

Hamid entered the tent, carrying yet another tray. Placing it on the carpet beside Nathan, he picked up the pot from the brazier, placed it on the tray that Lorna and Nathan had been eating from, picked up the tray, and again withdrew. Watching him from where she sat, Lorna thought the Arab looked ridiculous with his eyes downcast. Why, it was a wonder he didn't stumble over something and break his neck.

Nathan picked up the tray that Hamid had left and held it before her, saying, "Would you like some dessert?"

Looking down at the tray covered with dried figs, dates, and honey cakes, Lorna decided that she had made enough of a pig of herself and picked up a date, although she really would have preferred one of the small, sticky cakes. Leaning back on one of the cushions, she put the date in her mouth and chewed, enjoying the sweet taste before she swallowed it.

She gazed about her, for the first time noticing her surroundings. From the light of a brass lamp that hung from one of the tent poles, she could see that the tent was a little larger than the one they had used at their noon break and bare of all furnishings except for the low table they had eaten from, the brazier, the beautiful Persian carpet on the sand, and the large pallet she sat on. Then, spying the two chests in the shadows of the tent, she suddenly realized that Nathan would be sharing this tent with her. She had assumed that he would sleep in another tent. And my God, there was only one pallet!

"Where are you going to sleep?" Lorna asked. "There's only one pallet."

"I'll sleep over there," Nathan answered, motioning to the shadows at one side of the tent.

His sleeping in the same tent seemed much too intimate to Lorna, particularly in view of her strong attraction to him. "Why can't you sleep in another tent?"

Nathan hadn't been particularly relishing the thought of sleeping in the same tent with a woman he found so damn desirable, but her suggesting that he sleep in another tent put him on the defensive. Did she think she was so high and mighty that she couldn't bear to share a tent with a commoner? Or did she think he would make advances? That shouldn't bother her. She was obviously a woman who threw herself at other men; otherwise she wouldn't have worn that disgusting, revealing dress. No, undoubtedly she had known a variety of strange bedfellows—all noblemen, of course.

Nathan's eyes glittered with anger as he said, "If

you're worried about your supposed virtue, you can forget it. You're perfectly safe from me."

Lorna bristled. "And what do you mean by that remark, my 'supposed virtue'?"

"Oh, come now, m'lady," Nathan said sarcastically, "surely you're not going to play the virtuous wife, not after that indecent dress you were wearing. My God, it was obvious you were soliciting a new lover."

That damn dress again, Lorna thought. Suddenly she felt defensive on Lady Hampton's behalf. No one knew for certain that she was amoral. Everyone was just assuming it. Why, the noblewoman might be being misjudged, just as she would have been if she had stayed in England. It wasn't fair. "You have no right to assume anything about my morals simply because of my dress! For your information I didn't have any choice of what to wear that day. Only one of my trunks was delivered to me, the one with my clothes I was going to wear in Naples. And that happens to be the style all the women are wearing there. Just because I'm being stylish doesn't mean I'm immoral."

Nathan wanted to believe her, but knew better. "Then why didn't you cover yourself? You had a shawl. We weren't in Naples, where you claim such indecency is socially acceptable. No, m'lady, I don't believe you. You enjoyed teasing me with your body. But you could have saved yourself the effort." He raked her body coldly with his eyes. "Personally, I don't find you at all desirable."

Lorna felt his hurtful words to the quick. If nothing else, she had hoped he found her desirable. Suddenly she couldn't stand to be anywhere near him, knowing how strongly he felt about her. "Then since you have such low regard for me, I should think you would be more than happy to sleep in another tent!"

"I would, except that would arouse suspicion. I'm supposed to be your husband, and this tent is where I belong. We're both stuck with our sleeping arrangements whether we like it or not."

Nathan turned and stormed angrily from the tent, leaving Lorna to nurse her battered female pride.

Chapter 6

Lorna was sound asleep when Nathan returned to the tent much later that night. He stood for a long while and gazed down at her, thinking that she looked very beautiful with her long, reddish hair fanned out about her and her thick, dark lashes lying on her rosy cheeks. His eyes dropped to her mouth, the full bottom lip looking even more sensuous in its relaxed state, and then drifted lower to where her breasts rose and fell, the thin material of her *entarie* molding the soft mounds like a pale blue second skin.

Feeling his heat rise, he muttered a curse and turned away. Blowing out the candle and tossing down his burnoose, he stripped off his caftan and *kumya*—the long shirt he wore over his pantaloons—before he lay down on the burnoose and stared at the top of the tent, his self-disgust at war with his desire. Christ, what was wrong with him? He had hoped that by telling Lady Hampton he didn't desire her he could exorcise his strong attraction to her, but it hadn't worked. He still wanted her as he had never wanted any other woman, and for the life of him he couldn't understand it. Not only was she everything he hated, but she was a married woman, a woman who was clearly off limits for him. But dammit, he thought, coming to his own defense, he wasn't made of stone. It was downright unnatural for a man to sleep beside a woman as utterly desirable as Lady Hampton and be expected to keep his hands off her. Her husband should be here, not he.

Nathan's thoughts zeroed in on Lady Hampton's husband. What kind of a man would entrust his wife to a complete stranger for a long and dangerous trip such as they were facing? Didn't the man care anything about her? If Lady Hampton had been his wife, he would have gone to Tripoli and ransomed her himself, then seen to her safety. He certainly wouldn't have turned the woman he loved over to the keeping of another man, particularly not if the woman was as tempting as she. But Lord Hampton seemed to be content with letting everyone else, from the American government to the king of Naples, make the decisions and the arrangements on which the very life of his wife depended. Christ, the man must be a damned fool to trust any man with his beautiful wife.

Yes, she was beautiful, he thought with a certain amount of cynicism. But she was also spoiled, demanding, and impossibly irritating. But he had to admit she had a strong will and a strong constitution that he hadn't expected in one so delicate looking—and certainly not in one who had been pampered all her life. She hadn't been too exhausted from her hard day's travel to argue with him over their sleeping arrangements, he noted wryly. Yes, as much as he hated to admit it, she seemed to have a perseverance and an inner strength that he had never suspected.

Lorna was roused from her sleep early the next morning by the sounds of Arabic shouts and camels grunting. She sat up, feeling disoriented, and looked about her, seeing no sign of Nathan nor any evidence that he had even slept in the tent.

Realizing that all of the activity outside meant the Arabs were breaking camp, she hurried to bathe and dress, then walked to her pallet while she rolled her long hair into a chignon and scanned the bed for the wooden hairpins that had fallen out during her sleep. Spying three beside a pillow, she picked them up, slipping them into the thick roll of hair. Then she searched for the fourth, a feeling of panic coming over her when she couldn't find it, for these were all she had.

Throwing pillows everywhere and not finding the elusive pin, she bent over, picked up the pallet and peered beneath it. Then she froze when she heard Nathan's deep voice asking, "What's taking you so long? We don't have time for you to be primping. The caravan will be pulling out shortly."

His catching her in such an undignified position, with her rump up in the air, combined with his humiliating her the night before, angered Lorna. She threw the pallet down and slammed to her feet. "I'm not primping! I was looking for a hairpin."

Nathan bent and picked up a hairpin from the carpet. "Is this it?"

It irritated Lorna no end that he had found it so easily on the patterned carpet. "Yes," she snapped, snatching it from his fingers.

God, she is in a foul mood, Nathan thought. Even more waspish that usual. But he was in an irritable mood himself. He hadn't slept well, not with the desirable Lady Hampton so close by. "Are you through with your chest?" he asked impatiently. "Hamid and Jabir would like to load up everything while we eat."

"Yes, I'm through," Lorna answered sharply.

Lorna was prepared for the clapping noise Nathan made to summon the servants this time, and the two Arabs hurried into the tent, Hamid carrying a tray with their breakfast on it. As they ate, Lorna watched the two men scurrying around the tent, always keeping their eyes carefully averted, thinking Jabir an exact replica of his brother with his dark, swarthy skin and his little black beard. By the time they had finished eating, the two men had stripped the tent of everything but the rug, the small table, and Lorna's caftan, *haik,* and veil.

Helping Lorna to her feet and leading her off the rug so the servants could roll it up, Nathan said, "As soon as you've put on your veil and *haik,* they can strike the tent." Then handing the garments to her, he added, "We'll be waiting outside."

As Jabir carried out the small table, Nathan bent to help Hamid roll up the rug. Stopping at the opening to the tent as they carried it out, Nathan asked, "Do you think you can manage the *haik* by yourself?"

"Of course I can manage it! I'm not an imbecile!"

Nathan turned and walked from the tent, shaking his head in disgust and thinking it was going to be a very long, tedious day.

But despite Lorna's confident words she found, to her utter disgust, that she did need help in donning the *haik,* for no matter how she wrapped the long garment, she couldn't get it to stay in place. It slipped off her head or her shoulders or her hips. She was so frustrated she was almost to the point of tears when she suddenly remembered something she had noticed when Nathan was helping Hamid roll up the carpet. She stood with her hand poised to wrap the material around her again as the dawning came, then jerked the *haik* off and threw it on the ground. She was waiting for Nathan when he entered the tent to see about the delay, fully prepared to do battle.

When Nathan saw the *haik* laying on the ground where Lorna had thrown it, he said, "So you do need help with it."

"No, I don't need help," Lorna replied tightly, "because I'm *not* wearing it!"

Everything about Lorna spoke of rebellion, her stance, the glitter of her violet eyes, her tight-set mouth. He had never seen her so furious. Deciding the best way to handle the agitated woman before him was to remain calm, Nathan asked, "Oh? And why not?"

"Because it's utterly ridiculous for me to have to wear these clothes. Or you either. We're not going to fool anyone with this pretense. All they have to do is look at the color of our eyes and our skin to know we're not Arabs. Why, even as tanned as your face is, Hamid's is three times as dark."

"I didn't say we'd pretend to be Arabs. I said we'd pretend to be Berbers."

"I don't see what difference that makes! I'm talking about the color of our skin."

"So am I! Berbers are a fair-skinned, blue-eyed race who came from northern Europe and were the first inhabitants of North Africa. They were here long before the Arabs arrived on the scene, before the Vandals, the Romans, even the Phoenicians, and they fiercely resisted all who came to conquer them. To this day no one has subdued the *Imazighen*—the free men—as they call themselves. When the hordes of Arabs invaded this country, the majority of the

Berbers, except for the Masmuda tribe who remained on the northern coast, fled into the desert and mountains and claimed them as their own. The only thing the Berbers adopted from the Arabs was Islam, and it is pretending to be of this religion that protects us on this trip. A Muslim can war against another Muslim, even kill him, but the Koran—their Bible—strongly teaches against enslaving a brother Muslim."

Lorna knew by Nathan's rapid, clipped speech that he was very irritated at her, but she was amazed at what he had told her. "And they're actually blond and blue-eyed?"

"I've never seen a blond Berber. Most have brown hair. But their eyes are light-colored." Nathan bent and picked up the *haik*. "Now, put this on. You're holding us up."

As Nathan walked away, Lorna glared at his back. Then once again she wondered how he had learned so much about North Africa. She wished they were on better terms. Then she could ask him. But there didn't seem to be any hope for that. If anything, their relationship had gone downhill.

As soon as she had sat down in the sedan, Lorna decided that she wasn't going to think about Nathan and their strained relationship, nor was she going to let the heat defeat her as it had the day before. Deciding the best way to keep her mind from both things was to keep it occupied elsewhere, she forced herself to pay more attention to her surroundings. But there wasn't much to see. Other than a rare, sunbaked village with its inevitable walls around it and an occasional flock of sheep or ostriches here and there, the land was a dull monotony of browns with not a touch of green to be seen.

She sat back in the sedan, utterly disgusted. Well, she had wanted to see something of the world outside of London and now she was, she thought wryly. But not this desolate, godforsaken land. She had wanted to see America. She had heard it was a lovely country with its long seacoast, its thick virgin forests, its towering mountains. She had wanted to see beauty, not this ugly, parched land where the scorching sun beat down with a vengeance and the air seared your lungs. Besides being unbearably hot and thirsty, she was bored to tears.

Despite her vow not to think of Nathan, her thoughts turned to the rugged captain. His telling her he didn't find her desirable had hurt her deeply. But despite that and all of their little spats, she still found him the most exciting, attractive man she had ever met. Did he really find her unattractive? She knew that other men found her desirable. She had certainly had to fight off enough of them. Was it her hateful behavior that had turned him against her? Probably. There were times, when she was posing as Lady Hampton, that she couldn't stand herself. How ironic. If they had met under different circumstances, where she could have been herself, maybe things would have turned out differently. But she did know one thing. The strain of having to be so close to him and pretend to be someone else was beginning to wear on her nerves. She didn't think she could stand weeks of this, and yet she didn't dare to attempt an escape from him until she got out of North Africa. He had told her no Muslim woman traveled alone, and pretending to be one was the only thing that was protecting her. No, she wouldn't risk losing her freedom to the Arabs the second time.

When the caravan stopped for the noon break, Lorna found Nathan as irritated with her as he'd been earlier. Her mere presence seemed to annoy him. She was relieved when the unappetizing meal was over and she could lie down to take a nap, for the intense heat robbed her of all energy.

That afternoon it seemed to be even hotter than it had been the previous day, something Lorna found unbelievable. The heat was oppressive, the air still, not even a whisper of breeze as the blazing sun beat down on them. Glancing out the window, she saw a dark cloud coming over the horizon. It's going to rain! she thought in a mixture of excitement and tremendous relief.

Apparently others on the caravan spied the rolling black cloud at the same time Lorna did, for Arabic cries suddenly came from all around her, not cries of joy, but cries of alarm. The caravan came to an abrupt halt, and the next thing Lorna knew she was thrown backward as Hamid forced her camel to kneel, yelling frantic curses at it. She had hardly recovered from her jerking descent when the door opened and Nathan was pulling her from the sedan.

"What's wrong?" she asked. "Has everyone gone insane?"

"That's not a rain cloud. That's dust. We're in for a storm."

"You mean a sandstorm?"

"No, in a sandstorm the sand never gets above your chin. The granules are too heavy for the wind to lift any higher than that. You can ride on your camel or even walk without it getting in your face. That's dust, and that cloud goes a hundred miles up into the air. There's no escaping it. All you can do is try to protect yourself and ride it out."

Already the wind preceding the storm was whipping up the sand around them, and Lorna could hear a peculiar howling noise as the storm approached. Suddenly the sun was blocked out and a dark shadow fell over the earth.

"We aren't going to have time to set up the tent," Nathan said. "Here, give me your caftan."

Nathan quickly stripped the caftan from Lorna and tossed it down beside the kneeling camel. "Lie down," he commanded, pushing her to her knees.

Lorna felt the sand being whipped up stinging her face as she knelt on her caftan. "But wouldn't we be better off in the sedan? It's higher."

"No, we need to get behind something," Nathan said, stripping off his burnoose. "Now lie down. Get as close to the camel as you can. I'll try to shield you with my body."

Lorna was bewildered by the sudden turn of events. "But—"

Thinking she was objecting because they would be in such close proximity, Nathan's thin control snapped. "Dammit, do what I said!"

Lorna had no idea how fast the storm would hit or the dangerous situation they were in. Her resentment at him ordering her around came surging to the fore. She slammed to her feet and screamed, "Don't you yell at me!"

Nathan's eyes flashed. He caught her shoulders and slammed her to the caftan on the ground so hard it took her breath away, then lay beside her, shoving her against the side of the camel, and tossed his wide burnoose over them. Resenting the rough manner in which he had handled her, Lorna struggled to rise. He caught her shoulder with one hand and threw her back down. "Let go of me!" she shrieked.

"Shut up! Shut up or so help me God, I'll throttle you!"

Even with the burnoose thrown over them, Lorna could see the metallic glitter in Nathan's eyes, and remembering that he was a very dangerous man, she feared he might follow through with his threat.

She lay perfectly still while he struggled to pin the wildly flapping burnoose down with his body on one side, then tucked it between Lorna and the camel. She gasped in surprise when he took her in his arms and pushed his body against hers.

Thinking her gasp was one of outrage, Nathan said in a hard voice, "Don't make one move. I know you can't stand being so close to a lowly commoner, but I'm afraid it's something you're just going to have to tolerate, unless you'd prefer to go out in that storm and choke to death."

Lorna wasn't even aware when the storm hit full force seconds later, nor did Nathan's words fully penetrate her mind. Her attention was on their bodies pressed full length against one another, seemingly scorching her right through their layers of clothing. She couldn't distinguish his features, but she knew by his warm breath fanning her face that their lips were only inches apart. Suddenly she wanted him to kiss her so badly it was a physical ache within her.

Nathan was also very aware of Lorna. The feel of her soft breasts rising and falling against his chest, her long slender legs pressed against his, her silken skin beneath the thin *entarie* where his hands lay on her back, her intoxicating scent was attacking his senses. He longed to stroke that soft skin, to breathe deeply of her perfume, to taste the sweetness of the mouth that lay so close to his, but he didn't dare. She was another man's wife, forbidden fruit, and he knew his hunger for her would never be satisfied with just one kiss. To remove the temptation he pushed her head down, saying in a voice made harsh with desire, "Duck your head. You can breathe easier there."

Tears of disappointment stung in Lorna's eyes. With her face against Nathan's broad chest, she could feel the crisp dark hairs at the vee of his robe against her forehead, smell his exciting, manly scent. The ache inside her increased, centering in the pit of her belly as a strange heat suffused her. To be held so close by a man she longed for with every fiber of her being and yet be denied even a simple kiss seemed cruel. Had fate thrown him in her path only to torment her?

The passage of time as the storm spent its fury was an agony of hell for Lorna. Not only was she miserable at being so close to Nathan, but as the storm reached its crescendo and the wind shrieked so loud it made her ears ring, she was terrified. Were they going to die here, be buried alive under tons of dirt? She was already finding it difficult to breathe, for the dust had filtered through the thick material of Nathan's burnoose. Whimpering in fear, she pressed her body even closer to his and wrapped her arms about him, needing his strength desperately.

Nathan totally misinterpreted Lorna's action, thinking she was purposely taunting him. To his utter horror he felt himself hardening. Suddenly he found it difficult to breathe, and he knew damn well it had nothing to do with the dust in the air. Feeling himself at the very brink of self-control, he tried to pry Lorna's arms from him, but in her fear she had a death grip on him. "Let go, dammit!"

His harsh command brought Lorna to her senses. My God, she hadn't realized that she was embracing him and that their bodies were so close it made a mockery of their clothing. Then she felt it, the long, hard length of his readiness against her thigh. A little tingle of excitement ran through her. He'd lied! she thought. Despite all he'd said, he did desire her. Then she remembered that it was only his body speaking, a spontaneous reaction that he had no control over. Nathan himself couldn't wait to get out of their close proximity. No, undoubtedly he considered her even more of a wanton now, thinking she was throwing herself at him. Feeling both mortified and on the verge of tears, she pulled her arms away and squirmed even farther back into the camel's warm side.

To the immense relief of both of them, the storm ended soon after, as suddenly as it had come, and Nathan lost no time in throwing back the burnoose and rising to his feet. Even after Lady Hampton had removed her arms and moved away from him, he felt no relief from his raging desire. Looking at her still lying on the caftan, he knew he should help her up, but he didn't dare touch her. Instead he turned and looked around him, seeing the huge piles of sand the storm had blown against the camels and others of the caravan emerging from their impromptu shelters on the protected side of the animals. Several of the Arabs who had simply crouched and pulled their robes over them to protect them rose to their feet, shucking off the layers of sand that had all but buried them alive. In places, the wind had swept the sand completely from the bedrock beneath, leaving areas that looked like polished mosaic tile.

Hearing Lorna coughing on the dust behind him, he turned and saw she was on her feet. "Are you all right?" he asked with concern.

"Yes, but I don't think I can stand another several weeks of this."

Since Lorna had said weeks and not days, he knew she wasn't talking about the desert. He was left to assume that she meant she couldn't stand his company any longer. "Well, cheer up, m'lady," he said in a biting voice. "When we reach Tunis in a few days, I'll see what I can do to find another ship to take you to Naples. Then you won't have to endure my company any longer."

That night Nathan didn't dine with Lorna, and he didn't come to the tent until very late. Lorna was not asleep, although her eyelids were closed. She watched through lowered eyelashes as Nathan took off his caftan and tossed it on the ground, admiring the powerful muscles on his shoulders and back that strained at his shirt as he did. Then, as he stripped off the long shirt and bared his back, she gasped, seeing the horrible white ridges that crisscrossed his back.

Hearing her gasp, Nathan whirled and, seeing the shocked look on her face, said, "I didn't mean to offend you. I thought you were asleep."

Lorna was almost as disturbed by the sight of Nathan's broad chest with its furring of dark hair as she'd been by his back, but for a different reason, the sight sending little tingles of excitement racing through her. "No . . . no, I wasn't asleep," she muttered. Then, tearing her gaze away from his chest, she looked into his eyes, feeling herself drowning in their shimmering green depths before she finally managed to regain some semblance of thought and said, "Your back. You've been beaten."

Nathan stiffened, thinking she had been repulsed by the sight of the scars on his back. "Yes, I have," he replied tightly.

Lorna's eyes flashed with anger. "Who did that to you? And why?"

Nathan was not prepared for her reaction. He had expected revulsion, certainly not outrage in his behalf. He shot her a puzzled look before answering, "The Janissary captain in charge of the prison where I was taken after the ship I was on was captured by Barbary pirates."

"You were captured by the pirates too?"

"Yes. About ten years ago. They captured the ship I was on and threw us all into prison."

"How long were you there before you were ransomed?"

"About nine months, and I wasn't ransomed. I finally managed to escape."

"Escape?" Lorna asked in surprise. "But wasn't that dangerous? Weren't you taking a big chance?"

"It was the biggest gamble I ever made in my life," Nathan admitted. "But at that point I didn't care if I did get killed in the attempt. Anything was better than slaving in those stone quarries and being beaten. You see, I made the mistake of coming to the aid of one of my fellow seamen when he was being beaten for dropping a rock. Something inside me just snapped and I went berserk. Before the guards managed to overpower me, I had maimed one man and permanently scarred the face of the captain. He never forgave me. When my parents sent the money to ransom me, he told the Trinitarian priest who had been handling the negotiations that I had died in prison. He taunted me with this while he had me beaten almost daily, telling me I'd never escape him. I knew that I'd die there if I didn't get away, if not from disease in that filthy, vermin-infested prison, then laboring beneath the blazing sun being choked to death by the dust. To my way of thinking, I had nothing to lose and everything to gain."

Nathan felt his old hatred rising. Damn, he'd give anything if he could get revenge on the Janissary captain who had beaten him and tormented him. It infuriated him to know that bastard was still walking around someplace. If he only knew where to find him.

Lorna broke into his thoughts by asking, "But how did you ever get out of the country?"

"I knew better than to head for the coast, since that was the first place the Janissary would look for me. And there was no doubt in my mind that he'd search for me. Torturing me had become an obsession with him. I headed inland, figuring I could eventually veer west and find my way to the Atlantic coast, traveling under the cover of darkness and using the stars to guide me. But I hadn't taken my weakened condition into consideration, nor my lack of knowledge on how to survive in the desert. After three days without water, I collapsed. I was found by a tribe of desert Berbers on their way home from trading in Tripoli. They took me in, and I owe my life to them."

"And they helped you escape the country?" Lorna surmised.

"Yes, eventually. But I lived with them for several years before that happened."

"They held you prisoner too?"

"No, I stayed by my own choice."

Lorna wondered at Nathan's last words, but some inner sense warned her against questioning him about it. Instead, she said, "I wondered how you had learned to speak Arabic so fluently and knew so much about North Africa. Now I know. But it's extraordinary that you managed your escape at all, considering how well guarded the prison must have been and your youth and inexperience. You couldn't have been very old at the time. You said it was ten years ago."

Once again Nathan was astonished at the woman's perception. He *had* been hardly more than a boy when he was captured, and most of those to whom he had related his story assumed his escape was secured once he had freed himself from the prison, completely forgetting that he still had a hostile country to get out of. Lorna had immediately seen his predicament. But what surprised him even more was why he was so willing to talk about it. He had always been very closemouthed when people other than his family and best friends questioned him about his experiences in North Africa, not wanting their pity for what he had endured during his imprisonment and resenting that they thought him an oddity for having been willing to live so long with a desert tribe they considered no better than barbaric heathens. But Lady Hampton had shown no pity, only anger at how he had been treated, nor had she pried into his reasons for not leaving the tribe sooner. She seemed to possess an understanding that placed curiosity aside and surpassed compassion, an empathy that reached out to him and tugged at some vital part of him.

Realizing that she was awaiting his answer, he said, "Yes, I was young, only eighteen at the time. That was only my third voyage."

"You were a captain at eighteen?" Lorna asked in astonishment.

"No, I wasn't a captain then. Only second mate. It wasn't until I returned to the United States that I talked my father into loaning me the money to buy my own ship for a share of the profits. My mother was furious with him when he agreed. She had never wanted me to go to sea in the first place. But my father has sea water in his veins, too, and overrode her objections. He captained a privateer during the revolution."

Nathan was a little stunned at his own words. Why had he volunteered such personal information? It wasn't at all like him. His personal life was his business, and he usually guarded it as fiercely as he did his independence. Besides, the snobbish Lady Hampton wouldn't be interested in the details of his life.

But Lorna was more than interested. She was hungry to know everything she could learn about this fascinating man. "But your father isn't a sea captain anymore?"

"No, his health was too bad after the war for him

to return to sea. His ship was captured by the British in the last year of the war and he was imprisoned in the hulk of an old British ship that had grounded on the mud flats in New York harbor. The *Jersey* was the most notorious prison to be used in the war, so disease-infested that the majority of the prisoners died. My father was one of the lucky ones. He managed to survive, but it left him with weak lungs and subject to recurring fevers."

Lorna heard the bitterness in Nathan's words. Now she knew why he hated the British navy so much. His feelings went deeper than his resentment of their impressing his fellow Americans. And she couldn't blame Nathan's mother for not wanting him to go to sea or for being so angry when his father loaned him the money to buy his own ship. Both her husband and her son had been captured at sea and imprisoned by their enemies. She'd almost lost both of them.

For a long moment Lorna and Nathan stared at each other. She wondered if she should reveal her true identity to him. Having been captured by the pirates himself, he would understand her desperation to be set free. But would he understand about her flight from England? She decided to hold her tongue. It was simply too great a risk.

As Nathan stared at her, he was frankly puzzled. He hadn't expected her to be so sympathetic. It seemed that little by little she was revealing bits and pieces of herself that he had never expected to find in a spoiled noblewoman.

"Is something wrong?" Lorna asked. "You look baffled."

"To be perfectly honest, I am. I wouldn't have expected a woman like you, a woman who has never experienced any hardship until now, to be so under-standing."

Lorna smiled and answered, "Things are not al-ways as they seem, Captain. It may come as a surprise to you, but you don't know me at all."

Seeing his frown deepen at her cryptic remark, Lorna rolled to her side and said over her shoulder, "Good-night."

Long after Nathan had blown out the lamp and lain down on his makeshift bed, Lorna lay awake, feeling unbearably lonely and aching for the feel of his strong arms around her again. Maybe she shouldn't have made that last comment, but she couldn't help it. She wanted so badly to reveal her true self to him.

Only a few feet away Nathan lay with his back to her, also awake and feeling just as miserable. It was bad enough that he had been strongly attracted to her physically and was suffering sexual frustration such as he had never known, but he was even more alarmed at how comfortable he felt with her this evening. It was almost as if they shared some powerful, invisible bond. Yes, Lady Hampton was beautiful, spirited, and intelligent, a dangerous combination in any woman, and she had also revealed an amazing strength and fortitude, things he had always admired in anyone. And then tonight he had sensed an unusual sensitivity in her. Christ! She was beginning to get to him, in too many ways. But they were a world apart on the social ladder, and she was a married woman. But then, isn't that the way of the world? Nathan thought with a wry twist of his lips. Forbidden fruit is always the sweetest, the most enticing, the most unreachable.

It was a long time before either slept that night.

Chapter 7

The next morning Nathan didn't eat breakfast with Lorna, nor did he ride anywhere near her. Lorna was aware of his avoiding her. It seemed even more deliberate than before. Had she offended him with her questions about his personal life the night before?

Such was not the case. Nathan was simply trying to put distance between himself and temptation. But while Lady Hampton was out of sight and reach, she was not out of mind, not by any means. Visions of her loveliness and memories of his holding her soft, silken body in his arms the day before tormented him, and dammit, as ridiculous as it seemed, he missed just riding beside her. Again he wondered what Lord Hampton was like. He couldn't be too smart, letting a beauty like Lady Hampton get out of his sight, or was he such a catch himself that he wasn't worried about his wife's being attracted to another man? Nathan didn't like that image of the Englishman, and the thought of the man touching her, kissing her, making love to her filled him with such a jealous rage that it shocked him. My God, he *was* smitten with her—to the point where he was becoming possessive about another man's wife!

The heat was unbearable that morning in the small chaise, seemingly hotter than it usually was that early in the day, and soon Lorna was dying of thirst. She glanced out the window and saw the dark cloud rolling over the horizon. At first she feared it was another dust storm, until she saw the jagged flashes of lightning and heard the distant roll of thunder. It's going to rain! she thought. She was going to get relief from the scorching heat and her terrible thirst, for surely she could sneak a handful of it. Then, as they traveled closer to the black thunderhead, Lorna realized it was raining, but it was evaporating in the intense heat before it hit the ground. She could clearly see where the bluish veils of rain ended abruptly several hundred feet above the ground. What a cruel trick for nature to play, she thought bitterly, when both she and the parched land were thirsting for water, to make relief so close and yet so unobtainable. It was as cruel as the trick fate was playing on her, to throw the man of her dreams in her path and then snatch him away.

Lorna was miserable during the noonday break, not just because of the terrible heat, however. Just as she'd suspected, Nathan didn't join her. Maybe it would be best if he found another ship to take her to Naples, she thought. It would certainly relieve her of the strain she had been under. But the thought of Nathan walking out of her life made her feel even more wretched. It wasn't fair! Because of circumstances beyond her control, she was going to lose the man she had waited for all of her life. Damn Phillip!

And damn Lady Hampton! Why couldn't she have been single? Then she would have had only one obstacle to overcome, Nathan's dislike for royalty.

Seeing a movement on the ground from the corner of her eye, Lorna looked around and froze, her heart suddenly racing in her chest. A two-foot scaly monster with a long, spiny tail was moving toward her on its squatty legs, its beady eyes pinning her to the spot. She was too terrified to move, knowing she was looking death in the eye, for surely anything that looked that horrible had to be poisonous.

Then, as its long pink tongue flickered out from its ugly mouth, she flew to her feet and grabbed the first weapon she could find, which happened to be a tent pole. As part of the tent collapsed, she swung at the monster viciously, over and over, determined to beat it to death. But the reptile was amazingly agile and swift, darting here and there and managing to escape every blow, while Lorna silently cursed both it and the tent hanging around her and hampering her movements.

Outside, Nathan saw part of the tent collapse and then heard the commotion going on inside it. He ran to it, fighting his way through the folds of material where the opening was, entering the tent just as the terrified, hapless lizard was scurrying out. He looked up to see Lorna about to take another swing and caught her arm, saying, "No! It's just a harmless lizard."

"Harmless?" Lorna gasped in disbelief, lowering her arm.

"Yes, harmless. It wouldn't have hurt you."

"But . . . but it looked so dangerous, so lethal."

"Yes, I know. That's its protection against the other reptiles in the desert, some of whom *are* poison-

ous. The spiny-tailed lizard looks so dangerous they
scurry away in fear."

Well, Lorna thought wryly, at least she wasn't the
only one who was terrified by the sight of the ugly
lizard. But still she was embarrassed.

Nathan took the pole from Lorna and handed it
to Hamid, who had been fast on the captain's heels as
he ran to the tent. The servant replaced it, and as he
walked from the tent, keeping his eyes averted, he
said something to Nathan in such rapid Arabic that
Lorna couldn't understand him.

"What did he say?" she asked.

"He said my wife was very brave to attack the
lizard, even if it was harmless."

"I wasn't acting bravely. Just foolishly."

"No, Hamid's right. You were brave. You had no
way of knowing it wasn't poisonous. You were terrified, and yet you came to your own defense. That took
courage. Most women would have fainted or
screamed their lungs out," Nathan ended, secretly
admitting to an admiration for the way Lady Hampton had behaved and thinking she had revealed another unexpected attribute. Damn, she was just full of
surprises.

Lorna didn't feel very brave. Her heart was still
racing in her chest from her fright, and despite what
Nathan had said, she felt sheepish. Damn that bloody
lizard! He'd made her look the fool in front of Nathan.
Looking about her, she asked irritably, "How did it
get in here, anyway?"

"It was probably buried in the sand, and when we
put the tent up and everything turned dark, it
thought it was night and time to come out in search of
food."

"Could there be others buried in the sand in
here?" Lorna asked, her eyes darting about the small

tent. The lizard might be harmless, but she didn't care to share her lodgings with any of the ugly, slimy creatures. Why, just the thought of it gave her goose-flesh.

"I seriously doubt it. They don't usually travel in pairs."

Nathan stared at Lady Hampton, thinking it was a shame she had been born to nobility. She had the makings of what could have been a very extraordinary woman, if she hadn't been so spoiled. She had looked so damn beautiful with her violet eyes flashing as she swung at the lizard. And she was standing much too close. He could feel her heat and smell her sweet scent, an intoxicating scent that sent his senses reeling. An overpowering urge to kiss her rose in him, an urge that was too forceful to suppress.

Lorna gasped in surprise when Nathan slipped his hands beneath her caftan and pulled her to him. At first his kiss was rough, for he had misinterpreted her gasp as outrage. He hated himself for succumbing to his desire, and her for tormenting him. He meant to punish her, to teach her a lesson, but when Lorna made no effort to resist him, his lips softened; the kiss became more wooing.

Lorna had known that Nathan's kiss would be wonderful, but nothing in her wildest fantasies had prepared her for it. Even when he kissed her roughly at first, it excited her, but what he was doing to her now made her feel as if her bones were slowly melting. Incredibly warm, mobile lips pressed against hers before his tongue brushed back and forth across her full lower lip with a touch as light as a butterfly's wings, sending electric tingles of delight coursing through her. At the play of his tongue at the sensitive corners of her mouth, darting here, there, like a fiery dart, Lorna's legs suddenly turned to water and she

weakly sagged against him, her hands sliding over his
broad muscular shoulders to support herself.

Nathan groaned at the feel of her full breasts
pressing against his chest and pulled her into a tight
embrace, molding her soft curves to his long length,
his tongue demanding entrance to the honeyed recess within. Lorna opened her mouth to him, feeling
shock waves traveling up her spine as his tongue slid
along the length of hers, in and out, in an endless kiss
that brought her to her toes in a silent appeal for
more.

She gave a soft cry of protest when his mouth left
hers to rain soft kisses over her eyes, her forehead, her
temples. Stopping to nibble at one earlobe, he whispered huskily, "I knew you'd taste like this. So sweet.
So incredibly sweet."

She trembled as his tongue lazily traced the outline of her small ear, vaguely wondering where he
had learned such devastating, sensual use of it, then
gasped when he explored inside, a sudden heat suffusing her. When Nathan's mouth claimed hers again in
a deep, probing kiss that gave full rein to his passion,
Lorna began to kiss him back, her tongue at first moving tentatively in her inexperience, then urgently,
feeling herself drowning in a sea of feverish heat, her
senses spinning, her heart racing in her chest.

Her kissing him back with such uninhibited passion excited Nathan wildly. His hands rushed over her
back and hips before he shifted his weight, holding
her to him as his hand rose to cup her full breast,
massaging it through the thin silk of her *entarie,* his
thumb brushing back and forth over the nipple.
Lorna gasped, feeling a bolt of heat rush to her loins as
the aching peak rose and strained against the material
under his ministrations. Arching against him in a effort to assuage the throbbing that seemed to be cen-

tered in the very core of her womanhood, Lorna felt the long, hot, rigid proof of his arousal against her thigh, seemingly branding her through their layers of clothing. A brief tingle of fear was followed by a thrill of incredible excitement as she instinctively pressed closer to that rock-hard heat that threatened to consume her, clinging to Nathan's broad shoulders as if she would never let go.

As if from a far distance, Nathan heard Hamid calling to him. But it wasn't until the Arab called the second time even more urgently that Nathan finally came to his senses. Dammit, what in the hell was he doing?

Abruptly he pulled away, so rapidly and unexpectedly that Lorna swayed without his support. He looked down at her, thinking she looked even more beautiful with her violet eyes darkened with passion, her face flushed, her lips swollen from his kisses. God, how he wanted her, now even more so. Just a taste of her passion had left every fiber in his body screaming for release. Damn her!

He swept her *haik* up from the sand and shoved it into her hands, saying harshly. "Put this on. We're leaving!"

As Nathan rushed from the tent, Lorna stared at his broad back dumbly. Did I just imagine it all? she thought in bewilderment. No, she was still trembling in the aftermath of his sensuous caresses, and her lips still throbbed from his torrid kisses. He did desire her, despite everything, and he was fighting it. And by God, she was going to do everything in her power to see that he lost that battle. She wasn't going to let him just walk in and out of her life; she wasn't going to let fate cheat her of everything. If she couldn't have his love, she'd have his passion. She'd take whatever fleeting pleasure she could gain, for it was going to have to last her a lifetime. It was her right. Even a condemned prisoner is granted a last request.

Lorna found that the afternoon passed even more agonizingly slowly than the two previous ones. She was anxious for evening to come to see what transpired. As much as he had avoided her, Nathan always came to the tent at night for fear of arousing the Arabs' suspicions. Once they were alone, she'd do everything in her power to overcome his reluctance, even if she had to seduce him!

It was a rather shocking thought. Would she dare to go that far for what she wanted? But the alternative, a lifetime of knowing she'd had the man of her dreams within reach and had done nothing on her own behalf, strengthened her resolve. Yes, she had always fought for what was hers, and she was entitled to at least that much.

When Lorna saw the shimmering patch of green in the distance several hours later, she ignored it, thinking it was just another of those mirages she had been plagued with the past few days, yet another of nature's cruel tricks in this hostile land. Not until the green became distinct palm trees, which didn't go away when she blinked her eyes, did she finally realize it was an oasis.

As soon as she stepped down from the sedan, Lorna looked eagerly about her, seeing the caravan had stopped in a palm-shaded area a distance away from a small walled town that was flanked on both sides with citrus and almond groves and fields of melons and vegetables. Not finding what she was looking for, she turned and scanned the area behind her, seeing only the sandy desert that stretched to the horizon.

From where he had swung down off his camel a distance away, Nathan saw Lady Hampton looking about her in bewilderment. Ignore her, he told himself. She's nothing but a tease. But then, much to his disgust, he found himself walking toward her, as if his legs had a will of their own.

"Are you looking for something?"

Lorna knew by the terse tone in Nathan's voice that he was irritated with himself for momentarily succumbing to his desire for her. She decided the best recourse was to act as if nothing had happened between them. She turned and answered, "Yes, I am. Where's the lake? I always thought oases had small pools or lakes."

"There are oases in the desert where trees and vegetation surround pools of water, but in this case the water is pumped from artesian wells."

"There's not even a small stream?" Lorna asked, clinging to one last hope. "I was hoping there would be someplace I might bathe."

"I'm sure there's a public bathhouse in the town. Even the little villages have one of some sort, since the Muslims are required by their holy law to wash every day. You can bathe there."

Lorna thought not. Bathing in front of the women in the *iyal* had been embarrassing enough, but undoubtedly the women in this little isolated town would stare at her as if she were some freak. Besides, the Muslims might have some bathing ritual she didn't know. "No, I don't think so. I'll just make do with my pitcher and basin."

Lorna had hardly settled down after the tent was set up when she looked up to see Jabir and Hamid carrying in a large wooden tub filled with water. Lorna was momentarily stunned by the unexpected appearance of the bath, but as soon as the two men disappeared, she scrambled to her feet and hurried to the tub. Thirty minutes later she emerged feeling utterly refreshed, then sorted through her chest until she found an *entarie* and pantaloons that were of thinner, more clinging material. Then for good measure she carefully split the center seam of the loose shirt so the cleft between her breasts was visible.

Nathan didn't make an appearance for dinner, nor did he show up for a good two hours after the dishes had been cleared away. As the minutes ticked by, Lorna became more and more apprehensive. Maybe he would sleep elsewhere from now on, she thought, her spirits sinking.

Hearing a movement at the tent opening, she looked up and saw Nathan standing there. She knew by the glistening drops of water clinging to his dark hair that he had been to the bathhouse, and she thought he looked very handsome in his stark white robe. Then she noticed the hard look on his face and the glitter in his green eyes.

Nathan walked across the tent in a quick, agitated stride that told Lorna even further that he wasn't in the best of moods. It seemed she had her work cut out for her. When he reached his chest, he tossed his caftan and headdress down on it, then turned and said, "There's something I want to know —and by damn, I want an answer! Why didn't your husband come to ransom you? He could have traveled by caravan to Tripoli to pick you up. Doesn't he care what happens to you?"

Lorna wasn't about to let her supposed "husband" stand between her and what she wanted. She searched her mind for a plausible answer, then said, "Our marriage wasn't a love match. It was made for political reasons. To be brutally honest, we don't have very strong feelings for one another."

It sounded reasonable to Nathan. The nobility

was renowned for using their marriages to cement alliances, and with Napoleon running rampant across Europe, every country was looking for an ally to stand against him, particularly the smaller countries like Naples. "Am I left to assume that means you can both take lovers as you please?"

Lorna's heart raced. "Yes," she answered for Lady Hampton, then added for herself, "I'm perfectly free to choose my own lover."

Nathan didn't notice her singular usage. His gaze swept over Lady Hampton as she sat on the pallet, noting that the thin material of her apparel clung to every curve like a second skin and that from his viewpoint he could see the curve of one soft breast. Had he been secretly fantasizing about making love to her when he had bought that particular ensemble? Probably. And why had she picked it to wear tonight? Was she taunting him again? Or had his kiss that afternoon aroused her curiosity? She had shown no resistance.

He quickly covered the distance between them and sat on the pallet beside her. Looking her directly in the eye, he asked, "Have you ever made love to a commoner?"

If there had been any doubt in Lorna's mind as to what Nathan was leading up to, it was swept away. "No, I haven't," she answered breathlessly, her heart pounding hard in anticipation.

Nathan leaned closer, so close she could see the gold flecks in his eyes, and asked in a husky voice, "Have you ever wondered what it would be like? If it would be different? If it would be better?"

Lorna couldn't answer for the life of her. She seemed to be drowning in his overwhelming magnetic sexuality. Then, as he raised his hand and placed one finger on her full bottom lip, her breath came in little ragged gasps, an almost painful longing filling her.

Nathan, too, was deeply affected, very conscious of the softness of her lips, the desirability of her mouth, the quick rise and fall of her breasts. His desire came to the fore with a force that stunned him with its intensity. His eyes darkened to a deep emerald green as his gaze bored into her.

Nathan caught her shoulders and lowered her to the pallet. Lorna felt pinned to the spot by his hot, mesmerizing gaze. A smile crossed his lips as he said, "I think you are curious. I think you want to find out what it's like to be made love to by a real man."

As Nathan kissed her, Lorna was lost in the wonder of it, the beauty of it. His tongue brushed across her full bottom lip, teeth gently nipping the provocative curve of it, then flashed across her teeth before plunging into her mouth, exploring every inch of her sweetness before swirling around its interior, the taste of her heady nectar intoxicating him. Lorna felt her bones melting as his tongue slipped slowly in and out, in and out, in an excruciating erotic dance that foretold of a later, much more intimate act and brought Lorna straining against him and moaning deep in her throat.

Nathan covered Lorna's face with a shower of hot kisses, then blazed a trail down the long column of her slender throat, licking the racing pulse beating there, before stopping to kiss hungrily the sweet creamy flesh between her shoulder and neck, sending shivers of delight through her. She was floating on a warm rosy cloud when she felt Nathan push up her *entarie* and cup her naked breast, his fingers brushing back and forth with slow deliberation.

Her fingers threaded through the hair at the nape of Nathan's neck as his mouth replaced his hand, the soft curls twining around her fingers and holding them a prisoner there. At the feel of his tongue laving her breast, slowly circling then flicking the sensitive nipple before taking it into his mouth while his free hand tantalized her other nipple, sensation erupted in Lorna, a bolt of fire shooting to her loins as a sudden wetness flooded her there, leaving her throbbing and burning. She gasped, her hands frantically clutching his head, lost in a sea of pure sensation, thinking she would die of this exquisite torture if he didn't stop, feeling the strength from her muscles, the life from her body, the burning in her loins becoming a raging inferno of need. Sobbing incoherently and trembling uncontrollably, she arched her hips, pressing herself hard against Nathan's muscular thigh where he had insinuated his knee between her legs, a silent but eloquent plea for release.

Nathan raised his dark head, his eyes glazed with desire. His warm breath fanned her face as he asked in a ragged voice, "You want me, too, don't you? Just as much as I want you."

Dazed, Lorna looked up, seeing the tiny flames flicking in his passion-darkened eyes, an intent, almost painful expression on his ruggedly handsome face. The words wouldn't come, not with Nathan's warm lips nipping the ultrasensitive corners of her mouth, his tongue a flaming dart of sensual promise, his hand still caressing her swollen, aching breasts.

"Answer me!" Nathan demanded huskily, shaking her lightly. "Tell me you want me."

"Yes," Lorna muttered, then said in a louder voice, "Yes, I want you. Oh God, yes!"

A cry of exaltation escaped Nathan's lips before his mouth crashed down on hers in a deep, bruising, devouring kiss that left her breathless and spinning under a fresh onslaught of new sensations. Lorna kissed him back, her small tongue dancing around his in total abandon and driving him wild with excitement.

He undressed her, kissing and caressing each inch of skin he exposed, his passion tempered by awe at her high, creamy breasts, her tiny waist, the gentle flair of her hips, her unbelievably long, shapely legs, her silky softness, and drugging, sweet scent. His eyes locked on the dark curls between her thighs, his desire to possess her there coming to the fore in an urgent hot demand. He rose, tearing his garments from him.

Lorna watched breathlessly as he stripped before her, just as awed as he had been with her beauty as he revealed his magnificent male body to her. Exceptionally broad-shouldered, lean-flanked, long-limbed, there wasn't an ounce of fat on him, his skin a smooth sheath over hard muscle and sleek tendons. Her gaze drifted down over him in silent admiration, following the line of hair from the crisp dark curls on his broad chest to where it flared again at his groin. And then she stared, shocked by his blatant arousal. Feeling it pressed against her had excited her, but now, actually seeing it, a tingle of fear ran through her at its immense size and the power that pulsated from it.

Nathan was very aware of her eyes locked on his erection and her face draining of all color. What in the hell is wrong with her? he wondered. Surely she's seen an aroused naked man before, with all of her lovers. It galled him no end that there had been others before him. "Is something wrong, m'lady? Do you not find me to your liking?"

There was an edge to Nathan's voice that made Lorna realize she had almost given herself away. Were all men built alike? she wondered. No, what she had felt pressed against her when Phillip tried to force himself on her and what she had felt with Nathan were nothing alike. She forced herself to look Nathan in the eye and answer, "No, it's just that you're so big there."

Nathan knew that he was better endowed than most men. He chuckled and fell to his knees beside her. "My God, you haven't been loved by a real man have you?"

I haven't been loved by *any* man, Lorna thought, but answered, "No . . . no, I'm afraid I haven't."

His hand lightly stroked her arm as he said in a husky voice, "Don't be afraid. I promise I won't hurt you."

It was the sound of Nathan's deep voice, throbbing with desire, more than the feel of his hand caressing her arm that relieved Lorna of any lingering fear, bringing an answering throb of need from deep within her. She looked up into his eyes, seeing the hunger there, a longing so intense that it tore at her heart. She opened her arms to him.

A warm male body covered hers and a hot breath seared her flesh as he teased and tormented her with hands and lips, kissing, nipping, tonguing her clear to her toes, taking his time with her as he slowly and skillfully aroused her to a feverish pitch. He dallied with his kisses at the soft skin of her inner thighs, the sweet-musky scent of her womanhood just inches away a powerful aphrodisiac. God, how he longed to taste her there, but he was afraid the haughty aristocrat wouldn't allow him to make love to her in such a bold manner, and he wouldn't risk her rejecting him at this point. He had to have her! Possess her completely and totally. Breathing a sigh of regret, he blazed a trail of searing kisses over her taut abdomen and across her swollen breasts.

Lorna was drowning in a sea of marvelous sensa-

tions, her skin tingling and burning in the wake of
Nathan's caresses and fiery kisses. Then, as his hand
slipped between her thighs and cupped her there, in
the most intimate of all spots, she tensed, her legs
instinctively closing, before she realized that she had
almost given herself away the second time. But as
Nathan's slender fingers slid through her slickness,
parting the aching folds, seeking and finding the bud
of her desire, Lorna found that she didn't have to
pretend to acquiesce. Her legs opened of their own
accord as a whole new barrage of sensations attacked
her senses, searing her to the soles of her feet and
curling her toes. As Nathan worked his wondrous,
exciting magic there, teasing and tantalizing, she
moaned, her head moving from side to side as the
sweet, yet frightening ripples began, becoming powerful undulations that rocked her body and left her
weak and dazed, her breath coming in rapid gasps.

Nathan nuzzled her neck, his hands buried in the
wild tangle of hair that had come loose during her
head thrashing, wanting so badly for her to love him
back. He would have thought that a woman of her
experience would have been more demonstrative.
But then, he reminded himself, she was a selfish noblewoman, accustomed to receiving, not giving.

Still feeling overwhelmed by all of the new and
wonderful sensations Nathan had brought her, Lorna
wondered why he was just lying so quietly over her.
Was there something she was supposed to do next?
Suddenly it dawned on her that she hadn't been acting like Lady Hampton, a woman of the world, but
herself. She ran her hands lightly over Nathan's broad
back, feeling the powerful muscles contract beneath
his feverish skin. Knowing her touch was pleasing him
encouraged her. She kissed his shoulder, then licked
his salty skin, hearing his hiss of pleasure. Suddenly

she wanted to lavish her love on him. She covered his neck and shoulders with hot kisses, her hands running greedily over him, her body touching his male body that was so different from her own exciting her unbearably. Feverish with need, she clasped his rockhard buttocks and dug her nails in, arching her hips into his. Feeling his rigid length pressed against her, throbbing with a life of its own, so close to where she wanted him was an agony. "Please, please," she sobbed.

When Lady Hampton first touched him, Nathan thought her a little tentative. He wondered if it was because she had never given anything in return, or if it was just her way of teasing him further. When she threw herself into caressing him and kissing him so uninhibitedly, all of his cynical thoughts fled, his intense excitement taking precedence over all. Every fiber in his body was crying for release, his need to possess her completely and totally consuming him.

He nudged her thighs apart with his knee and rose over her, placing fiery kisses over her face and throat and breasts as his hands slipped beneath her soft buttocks and lifted her. Poised with the tip of his rigid manhood at the very portal of her womanhood, he looked deeply into her eyes and said in a demanding, husky voice, "Tell me your first name."

All Lorna could think of was the tip of Nathan's hard, hot flesh pressed against her. She was frantic with need, her breath coming in ragged gasps that seemed to burn her lungs.

"Dammit, answer me!" Nathan said harshly. "I'll be damned if I'll consummate this without knowing your first name. If we can't meet as equals in at least this much, simply a man and woman, then we won't come together at all!"

He couldn't deny her, Lorna thought, not now.

She was throbbing for him, burning for him, and she knew only he could put out that fire that seemed to be consuming her. She whimpered and answered weakly, "Lorna."

When Nathan softly repeated her name with his voice roughened with desire, Lorna realized that she had foolishly given him her real name. But her regret quickly vanished. She wanted him to consummate their loving thinking of her as Lorna, not as the hated noblewoman. "Please," she begged. "I can't wait any longer. I've never wanted anyone as badly as I want you."

Her admitting to her intense desire for him sent a surge of exultation through Nathan. With a cry that echoed his feelings, he plunged into her. He stiffened in surprise as he felt that thin membrane tear and heard her sharp gasp before he slid into her soft, moist void. For a split second, his mind reeled in disbelief. Then, feeling her tight heat surround his rigid member, the untutored muscles clutching him like hot greedy hands, he broke out in a fine sheen of perspiration, his body trembling with effort to keep from taking her by storm, wanting to give her time to become accustomed to the feel of him before he began his movements.

The brief, tearing pain that Lorna felt on Nathan's entry was quickly replaced with dull ache and then an acute awareness of him filling her, feeling enormous and hot, his flesh seemingly throbbing in unison with hers. She waited, breathless, for something else to happen, feeling a slow tension invading her, totally unaware of Nathan's hands soothing her, of his muttered endearments, his total concentration on their joining. Surely this wasn't all there was to it, she thought. There had to be more. Instinctively, she moved tentatively against him, then gasped at the sensation her small movement had brought her.

Nathan began his movements then, slow, sensuous thrusts that lit fires in nerve endings Lorna had never dreamed existed. Greedy for more, she moved with him, her eyes wide with awe, her heart beating a wild tattoo in her chest as he led her up that spiraling ascent. When the movements quickened, a fire consumed her and an unbearable tension began to build within her. Sobbing incoherently, Lorna locked her long legs around Nathan's waist, straining against him, desperately wanting something that she had never known and sensing that she was on the brink of it. At the feel of that sweet, tight vise around him, squeezing him in her liquid heat, Nathan groaned at the exquisite sensation and clenched his teeth, struggling to hold back his release until she had reached hers, his gaze locked on Lorna's face. Then feeling her stiffening in his arms, then convulsing, and seeing her eyes flying open with the wonder of it, he let out a victorious cry and followed her in his own explosive white-hot release that seemed to shake the earth and make the heavens tremble.

By the time Lorna had drifted back to earth after her own soul-shattering experience, Nathan had recovered from his. When she opened her eyes, feeling as if she was floating on a warm, rosy cloud, she saw him staring down at her in puzzlement. Feeling deliciously languid, she absently stroked his sweat-slick shoulders and asked, "Why are you looking at me so strangely?"

"I was the first."

The accusing tone of his voice brought her to her senses. Oh my God, she had completely forgotten about that! Quickly she searched her mind for some explanation, then remembering what she had told him of her marriage, said, "I told you my marriage was arranged for political reasons, that we have very little feeling for one another."

"That may well be, but I can't imagine any man not consummating his marriage, as desirable as you are, and particularly not a man as greedy and selfish as the men of your class are."

Lorna realized what Nathan said was true. Even if he hadn't cared for her, her noble "husband" would probably have forced himself on her to satisfy his lust, since it was his "right." She frantically sought some further explanation, then remembered a guest she had seen at one of the parties at the nobleman's house she had served in. The man had been so overdressed and effeminate that it had aroused her curiosity and she had questioned Maddie about it. "My husband preferred men to women."

Nathan was shocked, then filled with utter disgust. Well, he thought, rolling to his side, he guessed that explained a lot of things. But what a blow it must have been to Lorna's female pride. Well, if her noble husband didn't want her, he did, even more so now that he had made love to her. He pulled her into his arms possessively, feeling a secret elation that he had been the first.

Lorna was vastly relieved when Nathan didn't ask any further questions, but took her in his arms. She wanted to relish her happiness, savor all the wondrous delights he had introduced her to. She had no regrets. It had been absolutely beautiful, even more beautiful than she had imagined. With his hands smoothing over her and his chin nuzzling her hair, she thought this was the best part of it. She had halfway expected him to leave as soon as his passion was

spent. But his holding her in his strong arms, treating
her with such tender care, was something she had
craved long before she had come to know a woman's
passions. Feeling a deep contentment she had never
known, she drifted off to sleep.

But for Nathan sleep wouldn't come. He lay staring off into space, deep in thought. Surprisingly, he
wasn't puzzling over all the unexpected things he had
found out about Lorna, but rather his feelings for her.

He had known there was passion in her, had
meant to drink his fill, but now his thirst for her was
even greater, as if her sweet, heady passion was a
powerful drug and one taste had left him addicted. It
was an unsettling thought. He was a man accustomed
to controlling his own destiny, and yet, he had been
driven by some strange compulsion to possess her
completely, totally, to place his mark on her forever.
Somehow, by her uninhibited free giving of herself
there at the end, she had turned the tables on him, as
if during their shared passion and shattering explosion, *she* had placed a brand on *his* soul. And then
there was that urge to protect her that had been there
to some degree from the very beginning, stronger
now than ever, to say nothing of the peculiar tender
feelings for her that were emerging—new, frightening feelings that threatened his fierce independence.

Dammit, what the hell had he gotten himself
into? Despite everything she was still a married
woman. Besides, he wanted no emotional entangle-
ments with any woman, no attachments, no ties, no
matter how desirable she was. Yet he seemed to be
helpless against the feelings she aroused in him. She
seemed to hold him to her by some mysterious, invisible bond. Even now as she slept in his arms, so fragile

and seemingly so trusting, there was a choking feeling in his throat and a strange ache in his chest.

Bewildered and deeply disturbed, he finally slept.

Chapter 8

The next day when Lorna was riding in the sedan, she had entirely different feelings than she had
had the night before. Despite what she had thought,
she did have regrets. When she saw Nathan briefly
that morning, he seemed distant, so cold and indifferent. Why, he had hardly said a word to her. It seemed
that by giving herself to him so completely, so totally,
she had only gotten herself deeper into her duplicity.
Now he didn't just suspect that she was an unfaithful
wife. He knew it. Nor would the fact that he was her
first lover change that. Regardless of the circumstances of her supposed marriage, she was still a married woman, and she had thrown herself at him, offering absolutely no resistance, only proving to him that
she had no moral character. No wonder he had
treated her so coldly, considering his low opinion of
her. Oh, if only she could reveal her real self to him,
but after all the lies she told him last night, she feared

it was too late. That's when she should have admitted the truth to him, instead of sinking deeper into her deception. She had let her fear for herself override her basic honesty, something she had always prided herself on. She was nothing but a coward.

Riding before the camel that carried Lorna's sedan, Nathan was lost in his own gloomy thoughts. That morning when he awoke and found her in his arms, so soft and so desirable, it had been all he could do to keep from waking her and making love to her again. But he feared tasting her passion would only ensnare him deeper in the silken web she seemed to be weaving around him, a tender trap that would enslave his soul. Quickly, he dressed and left the tent, vowing that he would fight his attraction to her, squelch the strange, threatening feelings she was arousing in him. But when she stepped from the tent, a surge of spontaneous joy went through him, irritating him no end. He threw up his defenses, hiding behind a wall of pretended indifference.

Nathan frowned. There were things about her that still perplexed him, even after all she had told him about her marriage. Knowing that it was a forced union and that her female pride must have suffered terribly when she found out her husband didn't even desire her body, he could understand her taking lovers. But he had been the first. Why him? Did she enjoy only teasing and taunting men? Regardless of the explanation she had given him about her indecent dress the first day he had seen her, he still didn't believe her. It was clearly a dress meant for seduction. And then there were those flimsy garments she had worn last night. Did she take perverse pleasure in taunting men then spurning them? Had she not counted on her passion getting the upper hand? Or had it been only passion speaking? Was it possible that she felt more for him than just desire?

The thought sent a shot of joy rushing through him. But there was still that matter of class distinction between them. Would she divorce her noble husband and marry a commoner? He'd be damned if he'd play the role of just her lover in her life. He had too much pride for that. She'd give him her all, or nothing. Then, realizing what he was speculating, Nathan was shocked. What in hell was wrong with him, contemplating marriage? He wouldn't give up his independence for any woman. Dammit, it wasn't enough that she had his guts tied in knots, she had him completely befuddled too.

Inside the sedan Lorna forced herself to turn her thoughts from Nathan and tried concentrating on her surroundings. Thinking of the mess she had gotten herself into with Nathan was just too painful. As she gazed out her window, she noticed that there was something different about the area they were passing through. Before, the caravan had weaved its way across the desert, seemingly following some invisible trail that only the Arab guides knew, but now they were on a very well-defined road, a strip of packed earth a good fifty feet across. Amazed, she asked herself aloud, "How did this road get here, in the middle of the desert?"

Nathan was unaware that he had slowly slipped back until he was riding beside Lorna's chaise, once again gravitated to her by some mysterious force. Thinking that her question was directed at him, he cursed himself under his breath for being a fool and answered, "The Romans built it. We left the trail we've been following about a mile back and are now on the old Carthage Road."

Lorna heard the terseness in Nathan's voice. He

can't stand to be around me, she thought. Well, she couldn't stand being anywhere around him either, not knowing how he felt about her. Perhaps she should try to escape him now. She hadn't dared to attempt it before because she had known she would get hopelessly lost. "Where does it go to?"

"To the old Carthage ruins outside of Tunis."

Tunis? Lorna thought in surprise. Why, that was their destination. "Are we that close to Tunis?"

"Yes, we should be arriving there tomorrow."

Did she dare to make her escape? If so, she should wait until tonight, when she could slip away under the cover of darkness. But what if the road wasn't this wide everywhere. She could lose her way, particularly at night. "Is it this wide all the way into the city?"

Nathan thought her question a little odd. Then he assumed she was just bored to tears and trying to engage him in conversation. "Yes, it's one of the main caravan routes across the Sahara and goes back a long way. Not only did the victorious Roman legions use it, but the Arabs swept westward over this road on their holy wars. Even the Crusaders used it. That's why the ground is so packed."

Did she dare to try her escape here? Lorna wondered. Then she realized that even if she did get to Tunis, she wouldn't be safe. She would still be in a hostile country where women were forbidden to travel alone. Nor did she have any money to buy passage with, providing she could even find a European ship in the harbor. No, she had only been entertaining crazy, wild thoughts in her desperation to get away from Nathan. Blinking back sudden tears, she turned her head away and gazed out the open window.

Nathan had seen the fleeting expressions that crossed Lorna's face before she turned her head. She

seemed to be very upset about something. Again he
was puzzled. He couldn't imagine what in their brief
conversation had upset her so much, but he was reluctant to leave her side. He found himself wanting to
crawl into the chaise, take her in his arms, and comfort her. It was an unsettling urge, but he couldn't
fight it off.

Lorna was very aware of Nathan's eyes on her.
Damn, why didn't he just go away and leave her alone
if he didn't want to be around her? She forced herself
to lean closer to the window, trying to show him that
she was just as indifferent to him as he had appeared
to be to her earlier. Then, seeing the big holes in the
ground all around her, she was puzzled. They seemed
to be much too large to be made by some burrowing
animal. She was curious to know what had made them
but determined she wouldn't ask Nathan. Tearing her
eyes away from the holes, she looked about the barren
land all around her. Well, at least she had one consolation. She might have to bear Nathan's company for a
while longer, but in a matter of a few days she would
be out of this ugly, harsh land with its scorching sun
and its glaring hot sand that waited for rains that
never came. At least she would be getting rid of a part
of her misery.

Catching sight of something at the top of a rise in
the distance, Lorna squinted against the glare of the
bright sunlight. As the riders rolled over the hilltop in
a wave of blue, she stared at both their numbers and
the grace with which they rode their pure white racing camels, wondering who these tall, skillful riders
were. Dressed completely in blue, even the turbans
they had wrapped around their lower faces, they
looked magnificent as they came sweeping down the
hill, their bright robes billowing in the wind.

Then a bloodcurdling, shrill cry rent the air, fol-

lowed by the long, lugubrious beat of drums, and then
the Arabs' terrified screams, *"Razzia! Razzia!"* Lorna
was stunned. A raid? she thought in disbelief. Sudden
fear clawed at her heart. She turned her head, seeing
the tan on Nathan's face pale as he watched the horde
of camel riders bearing down on them.

"Who are they?" she asked.

"Tuareg," he answered, grim-lipped. "The fiercest desert raiders and warriors in North Africa."

The ominous tone of his voice terrified Lorna.
"Then we'll all be killed?"

"No, they won't kill you. As a woman, you'll be
part of the plunder." Seeing Lorna's face wash of all
color, he quickly added in a fiercely determined
voice, "But that's not going to happen. Not if I can
help it!"

Lorna had no time to wonder over his words. He
gave her a quick, profound look that would have spoken volumes had Lorna not been too terrified to notice, then yelled to Hamid in Arabic, "Run! Get her
out of here! Make for those rocks over there and
hide!"

Lorna's head snapped back on her slender neck
as the camel beneath her suddenly took off at a dead
run. Behind her she could hear screams and yells, the
sounds of gunshots and javelins shrieking through the
air. Holding onto the wildly swaying sedan for dear
life, she stuck her head out the window and looked
back, seeing the furious battle that was taking place as
the Arabs and the raiders swung at each other with
their razor-sharp swords, the dust swirling about
them. But the Arabs on the ground were at a distinct
disadvantage, those poor men who weren't being shot
by the raiders' long muskets being cut to pieces
where they stood. Lorna felt sick. It was a massacre!

But where was Nathan? she wondered, looking about wildly, her heart racing in fear for him.

Then, seeing that they were being pursued by six Tuareg who had spied them fleeing the scene, Lorna's heart raced even faster. A flurry of gunshots followed, bullets whizzing all around the sedan. Lorna watched as one of the Tuareg pitched forward and fell off his camel, for a moment bewildered before she realized the shot had come from Nathan, who was riding behind her camel. Oh, thank God, he's alive, she thought, feeling weak with relief. Now if they could just outrun them.

But such was not to be the case. Their bullets spent, the Tuareg slipped their muskets into their long saddle scabbards and drew their swords, screeching like madmen and urging their mounts forward. The drumming of the camels' hooves pounded in her ears as the raiders came closer and closer.

Then Lorna froze in terror, seeing Nathan doubling back to meet the Tuareg and a minute later racing his camel headlong into the group, swinging his sword like a vengeful god, the clatter of steel hitting steel ringing in the air. Another Tuareg fell from his camel, the blood draining from the mortal chest wound staining his bright blue robe. Then Nathan seemed to be swallowed up by blue as the Tuareg surrounded him, their swords flashing in the sunlight as they viciously wielded them.

Frantically Lorna tried to open the door to the sedan, her only thought to go to Nathan's aid. But the handle was on the outside, and much too low for her reach in the wildly swaying sedan. She clung to the window for dear life, her eyes glued to the fierce battle in the distance, holding her breath, too terrified for Nathan's life even to scream. Then, as the Tuareg burst from the cloud of dust raised by the camels' hooves, leaving Nathan lying lifeless on the sand, his kaffiyeh ripped to pieces, his entire body covered with blood, and his head lying in a pool of it, she thought, My God! They cut him to ribbons! Then a scream did come from her, an anguished cry that came from the depths of her soul. "Noooo! No, not Nathan!"

Nathan's play for time in rushing headlong into the Tuareg and attacking them was a valiant but futile effort. Hamid was running as fast as his short legs could carry him, all but dragging the reluctant camel behind him, but it wasn't fast enough to escape. A blue-veiled raider tore past the sedan, brandishing his sword, the long tail of his turban following him like a bright streamer, and cut Hamid down in his tracks, the servant's death cry yet another horror to Lorna. A moment later the camel slowed its speed, no longer urged forward by the slim Arab who had put all his heart into trying to secure Lorna's escape.

When the raider who claimed the camel with the sedan as his plunder opened the door a few moments later, he found a beautiful woman with tears streaming down her face. "You bastard!" Lorna hissed, baring her nails and flying at him with murder in her eyes.

Caught unaware, Lorna almost tore the wrappings from his face—causing a look of absolute horror to come into his eyes—before the man caught her arms, struggling to subdue her, shocked at her strength as she wildly kicked and swung at him with her fists. It wasn't until another Tuareg came to his aid that he was finally able to force her back into the sedan, where she collapsed among the pillows, sobbing hysterically.

Lorna cried until there were no more tears left. Then she stared at the ceiling of the sedan, feeling empty, as if her life had been snuffed out along with Nathan's. Again she wondered at the cruelty of fate. She had found the man of her dreams, shared one incredible night of passion with him, and then lost him. She had known that he would walk out of her life, but at least he would have been alive. No, it was the knowledge that he had died in a brave and noble effort to secure her escape that was an agony to her tortured soul. If she had not impersonated Lady Hampton, he'd be alive today. Now, because of her, he was dead. That he had gone to his death thinking of her as nothing but a spoiled adulteress who had no feelings for him was an added burden to her soul.

If only she'd had the courage to reveal her real identity to him, to tell him that she loved him, she could at least have spared herself that awesome guilt. A single tear squeezed from her eye as she muttered in an anguished voice, "Oh, my love, forgive me."

Chapter 9

That evening when the Tuareg stopped and opened the door to the sedan, they stood back, warily watching Lorna as if they were afraid she would attack them again. But all the fight had gone out of Lorna, along with her will to live. She had decided that without Nathan her life was meaningless, that she would be nothing but an empty shell going through the motions of living.

But Lorna found over the next days that it was not easy to will death, particularly when there was a part of her that so desperately wanted to live. She had always been a fighter and a survivor, and she couldn't deny her true nature. Without her willing it, a hard core of fierce determination came to the fore.

The Tuareg took their plunder south, deep into the Sahara, driving the camels hard and relentlessly, sometimes traveling far into the night, an exhausting pace calculated to discourage any resistance on the

part of their captives. The days that passed became
one long agony: days of grueling heat and endless
golden sand that stretched to infinity and blended
into a golden sky where the white-hot orb of the sun
blazed down on them, nights of shivering cold when
the temperature plunged fifty to sixty degrees and
the black canopy above them was covered with glittering stars or the desert was bathed in eerie moonlight.

Then came the sand dunes, a virtual sea of cres-
cent-shaped piles of sand that towered five hundred
feet into the air, looking like a mountain when one
gazed up at them from the foot of the dune. The
camels labored up one dune, then down, up and
down, over and over, and Lorna knew why the animals were called "ships of the desert." Her heart filled
with despair each time they reached the crest of one
tall dune only to discover another facing them, wondering if they would wander out here forever in this
endless sand—or until they fell off the ends of the
earth.

A week into their trek they stopped at an oasis,
the pitifully small pool of water surrounded by a few
scraggly palm trees. The Tuareg filled up their water
bags before allowing the thirst-crazed camels to
drink, the animals bellowing pitifully as the men held
them back. Then the camels rushed in and drained
the pool, leaving only a wet patch of sand.

Three days later Lorna saw mountains in the distance, their peaks covered with snow. The sight was
enough to drive one as crazy as the mirages on the
shimmering sand, the thought of cold water a torment to her cracked lips, swollen tongue, and
parched throat. She kept her eyes glued on the mountains, somehow sensing this was their destination and
the end to her long agony.

When they entered the foothills and left the sand behind, Lorna would have cried with relief had she been able to summon the moisture from her dehydrated body. Two days later when they crested a hill, Lorna looked down and saw the city of red leather tents in the valley below and knew their trek was finally ended. She had dropped twenty pounds; her face was blistered from the hot winds; her lips were so cracked that she doubted they would ever heal—but she had survived!

It seemed the whole town came out to greet them when the victorious raiders led the camels with their plunder into the maze of tents, the Tuareg on the ground pushing and shoving and the sounds of their excited yells and the babble of a strange tongue grating on Lorna's nerves. Even the goats and sheep grazing in the hills around them were bleating, only adding to the din.

Lorna was led into a large tent by her captor, and even though his lower face was still swaddled in the blue cloth, she knew by the sparkle in his hazel eyes that he was grinning beneath the material. Coming into the dim light of the tent, it took a moment for her eyes to adjust and for her to see the plump woman, about five years older than herself, standing there. Lorna stared in amazement, for the woman's skin was almost as light as her own, and her eyes were a distinct blue.

There was the rattle of the strange tongue between the two Tuareg before the woman stepped forward and asked in Arabic, "Who are you?"

Lorna remembered Nathan's telling her that Muslims didn't enslave fellow Muslims, and Lorna hadn't struggled to survive the trip across the desert only to become a slave. She threw back her shoulders and answered, "I am a Berber."

"I am Berber, too. But I have never seen a Berber with eyes the color of yours." In a lightning-swift movement the Tuareg woman pushed back the sleeves of Lorna's caftan and *entarie,* revealing her milky white skin. "Nor skin that pale."

Lorna's heart hammered in her chest. Would they punish her for lying to them? She decided to stick to her story no matter what. "I am still a Berber, and a Muslim."

"From what tribe?"

Lorna frantically searched her memory, then answered with a smug smile, "I am of the Masmuda tribe, from the coast."

The woman's eyes widened in surprise, then narrowed suspiciously as she said, "I still do not believe you. What year is it?"

"Why, it's eighteen oh four," Lorna answered a little hesitantly, wondering at the strange question.

The woman threw back her head, made a strange kissing sound with her mouth, and said in a victorious voice, "You lie! You gave me the Christian year, not the Muslim."

At the look of horror that came over Lorna's face when she realized she had been tricked, the woman laughed huskily, saying, "Ah, I see you did not know the Muslims have a different calendar than the Christians. Our calendar begins in your Christian year of six twenty-two, when our prophet Muhammad made his flight from those who plotted to murder him. You are not a Berber or a Muslim. You are a Christian. Now, tell me who you are!"

Lorna knew she had been foolish to try to pretend to be a Muslim. She knew only a smattering of the religion, and if the woman hadn't tripped her up on the Muslim calendar, she would eventually have made some slip that would have given her away. Her shoulders slumped in defeat as she said, "My name is Lorna Winters."

Lorna gave her name in English, since she had no idea what the Arabic translation might be. The woman rolled the strange words around her tongue, swallowing the *n* in Lorna's first name so that it came out sounding like, "Lor'a," then asked, "And where are you from?"

"Great Britain," Lorna answered, again in English.

"Where is that?"

"It's a big island, in a large ocean, far, far away from here."

"And where did you learn to speak Arabic?"

"The ship I was on was captured by Barbary pirates. I spent nine months in the pasha's *iyal* in Tripoli before I was ransomed."

The woman again jerked her head back and made the strange kissing noise, saying, "The Arabs are nothing but thieving, murdering pigs. A curse on them!"

Lorna remembered the Tuareg killing Nathan. Without even stopping to consider the consequences, she threw back, "The Tuareg are no better! Your men attacked the caravan, massacring the men on it, stealing their property!"

The woman's eyebrows rose in surprise. She had been fascinated when the girl told her she was from a strange land, but she had never expected such spirit. And if there was anything a Tuareg woman admired, it was spirit in another woman. Intrigued with the girl who stood so defiantly before her, the woman shrugged off Lorna's accusation and said calmly, "I am Chedlya, wife of Abu Bakr, your captor. You will be my personal slave. You will tell me of this strange country you come from."

Abu Bakr stepped forward to object, but the scathing look his wife gave him silenced him before he got two words out. He turned and rushed from the tent, obviously angered.

Abu Bakr's anger didn't surprise Lorna. She had seen him casting admiring glances her way and knew he desired her. But she was amazed at Chedlya's dictating to him. A Muslim woman who overrode her husband's authority? Why, it was unheard of! Then, remembering what Chedlya had said, tears of bitterness sprang to her eyes. It seemed she had gone a complete circle, and everything she had done before was all for naught. In the end she was to become a slave, the very thing that she had lied to the pirates to avoid, her freedom taken away forever.

Over the following months Lorna learned to accept her new way of life with a grudging resignation. Except for losing her precious freedom, she was treated well, certainly faring better than the multitude of black slaves, known as *bouzous,* who did all the work, the men tending the huge herds of sheep, goats, and camels, working in the irrigated fields, lugging the buckets of water from the deep artesian wells, while the women pounded and cooked millet, gathered camel chips for fires, swept the camp, and searched the hills for wild melons. A Tuareg male would not even saddle his own camel, and the women were ladies of leisure, overseeing the black female slaves, reading poetry, playing a peculiar instrument that looked like a violin, or just passing their time gossiping.

But despite the fact that the Tuareg society was founded on slavery, even the blacks fared much better than Lorna would have thought. They lived in the same camp, in similar shelters, and ate the same meals, often from the same pot, in many ways treated like members of the family. The only punishment Lorna saw given to them was a few swats with a light stick, as if the slaves were naughty children instead of chattel. They were even clothed well, but always in white, as blue, the only color the Tuareg wore, was reserved for the masters. Lorna was glad she was given white clothing, for the blue, made from a strong indigo dye, rubbed off on the Tuareg, tinting their skins beneath their robes, the color resisting even the most vigorous scrubbing.

It turned out that Lorna's only chore was to brush Chedlya's long brown hair and answer the millions of questions the young woman asked about the outside world. She wanted to know everything in minute detail—what the people in Great Britain ate, what they wore, how they traveled, how they entertained themselves, how they made their living—until Lorna's throat ached from swallowing letters of the difficult Arabic. When Lorna told her about forests where the trees towered into the air, so thick that you could hardly see light through the leaves, Chedlya was filled with wonder, and the description Lorna gave of the Atlantic Ocean awed the Tuareg woman, who couldn't envision water stretching from horizon to horizon. But it was when Lorna told her that rain was an almost daily occurrence in England at some times of the year that Chedlya eyes filled with utter disbelief, for the Tuareg woman had seen rain only once in her lifetime.

Talking about England made Lorna feel homesick, even though she had been anxious to leave her homeland to get away from the snobbish nobility. She yearned for the pleasant climate, the sights and sounds, even the smells of her country. She missed Maddie and her other friends among the servants and longed with desperation to get back to a civilized country where she could be among those who shared her own language and culture. And talking about her previous life reminded her too much of Nathan. Anytime she thought about the rugged American, whether it was Chedlya who reminded her, or if she were lying at night in her lonely bed, or if his memory just happened to flash across her brain, she was filled with a terrible sadness that left her with an aching emptiness, an emptiness that she knew could never be filled by another man. For these reasons, when Chedlya demanded her presence, Lorna deliberately turned the discussions away from England and to Chedlya's Tuareg society, pretending a halfhearted interest.

She learned that the Tuareg were an offshoot of the warlike Sanhaja Berber tribe, that by virtue of their profitable raids on caravans and their huge herds of animals, they were very wealthy, that they were the most feared of all the desert tribes. And yet the Tuareg society was a paradox. Even though they were Muslims, the women wore no veils; rather, the men kept their faces hidden, not just when they were outside, but at all times, even eating with their hand covering their lower faces and sleeping in the twelve-foot-long wrapping they wore around their heads. What amazed Lorna even more was that the women clearly ruled the roost, often intimidating their husbands, despite the fact that the men were renowned for their fierceness. Nor did they allow their husbands to have more than one wife, although the Koran allowed a Muslim male four.

Curious to learn just how the Tuareg women had managed to get such a firm upper hand over their husbands, Lorna finally asked Chedlya about it.

Chedlya shrugged her shoulders and answered,

"They are afraid if they do not do what we wish, we will divorce them."

"Divorce them?" Lorna asked in surprise. "I didn't know a Muslim woman could divorce her husband."

"She can't. Only the man can divorce. But a Tuareg man who clings to a woman who no longer wants him is considered ignoble by our people."

"But why should divorce be such a threat?"

"Because the women own most of the wealth. We are a matriarchal society. The women inherit, not the men. We even trace our lineage through the woman, an ancestry that goes back to one powerful woman who lived long, long ago."

"And have your men always kept themselves veiled? Was this some edict that this woman decreed?"

"No, when the Tuareg first embraced Islam, we kept ourselves veiled like the other Muslim women."

"Then what happened to change it?"

"According to legend one day our men came home from a raid empty-handed, having even lost their camels. The women were furious and severely berated them, calling them weak. They threw down their veils and said from now on the men would wear them. The men were so shamed that from that day on they wore the veils." Chedlya laughed huskily, saying, "Of course our men deny this. They claim they keep their faces covered for fear an evil spirit will enter their soul if someone gazes upon it. But we women know better."

Considering how the women intimidated the men, Lorna was inclined to believe the women's claim. "But how can you tell who is who with the men's faces covered and only their eyes showing.

"It is not difficult. They all have a different look

about the eyes and distinctive mannerisms. But if a Tuareg is killed in battle and his veil is torn off, it must be replaced before he can be identified. Without his veil, no one recognizes him."

Chedlya gave Lorna a penetrating look, then said, "Christian women do not wear veils either, nor do they allow their husbands to have more than one wife. Are they allowed as many lovers as they wish, as we are?"

"You mean your husband allows you to have lovers?" Lorna asked in surprise.

"Why not? He has his lovers."

"You mean his black concubines?"

"No, other Tuareg women."

"But . . . but isn't that . . . awkward?"

"No. If a man tires of his wife and concubines and desires to make love to another woman, he simply rides through camp until he finds a woman alone in her tent who is pleasing to his eyes and asks, *'Isalan?'* —What's your news?—If the woman finds him pleasing to her eyes and is agreeable, she answers, *'Nan-i'* —I have a lot of news. Then he dismounts, embraces her, and spends the evening."

Free love? Lorna thought in horror. Everyone dallying with everyone else's husband and wife? Oh, she knew there was a certain amount of adultery that went on in her civilization, too, but it wasn't acceptable, nor did everyone practice it. Why, it was the most amoral thing she had ever heard.

"Ah, I see you do not approve." Chedlya threw back her head and gave her kissing sound, a characteristic mannerism that Lorna had learned showed her disgust or impatience with someone. "You Christian woman are as prudish as the other Muslim women." She cocked her head, asking, "Are you still a virgin?"

"That's none of your business!"

Chedlya chuckled. "Why didn't you just say no instead of getting angry? You gave yourself away. And you have already told me you are not married. Perhaps there is hope for you after all."

"It wasn't like that!" Lorna replied hotly. "I loved him. And I'll never love another man."

Chedlya threw up her arms in exasperation, saying, "What has love got to do with it? I'm talking about passion!"

"To me, one doesn't exist without the other."

"Ah, I should have guessed it is a man you are thinking of when you look so sad so often. Who is he?"

"It doesn't matter. He's dead now. And I don't want to talk about it!"

Chedlya sat back on her pallet, her eyes narrowing. "It is a shame that you have given your all to one man, particularly one who is dead. And so utterly foolish. It would be easier for you if you could learn to accept passion for passion's sake."

There was something in the tone of Chedlya's voice that made a tingle of fear creep up Lorna's spine. She could hardly force the words from her mouth; "What do you mean by that?"

"I am selling you. Word went out to all the desert tribes over two weeks ago. Tomorrow you will be auctioned off to the highest bidder."

Lorna was shocked speechless. And now she knew what Chedlya had meant when she made that remark about passion for passion's sake. She was to be sold as some man's concubine, his plaything. No! She couldn't stand it. She'd never live through it, particularly not after having experienced Nathan's beautiful lovemaking. Her anger came to the fore. "Why are you doing this? Have I displeased you?"

"No, that is not the reason. Talking with you has

been stimulating, enlightening. I have enjoyed your company immensely. But I have seen the way my husband looks at you. You are a beautiful woman, even if you are skinny. Too beautiful. Despite the great wealth and the power I hold in our tribe, he might be tempted to divorce me and take you for his wife."

"But what if I refuse to be his wife?"

"You cannot refuse. You are a slave."

"But I'm *your* slave, not his! You said so yourself."

"To refuse to sell you to him would make me look petty in the eyes of the others. Either way, I would be disgraced before my people."

"If I'm to be put on the auction block, what's to keep him from buying me then?" Lorna argued.

"I told you, I hold the wealth. My husband is too poor to compete with the bids that your beauty will bring. Besides, he has not whipped up his courage to divorce me yet. But with you around as a constant temptation, your body filling out more and more, it would be only a matter of time."

Lorna didn't bother to tell Chedlya that the weight she had gained was what she had lost on her trip across the Sahara. Instead, she took another approach. "Then I'll do like the *bouzous* do when they are dissatisfied with their master. I'll cut a slit in the ear of one of your neighbors' sheep. Then you would have to give me to the owner as compensation."

"No, that will not work in this instance. They will know why you are doing it, because you are angry with me for selling you, and not because you prefer them as a master over me. Besides, there is not one woman in this tribe who would accept you or allow her husband to do so, for the same reason I am getting rid of you."

As Lorna glared at her, Chedlya said in a soothing

voice, "Ah, don't be angry with me. I hate to give you up. I will miss you. But you are too much of a threat. I only do what I must."

Chedlya rose to her feet, saying, "Now go and take a long walk. Resign yourself to your fate. *Inshullah.*"

God wills it be damned, Lorna thought furiously. Chedlya wills it—not God! Fighting down the urge to scratch out the woman's eyes, Lorna turned and stormed from the tent.

Angrily, she walked through the camp, threading her way through the maze of tents and passing a row of *ziribas*, houses made of dried grass that some of the Tuareg preferred to live in, almost stumbling over a *bouzou* woman milking a goat. Leaving the camp behind, she rushed past a small herd of camels eating the boughs and leaves of adras and thorn trees, the goats below them scrambling for the leaves that were being shook loose. She didn't stop until she reached the hillside above the camp, and there she sat on a rock among a herd of grazing sheep, the *bouzou* herdsman with his white turban wrapped around his face like his master looking at her curiously.

Lorna couldn't understand Chedlya. The woman had been kind to her, treating her with an almost courteous hospitality, until today. How could she be so cruel, so treacherous, as to throw her to the wolves?

She gazed down on the camp below her, seeing two Tuareg men meeting in one of the dusty streets and greeting one another by kissing the crossed thumb and forefinger of their right hand, a puzzling Tuareg custom, for Lorna had once read that the gesture was a secret sign of the early Christian Church. As the two men walked away, Lorna watched them in admiration in spite of her agitation. Unusually tall, as slim and hard-muscled as their wives were fleshy and flaccid, with small wrists and slender, refined hands, they all had a striking grace of carriage, moving like princes of the earth. There was only one other man Lorna had ever seen who strode so easily, so confidently, so gracefully. Nathan.

Tears swam in her eyes, the pain from the still-raw wound of his death deep in her soul, almost unbearable. Tuareg meant "forsaken to God" in Arabic, and who was she to be forsaken to? A brutal, cruel man who would use her to slake his lust? Maybe she shouldn't have run away from Phillip's accusation. Even imprisonment in her home country would be better than that. Not only had she lost her freedom, but now she would be subjected to a lifetime of humiliation at the hands of some lusting Muslim man, for there appeared to be no hope of her ever returning to her own people. Again Lorna's strong will came to the fore. Well, he could claim mastery of her body, but never her heart and her soul. He couldn't claim something that could never be enslaved, something that could only be given freely and, for her, once.

The setting sun slipped behind the mountains, taking its warmth with it. It was winter now, and at night a cold wind came howling down from the mountains. Lorna shivered, as much from dread at what the morrow would bring as from the chill in the air. Rising, a heavy heart in her chest, she walked back down the hill to tents that glowed an eerie red in the dusk as the lamps within them were lit.

The next morning, Lorna was so apprehensive she couldn't eat her porridge made from goat's milk and ground millet. Even the cup of green tea that she managed to force down rolled in her stomach, threatening to come back up at any second.

While she was bathing with the ewer and basin

provided her, Chedlya pushed aside the curtains that separated her cubicle from the rest of the tent and entered, followed by a husky female *bouzou* carrying a chest.

Lorna recognized the chest with its beautiful bone and wood inlays. She hadn't seen it since the day she had been captured. The chest brought back memories of Nathan, and she closed her eyes as an immense wave of longing ran through her, a painful yearning for what could never again be.

"Today you will dress fitting your beauty," Chedlya announced after the *bouzou* had set the chest down on the carpet and left. She knelt beside the chest and opened it, rummaging through it, then pulling out a deep violet caftan. Glancing at Lorna's eyes, she seemed to hesitate, then tossed it aside to pull out a white silk, shot with gold and scalloped with gold metallic thread along the edges, a matching *entarie* and pantaloons and gold leather *babouches.*

When Lorna was dressed, Chedlya tied the gold cord around her slender hips and then stepped back, looking her over critically before saying, "Yes, the color does not detract from your natural beauty."

But Lorna knew better. Even though the white ensemble was as beautiful as the violet, Chedlya had chosen the white on purpose, to remind her who she was—a slave.

As Lorna started to roll her long auburn hair into the chignon she always wore, Chedlya said, "No! Leave it down. With its lustrous red highlights and as long as it is, it will only serve to entice them all the more."

Lorna's eyes glittered with anger. "And drive up the price?" she asked in a brittle voice.

Chedlya shrugged, answering, "I am a shrewd businesswoman, like my mother and her mother before her. We did not attain our wealth by being fools. If you have an exquisite jewel to sell, you do not display it among sacking or hide the facets that glitter the brightest."

Yes, Chedlya was shrewd, Lorna thought, and cruel and deceitful. And to think that she had begun to think of her as a friend of sorts. She felt both angry and betrayed.

Seeing the expression on Lorna's face, Chedlya said, "Ah, I see you are still angry with me."

"Yes, I'm angry!" Lorna spat, her violet eyes flashing. "How would you feel if you were me, sold to some filthy man to use as he saw fit, forced to share his pallet. You're a woman. How could you do that to another woman?"

"If you could learn to accept passion—"

"I'm not talking about passion," Lorna threw back. "I'm talking about lust! There's a difference." Lorna glared at Chedlya, looking so cool and undisturbed under her heated attack, then said bitterly, "But then, you wouldn't know about that, would you?"

"Yes, Lor'a, I do know how it feels to be used to satisfy a man's lust. My first husband was like that. There was nothing in it for me. I couldn't stand for him to touch me. He was a rutting pig!"

"Your first husband?" Lorna asked in surprise.

"Yes, I was married once before."

"Well, if he was so repulsive, why did you marry him?"

"First marriages are arranged by families. The Tuareg are no different from other Muslims in that respect. But unlike our Muslim sisters, a Tuareg woman can escape the clutches of an insensitive, brutish husband, or even one who simply bores her. All she has to do is demand a divorce. It is the second marriages that are made for physical attraction and love."

"Then you love Abu Bakr?" Lorna asked, having assumed Chedlya had no tender feelings for her husband if she took lovers so casually.

Chedlya sighed deeply, admitting almost as if she were embarrassed, "Yes, I love him. I am afraid when it comes to loving a man, we Tuareg women are just as weak and foolish as any other. It seems we can rule our men, but not our hearts, and there is no accounting for what our hearts choose. Yes, I love my husband. Very much. I could not bear to lose him to another woman."

For the first time Lorna could appreciate Chedlya's position. The woman's deep love for her husband put an entirely different light upon everything. She wasn't trying to protect her fierce pride, or even her position of respect in the tribe. She was fighting to retain something that women have fought for since the beginning of time—her man, her only love.

"So, you see, Lor'a, I do not do this because I have any ill will for you. Living here in my tent, a day-to-day temptation, you are too much of a threat. You must go."

Strangely, Lorna understood. Given the circumstances. Chedlya couldn't set her free and send her off. Manumission was prohibited in the Tuareg society. A master was obligated to feed, clothe, and shelter his slaves until they died, ran off, or were sold.

Grimly resigned to her fate, Lorna muttered, "I understand."

The sound of hooves drumming on the packed dirt outside the tent startled both women. Recovering from the her fright at the sudden thundering noise, Lorna frowned, saying, "That sounded like horses running, not camels."

"It was. I have invited men from both the Zenata Berber tribes and a few of the local Bedouin tribes, besides Tuareg from the surrounding confederacies and a few of our Sanhaja cousins. Naturally, some of the Bedouins ride horses, being Arabs and fools," Chedlya informed Lorna, "but I will never be able to understand why the Zenatas are so enthralled with them. They are Berbers. You would think they would know better. Horses are ugly and impractical creatures. Why, you can't even use their droppings for your fires, and they have none of the nobility and beauty of the camel."

Lorna couldn't believe her ears. She thought camels were the ugliest, most misshapen creatures she had ever seen, with their humped backs, small heads, long necks and legs, and knobby knees. Besides, they had the disgusting habit of chewing on their cuds, to say nothing of the fact that they smelled to high heaven. But then, she supposed, beauty depended upon the eyes of the beholder.

"Come, it is time to go. Everyone should be waiting in the tent I have set up for this occasion."

A lump came to Lorna's throat, her mouth suddenly dry. With trembling hands she reached for the veil sitting on top of the clothing in the trunk. Chedlya snatched it from her hand and threw it on the ground, saying, "No, you will not go veiled!"

"Oh, yes," Lorna said, a fresh wave of bitterness sweeping over her, "I forgot I'm only property that's being displayed."

A frown came over Chedlya's face at Lorna's biting words. In her own way the Tuareg woman had a fondness for this spirited English girl, and what she was being forced to do was growing more and more distasteful to her. "It is not that. You are the slave of a Tuareg woman. No woman wears a veil in this camp.

If the other Muslim males are offended by our customs, so be it. We hide nor cower from no one!"

Despite her bitterness Lorna had to admire the Tuareg woman's fierce independence, and she secretly applauded her courageous refusal to be dominated by the male in a country where all women were traditionally silent slaves and nothing but chattel. And she would not cower to the male either, Lorna vowed with equal determination. The man who bought her was going to be in for a big surprise if he thought he was getting a meek, cowardly, submissive woman. She would create her own living hell for him, preach rebellion, and disrupt his *iyal* so badly he would regret the day he laid eyes on her. The thought lifted her spirits.

She squared her shoulders and followed Chedlya through the tent, bringing gasps of awed admiration from the *bouzou* women at her breathtaking beauty and proud, regal carriage. To them she looked like a queen going to review her subjects, rather than a slave about to be humiliatingly sold to a new master.

Chapter 10

When Lorna walked into the tent where she was to be auctioned, the men were already seated cross-legged on the carpet, a good fifty or more Muslims dressed in a rainbow of silk robes and headdresses, the huge jewels on their fingers and hanging from their necks a silent testimony to their great wealth. Only the Tuareg scattered through the crowd wore no jewelry, the vibrant blue of their robes and turbans enough decoration for the fierce desert warriors who valued the worth of a man more by his courage than by the outward trappings he wore on his body.

As Chedlya led the way down the aisle in the center of the tent, Lorna could feel every male eye on her, and despite her fierce vow not to cower, her legs were trembling badly. Stepping on the dais provided for her, Lorna turned and faced the Muslims, her heart thudding in her chest, sickened by their lust-filled eyes. Then, renewing her vow, she stared back, her eyes glittering with defiance.

The Muslims who had come to the auction had not expected to see such a beautiful Christian slave, despite the fact that the Tuareg who had brought the invitation had assured them of such. This girl was exquisite and breathtakingly lovely, a morsel that would tempt even the most jaded appetite. But when Lorna glared her defiance back at them, a few of the more astute had second thoughts, while others were even more intrigued, the prospect of breaking her spirit adding spice to the sexual fantasies they were already weaving.

Lorna had never felt so humiliated as she did when the men slowly eyed her up and down, stripping her with their eyes. Then, coming from the back of the tent where some of the late arrivals were standing in the deep shadows, she felt it, a strange power crossing the distance between them, touching her, filling her. She had the most curious feeling that there was some protective influence near. Then Lorna decided that her mind must be playing tricks on her. Why, she was so terrified of these repulsive, animalistic men that she was imagining things.

Chedlya had been very proud of way Lorna had walked into the tent, as regal as a queen, and then glared her defiance at the men, refusing to be intimidated by their rude stares. She was truly going to miss the spirited girl. It was a shame she had to sell her.

"Strip her!" a hawk-faced Bedouin sheik sitting at the front of the tent demanded. "We want to see what we are bidding for."

Lorna tensed, terrified that Chedlya might do as the Arab had demanded, display her entire body to the lustful eyes of those present, and she couldn't bear that supreme humiliation. She turned her head to Chedlya, her eyes silently pleading for mercy.

Chedlya had no intention of stripping Lorna. The

demand infuriated her. Rutting Arab pig! she thought
hotly. She wished now she hadn't invited the brute,
nor any of the hated Arabs, but at the time she sent
out the invitations, she had been thinking of their
wealth and the heavy bids they would make. She
whirled, spitting out, "No! It is enough that you see
her face. This is a Tuareg camp, a private auction, not
one of your disgusting Arab slave markets where the
woman is stripped and her body violated with your
filthy probing fingers."

Seeing every Arab in the crowd stiffen with outrage, Chedlya felt an immense satisfaction at knowing
she, a woman no less, had insulted them to their faces.
She secretly hoped that they would all rise and leave.

"And if we agree not to touch her?" a Berber
asked.

Chedlya wanted the Arabs to leave, but not the
Berbers. And she was very aware that every man
present, except for the Tuareg, resented her bared
face and her position of authority. Hoping to soothe
their ruffled Muslim male egos and yet stick to her
word, she said, "No, I still will not strip her. The man
who buys her will not want her flawless beauty ogled
by every man present. The privilege of viewing her
naked belongs exclusively to her master and no
other."

At the nods of approval Chedlya had to bite back
a laugh. Her appeal to their possessiveness had
worked, for every man present was supremely confident that he would be that man. "And now I will
accept your bids for this lovely creature."

The bids came fast and furious, climbing higher
and higher. Lorna felt sick with despair, knowing her
fate was sealed. She fervently wished she had been
killed along with Nathan. Then, at the back of the
tent, the very man she had just thought about stepped

from the deep shadows. I must be hallucinating, Lorna thought. My eyes must be playing tricks on me. This Berber can't be Nathan. Nathan is dead.

And then, as Nathan made his bid, his deep, musical voice washing over Lorna like a warm, sensuous caress, she knew it was Nathan. He was alive! She was so shocked she felt faint and would have fallen if Chedlya hadn't caught her arm to support her. Then, as an overwhelming happiness rushed over her, she started to run to him.

Chedlya had no idea why Lorna was acting so strangely all of a sudden. She was left to conclude that the English girl was trying to make a desperate, last-minute escape. It took both of her hands on Lorna's shoulders to restrain her. "Stop it!" she demanded, shaking the girl. "You can't escape!"

Suddenly Lorna realized that she had almost given away Nathan's true identity. Surely the Muslims present would think it suspicious if she got loose from Chedlya and threw herself into his arms. Like the rest of them he was supposed to be a stranger who had come here to bid for her. She forced herself to remain still and hung her head, trying to look submissive, but from beneath lowered eyelashes she kept her eyes glued to Nathan, feasting on the sight of him and wondering how in the world he had managed to survive.

Lorna's hanging her head and looking submissive bewildered Chedlya even more. Her eyes narrowed suspiciously as the bidding went on. She knew the English girl didn't have a meek bone in her body. She peered closer, seeing the girl was staring at the back of the tent.

Chedlya turned and for the first time saw Nathan. When he had stepped from the shadows and made his bid, she had been too busy trying to restrain Lorna to notice. She knew instinctively that this was the man Lorna was staring at. And no wonder. Towering over the other Zenata Berbers standing beside him, his exceptionally broad shoulders straining at his robe, he radiated masculine strength and sexuality as the Saharan sun did heat waves, sending tingles of excitement up her spine. Then Chedlya frowned, noting the expression on the handsome Berber's face. While his green eyes looked just as hungry as the other men's, they lacked the hard glitter of unadulterated lust that the others' had taken on. Instead his eyes were filled with a warmth and yearning. Suddenly she sensed that this fascinating Berber and Lorna weren't strangers. Somewhere along the line their paths had crossed before.

As Nathan made yet another bid, every head in the tent turned, the Muslims staring at him in disbelief. Even Chedlya was stunned. Why, it was a fortune! As a long silence filled the tent, Chedlya felt an immense relief, knowing the auction was over and taking satisfaction that the handsome Berber, whoever he was, had bought Lorna. And that was something she intended to find out as soon as she had Lorna alone. She smiled and stepped forward, saying, "I accept your—"

"No! Wait!" the hawk-faced Arab at the front of the tent called out, cutting across Chedlya's words and slamming to his feet. "I will match the sum and throw in a hundred camels."

Chedlya had been aware of the Arab's increasing agitation as the bids went higher and higher. And she had not wanted Lorna to go to him. There was a cruel glint in his eyes that bespoke a sadistic nature. She whirled, saying, "Bah! What do I want with camels? I have thousands of them. This auction is for gold. Nothing else! Can you top this man's bid?"

Chedlya already knew the Arab couldn't top the bid, or he would have done so. She watched as his face turned beet red with fury.

"The bidding is deadlocked," another Arab pointed out. "How will you decide which man gets her if you will not accept anything but gold? Both men have made the same offer."

"We will fight for her!" the Arab cried out, drawing his dagger.

There was no hesitancy on Nathan's part. He shrugged back his burnoose with his broad shoulders and reached for the dagger at his belt, stepping forward. Seeing the murderous gleam in his eyes, a look that would have brought terror to the heart of even the fiercest Tuareg warrior, Chedlya thought in silent admiration, By the Prophet, he is magnificent! Why, he'd cut the insolent Arab to ribbons. But even though there was no doubt in Chedlya's mind about who would be the victor, she knew she couldn't allow the two to fight. The tent was charged with electricity, the old hatred between the Berbers and the Arabs coming suddenly and dangerously alive. It wouldn't simply be a contest between two men for a prize, it would be all-out war, and the Tuareg, as hosts, would be caught in the middle, their camp torn to pieces, their women and children endangered.

"No!" Chedlya cried out, stepping between the two men, who were already rushing forward. "You will not fight!"

For a moment Chedlya feared it was too late to stop the forces that had already been set into motion as the Berbers and Arabs murmured in angry discontent, coming to their feet and drawing their weapons all around her. It was the sudden appearance of over fifty fierce-looking Tuareg crowding into the tent with their swords drawn that made the seething mass of men take pause.

"This is an auction!" Chedlya cried out angrily. "Have you forgotten that you are invited guests here? Will you disgrace yourselves and insult the Tuareg hospitality by turning it into a bloodbath?"

Chedlya's words were like a dash of cold water on the hot-blooded Muslims' heated tempers. Suddenly they remembered where they were, in the camp of one of the most feared and formidable Tuareg tribes in the Sahara, a tribe whose fiercely proud warriors would not take an insult to their hospitality lightly, not only slaying the offenders, but very likely seeking revenge on the tribes of every man present.

Seeing the daggers being sheathed and knowing she was once more in control of the situation, Chedlya said in a firm voice, "I, and I alone, will decide how the deadlock will be broken. While you are partaking of the feast that is being set up for you in the adjoining tent, I will think on this. When I have reached my decision, I will call you back together."

Chedlya turned to Lorna, seeing the English girl was pale-faced and obviously shaken by the near disaster. "Come," she commanded softly, "we will retire to my tent."

As the two women walked past Nathan and the Arab, both men still glaring at the other and seething with anger, Chedlya wondered how she was going to get herself out of this mess without precipitating another near disaster. Then, seeing Lorna glancing back over her shoulder at the handsome Berber, a surge of irritation ran through Chedlya. She caught the girl's hand and jerked her forward so hard she could hear the snap of Lorna's neck. She rushed her from the tent.

* * *

The second they had stepped into Chedlya's tent, Chedlya whirled around and asked, "Who is that man?"

Realizing Chedlya must have seen her staring at Nathan, fear for him rose in Lorna. If Chedlya knew he was a Christian, would she have the Tuareg warriors capture and enslave him too? "I don't know what you're talking about."

Chedlya shook her, saying, "Don't lie to me! Do you think I'm blind? I saw the way you looked at him and the way he looked at you. You are not strangers. No, I strongly suspect he is your lover."

"What you're suggesting is insane. I told you my lover is dead!"

Chedlya was a very shrewd woman. She had a knack for smelling deception. "I told you, don't lie to me! How did you, a Christian, come to meet a Zenata Berber?"

Lorna glared at Chedlya, stubbornly silent, determined she wouldn't betray Nathan.

"You crazy fool! How can I help you if I don't know what's going on?"

"Why should you want to help me?" Lorna asked bitterly.

"Ah, you are hopeless!" Chedlya answered, throwing her arms up in exasperation. "I have no ill will toward you. I have already explained my reasons for selling you. I would much rather see you go to the man you love than to that filthy Arab pig. Now answer my question."

Lorna fought a desperate battle with herself, wanting to trust Chedlya, but still fearful of what she might do if she knew of Nathan's true identity.

Chedlya's eyes narrowed. "Would you have me summon him and question him instead? Do you realize how that would look to the others? How it would arouse their suspicions? The Arabs would suspect a plot, that I was showing favoritism to another Berber. You saw yourself how close the two groups were to doing battle. Would you have innocent women and children in this camp killed because your stubbornness caused a bloodbath?" Chedlya could see her appeal to Lorna's tender heart had worked. "Now answer my question, and don't try to lie to me," she warned in a steely voice. "I can read you like a book. You are not devious enough to fool me."

Since Lorna couldn't think of any plausible way she could possibly have met and fallen in love with a desert Berber, she broke down and told Chedlya the truth, starting from the moment she had first seen Nathan from the *iyal* window and ending with how she thought he had been killed in the Tuareg raid on the caravan. Chedlya was amazed to learn the exciting, fascinating man was a Christian, too, and was touched by the love in Lorna's eyes when she spoke of him.

When Lorna finished her story, she asked in a trembling voice, "You won't try to capture him, too, will you?"

So that's what she feared, Chedlya thought. And undoubtedly if the others knew his true identity, they would do just that. Muslim fought Muslim and Berber fought Arab, unless there was a Christian around. Then everyone fought him. And there was no doubt in Chedlya's mind that the man would fight to the death before he would give up his freedom—and that would be a terrible waste of the most splendid, magnificent specimen of manhood she had ever seen. She felt a twinge of envy at Lorna for having such a fascinating, exciting man desire her, then answered sharply, "And have you go by default to the Arab pig? Never!"

"Oh, thank you!" Lorna cried out, tears of relief streaming down her face.

Chedlya was deeply touched by Lorna's tears. She had never seen the girl openly cry, not in despair or anger or when she had looked so terribly sad. Somehow, someway, she was determined to see the girl she had become so fond of attain her happiness. But just how she hadn't figured out. "There is something I am curious about. How did your lover come to be in the midst of Zenata Berbers? Those around him did not bid for you, as friends will not do, and they were the first to step forward when it looked as if there would be a fight."

"He was captured and imprisoned by the Barbary pirates, too, but managed to escape into the desert. He almost died there, but was found by a tribe of Berbers who took him in. He lived with them for some time after that," Lorna explained. "Those men must be from the same tribe."

With this information more pieces of the puzzle fitted into place. Lorna's lover must have gone to his old friends to help him find her, and surely they knew his true identity, that he was a Christian.

"How are you going to break the deadlock without offending the Arabs?" Lorna asked.

"I haven't decided yet. I have to think this over very carefully." Chedlya paced the carpet, then turned to Lorna, saying, "Go to your cubicle and rest. This has been an ordeal for you."

Seeing the apprehensive expression on Lorna's face, Chedlya laughed huskily and said, "Stop worrying, my friend. Did I not tell you I was shrewd? I will figure out some way for you to go to the man you love. Now go. I need privacy so I can think."

After Lorna left, Chedlya sent for her husband and, when he entered the tent, said, "Have our men seat themselves among the Arabs at the feast. I want them to find out as much as they can about the hawk-faced Arab. But warn them to be careful. The Arabs are already suspicious. And bring out the water pipes."

"You would waste our hashish on Arabs?" Abu Bakr asked in disgust.

"It will not be a waste. It will loosen their tongues. Now go, before the men are seated. After they have eaten come and tell me what you have found out."

Two hours later Abu Bakr was back, relaying the information he had found out, ending with, "You should have decided on some way to end the deadlock while it was still in your hands if you do not want your slave to go to the Arab. The Bedouin sheikh has made good use of the past two hours, borrowing gold from his wives' kinsmen who are present."

"And the Berber?" Chedlya asked, alarmed at this new development.

"He, too, has been trying to borrow more gold. But the Zenatas he came with did not come prepared to bid and could not loan him much, and the other Berbers were reluctant to give him a loan. He is a stranger to this part of the Sahara, a guest who has been visiting the Zenatas who brought him to the auction."

Chedlya frantically rolled the information her husband had brought her around in her head, her crafty mind searching for a way to prevent the Arab from buying Lorna. Suddenly the solution came to her, making her blue eyes light up as she laughed outright.

"You have thought of a way to outwit the Arab?"

Abu Bakr guessed, for his wife had a keen mind, something he admired that held him to her as much as her fiery passion.

"Yes. A plan that is pure inspiration," Chedlya answered with a smug smile.

"What plan?" Abu Bakr asked excitedly, for he was anxious to see the insolent Arab brought down.

"No, I will not spoil it for you, my beloved. You will appreciate it much more if you are as surprised as the others. Now go and summon the men back to the auction tent."

As soon as Chedlya walked back into the tent where the men were assembled, the hawk-faced Arab rose, the supremely confident expression on his face making Chedlya thank Allah for her inspiration. Before he could open his mouth Chedlya faced the crowd of men, saying, "I have an announcement to make. I have decided not to sell my slave. Instead, I am offering her in marriage and am willing to accept the sum bid as her dowry price."

If Chedlya had thrown a bombshell into the midst of the Muslims, they couldn't have been more shocked. The men were stunned speechless. Before any could recover from her announcement, Chedlya continued, saying, "I ask your forgiveness for my female weakness, but I have become fond of this particular slave and wish to see her placed in a position of respect if at all possible."

As the expressions on the men's faces turned from shock to utter disgust, Chedlya knew they had swallowed her excuse for her change in plans. She knew what they were thinking. She could almost see the wheels turning in their arrogant male minds. Only a weak, emotional woman would become attached to a slave, would entertain such silly romantic notions. Bah! Women knew nothing about conducting business. What had started as an auction for a slave had turned into a marriage mart. But then, in essence, there really wasn't much difference between a slave and a wife, and the girl being offered was incredibly beautiful. They glanced at the tall Berber and the Arab, wondering if they had come to the same conclusion.

The Arab had recovered from his shock and was furious with Chedlya's change in plans. "I was prepared to offer a higher price for the slave," he said angrily.

"Oh? I didn't realize that," Chedlya answered, looking the picture of innocence. She chewed her lips as if in indecision, then sighed deeply, saying, "That was generous of you, but I'm afraid I still can't sell her. You see, I promised her marriage."

Chedlya heard the groan of disgust coming from the crowd of men and knew they thought her an even bigger fool. She smiled sweetly at the Arab glaring at her and said, "In view of your being prepared to offer even more for her as a slave, I feel it is only fair to offer you the opportunity to make the first offer for her hand."

Chedlya knew even before the Arab spoke what he would say. From the information her husband had brought her, she knew the sheik already had four wives, marriages that had been made to cement alliances with other Bedouin tribes, all powerful tribes that he dare not insult by divorcing their kinswomen.

The Arab strongly suspected the shrewd Tuareg woman knew his marital status and had cleverly outmaneuvered him, which infuriated him all the more. "No. I have the wives allowed me by the Koran," he answered tightly, his black eyes glittering with rage.

"You could put one aside," Chedlya taunted.

Aware of his wives' kinsmen's eyes on him, feeling like daggers at his back, the Arab answered, "No. I will not dishonor any of my wives."

The honor of your wives has nothing to do with it, Chedlya thought with disgust. You care nothing for them. No, it is fear of their kinsmen that makes you refuse. Yes, it was just as she had calculated. Like all inherently cruel men, the Arab was a sniveling coward. She turned, facing Nathan, asking, "And you? What do you say? Will you marry her and give her a place of respect in your household?"

Nathan reacted to Chedlya's question before he even thought. He had never probed into his motives for finding Lorna and rescuing her, the consuming need that had driven him. He had known that somehow, someway he would find her, even if he had to search the entire length and breadth of the Sahara to do so, and that he would get her back, even if he had to kill for her. But he had not come prepared to offer marriage. For a moment his fierce independence flared before it was smothered by the same powerful emotion that had driven him, an emotion he stubbornly refused to identify. Then he remembered that Lady Hampton was married and he realized why Chedlya had chosen this alternative. Lorna must have told her everything, and the Tuareg woman knew the marriage would be a sham since Lorna was already married. He smiled, thinking that Chedlya was a very crafty woman to have figured out such a clever means for him to rescue Lorna—as well as keep the gold he had offered for her. Then, becoming aware that everyone was waiting for his answer, he said, "Yes, I will marry her."

The hawk-faced Arab whirled to face him, asking, "How do we know you do not already have the wives allowed you by our Koran?"

An older Zenata Berber stepped forward and stood beside Nathan, saying, "I can attest to this man's marital status. He has no wives."

Everyone in the tent recognized the Zenata emir. Ali bein Ghaniya was a powerful leader of several Zenata tribes, a man greatly respected by the Berbers and much feared by the Arabs; and for those reasons, no one questioned his word.

"Then it is settled," Chedlya announced, smiling with pleasure at the coup she had pulled off.

"I request to act in behalf of my friend in the wedding arrangements," the emir said, laying a hand on Nathan's broad shoulder. "With your permission I will set up a tent in the hills above your camp to act as the groom's home, and in place of his father, who cannot be present, act as his host."

Chedlya had no objections. If the emir wished to take on the burden of the groom's father and provide the groom's wedding feasts, that was fine with her. "Agreed," she answered.

The hawk-faced Arab stepped forward, saying in a hard voice, "And I and my kinsmen shall stay to make sure the wedding takes place."

He's suspicious of a plot, Chedlya thought. "Of course you will stay," she replied smoothly, pretending she did not realize his words were a threat. "Everyone here is invited to the wedding. And since I know you're all anxious to get back to your homes and families, the festivities will begin tomorrow."

Chedlya walked from the tent, feeling even prouder of herself. By inviting the hated Arabs to the wedding she had put them in the position of having to give gifts to a Tuareg slave girl and a hated Berber, something that would undoubtedly irritate them no end, since they didn't dare give miserly gifts for fear of making themselves look petty in the eyes of the other Muslims. No, if she knew them, the vain, arrogant Arabs would break their necks trying to top the next man's gift. And right now, she wouldn't want to be in the hawk-faced Arab's sandals. His brother Arabs weren't going to forget who put them in that position. Oh, this wedding was going to be great fun! And she could hardly wait to tell Lorna what a coup she had pulled off in her behalf.

Chapter 11

As soon as Chedlya returned to her tent, she sought out Lorna and told her what she had done, feeling very proud of herself and pleased with how well everything had turned out. But instead of being excited and thrilled at the prospect of marrying Nathan, Lorna's fierce pride came rushing to the fore, and she was furious with Chedlya.

"How could you do that to me?" Lorna asked in an accusing voice. "Put him in the position where he *had* to offer marriage?"

"But I thought you loved him," Chedlya answered, bewildered by her anger, "that you wanted to be his wife."

"I *do* love him, and there is nothing in the world that would make me happier than to have him ask me to marry him. But I didn't want him to be forced into it. Why, he doesn't even care for me. The only reason he came to rescue me is because he felt obligated to do so. After all, I was entrusted into his care by both his government and mine."

"No, you are wrong. He is not marrying you out of duty, to himself or anyone," Chedlya said with conviction. "Nor is he being forced, as you say. That one could never be forced to do anything against his will. He agreed to marry you for the same reason he came searching for you. He wants you. I saw the way he looked at you, devouring you with his eyes."

Lorna knew Nathan had thought her desirable, but she also knew what a terribly low regard he had for her, and surely no man would agree to bind himself legally to a woman he despised, no matter how desirable she was. Then, remembering that Nathan still thought she was Lady Hampton, a sudden dawning came. "I think I understand now why Nathan agreed. He thinks the ceremony will be nothing but a sham, since he believes I'm already married."

"Then you never told him any differently, even after you became lovers?" Chedlya asked in surprise.

"No."

"Why didn't you tell *me* that?" Chedlya asked in an accusing voice.

"I didn't think it was important at the time!" Lorna snapped. "And I had no idea what you were going to do."

Seeing the look of disgust on Chedlya's face, Lorna said, "I had my reasons for not telling him, even then. At the time they seemed reasonable to me."

"What reasons?"

"It's too complicated to go into right now. The point is Nathan is under the impression that he can't really marry me because I'm already married."

Chedlya shrugged her shoulders. "So he will be surprised."

"Are you suggesting that I trick him?" Lorna asked in outrage.

"What choice do you have?" Chedlya threw back. "He has already agreed before the others. It's too late to back out. Would you rather go to that Arab pig by default?"

"Yes, I would! I won't deceive Nathan anymore, for any reason." Then a sudden thought occurred to Lorna. "Wait a minute," she said with obvious relief. "I just thought of something. The marriage won't be legal anyway. We're both Christians."

"No, it will be legal and binding. You will both have to convert to Islam before the ceremony."

"Convert to Islam?" Lorna asked in a shocked voice.

"It is a simple thing to do. All you have to do is recite the necessary words in front of Muslim witnesses."

"Does Nathan know that?"

"I assume he does or he wouldn't have agreed."

Yes, he probably does realize it, Lorna thought, as much as he knows about the Muslims and their religion. She racked her brain for another solution, then asked, "Can a Christian marry a Muslim?"

"No. Why do you ask?"

"Then we can just say that I recited the necessary words in front of you, and I won't convert. Then the marriage will be void."

"No. Everyone is expecting your conversion to be in public. And with the Arabs staying for the wedding, at the insistence of the hawk-nosed sheikh, we do not dare try any more tricks. He is already suspicious of a Berber plot. He will be watching everything very closely to see that it goes exactly according to Muslim law."

"Well, I won't go into this marriage deceiving

Nathan. I have to talk to him. I have to tell him who I really am."

At this point Chedlya wasn't so sure that Lorna's lover hadn't agreed to marry her because he thought the marriage would be a sham. He had given her a knowing smile right before he agreed, a smile that told Chedlya he knew she was plotting. But Chedlya had assumed he was thinking of how cleverly she had plotted for him to have Lorna. "You would risk his refusing to marry you and lose the freedom you value so highly?" Chedlya asked in disbelief.

"Trying to keep my freedom is what got me into this mess in the first place." A fiercely determined expression came over Lorna's face. "No, I'm through with lying and deceit!"

Chedlya groaned with disgust. Of all of the people for her to choose to champion, why did she have to pick someone so stupidly noble? She threw her hands up in exasperation and said, "You are as obstinate as a camel! I would take a stick to you if I thought it would do any good. I will summon your lover." Chedlya whirled and walked angrily from the cubicle, throwing over her shoulder just as she pushed the curtains aside, "But don't blame me if you have to go to that Arab pig!"

Chedlya's last words preyed on Lorna's mind while she waited for Nathan to appear. Deep down she didn't think Nathan would abandon her to the Arab, knowing how strongly he felt about slavery. But she didn't believe he would be willing to marry her either. That was too high a price to pay to fulfill an obligation—if that's why he had sought her out. Perhaps his motive for rescuing her wasn't even that personal. Maybe his government had ordered him to find and rescue her. And now she was going to have to tell him that she was of no value to his government.

Maybe she had been wrong. Maybe in view of all of her deceit he would leave her to face her fate.

By the time Nathan pushed aside the curtains and stepped into the cubicle, Lorna's nerves were tied into a million knots. But just the sight of him standing there, looking so calm, so utterly in control, his powerful presence filling the small room and crowding out everything else, made the tension within her disappear like a puff of smoke in the wind, to be replaced with renewed wonder that he really and truly was alive.

When Nathan stepped into the cubicle, he came to an abrupt halt, his eyes hungrily taking in the sight of Lorna. He completely forgot his puzzlement over Chedlya's urgent summons or that Lady Hampton was completely off limits for him. All he could think of was kissing her. He crossed the distance between them in two swift strides, and then, when he was almost upon her, Lorna said with a sob, "I thought you were dead!"

Seeing a tear trickle down her cheek, Nathan felt that strange twisting pain in his chest, and his passion drained from him. "I know," he answered softly, coming to a complete stop and tenderly brushing the tear from her cheek with the tips of his fingers. "It must have been quite a shock to see me standing there."

"It was. I almost fainted. And then I wanted to run to you."

"Yes, I know, but it's a good thing Chedlya stopped you. She said that's what aroused her suspicions," Nathan continued, "the peculiar way you were staring at me."

"You talked to Chedlya?" Lorna asked, suddenly alarmed.

"Yes. She summoned me, remember? She told

me she knew who I was, but then I'd already figured that out."

"Is that all she told you?"

"Only that you insisted upon talking to me."

Thank God, Lorna thought. Chedlya had an irritating way of taking everything into her own hands, and Lorna wanted to tell Nathan her real identity in her own way. Then, realizing that he was waiting, she was suddenly filled with trepidation. She didn't know where to begin. "You can't marry me," she blurted. "You can't marry me because I'm not Lady Hampton. I was just impersonating her. My real name is Lorna Winters. I was on the same ship that she was, and when she was killed by the pirates, I told them I was her since we looked so much alike. You see, I knew there was no one to ransom me, but I knew Lady Hampton's husband was bound to have the money for *her* ransom. So I lied. I didn't mean to do anything dishonest. I was just trying to save myself from the slave block. I didn't even stop to think what kind of a mess I might be getting myself into, and I certainly had no idea how involved it would become, with the king of Naples and your government getting in on it. But by that time I was so deeply enmeshed, I didn't know how to get myself out of my predicament. So I just played along with the charade, hoping that once we reached Naples I could escape from you." Lorna paused, and when Nathan just stared at her, she wondered what he was thinking. "I hope you aren't angry with me for deceiving you."

Nathan was a little stunned by all Lorna had told him. Everything was still whirling around in his head. He concentrated on her last statement and found he couldn't whip up any anger at her. If anything, he admired her for her quick thinking and her perseverance. "No, if I had been in your position, I would have done the same thing. In fact, I've done a lot worse than lie to secure my freedom. The night I escaped from my prison I killed my guard by slipping a knife I had managed to steal into his back. But why didn't you tell me truth? You know how strongly I feel about slavery."

"I might have if there hadn't been something else in my past," Lorna admitted. "You see, I'm also a fugitive from the law."

Seeing the shocked expression on Nathan's face, Lorna quickly said, "But I'm innocent! I swear I am! I didn't steal any jewels."

"What jewels?" Nathan asked in confusion. "What jewels are you are talking about?"

"The son of the nobleman I was in service to in London accused me of stealing his mother's diamond jewelry. He did it out of spite, because I kept spurning his advances. While the constables were searching the house for me, I managed to escape. You see, I didn't think they would take my word against his, so I fled. That's what I was doing on the same ship with Lady Hampton. But in view of my impersonating her, I was afraid you might not believe my story about the jewels."

Nathan didn't doubt Lorna's story for one minute. He knew the nobility too well, and Lorna was a very desirable woman. And unfortunately the law probably *would* have believed the nobleman over her. But something was puzzling him. "I believe your innocence about the jewelry, but where did you get the money to buy your passage?"

"I didn't steal it," Lorna answered defensively, "if that's what you're thinking. I'd been saving money for some time to go to America. But the day I had to flee, the only convoy leaving London was the one going to Cadiz and then to the West Indies."

My God, Nathan thought, she had gone through hell, and faced it all by herself, with no one even to confide in. His admiration for her soared to new heights. Then suddenly the full realization hit him. She *wasn't* Lady Hampton, a married woman and a hated aristocrat. She was no longer unreachable! A shot of pure joy ran through him. Then, remembering something, he frowned, gave her a penetrating look, and said, "There's only one thing I want to know. Was that last night a charade too? Were you only pretending to be Lady Hampton?

A furious blush rose on Lorna's face at his reminding her of how bold she had been. My God, had I only redeemed herself in his eyes to lose it again? she thought in horror. But she had promised herself she wouldn't lie to him again. She squared her shoulders and bravely looked him in the eye. "No. I did that for myself. You see I . . . I wanted you."

Her candid answer pleased Nathan enormously. He smiled, a devastating, warm smile that played havoc on Lorna's senses, then said in a husky voice, "In that case I'm going to do something I've been wanting to do ever since I walked in here."

He swept Lorna into his arms and crushed her to him in a fierce embrace, his mouth covering hers in a deep, passionate kiss that seemed to suck the breath from her lungs and sear her soul.

Lorna felt as if Nathan would squeeze the life from her, and yet she pressed even closer to him, standing on her tiptoes and straining against him, wanting desperately to absorb him, take him completely within herself. She kissed him back with naked abandon, their tongues dancing wildly, breaths rasping, hearts thudding, bodies trembling with need, trying to assuage their starvation for one another in one desperate, urgent kiss.

Feeling Nathan's long, hot length hardening through their layers of clothing, Lorna moaned deeply in the back of her throat, grinding her hips against him, sending a bolt of fire through Nathan. Strangely, the shock brought him to his senses and he remembered his reason for being here—to secure Lorna's safety. With superhuman effort he jerked his mouth away and stepped back, holding Lorna tightly at arm's length with an iron will.

His breath was ragged and his deep voice even huskier than usual as he said, "If we don't stop, I'm going to take you right here and now. And I'm not supposed even to be here. By Muslim custom the groom isn't supposed to see his bride until after the wedding."

"Then you still intend to marry me?" Lorna asked in utter surprise. "Knowing that it will be a real marriage?"

"Yes, I came here to rescue you, and that's what I intend to do."

"But can't you figure out some way for us just to escape?"

"With all these suspicious Arabs watching every move we make? No, I'm afraid that's impossible."

A sudden thought occurred to her. "You don't have to convert to Islam. Everyone already thinks you're a Muslim. It won't be a real marriage after all."

"No, Lorna, I'll have to convert, too, but I'll do mine in private in front of Berber friends. You see, they won't stand by and watch anyone make a mockery of their marriage ceremony. They feel very strongly about their religion."

He was certainly having to go to great lengths to rescue her, Lorna thought. "How do you feel about that?"

"Becoming a Muslim?" He shrugged his broad

shoulders, saying, "That doesn't bother me. To become a Muslim all one has to do is recite the words 'There is no God but Allah, and Muhammad is the prophet of Allah' before witnesses and in sincerity. There is only one God, Lorna, regardless of what name He goes by. God, Allah, Yahweh, Jehovah, He is the same God. To say the words would only be confirming what I already believe."

"But Muhammad—"

"A prophet, nothing more. He never claimed divinity, any more than the prophets of the Old Testament did, prophets the Muslims also recognize. They even acknowledge Christ as a great prophet, although they deny his being the son of God. But they're not asking me to renounce Christ as the son of God, only to proclaim that there is but *one* God."

Nathan gave Lorna a penetrating look, then asked, "Does becoming a Muslim bother you?"

"No, particularly not in view of what you just said."

Lorna hadn't expected Nathan to agree to marry her so readily. Oh, she knew he was doing it to save her from a life of degradation, but he was a seaman by trade, a breed of men notorious for their love of freedom and their fierce independence. Did he find the idea totally repugnant, something he was being forced to do? She worried her bottom lip nervously, something that Nathan thought very provocative and knew was a dead giveaway to her anxiety.

Forcing his eyes away from the enticing lip, he asked, "Is something bothering you?"

"Well . . . yes," Lorna admitted hesitantly. "I know you didn't plan on marrying me when you came for me. I was just wondering . . . how you felt about it?

Strangely the idea of marriage to Lorna had

grown more and more appealing the more Nathan thought about it. She was a beautiful, desirable woman, intelligent and spirited, a woman any man would be proud to call his wife. And then there was that driving need to find her, making him completely desert his ship and the profitable business he had been enjoying. But Nathan wasn't about to admit to an emotion that he was still struggling to come to terms with himself.

He found himself wondering how Lorna felt about the marriage. She was being pushed into it by circumstances beyond her control just as much as he. A sudden, deeply disturbing thought occurred to him: Maybe she didn't want him for a husband. "Do you object to being my wife?"

I'd glory in it if I knew you really loved me, Lorna thought, but said, "No, not really."

Nathan should have felt relieved, but he didn't. Somehow, he had hoped for something more and, instead, found himself disappointed in her lack of enthusiasm. Aware that she was waiting for his answer, he shrugged his shoulders, saying, "Marriage might not be so bad. After all, we're not exactly averse to one another."

Lorna remembered their earlier passionate kiss, the way they had pressed their bodies together as if each were trying to crawl into the other's skin. No, they certainly *weren't* averse to one another.

"And there are a lot of marriages of convenience that have started out with less than that in their favor," Nathan continued. He paused and searched Lorna's face, seeing no particular reaction to his words and having no idea of the tremendous struggle she was fighting to keep her emotions hidden from him. "And then, if it doesn't work out, our being married in the Muslim religion would be a distinct advantage. Divorce is a simple matter for a Muslim."

As soon as the words crossed his lips, Nathan wondered at them. Why had he said that? Was it because Lorna wasn't acting particularly enthusiastic, or was it his fierce independence making a last-ditch effort to ensure his freedom? Whatever, the thought of divorcing Lorna didn't sit easily with him.

Still perplexed, Nathan said, "I'd better go before someone other than Chedlya discovers I'm here." He bent and gave her a quick kiss. He smiled, an engaging grin that tore at Lorna's heartstrings and said, "It doesn't look like I'm going to make a very good Muslim, does it? That's the second time I've stolen a forbidden kiss."

After Nathan left, Lorna stood pondering his words about divorce. Was that what he had in mind? Was their marriage only to be a temporary thing, a means to secure her freedom and see her safely out of the country, and nothing more? She was so occupied with the painful thought that she didn't hear Chedlya come in.

"Well?" Chedlya asked. "Is he still going to marry you now that he knows who you really are?"

"What?" Lorna asked, still distracted.

"I asked if he agreed to marry you now that he knows your real identity."

"Yes, he agreed."

A big grin spread over Chedlya's face. "See? I told you he wanted you."

Lorna turned to face her, saying, "Oh, he's physically attracted to me. I know that for sure, but . . ."

"But what?" Chedlya asked, wondering why Lorna seemed so distressed.

"He said if our marriage didn't work out, divorce was easy for a Muslim to attain."

"Yes, all the man has to do is renounce his wife three times in front of witnesses. But why should that worry you?"

"Because I'm wondering if that's what he plans to do eventually. Divorce me."

"Bah! He did not say he plans to divorce you, only that he could if it did not work out. It was just a statement of fact."

"But if he only agreed to marry me because he's physically attracted to me, he might divorce me when he tires of me."

"And he might never stop wanting you," Chedlya argued back. "You are worrying about something that may never happen."

Lorna acted as if she had never even heard Chedlya's words. "I'm afraid of losing him. I did once. Or thought I had. That was bad enough. But to marry him, to know the supreme happiness of being his wife, and then to lose him would be more than I could bear. It wouldn't be worth the pain."

Chedlya's patience was at an end. She caught Lorna by the shoulders and shook her so hard the English girl's head bobbed. Her eyes boring into Lorna's, Chedlya spat, "By the prophet, you are the biggest fool I have ever seen! Because you are afraid you will starve tomorrow, do you refuse to feast today? Take the happiness that is being offered you and do not question it. Savor your marriage. Enjoy it to the fullest. Even if it turns out to be only a season of joy—it is better than a lifetime of nothing!"

Chedlya dropped her arms, ashamed of her loss of control. But sometimes Lorna infuriated her with her stubborn persistence. Once the girl got a notion into her head, she worried it to death, making mountains out of molehills. Why couldn't she just accept things as they were? *Inshullah.*

"Now," Chedlya said in a firm voice, assuming her usual businesslike manner, "stop your worrying. It is time to prepare for your becoming a Muslim."

Later that night, as Lorna lay on her pallet, Chedlya's words kept floating through her mind. Yes, she would do as the Tuareg woman had urged her, she decided. She wouldn't let her fear of the future spoil her present happiness. She would take the precious time with Nathan being given her, live each day of her marriage to the fullest, savor her happiness—for as long as it lasted.

Chapter 12

The Muslim wedding festivities began the next morning. For three days the guests were feasted at the bride's home—in this instance, Chedlya's tent—then for three days everyone traveled to the groom's tent on the hillside overlooking the Tuareg camp and were feasted there. During this time Lorna never even got a glimpse of Nathan, for the men and women were separated by heavy draperies hung from the middle of the tent. By the seventh day Lorna was growing irritable, anxious to begin her new life as Nathan's wife and fulfill her vow to live it to the fullest.

The minute Chedlya walked into her cubicle that morning, Lorna snapped, "When is everyone going to stop gorging themselves and let the wedding take place?"

Chedlya smiled, having been aware of Lorna's growing impatience with the festivities and knowing the English girl was anxious to be alone with her husband. And she really couldn't blame her. By the prophet, with his superb physique and profound masculine virility, that one must be a magnificent lover. "Don't fret, Lor'a. This is the last day of the festivities. In a few hours you will be his wife."

A thrill ran through Lorna, her heart racing with anticipation. She hurried to the chest of clothes that Chedlya had given her as a wedding trousseau—the same clothing that had been taken away from her when she was captured, Lorna remembered wryly— and knelt, searching for and pulling out the white ensemble that she had worn the day of the auction.

"No," Chedlya objected. "Do not wear that one."

"But it's the only white I have," Lorna pointed out.

"You would wear the slaves' color on your wedding day, the day you become free?"

"In England all wedding gowns are traditionally white. It's a symbol of purity." Seeing Chedlya's eyebrow rising at this bit of information and guessing what she was thinking, Lorna snapped, "Well, it's just a symbol!"

"It may be a tradition in England, but it is not done here." Chedlya walked to the chest and pulled out the lavender silk *entarie* and pantaloons and the deep violet caftan edged along the sides, hem, and cuffs with gold-embroidered leaves. "You will wear this, the color of joy, not servitude."

"It's too colorful. I'll look like a gypsy."

"No. You will look like a queen. Now do not argue with me or I will take a stick to you. Until the festivities are over, you are still my slave." Then, seeing the flash in Lorna's eyes, Chedlya smiled and said, "No, Lor'a. Do not be angry. Trust me in this. You will look beautiful."

When Lorna was dressed, her hair left free to hang in a shimmering cascade around her shoulders and down her back, Chedlya handed her the lavender *yashmak*. Lorna looked at the veil in disbelief, then said, "I thought you said no woman goes veiled in a Tuareg camp, not even a slave."

"Only in this one instance. It is tradition in the Muslim ceremony. You will go veiled until your husband removes it. It is a symbol of his ownership."

"And since when does a Tuareg woman allow her husband to own her?"

Chedlya's blue eyes twinkled as she threw Lorna's own words back at her, "Well, it is just a symbol."

Both women laughed, then Chedlya said, "Now let me tell you what to expect."

Lorna would have been alarmed an hour later when four strange men walked into her cubicle had Chedlya not forewarned her what to expect. Each of Nathan's Berber friends lifted her veil and praised her beauty, as custom dictated, and Lorna pretended to resist when they took her from the tent, feeling a little foolish at playing out this planned "abduction." She was placed in her old sedan, which had been converted into a litter, and rushed up the hillside to the groom's "home," while the Tuareg, "the bride's family," pretended hot pursuit and yelled Arabic threats and curses.

Left alone in the groom's tent, Lorna looked about her and frowned, disappointed that there were no decorations for the ceremony and wondering where the guests were going to sit, for there wasn't even a carpet on the ground. Then her breath caught in her throat as Nathan stepped into the tent, dressed in a green and white striped gown and *kaffiyeh* and an emerald green caftan, his wedding apparel enhancing the color of his remarkable eyes. Her heart did crazy flip-flaps as she gazed into those deep, sensual pools, a heady warmth flooding her clear to her toes and making her fingertips tingle.

Time seemed suspended as the two stared at each other. To Nathan, Lorna was a vision of exquisite loveliness that he couldn't believe was real, afraid even to blink his eyes for fear she would disappear.

"When . . . when is the ceremony going to take place?" Lorna asked, breaking the long silence, shocked at how breathless she felt.

"There is no official wedding ceremony in the Muslim religion, since there are no priests or ministers. The days of festivities we just finished was our wedding."

"Then we're married?" Lorna asked in disbelief, feeling cheated by the lack of pomp and ceremony.

"Yes. Except for one last thing," Nathan answered, closing the distance between them, then looking deeply into her eyes as he said softly, "this."

Nathan removed the veil from Lorna's face and dropped it, the semitransparent piece of material fluttering to the ground between them. As the significance of the act hit him, a surge of joy ran through Nathan when he realized that this beautiful creature standing before him was his wife, to be followed with a profound sense of awed humility to think that God had entrusted this precious treasure into his care.

Nathan's long fingers trembled with emotion as he traced Lorna's features ever so carefully, as gently as if she were made of the most fragile crystal instead of skin and bone. Cupping her chin in his hand, he raised her head and kissed her, long, lovingly, with such aching tenderness and excruciating sweetness that he bonded her to him as no words, pomp, or ceremony ever could have. When he lifted his head,

Lorna's eyes were swimming with tears as she was filled with the wonder of it, the beauty of it, knowing the true meaning of being cherished.

"I know you expect your wedding day to be one of celebration, but I'm afraid I'm going to have to disappoint you," Nathan said with an apologetic smile. "We're leaving for the Zenata camp as soon as possible. The Arab sheikh has managed to convince some of his kinsmen that our marriage was a Berber plot contrived to insult them all. My friends are afraid if we wait until tomorrow to leave, the Arabs will sneak out during the night and set up an ambush for us in the hills. We've decided to slip away while they're occupied with the noon meal."

Lorna *was* disappointed. She had waited for days to be alone with Nathan, but she certainly didn't want to take the risk of being ambushed. "But won't they get suspicious when you don't show up for the meal."

"No, they'll assume the bride and groom are dining with the groom's friends in his tent. That's why we're not striking the tent. With it still standing here it should take awhile for them to realize we've left, and hopefully by that time it will be too late for them to follow."

Nathan bent and picked up the veil. As he started to place it over her face, Lorna stepped back, saying, "No! I won't wear it. I told you when I became a Muslim that I'd say the words but nothing more. I won't play the role of a meek, subservient Muslim wife. Besides, your friends have seen my face, both today and at the auction. There's no point to it."

Nathan was pleased with her spirit, but he didn't give her any hint of it. Instead he frowned and, with a perfectly straight face, said, "Well, I guess I can tell them you lived with the shamefully indecent Tuareg women too long and refuse to obey me. Of course, it's

going to be embarrassing for me to have to admit to
being intimidated by my bride of less than an hour."

"The Tuareg women aren't indecent just because
they refuse to cover their faces!" Lorna threw back
hotly. "And I'm *not* intimidating you. I'm just refusing to bow to a stupid male law."

When Nathan started laughing, Lorna realized
he had been teasing her and felt a little foolish. His
eyes still twinkling with mirth, he took her arm and
led her to the tent opening, saying, "I don't think my
friends expect us to embrace their customs wholeheartedly. They realize we became Muslims under
duress and are still very European at heart."

As Nathan and Lorna stepped from the tent, the
four men who had "abducted" her walked up to them
from where they had been standing waiting with the
horses. When the Berbers stood before the couple,
Nathan said in Arabic, "Lorna, I'd like to introduce
my good friends. This is Ali bein Ghaniya, the man
who found me in the desert and who's responsible for
saving my life."

The tall, distinguished older man, his short beard
neatly trimmed, touched his forehead and his heart,
then bowed slightly, saying, "The honor is all mine."

Lorna returned his smile, saying nervously,
"How do you do," wondering if she was doing it correctly by Muslim etiquette. She had been in North
Africa for over a year, but this was the first time she
had been officially introduced to any of the Muslims.

"And these are his sons, Mustafa, Abu, and Jabir,"
Nathan continued, drawing Lorna's attention to the
three younger men.

The introductions had hardly been completed
when Lorna saw Chedlya coming down a path on the
hillside from the opposite direction that faced the
camp, her husky female *bouzou* following her and

carrying Lorna's chest. One of the Zenatas took the chest from the slave and started tying it to the back of his horse as Chedlya said to Nathan, "The Arabs are occupied with their meal now." She pointed to a path that disappeared in a outcrop of large boulders, saying, "If you follow that path, the Arabs will not be able to see you when you leave. It circles the camp and comes out on the main road several miles away."

Nathan nodded in acknowledgment of Chedlya's instructions and accepted the reins to the horse that Ali was handing him. Pulling the beautiful bay mare forward, he said to Lorna, "This will be your horse. I'm afraid you'll have to ride astride, though. Muslims don't have sidesaddles."

Although the mare wasn't as large as the horses Lorna had seen pulling carriages in London, the animal was heavily muscled and the saddle looked a long way from the ground. And she'd be up there, all by herself, trying to control the powerful horse with just two thin little reins, Lorna thought. She swallowed hard, then admitted, "I don't know how to ride a horse. I've never been on one in my life."

Seeing the look of surprised disbelief on Nathan's face, Lorna asked testily, "Where would I learn to ride a horse? The only women who ride horses in London are the wealthy who frequent Hyde Park."

"I thought when you asked why you couldn't ride a camel like me, instead of traveling in the sedan, you knew how to ride," Nathan answered.

"No. I was thinking Hamid could lead the camel, and all I'd have to do is just sit on it."

"I do not blame you," Chedlya said, entering the conversation and eyeing the beautiful animal with disgust. "I would not get on that ugly creature either. I will send word to have Abu Bakr bring a camel and the sedan up here for you."

"No, Chedlya," Nathan said. "We appreciate your offer, but my friends and I plan on traveling fast, and a camel would slow us down."

Lorna hated herself for not knowing how to ride. Here she had been married to Nathan less than an hour and she was already causing problems for him. "Maybe you can lead my horse," she suggested.

"No, trying to keep your seat when you're not accustomed to riding at the pace we intend to travel would be awkward for you, if not downright dangerous," Nathan answered. "You'll ride with me, and we'll switch off between horses when one tires. Even riding double, we'll make better time than dragging a camel behind us."

Nathan led Lorna around the bay to where his black stallion stood and helped her mount. Sitting astride the horse, Lorna was terrified the animal would take off before Nathan could mount and she wouldn't know how to stop it. When Nathan swung into the saddle behind her and picked up the reins, she breathed a silent sigh of relief.

Chedlya walked up to the stallion, watching it warily from the corner of her eyes as if she didn't trust it either. Nathan smiled down at her, saying, "Thank you, Chedlya, for helping us."

"You are welcome," she answered. She turned her attention to Lorna, saying, "Farewell, my friend. *Inshullah*, we will meet again. If not in this world, perhaps the next."

Tears swam in Lorna's eyes. She was going to miss the Tuareg woman. "Good-bye, and thanks for everything."

Chedlya took Lorna's hand and squeezed it, looking deeply into her eyes and saying, "Remember what I said. Enjoy your happiness."

"I will," Lorna promised, swallowing the lump in her throat.

One of the Berbers leaned from his saddle and took the reins of the bay mare; then he and the emir led the way to the path that Chedlya had pointed out, Lorna and Nathan following behind them, and the other two Zenatas bringing up the rear, leaving Chedlya standing in a flurry of dust. They followed the narrow path that weaved through a ravine and then through the hills where herds of sheep and goats grazed indolently in the warm winter sun. Then, when they reached the main road, the men gave their horses their heads, and the spirited animals galloped off, long necks stretched out, manes and tails flying, powerful legs gobbling up the ground.

When Nathan's stallion raced away, Lorna held her breath, terrified as they sped along the road, the sounds of the horses' hooves pounding on the packed ground seemingly beating in unison with her thudding, racing heart. Then, aware of Nathan's strong arms around her and his masterful skill in handling his mount, her fear was replaced with an exhilaration. She had never moved at such a rapid speed in the wide open with nothing around her, felt the wind rushing past her, or seen the scenery racing by. Why, she felt as if she had sprouted wings and was flying, soaring through the air.

She laughed outright, crying out, "This is exciting!"

Nathan laughed, too, raising his voice to be heard over the thundering hooves and saying, "Yes, horseback riding can be an invigorating experience. I'll have to teach you how to ride when we reach the Zenata camp. Then we can go on long rides together."

Lorna didn't see anything wrong with the way

they *were* riding. Part of the fun was being in Nathan's arms. But then, riding beside her new husband would be a second best. Doing anything with him would be wonderful.

As Nathan had said, they rode hard and fast that day, wanting to put as much distance between them and the Arabs as they possibly could. They stopped only long enough for Lorna and Nathan to switch horses periodically, and by nightfall, when they finally made camp in an outcrop of boulders, Lorna was exhausted from the grueling pace.

When Nathan swung her off the horse and set her on the ground, Lorna gasped, feeling a sharp jabbing pain shoot up her legs and hips. She clung to him, struggling to straighten her legs, fearing they were permanently bowed from sitting astride the horse for so long and acutely aware of the burning coming from the chafed skin on the insides of her thighs.

Seeing the exhausted lines on her face for the first time, Nathan frowned deeply. His concern for her safety had taken precedence over her comfort, and he silently cursed the Arabs who had made such tortuous traveling necessary. "Here," he said, bending to pick her up, "I'll carry you to that grassy spot over there."

Lorna was aware of the Berbers watching from the distance as they unsaddled their horses and didn't want them to think Nathan had married a weakling. "No, I'll walk. It will help work out the stiffness."

"You're sure?" Nathan asked.

The look of concern on Nathan's face touched Lorna deeply and made her even more determined. She managed a smile and answered, "Yes, I'm sure."

By the time Lorna had limped to the clump of grass, with Nathan supporting her with his hand on her elbow, the circulation in her legs had returned

and the tingling had disappeared. Even a lot of the
stiffness was gone, surprising Lorna. But her bottom
felt numb and she longed to give it a good, brisk
rubbing, something she didn't dare do until she was in
the privacy of her tent.

It was then that she discovered there would be no
tent. The Berbers traveled lightly, eating in the open
and sleeping on small rugs they carried rolled up behind their saddles with their burnooses wrapped
around them for warmth when the meager fires had
burned out.

That night Nathan placed their small carpet on
the ground at a discreet distance from the others, and
he and Lorna lay on it. With his arms wrapped around
her and his burnoose covering them, Lorna felt safe
and cozy, but it was hardly what she had expected for
her wedding night. Ever since Nathan had kissed her
so passionately the afternoon she agreed to become a
Muslim, she had been looking forward to his lovemaking on this night, and he hadn't even kissed her except for that chaste little kiss on her forehead.

Nathan didn't dare more, not trusting himself to
leave it at that. Holding her in his arms all day and
lying beside her at night without even being able to
make love to her was going to be a living hell, the fact
of her being his bride and therefore his to make love
to making it all the harder. Then, seeing the moon
rising, he smiled and said softly, "Look at the moon."

To Lorna even the moon was a disappointment.
Instead of a romantic full moon, it was a just a miserable little sliver of light in the dark sky.

"That's the crescent moon that follows the new
moon, and it has special significance for the Muslims,"
Nathan said, his deep voice washing over her like a
sensual caress. "They regard it as a symbol of new
strength. That's why their swords are crescent

shaped. I didn't realize it at the time, but we were married on the day of the crescent moon. Our marriage is blessed."

Nathan's words helped put things in their proper perspective for Lorna. She felt ashamed of herself. Here she had been feeling sorry for herself because her wedding night was not what she had always imagined it would be, when less than a week ago she had thought that Nathan was dead and she would be facing a lifetime of emptiness. Now he was her husband and her new life stretched out before her like a beacon of shining light in the darkness. Yes, she was blessed.

"How did you find me?" Lorna asked. "I thought you were dead. Your clothing was ripped to pieces, and there was blood all over you. Your head was lying in a pool of it."

"Those cuts I took on the body were just surface scratches. It was the blow to the head that felled me, and it isn't unusual for scalp injuries to bleed something fierce. I was unconscious for a week."

"You lay out there on the desert for a week?" Lorna asked in disbelief.

"No. If that had been the case, I'm sure I would have died from exposure. Do you remember seeing the large holes in the ground in the area we were passing through when we were attacked?"

"Yes, I was curious about them. They seemed to be too large to have been made by a burrowing animal."

"You're right. They were made by Berbers who live in underground caves in that area. After the Tuareg left, those people came up and investigated. They found me and, because of my light skin, assumed I was Berber. They took me back to their caves and nursed me back to health. But even then it was another two weeks before I could travel."

"Because you were weak from losing so much blood?"

"No. Because of the headaches. I couldn't even raise my head off the pillow for a week after I regained consciousness. When I was able to travel, I went to the American consul in Tunis. He had already heard about the caravan's being attacked. He had been told there were no survivors. I told him that there was a possibility that you were alive and that I was going to go looking for you because I felt responsible for you."

Then his government hadn't ordered him to find her and rescue her, Lorna thought. But then, knowing that it had been a personal choice didn't give her any satisfaction. He had only come because he was such a noble person and was helping her because he identified with her as someone treated unfairly.

In her shock at finding Nathan alive and her subsequent happiness at their marriage, Lorna had never even thought about what would happen to her when she went back to civilization. "I wish you hadn't told the consul that you thought I was alive. When we go back and everyone finds out about our marriage, they'll all know about my deception. My God, I'm right back in the same mess I was in!"

Nathan shifted his weight, rose on his elbow, and looked down at her. "No one has any way of knowing that you're the woman I came looking for," he said in a firm voice. "I'll simply tell them that I found out Lady Hampton had been killed in the attack after all, but during my search for her I heard about another Englishwoman being held as a slave in a Tuareg camp and went to investigate. We can say you were taken captive by the pirates off another boat that sailed much earlier than the one you were on."

"What about my supposed crime in England?"

"Did you give your real name when you boarded the ship?"

"No."

"Then the authorities have no way of tracking you down either. Besides, we'll never have any reason to travel in England, where you might be recognized, and we'll be living in America."

She was finally free, Lorna thought. Free from slavery, free from her deception, and free from running. It was a wonderful feeling. She savored it for a moment, then said, "But you still haven't explained how you found me."

Nathan lay back down before continuing his story. "After I left the consul, I sent word by a neutral ship to my first mate in Malta to bring the *Seabird* to Tunis. I took the money from my safe, turned command of the *Seabird* over to him, and instructed him to do some trading in the Mediterranean in my absence, but to check in at Malta between runs to see if there was any word from me. Then I came looking for you."

"It was a miracle that you managed to find me," Lorna commented.

Yes, it was, Nathan thought. But he had refused to accept the possibility that he might not—or that Lorna might not have survived the trip across the Sahara. He kept telling himself that she was strong, that she would survive, that she would hold out until he found her. He refused even to contemplate her being dead. "Yes, considering the Sahara covers three and a half million square miles and that the Tuareg roam all over it from Morocco to Egypt, it was nothing short of a miracle. That's why I went to my Zenata friends. I knew I would need help. Ali is an emir, the leader of several Zenata tribes. He sent riders to the other Zenatas to keep an ear out for information regarding the whereabouts of a beautiful Christian woman who was just recently taken captive by the Tuareg. When the invitation to the auction arrived, I knew it had to be you. Frankly, I was surprised. I had expected it to take at least a year, maybe longer, for any word of your whereabouts to filter back."

Lorna was shocked. He had been prepared to search for her for a year or longer? Would a man go to such lengths just to satisfy a feeling of obligation? Lorna didn't know the answer, but a little glimmer of hope that Nathan might have had other motives was born in her, making her feel warm all over. She snuggled closer, muttering sleepily as her eyelids fluttered closed, "But you found me. That's all that matters."

Nathan held Lorna in a tight, possessive embrace as she lay sleeping in his arms, the strange emotion that had driven him to find her welling up inside him and threatening to smother him with its intensity. As he surrendered to sleep, his subconscious mind spoke with a fierce will of its own. And now that I've found you, I'm never going to let you go. Never!

The next day they left the foothills of the mountains and rode out onto the flat area between the mountains and the sand dunes farther north, passing by several of the strange pedestal rock formations that were formed by the sand eroding the lower portion of the rocks, many of them towering into the air and looking as if they would topple over at any minute. Seeing the mountains of sand in the distance before them and remembering the grueling trip over them, Lorna felt a strong sense of dread. Crossing that desolate, barren area once in one's lifetime was enough, but twice? "How far is the Zenatas' camp?" she asked, hoping Nathan would answer only a day or two away.

"It's on an oasis in an area north of here known as the Fezzan, about five days' ride from here."

Lorna blinked back tears of disappointment and set her shoulders with grim resignation, knowing what was before her.

It turned out the trek was almost as unbearable as her first trip across the huge dunes. Even though it was winter, the sun beat down on the them unmercifully, the sand reflecting the heat rays and turning the area into an oven, and the horses had to labor even harder than the camels to cross the deep piles of sand. Up the side of one dune they traveled, the struggling horses taking the steep incline by leaps instead of steps, the sun bearing down on them, then sliding down the other side, relishing the feel of the shade and the brief respite from the burning sun until they climbed the blistering side of yet another dune, over and over in a never-ending world of sand and glaring white light.

Spying something to the side of them that traversed the huge dunes, Lorna asked, "Why don't we follow that ravine, instead of going up and down? It seems like it would be easier."

"That's a wadi, a deep-cut water channel, and anyone who has any sense about traveling in the Sahara knows to avoid them for fear of being caught in a flash flood."

"A flood, in the middle of the Sahara?" Lorna asked in disbelief.

"Yes. It can be raining miles away, without our even knowing it. The next thing we'd know, a huge wall of water would come down that wadi so fast we couldn't get out of its way. More than one caravan has been totally wiped out by foolishly traveling in a wadi, every person and animal in it drowned in an onslaught of swirling, rushing water. Then an hour later, there's nothing left. Not a drop of water. Just the dead bodies and carcasses."

It seemed impossible anyone could drown in the middle of the Sahara, but Lorna didn't doubt Nathan's words. A shiver ran through her despite the heat. Then she asked, "Then why don't the Zenatas use camels if they're going to travel over these tall dunes? It seems almost cruel to make these horses labor so hard."

"You have a good point there, but the Zenatas are as fanatical about horses' being the superior animals as the Tuareg are about camels. The Zenatas' preference for horses goes way back. They had them before the Arabs showed up on the scene, even before the Romans introduced camels to this area. The horse has become a way of life for them as much as for the Plains Indians back in my country. And they're fantastic horsemen. A Zenata can pick up a coin from the sand from a horse going at full gallop. I thought I could ride passably well until I lived with the Zenatas and they taught me some of their skills."

Lorna had wondered where Nathan had learned to ride so well. Mounted, he and his horse seemed to blend into one magnificent, powerful unit, and she knew seamen weren't noted for their horsemanship. If anything, most were probably like her, having never been on a horse. Curious, she asked, "Where did you learn to ride?"

"On my father's plantation in Virginia. But as I said, it was the Zenatas who made me a real horseman. Compared to them I was just a novice."

From then on Lorna and Nathan didn't do much talking. The heat drained them of all energy, making even something as simple as conversation seem too much of an effort.

Several nights later Lorna said to Nathan as they prepared to bed down for the night, "I don't think your friends like me. They seem to be avoiding me."

"It's not that they don't like you, Lorna. They're Muslims and unaccustomed to being around another man's wife. If anything, they feel awkward. But each and every one of them has commented on your amazing strength and fortitude, the fact that you've never complained, that you keep going even though they know you must be exhausted. You've made quite an impression upon them."

Lorna heard the pride in Nathan's voice and was glad for it. It nothing else, she could have his respect.

Later, in the still of the night, Lorna was awakened by a sudden, deafening beating sound. She sat bolt upright, her eyes filled with fear, looking wildly about her. Then, seeing nothing, she yelled over the loud noise, "What's that?"

"It's a phenomenon you'll find only in the sand dunes. It's caused by sand flowing over the slip side of a high dune," Nathan yelled back.

The noise lasted for a good five minutes before it stopped. Lying back down, her heart still racing, the only sound the gentle sighing of the wind, Lorna said, "That was the eeriest thing I've ever heard. It sounded like bells tolling."

"Yes. Perhaps that's where the legends of buried monasteries in the Sahara came from."

"But there aren't any?"

"No, the Christians who might have ventured this far south were few and far between, and there were certainly not enough of them to build a monastery."

* * *

Two days later Lorna spied a touch of green in the distance and knew it had to be their destination and not a mirage. Nathan had told her mirages occurred only on windless days, and there was a stiff breeze blowing. Tears of relief shimmered in her eyes, knowing that the grueling trip across the towering dunes was finally over.

Nathan's eyes were locked on the speck of green also. "When we reach the Zenata camp, we can begin our seven fig days."

"Our what?"

"That's what the Muslims call the honeymoon."

Lorna's heart raced in anticipation at the sensual promise of Nathan's words. Tonight would be her long-awaited wedding night. Suddenly she was acutely aware of him, his warm breath fanning her neck, his powerful arms at both sides of her, his exciting male scent enveloping her and leaving her feeling weak with need.

Nathan was very conscious of Lorna, too. Over the past days, he had rigidly schooled himself not to let her nearness affect him, but knowing that the consummation of their marriage lay only hours away, his control fled and his manhood rose in anticipation, testimony to the desire he had kept at bay with an iron will.

Feeling his hardness pressing against her buttocks through their layers of clothing, Lorna's eyes widened. Then, with a throaty moan, she leaned back against him, squirming in the saddle to get closer to that part of him that she so desperately wanted inside her.

Nathan groaned and pulled her even closer with one arm, nuzzling her neck and whispering, "After waiting for six days, I don't think I can wait another second."

"Neither do I," Lorna admitted in a breathless voice, her total honesty pleasing Nathan very much.

But they were forced to wait, the remaining miles to the camp an eternity of hell for both of them. Then, when they rode into the maze of tents sitting beneath the cool shade of the gently swaying palm trees, they were suddenly surrounded by Zenatas, a tide of humanity flowing from the tents and congratulating them on their marriage.

Nathan glanced across at Ali and knew by the smile on the emir's face what had happened. Ali had sent word ahead, and now he and Lorna would have to go through yet another ritual before they could be alone. Sighing in a mixture of irritation and frustrated resignation, he dismounted, swung Lorna from the saddle, and relinquished his bride to the keeping of several slaves who rushed her into a nearby tent that had been set up for them.

Inside the tent Lorna looked around her in amazement. While the tent wasn't as large as Chedlya's, it was much more luxurious. Plush Persian carpets in deep rich colors covered the ground and sheer pastel-colored draperies were hung inside the tent poles to soften the stark lines. In one corner there was a royal blue carpet surrounded by colorful cushions, with a low table sitting in the center. On the opposite side of the tent was a dais on which the bed sat, the silken sheets covered with a rainbow of pillows and the gauze canopy over it flowing down the sides and surrounding it like a shimmering waterfall.

Before Lorna could even recover from the surprise of her luxurious surroundings, the slave girls were urging her to strip, telling her they had a bath prepared for her. As soon as they had finished bathing her in perfumed water, she was given a caftan of the palest gold to don, the garment slipping over her head, the V-shaped neckline revealing a great deal of cleavage and the thin silk clinging to her curves, a gown that was clearly made with seduction in mind.

While Lorna waited for Nathan to appear, sitting on the blue carpeting where the slave girls had positioned her, the slaves busied themselves, one brushing Lorna's long hair until it gleamed, while the others lit the brass lamps hanging from the tent poles, the small braziers, and the lamps filled with incense sitting about. Soon the odors of spicy food mingled with that of incense as the slaves carried in trays of food and pots of tea, setting them on the glowing braziers to keep them warm. And then the girls were gone, leaving Lorna with only the spitting braziers to keep her company.

Peering out the tent opening, Lorna saw it was growing dark and wondered where Nathan was. Obviously all this had been done to set the scene for the wedding night. The bride was primed and ready, so where was the groom? Then, seeing a shadow cast by the torch that was blazing outside the tent, Lorna stiffened, a tingle of fear running through her. Then, when Nathan entered, ducking his head to keep from hitting it on the low tent opening, she went weak with relief.

As he walked toward her, a smile on his face, Lorna took in the sight of him hungrily, finding it hard to believe that this magnificent specimen of manhood was actually her husband. Then, noting the drops of water that were glistening in his dark hair, she asked, "You've bathed too?"

Nathan seated himself at the table across from her before answering. "Yes. I told you the Muslims were very clean. A groom wouldn't think of going to his bride without a bath."

Nathan remembered his urgency that afternoon and thought the bath had been a good idea, despite his irritation at the time. Not only was he more presentable, but it had cooled his raging passion. A wedding night was like a sumptuous feast, its pleasures meant to be enjoyed at leisure, savored, not hurriedly gobbled up.

As soon as Nathan sat down, the slave girls reappeared, much to Lorna's disgust. She wanted to be alone with Nathan. To her utter frustration they didn't leave until the meal was finished, handing both Nathan and Lorna a cup of tea before they departed, dropping the tent flap down behind them as they went.

Lorna realized the time had arrived and suddenly felt shy. Dropping her eyes, she started to take a sip of tea when Nathan stopped her saying, "I would prefer you didn't drink that."

"Why not?"

Nathan set his cup down and reached for hers, setting it aside on the carpeting beside his before answering, "Because it contains an aphrodisiac. Didn't you notice the tea we drank with our meal came from the other pot?"

"No, I didn't."

"I would like to think that the pleasure we find in each other's arms tonight comes from our mutual desire and not from some artificial stimulant." He smiled, adding, "Besides, I don't think we need aphrodisiacs to get us through this night—and hopefully none of the others that will follow."

Lorna felt as if she was drowning in Nathan's warm gaze. No, she certainly didn't need anything to make her want him. Wanting him was an ache deep inside her, and if he didn't kiss her soon, she'd scream in frustration.

As Nathan leaned toward her, the look in his eyes promising heaven and more, Lorna's heart hammered erratically beneath her breast, a tremor of anticipation running through her. Pushing her down among the cushions, his warm male lips sought the tender shape of her mouth, nibbling at one sensitive corner, then the other, catching her provocative lower lip in his teeth and biting it gently before his tongue slowly traced the outline of her mouth, brushing back and forth, driving her wild with frustration. She caught his head with her hands, her lips parting in silent invitation, but still he tormented her, teasing, tantalizing, before he finally gave her what she wanted, his tongue plunging in and swirling around hers in a torrid kiss that went on and on and left her breathless and swimming dizzily, her entire body tingling.

His mouth left hers to explore her neck and shoulders, dropping love bites over the creamy skin and leaving a trail of fire in his wake, slowly, ever so slowly, moving lower until he was nuzzling her breasts between the deep opening of the neckline of her caftan, breathing in her intoxicating scent while his hand cupped and massaged one incredibly soft mound.

Anxious to taste her there, he stood, bringing her to her feet with him, saying in a husky voice, "Let's get rid of this damned thing," before he whisked the caftan over her head and tossed it aside.

Lorna watched as Nathan's eyes darkened with passion while his gaze slowly roved over her nakedness and then flushed under that hot, smoldering look, a look that seemed to admire, possess, and ravish all at the same time. Suddenly becoming aware of his being still dressed, she felt cheated.

"Take off your clothes," she commanded softly. "I want to see you too."

She waited anxiously as Nathan shrugged out of his caftan and stripped off his long shirt, her eyes greedily taking in each inch of flesh he exposed. When he reached for the drawstring of his pantaloons, Lorna stepped forward, saying, "No. Let me do it."

Aware of the surprised expression on Nathan's face, Lorna blushed even deeper at her own boldness. With trembling fingers she untied the string, acutely aware of Nathan's stomach muscles contracting beneath the brush of her hand, then pushed the full pants down his slim hips, kneeling as she slipped them over his long legs.

At the feel of Lorna's fingers trailing down his flanks and the length of his thighs, Nathan's breath caught in his throat. He lifted one foot, then the other, shaking his slippers free and kicking the pantaloons aside. Then he stood, acutely conscious of his straining erection and remembering Lorna's shocked expression when she had seen him in that state of blatant arousal before. He hadn't realized it at the time, but she must have been afraid. He held his breath, not knowing what her reaction might be.

But when Lorna sat back on her heels and looked up at him, she wasn't in the least frightened. Instead she was awed by his magnificence. He's beautiful, she thought, her eyes drifting over the powerful muscles in his shoulders and arms, his broad, ridged chest and flat abdomen. Her gaze locked on the rigid proof of his masculinity, standing proudly before her, a silent, but eloquent, testimony of his desire for her. Fascinated, she reached for him, touching him tentatively, then wrapping her hand around the hot flesh, amazed at how soft the skin felt, thinking that it felt like warm velvet over steel. Then, feeling him growing even larger in her hand and the powerful muscle throbbing with a life of its own, an incredible excitement filled her. Instinctively, she slid her hand back and forth over his long length, needing no tutoring in the movements.

Nathan had been immensely relieved at Lorna's reaction to his nakedness and extremely pleased when she fondled him of her free will. As she stroked him sensuously, he clenched his teeth and hands, his groan of pleasure encouraging Lorna in her new, bold venture. A fine sheen of perspiration covered him, and his legs trembled, awash in sensation as she continued with growing enthusiasm, feeling as if he would explode at any minute. His hands reached to still hers as he whispered urgently, "No more!"

"But . . . but I thought you liked it," Lorna answered in bewilderment, removing her hand.

Nathan dropped to his knees and caught her shoulders, pulling her to the carpet with him. He nuzzled her neck, saying softly, "I did like it. Too much. If you had continued, it would have been over with too soon."

But Lorna hardly heard Nathan's explanation. She was too absorbed with the feel of his heated skin against hers, the crisp hairs on his chest tickling her swollen, tender nipples, his powerful heart thudding against hers, his rigid, throbbing manhood pressed against her loins, his lips trailing liquid fire down her throat. From every direction her senses were being assaulted. Then, when his head slowly descended to her breasts, tonguing every inch of skin along the way, Lorna held her breath in intense anticipation, knowing the delights that were in store for her.

Again, he tormented her, dropping tiny love
bites in slowly decreasing circles around the throbbing peak that ached for his mouth, licking away the
little stings, leaving Lorna sobbing in frustration and
clawing at his shoulders. When his mouth finally
closed over the turgid nipple, tongue rolling it
around, Lorna cried out softly, a terrible ache possessing her, her muscles trembling at the exquisite sensations he was invoking. When his mouth left her
breast, she moaned in objection, then sighed in utter
bliss as he paid homage to its twin, exciting her even
more.

Lorna's senses were spinning as Nathan continued his erotic exploration. His hands stroked her sides
and hips with whisper-soft caresses as he dropped
fiery kisses at random over her chest and soft abdomen, slipping lower and lower. When he gently
pushed her legs apart, his fingers tantalizing the ultrasensitive skin on the insides of her thighs, Lorna
offered no resistance. With passion-dulled eyes, she
looked down and saw him kneeling between her legs.
When the palms of his hands slipped up the back of
her thighs and cupped her buttocks, lifting her hips,
she arched her back in anticipation of his entry. Then,
seeing his head lowering, she stiffened in shock, intu-
itively knowing what he planned.

Her hands flew down, fingers tangling in his dark
hair as she pulled his head up. "No!"

Nathan's eyes were shimmering green fire as he
gazed up at her. "Why not?"

"Because . . . because it's wrong. It's indecent!"

"No, Lorna," Nathan answered in a firm voice.
"Nothing is forbidden between a man and his wife.
Now hush. Let me love you."

Lorna tried to clamp her legs shut, but Nathan
was determined to taste her sweetness there. He held

her hips firmly to keep her from squirming away from him, ignoring her ragged pleas to stop, his tongue laving her moist lips, the taste of her nectar and the musky scent of her womanliness exciting him wildly.

When Lorna felt Nathan's warm tongue circling the tiny bud, stroking sensuously, then flicking like a fiery dart, her loins were flooded with heat as an insidious warmth crept through her, sapping her will and leaving her boneless and yielding. With a will of their own, her legs parted, giving him free access, the hands that had tried to pull him away cupping the back of his head and pressing him closer.

Her head was spinning as her smoldering passion burst into a raging inferno. It was wicked what he was doing to her. It was wonderful! Then, as his strong tongue dipped to explore inside her warm, wet recess, then back to tease her swollen bud of desire, back and forth, over and over, Lorna trembled all over as wave after wave of hot, searing sensations washed over her, her heart pounding as if it would leap out of her chest, her breath coming in ragged gasps. He'd kill her if he didn't stop this exquisite torture, Lorna thought wildly, an incredible excitement filling her and threatening to burst her skin. And then, as her whole body convulsed, a blinding flash exploding in her brain, she did think she was dying. She cried out as the world seemed to tilt crazily on its axis and she was hurled into space.

Lorna never knew how long she drifted in that dark void. Her first awareness was of Nathan softly kissing her lips. Her eyelids fluttered open to gaze up at him with dazed eyes.

Nathan smiled down at her and taunted softly, "Now, tell me you didn't like that."

Lorna thought to deny it. Surely anything that wickedly wonderful must be sinful. But the words wouldn't come. A hot flush crept up her face and she averted her eyes, muttering, "Yes, I liked it."

Nathan laughed at her reluctant admission, then nibbled her ear, whispering, "Little liar. You loved it."

At the feel of the deep rumble of laughter in Nathan's chest pressing against her own and his lips playing at her ear, Laura shivered in renewed excitement. My God! she thought. I must be a wanton. How could I possibly respond to his touch so soon after that explosive release?

But when his hand slipped between her legs, his fingers teasing and tantalizing just as his tongue had so recently done, Lorna felt the bolt of fire running up her spine, her muscles quivering with renewed anticipation, knowing he meant to bring her to that maddening brink once again.

"What . . . what about you?" she gasped.

"I can wait. I enjoy pleasuring you."

Nathan meant what he said. He wanted to give instead of take, make this first night of their marriage a memorable one for her. He refused to delve into his reasons. His pleasure in giving her pleasure was enough.

After he had brought her to another shuddering release, Nathan rose over her and knelt between her thighs, lifting her hips. Still trembling in the aftermath of the spasms that had just rocked her, Lorna felt the hot, moist tip of his manhood pressing against her. A cry of gladness escaped her lips, thinking that the final act was finally at hand and he would stop tormenting her. But if Lorna thought Nathan's torture with his hands and lips was excruciating, it was nothing compared to what he was doing now.

With agonizing slowness, he entered her, inch by inch, then withdrew, over and over, each sensuous thrust an ecstasy, each retreat an agony, until Lorna was desperate for release and sobbing incoherently. Then, when his mouth covered hers, his tongue moving in unison with his powerful thrusts, she wrapped her long legs around him, squeezing as if her life depended upon it.

Beads of perspiration broke out on Nathan's forehead and he clenched his teeth against the exquisite feel of Lorna's sweet flesh surrounding him, the muscles gripping at him like hot hands. With an iron will, he peeled her legs from him, whispering hoarsely, "There's no hurry. We have all night."

"No! You're killing me," Lorna sobbed. "I can't stand any more."

But Nathan ignored her protest, bringing her over and over to the shuddering brink, then backing off, until Lorna was frenzied beneath him, every nerve screaming for release, her pulse pounding in her ears, her body consumed in flames. Finally Nathan's own need came to the fore, the floodgates of his passion bursting through and drowning out his steely control. With deep, powerful, masterful strokes he drove them both up that thundering height, taking her in a sweet-savage storm of primitive urgency until he brought them both to that mindless, searing burst of passion, an explosion that rent their souls from their bodies and sent them hurling among a starburst of flaming, glorious colors.

Slowly they spiraled back to reality, muscles still trembling in the aftermath of their explosive release, their breath ragged. Then, realizing that he had collapsed over her and fearing he would crush her with his weight, Nathan raised himself on his elbows, shocked at how weak he felt.

Gazing down at her, he saw the tears trickling down her cheeks. "My God! Did I hurt you?" he asked in alarm.

Lorna looked up at him, her violet eyes gleaming with happiness. "No. It's just that it was so . . . so beautiful."

Nathan felt that strange twisting pain in his chest. He bent and tenderly kissed her swollen lips, then whispered against them, "Yes, it was beautiful."

He lifted himself from her and rolled to his side, bringing her with him, loath to let her go for even a moment. Lorna snuggled close, relishing the feel of his strong arms around her, the salty taste of his warm throat against her lips, her hand playing absently in the damp curls on his chest. Then she laughed softly.

Nathan raised his head and asked, "What's so funny?"

"I was just thinking about what you said earlier about us not needing any aphrodisiacs. It just occurred to me that we never even made it to the bed."

Nathan raised himself on his elbow and glanced at the bed. Then, before Lorna could even guess his intent, he scooped her up in his powerful arms and rose, carrying her to the bed, shouldering the gauzy waterfall aside as he placed her on the silk sheets, following her down, saying in a thick voice, "We can't have this going to waste."

Lorna looked up and saw the molten glitter in his eyes. Her heart beat a crazy tattoo as he lowered his head once again to her lips. All that and more? she thought in disbelief. Then her mind was reeling dizzily as all thought fled to be replaced with sheer sensation.

Over and over Nathan loved her in a long night of blissful ecstasy. The rising sun was tinting the eastern horizon in rosy pinks before he finally slept in utter exhaustion. Feeling wonderfully contented and totally satiated, Lorna lay in his arms, thinking no bride had ever been loved so sweetly and tenderly, so completely, so beautifully. A tear slipped down her cheek and a lump came to her throat. Yes, she was blessed. Regardless of what lay ahead of them, she had this night to remember, a priceless treasure she would carry in her heart forever.

Chapter 13

When Lorna awoke later that day, Nathan was hovering over her and gazing down at her. Once again Lorna was stunned by the startling green eyes in his tanned face, wondering if she would ever become accustomed to his beautiful eyes or if they would always have that breathtaking impact on her.

Nathan kissed her softly on the lips, saying, *"Sahbah el-khayre."*

"Sahbah innoor," Lorna answered, thinking what a wonderful way to start the day, being kissed and told "good morning" by your exciting husband.

Nathan chuckled and said, "Or maybe I should have said good afternoon."

"What time is it?"

"Around two, I'd guess. I'm afraid we've slept through both breakfast and lunch. Are you hungry?"

Lorna's stomach answered for her with a loud growl. She flushed in embarrassment, bringing another chuckle from Nathan. He rolled from the bed, saying, "I'll see if the slaves can find something to tide us over until dinner."

As he walked to where he had tossed his clothing the night before, Lorna admired his long, muscular legs and lean flanks. It wasn't until he was pulling on his pantaloons that she looked at his back, then gasped.

Hearing the sound, Nathan turned, asking, "Is something wrong?"

"Your back. It's covered with scratches."

Nathan grinned, answering, "That's the price a man has to pay when he excites his wife to the point where she doesn't know what she's doing."

"I did that?" Lorna asked in horror.

"Well, you're the only wildcat I've been in bed with," Nathan answered with a teasing glimmer in his eyes as he tied the drawstring; then, seeing the look coming over her face, he walked quickly back to the bed and sat on it, saying, "No! I don't want you to regret it. I don't want you ever to regret what happens between us in the throes of passion. A few scratches is small price to pay for the immense pleasure you gave me last night. And I want our lovemaking to stay that way, uninhibited and without restraint."

Seeing the doubt in her eyes, Nathan said, "Don't you see? Your wild response excited me, spurred me on. A man likes to know the intense pleasure he's giving a woman, even when he's receiving it himself. Doing what you feel like doing at that moment is what makes it so special. Where else can you scratch me and I bite you if not in the throes of passion?"

"I don't remember you biting me."

"And I don't remember you scratching me. But

the proof of our excitement is on both of us. Look at your breasts."

Lorna looked down, seeing the little red marks where Nathan had placed his love bites. "But they didn't hurt. Not really."

"Neither did your scratches." Nathan rose, saying, "Now, enough of that. Our little wounds are only a testimony to the intense pleasure we received, a reminder of our deep mutual passion."

After Nathan had dressed and left the tent, Lorna slipped from the bed, quickly bathed in the water she found behind the screen, and dressed. Then she sat on the carpeting where they had eaten the night before and waited for Nathan's return, her stomach grumbling in hunger. Several minutes later she heard the Zenatas cheering outside the tent and wondered what was going on and what was delaying Nathan. By the time he walked back in, she was a little irritated.

"What took you so long? I'm starving."

Nathan seated himself beside her before answering, "I had to fulfill the last of my Muslim obligations in our marriage before I summoned the slave women."

"And what obligation was that?"

"Announcing to the tribe that you were a virgin on our wedding night."

"What?" Lorna gasped.

"It's custom. If the woman isn't a virgin, the marriage is annulled and she is sent back to her family in disgrace."

Lorna remembered the cheers and was mortified. "Why, that's horrible! It's embarrassing to the couple and degrading to the woman."

"Yes. I'll admit I was tempted to say the hell with them and tell them it wasn't any of their damned business. But if I had refused, they would have been suspicious. Thank God we don't have to display the wedding sheet."

"What are you talking about?"

"Up until a few centuries ago it was custom in Europe for the wedding sheet to be hung for all to view. If there wasn't blood on it from the woman's maidenhead being broken, the marriage was void. At least the Muslims take the husband's word for it."

Lorna thought both were barbaric customs but didn't comment, as the slaves arrived with their food at that moment.

As the women served them and they ate, Nathan wondered why he had pronounced Lorna a virgin in public. It wasn't like him to offer any explanations to anyone, particularly an announcement that he found so distasteful. And it hadn't been because the Muslims might get suspicious if he refused, as he had told Lorna. He didn't give a damn what they thought. But for some strange reason he wanted to fulfill every detail of his marriage to Lorna, make their union irrevocable before God and man.

While Nathan was pondering over this, Lorna's attention was on the slave women. She wondered how they felt about their enforced captivity. The trio was well clothed and obviously well fed, all being on the plump side, and they didn't appear unhappy. But Lorna had been a well-treated slave, too, and might not have appeared unhappy to others, but she had burned with resentment at having her freedom taken away from her, at being at the beck and call of others.

As the women left the tent, Nathan asked, "Why are you frowning so?"

"I was wondering how those women feel about being slaves." Then, suddenly remembering something, she said, "Didn't you tell me your father owns a plantation? Does he have slaves?"

Nathan heard the subtle hint of outrage in Lorna's voice and guessed what she was thinking. "No, Lorna, I'm not a hypocrite. I hate slavery with all my heart and all my being. My father did own a plantation, and yes, he did have slaves. But when I returned from Africa after my capture and enslavement, he knew how strongly I felt about the matter and sold it." He sat back with a thoughtful look on his face, saying, "You know, it's strange. I grew up with slaves, yet I never once stopped to wonder how they might feel. I accepted the institution because it was accepted by my society. It wasn't until I was put in their place that I became so antislavery. Perhaps if all of us could walk in the other's shoes more often, we might have a kinder world."

"What does your father do now?"

"He bought a shipping firm. He told me several years later that he was glad he sold the plantation, that his heart had never been in it, that just being around ships and smelling the salt air every day made a new man out of him. But what really surprised me was my mother. She had been born and raised on a plantation. But she confessed she was glad, too, that my father's being happier made her happier."

Lorna decided that she liked Nathan's mother. Any woman who would put the happiness of her husband before her own had to have a kind heart.

"What would you like to do today?" Nathan asked.

"There isn't much of the day left," Lorna pointed out.

"We could go for a walk. Would you like to see the encampment?"

Lorna knew after Nathan's public announcement everyone would probably stare at her. But then, they would probably stare at her anyway, since she refused to wear a veil, and she'd be damned if she'd hide away in a tent the whole time they were in the Zenata camp. Why, she'd go crazy! "Yes, that would be nice."

When they stepped from the tent, Lorna realized the settlement was much larger than she had thought. The tents stretched both ways as far as she could see, and they weren't made of leather, like the Tuaregs' tents, but of heavy cloth in every color imaginable, some solid and some striped. In the center of the camp a large, circular striped tent sat, pennants fluttering from the pole on top of it and from the standards on both sides of its entrance, leaving Lorna to assume that it was the emir's lodgings.

Nathan led Lorna through the maze of tents that seemed to be set at random around the oasis and through a thickly palmed area until they reached the pool of water. Lorna was amazed. Why, it was almost as wide as the Thames River and stretched several hundred yards.

"I didn't expect the pool to be so big," she commented.

"There's another pool past that thick grove of palm trees," Nathan informed her, pointing at one end of the pool, "and another beyond it, and another. There are nine pools in all, some as large as this and some much smaller, and they stretch out across the desert for a good five miles like a ribbon."

"I can't get over how cool it is here," Lorna remarked.

"Yes, it is pleasant. Why don't we sit down and enjoy a few moments of it."

As soon as they sat down under the shade of a towering palm, Nathan said, "You know practically everything there is to know about me, but I know very little about you, other than the fact that you were in the service of a nobleman. Where were you born?"

A deep frown came over Lorna's face. "I don't know. You see, I was an orphan. I don't even know who my parents were. All I know is that they were killed in a fire when I was a baby."

"Then who raised you?"

"The orphanage I was taken to."

Nathan scowled. "That must have been pretty rough."

"Oh, I suppose I was luckier than the street urchins. I didn't have to search through garbage to find something to eat, and I did have a roof over my head."

"Did they mistreat you?" Nathan asked, vowing if they had they would answer to him.

"Do you mean did they beat me? No. In fact, there were so many of us children and so few of them, that we hardly got any attention, let alone discipline. I'm afraid I grew up rather wild."

No wonder she was so strong and self-sufficient, Nathan thought. She'd had no one but herself to rely on. It must have been terrible growing up with no family, no one who cared, no one to shield and protect her. He couldn't imagine that kind of childhood. His had been so loving and secure. And she must have gone without material things, too, if the place was that crowded. Well, he'd make it up to her, he vowed. She'd never want for anything again.

"That's why it was so difficult when the director placed me in the service of a nobleman when I was deemed old enough to earn my own living," Lorna continued, unaware of Nathan's being deeply engrossed in thought. "I was too independent for my own good. I resented taking orders terribly, particularly from those snobs. I didn't even know how to curtsy. I had to be taught. But even then it galled me no end to have to bow to them. I always considered myself just as good as they were. That's why I was saving my money to go to America. I had heard that there wasn't so much class distinction there, and no nobility."

"There isn't, and you aren't just as good as they are. You're better! They've become weak and soft with their luxurious living and pampered existence. It's rather ironic that you had to play the part of a noblewoman, one of the very people you disliked so much."

"Yes, I hated it, and the horrible way I had to behave. I couldn't blame you for thinking so badly of me, and I longed so much to reveal my real self to you."

"In many ways you did, and frankly, I was puzzled. I couldn't understand where you had gotten your strength and your fortitude. And that night when you sympathized with me when I told you about my imprisonment and you made that strange remark about my not knowing you at all, I was really baffled. But I'll have to admit that you fooled me, despite all the surprising attributes you had revealed to me. I even swallowed that story you gave me the night we made love. And I hated myself for succumbing to my desire. I couldn't understand how I could be so attracted to a woman who represented everything I disliked. And then, too, there was the fact that you were married."

Lorna hung her head and admitted, "I regretted that later, particularly when you acted so cold and distant. I thought all I had accomplished was to prove I deserved your low regard for me."

Nathan started chuckling.

"What are you laughing at?"

"Your having to wear that indecent dress. That must have galled you."

"I was furious with Lady Hampton for putting me in that position!" Lorna answered with renewed anger. "And to be perfectly honest, I was furious with you, too. I didn't think it was fair for you to judge me just on what I was wearing. Then when I saw it was making you angry, I decided to goad you."

"Well, you certainly succeeded there. You had me so sexually frustrated with your 'you can look but not touch' attitude that I wanted to punish you. That's why I took every opportunity to put you in your place."

Lorna started laughing. "Looking back on it all now, it does seem amusing. We both had our defenses up." She sobered and said, "But I'm glad it's behind us."

As they walked back to their tent, Nathan was glad it was behind them, too, and that they could be more open and honest with one another. But he still didn't know where he stood with Lorna. Oh, yes, they were physically attracted to one another. There was no denying that. But that didn't mean that Lorna had any tender feelings for him. She had married him out of necessity, as a means to escape slavery. And then, too, there was that bit about her wanting to go to America. Had that played any part in her decision? She had proven to be a very resourceful woman. No, he couldn't let his defenses down, not yet, not until he knew if the protection he was offering her was the only reason she had agreed to become his wife. He'd be damned if he'd make a total ass out of himself and admit that he had fallen in love with her. It was the first time Nathan had admitted his feelings to himself, and the thought came as a shock. But he found he couldn't take it back. Like it or not, he was in love with a woman who had admitted she only desired him. Christ! How in the devil had he gotten himself into this mess? Living with her day by day, loving her and not even being able to admit it, was going to be sheer hell.

"How long did you live with the Zenatas?" Lorna asked, breaking into Nathan's gloomy thoughts.

"Three years."

Lorna was stunned. He had said for some time, but she had never dreamed that long.

Seeing the expression on her face, Nathan said, "I was in a weakened condition by the time we reached this camp, practically down to skin and bones after a year of slaving in the stone quarries. It took me several months to regain my strength. During that time I realized that I had an opportunity that few Americans, or even Europeans, had in this day and age. Not since the Crusades had a Christian come this far into the Sahara—at least not to return and tell about it. The Muslims guard North Africa jealously, keeping all others out. It's a country shrouded in mystery, and I had an opportunity to see it, to live in a culture so different from my own. The desire to see the world was one of the reasons I wanted to go to sea. I was young. There was no urgent business awaiting me at home. So I stayed."

"And you lived here, in this camp, for three years?"

"No. Had that been the case, I would have left much sooner. As I said, I wanted to see as much of North Africa as I could. The emir does a lot of traveling, on tribal affairs and on business, seeking the best contracts for the tribe's date harvest. I tagged along with him. I got to see North Africa from Morocco to the Nile in Egypt. In my Berber disguise I dined with sheiks, beys, and even a few pashas. They all thought I was his son."

Nathan chuckled, saying, "The emir did want to adopt me. But I knew I wasn't going to stay in Africa. I told him I preferred we just remain close friends. Besides, I don't know why he wanted another son. He already had three."

Lorna knew why the emir wanted Nathan for a son. Because he was special, a cut above other men.

"So you just remained good friends?"

"Yes. There's nothing Ali wouldn't do for me. I saved his life during an Arab attack on this camp. The way I figured it, we were even. But not Ali. A Muslim never forgets an insult or a favor. When I decided I was ready to leave, he accompanied me all the way to the coast and paid my passage back to America. He insisted upon accompanying me to the Tuareg camp, took on the burden of the groom's feasts, just as if he were my father, and you've seen the tent he had set up for us. Sometimes I feel guilty, giving so little in return, but I know I don't dare refuse his generosity. That would be the greatest insult I could offer him."

"Perhaps he doesn't feel you're giving so little in return. The gift of true friendship can hardly be taken lightly."

Nathan shot Lorna a sharp look, surprised at her astute observation. "Maybe you're right. And if our positions were reversed, I'd do the same for him."

At that time they were passing a herd of horses grazing on the grass that grew around one of the pools. Taking note of them, Lorna asked, "When are you going to start teaching me to ride?"

"How about tomorrow? But we'll have to ~~se would~~ up early, before it gets too hot. Just after ~~up that early?~~ be ideal. Do you think you can g~~et up~~

Was he referring to how late she had slept that

day? Lorna wondered. "I can if my husband doesn't keep me up all night," she replied saucily.

Nathan chuckled and drew her closer, hugging her and replying, "I'm afraid your husband can't make any promises."

Nathan woke her with a kiss the next morning. As he rolled from the bed, Lorna saw that he had already lighted brass lamps. "But the sun isn't even up," she objected sleepily.

"It will be by the time we get dressed and pick up our horses."

Lorna wished she had kept her mouth shut. She didn't want to go horseback riding this morning. All she wanted to do was go back to sleep. While Nathan hadn't kept her up all night, he had at least half of it, and she sorely needed some rest.

Sitting up, she glanced around for her gown. Spying it lying halfway across the tent, she picked up Nathan's caftan from the foot of the bed, climbed from the bed, and slipped it on, the hem dragging a good foot on the carpet as she walked to her chest. Then, seeing Nathan walking back from his chest with his razor, shaving mug, and a small mirror in his hands, she stumbled on the hem. Why, he was stark naked!

She watched, both shocked at his total lack of modesty and awed by the sight he presented as he hung his mirror from a tent pole. Her eyes drifted over the rippling muscles in his back, his lean hips and taut buttocks, the long legs with their sprinkling of screen hair. Then, as he turned and walked to the a little ashamed for staring at him so brazenly.

She walked to her chest and bent, lifting the lid. At that moment Nathan came from around the screen, carrying a basin of water, this time presenting his naked front to her. Lorna was so stunned, for she had assumed he had gone behind the screen to dress, that she dropped the lid on her finger. Muttering a very unladylike oath beneath her breath, she sucked the injured digit, then looked up to see Nathan lathering his face before the mirror, the powerful muscles on his back flexing and relaxing. She remembered only too well the feel of those muscles under her hands the night before, and her mouth turned dry.

She tore her eyes away and opened the lid to her chest. But her eyes kept drifting back to Nathan. She wondered when he had shaved the day before. It must have been before he had awakened her. Did he always shave naked? Parade around like that with nothing on?

Forcing her attention back to the task at hand, she rummaged through the trunk until she found the ensemble she wanted and pulled it out. Walking across the tent to the screen, her eyes once again strayed to her husband's magnificent physique. This time she tripped over one of her slippers. For Lorna it was the last straw. "For heaven's sake!" she snapped. "Why don't you put on some clothes?"

Nathan turned, once again presenting his male body in all its splendid glory. "Why? Does my nakedness offend you?"

It was all Lorna could do to force herself to look at his face. "No . . . no, it doesn't offend me," she admitted in all honesty. "It just distracts me."

"Distracts you from what?"

"From what I'm doing!"

Nathan chuckled, picked up his razor ⟶ the small table where he had laid it, and ⟶ back to the mirror.

So he thinks it's amusing that I can't keep my

eyes off him, Lorna thought. Well, two can play at that game!

Lorna stripped off the caftan and walked right behind where Nathan was standing, holding up the entarie she had chosen as if trying to decide to wear it or not. It was impossible for Nathan not to see her in the mirror as she presented him a tantalizing view of her profile, her full breasts jutting out proudly. The razor slipped and he nicked his jaw. Swearing under his breath, he schooled himself to pay attention to what he was doing, but when Lorna started brushing her hair, the long tresses flowing around her nakedness like a shimmering waterfall, he nicked himself again.

Little vixen, he thought. I know what's she doing. All I have to do is ignore her.

He was just passing his razor up his Adam's apple when Lorna again came into view. Facing him fully, she stretched and pretended a yawn, the sensuous movement taking his breath away as he sliced a good inch of skin from his neck.

Holding his bleeding wound, Nathan whirled, threw his razor down in the basin so hard it clattered, and snapped, "All right! You've made your point!" He walked rapidly to his pantaloons and jerked them on, saying, "Now put some clothes on before I slit my goddamned throat!"

Lorna laughed softly at her little victory, picked up her clothes, and made a beeline for the screen.

When she stepped back out, Nathan was fully dressed in his gown and headdress. She looked at the ever on his chin and throat and asked, "Have you "Why ered a beard?"

And cover han ld you prefer me in one?" "No, I don't think so."

"Good. Because I would have to disappoint you. I tried growing a beard when I was living in Africa before. The damned thing itched like crazy. I could hardly wait to shave it off."

Lorna bent to pick up her caftan where she had left it on the bed. "Why don't you wear one of your waistcoats?" Nathan asked. "It would be less bulky for you, particularly riding a horse."

"What waistcoats?"

"The waistcoats in your chest. I distinctly remember buying at least three."

"You bought my clothes?" Lorna asked in surprise.

"Yes. Who did you think bought them?"

"Lord Hampton."

"No, Lorna. They only sent the ransom money for Lady Hampton. No one thought about what the poor woman was supposed to wear."

As Nathan walked to her chest, Lorna remembered how shocked she had been when she first saw the beautiful clothes. Nathan had spent that small fortune on them, not Lord Hampton. She wondered why. Had he assumed Lady Hampton would expect such lavish clothing, that he would later be reimbursed? Then, seeing Nathan throwing her clothes everywhere, she rushed forward, saying, "No, let me look! You'll get everything wrinkled."

But before she reached him Nathan pulled out a wispy garment, saying, "Here's one."

Lorna could see where the black waistcoat embroidered all over with silver threads would be much cooler and less cumbersome than the caftans she had been wearing. Besides being made of a thin silk, the garment was sleeveless. She slipped it on and buttoned it up, saying, "I wish I had known about them earlier. All this time I've been running around in those hot caftans."

"I assumed you never wore them because you didn't care for them. How is it you didn't know they were in there?"

"Because I've never gotten a chance to go completely through that chest. It was taken away from me when I was captured by the Tuareg. Chedlya chose what I would wear after she gave it back to me, and since then I've just been taking out what's on the top."

It turned out that Lorna's ride consisted of Nathan's leading her horse around while she became accustomed to sitting in the saddle by herself. He gave her a few instructions on the use of the reins and mounting and dismounting. Promising her she would actually get to ride by herself the next day, the two returned to their tent about midmorning.

As soon as they had finished eating their breakfast, Lorna walked to her chest, saying, "Now I'm going to finally find out what all is in there."

"While you're taking them out, why don't you hang them up?" Nathan asked.

"On what?"

"On a thin rope strung from one tent pole to the other. That's the way the Zenatas do it. Why, the majority of them have probably never seen a trunk in their entire lifetime, much less wardrobes like we have."

"I've been wondering about that," Lorna said. "I can understand the nomad tribes not having furniture. It would be too difficult to carry about. But you said these Zenatas are sedentary. Why don't they have furniture like we do, or do all Muslims just have a fondness for sitting on the ground?"

"Where would they get the wood to make trunks?" Nathan asked. "Trees are almost nonexistent in all of North Africa, at least the kind that you can make furniture from. And you certainly can't make anything substantial out of a palm trunk. It's nothing but fiber."

"That was stupid of me. I should have thought of that."

"No, you were just thinking like a European or an American. You'd be surprised how many people back home have asked me why the Barbary States declare war by chopping down a country's flagpole. It sounds silly to them. Then when I explain the lack of tall trees in North Africa, and that the flagpole is a mast from one of the country's ships, they understand. Not only are the Muslims insulting their flag, but destroying something valuable and the pride and joy of their consul."

Wood and water, Lorna thought, two things that she had always taken for granted, and yet, so valuable in this desolate country. She stroked the wooden chest. She had always thought it lovely, but never realized its worth.

As she opened the lid and started pulling out garments, Nathan said, "I'll see if I can find some rope to hang them on."

After Nathan had hung the rope, Lorna decided to hang the garments as she went, rather than just pile them up. Seeing her go back and forth across the tent a few times, Nathan carried the chest to where the rope was and said, "Now, if you'll hand them up to me, I'll hang them for you."

Lorna was amazed as she dug farther down into the chest and pulled out garments she had never seen, stopping to admire them before she handed them to Nathan. She was even more surprised when she found several bars of scented soap and a vial of perfume that she hadn't known was in there. But when she reached the bottom and saw the bulky oilskin pouch, she was puzzled. "What's in this?" she asked holding it up, shocked by how heavy it felt.

Nathan looked down, an expression of disbelief coming over his face, then tossed the last garment she had handed him aside and knelt beside her. Taking the pouch from her, he looked inside, then said, "This is the gold I paid Chedlya for your dowry."

He pulled a piece of parchment from the pouch and unfolded it. To Lorna the Arabic writing looked more like decoration than words. "Can you read Arabic?" she asked.

"Enough to read this. She says she could not accept my gold. That she could not sell a friend, or even take it under the guise of a dowry. That she will always treasure the time you spent with her and wishes us much happiness."

Tears glittered in Lorna's eyes. Yes, Chedlya had been a friend, but the strangest friend Lorna had ever known. She could be so overbearing and domineering at times that Lorna had longed to hit her, and then at others, so kind. She was like a little queen, bossing everyone around, intimidating even her husband, whom she professed to love, and then behaving benevolently, as the mood suited her, but always in complete control of the situation. No, there would never be another Chedlya.

Shortly thereafter Nathan left the tent to ask the emir to lock the gold in his strongbox. When he returned about an hour later, Lorna noticed he was carrying a pair of leather boots. "Did you buy a new pair of boots?" she asked.

"No, these are for you. If you're going to be riding, you'll need something to keep your ankles from getting chafed and something more substantial than those slippers. See if they fit. I had to guess at the size."

It wasn't until Lorna had struggled into the boots made of soft cordovan leather that she realized the boots were much shorter than the boots the men wore in Europe, coming to her calf instead of the knee, and had almost no heel. She walked back and forth a few times, then smiled, saying, "They fit fine."

It was then that she noticed the leather pouches hanging from Nathan's neck. She stared at them, asking, "Where did you get those?"

"Ali insisted that now I was a Muslim, I needed to wear them," Nathan replied in disgust. "The red one contains a copy of the *fatihah*, the opening chapter of the Koran. Now maybe I can see that. But the other three he tried to foist off on me when I was here before. They're amulets."

"For what purpose?"

"One is for the evil eye and there's no telling what the other two are supposed to be protecting me from."

Lorna laughed, saying, "The evil eye? You can't be serious."

"All the Muslims believe in the evil eye, Arabs and Berbers alike. It goes all the way back to the ancient Carthaginians." He reached for the string of one of the pouches, saying, "Well, one thing's for sure. I don't have to wear them in here."

As Nathan tried to remove the pouches, they got all tangled up and he couldn't get them over his head. Lorna laughed at his struggles. "Fine wife you are," he grumbled. "I could hang myself while you just stand there and laugh."

Lorna walked forward and pushed his hands aside, saying, "Here, let me."

After Lorna had untangled the pouches and slipped them over Nathan's head, he caught her to him and kissed her long and deeply. When he raised his head, Lorna said breathlessly, "That was a trick. You could have gotten them off yourself."

She watched as Nathan's eyes darkened with desire. "Maybe, maybe not," he answered thickly, his fingers smoothing down the hair at her temple and then trailing down her jaw line and brushing across her lips.

He picked her up in his arms and carried her to the bed. Lorna's heart raced in anticipation, loving the feel of being held in his strong arms. She snuggled closer, burying her face in the warm crook of his neck, drinking in his heady male scent.

He placed her gently on the bed and then to her surprise stood and asked, "Do I have your permission to remove my clothes? I wouldn't want to distract you."

Lorna stared at him in dismay, then sputtered, "Oh, you—you—" Picking up a pillow, she threw it at him with all her might.

Nathan deflected the flying pillow with his arm, then laughing, he came down on her. Their tussle was brief but exciting before he subdued her with torrid kisses and tantalizing caresses. And later, much later, Lorna wondered at the many moods of lovemaking.

Chapter 14

On the last morning of Nathan and Lorna's "seven fig days," they walked through the settlement as the sun was just rising and sending golden shafts of light into an azure sky; the desert larks in the palm trees all around them greeted the new day with joyous trills and warbles. Saddling their horses, they mounted and rode out into the desert.

Clearing the trees at a canter, Nathan asked, "Do you think you're ready for a full gallop?"

Lorna felt a tingle of fear. "Do you?"

Nathan smiled reassuringly at her, answering, "Yes, I do." Then, giving his mount a nudge with his heel, he said, "Let's go!"

As Nathan's horse flew off at a full gallop, Lorna had no choice but to follow, the spirited mare beneath her anxious for a hard run. As the ground flew by beneath her, Lorna's heart pounded furiously in her breast as she hung onto the reins for dear life. And then, when the mare pulled up to Nathan's stallion, the wind billowing his robe and ruffling his dark hair, the excitement of the race caught Lorna. She urged her mount on, fear forgotten, glorying in the feel of the wind racing past her and tearing at her clothing, the tendrils of hair that had escaped her chignon flying wildly about her face. Over one rolling dune, then another, and another, they sped, the horses' hooves pounding on the ground and sending sprays of golden sand into the air.

When they finally came to a stop at the crest of a tall dune, their mounts lathered with sweat and muscles quivering from their exertions, Lorna laughed, saying, "Oh, that was exhilarating!"

Her sparkling laugh was a sensual caress to Nathan's ears, sending tingles through him. He looked across at her. With her face flushed with excitement, her exquisite eyes dancing, and her lips parted in laughter, he thought her the most beautiful and desirable creature he had ever seen. His passion rose, hot and urgent.

He flew from his saddle, caught Lorna's waist, and swung her down. Seeing her startled expression as he stood her on her feet and afraid she would object, he said in a roughened voice, "No! I want you. Here! Now!"

Lorna didn't object. The race had excited her, and the naked look of urgent desire in Nathan's smoldering eyes only raised that excitement to a feverish pitch. Their clothes flew everywhere as they stripped, and when they came together, both gasped as heated flesh met heated flesh.

He bore her to the sand with him, his chest hot against her heaving breasts, his naked loins a hard fire against hers, his mouth slashing across hers in a deep, demanding kiss. They needed no foreplay, no priming. He thrust into her like a lightning bolt, sending fiery sparks dancing up their spines and making both tremble as they were rocked with spasms of intense pleasure.

He took her like a storm, pounding at her as she pounded back, bodies straining, mouths clinging, hearts hammering as he carried her to a wild, primitive world of their own making, riding that white-hot crest of frenzied passion until they reached a violent climax of thousands of exploding stars, their cries of rapture ringing in the air around them.

They lay sprawled in the sand, dazed, drinking in deep draughts of air. Finally becoming aware of the glaring light and the sun beating down on them, Lorna's first rational thought was, My God! I'm a total wanton, making love stark naked in broad daylight in the hot sand.

There were times when her desire for Nathan irritated Lorna no end. It was as if she no longer had any control over any of her emotions, and Lorna had always prided herself on her self-possession. It was bad enough that Nathan could turn her into a mindless, spineless creature with no will of her own with just a look, but she was always afraid she would give herself away in the throes of passion and foolishly tell him how much she loved him, and if she did that, she would be throwing away the last vestiges of her pride. She was going to have to learn to practice more *ismak*, the control of her fierce passion.

When Nathan lifted her to her feet, Lorna was even more irritated to find herself covered with sand, the gritty material clinging to her damp body with a fierce tenacity. She tried to brush it away with quick, agitated strokes, saying, "Now look what we've done! We've got sand all over us."

Nathan grinned and answered, "That's what happens when you play in a sandbox."

"Well, I wish we hadn't done it! Now I'm going to have to go back and bathe again."

Having no idea of what was really irritating Lorna, Nathan frowned, feeling a little hurt. He had thought their spontaneous, uninhibited lovemaking terribly exciting and, from the way she had responded, assumed Lorna had too. Well, I guess the honeymoon is over, he thought cynically. Tight-lipped, he handed Lorna her clothing.

As they rode back to the camp, both were silent, Nathan nursing his hurt and thinking that he'd been a fool to think their passion could hold their marriage together until they got to know one another better and Lorna came to love him. Since he had admitted to his feelings for her, wanting her to return the emotion had become paramount to him. He had never known that the soul could hunger for love, leave him aching as much, or more so, as his body did for physical release. It was as if in giving of his love so totally and irrevocably, he felt drained and incomplete without something of a like intensity to fill the void. And now it seemed they didn't even have a mutual passion to bind them, to soothe that deep ache if not fill that strange emptiness. Apparently the newness and excitement of physical love had already worn off for Lorna.

Lorna was very aware of Nathan's silence and knew she had been unnecessarily sharp with him. She longed to apologize but didn't quite know what explanation to give him, and she certainly couldn't tell him the truth, that trying to hide her deep feelings for him was beginning to wear on her nerves. The ride back to the camp was a misery for her.

As soon as they got back to their tent, Lorna

rushed behind the screen to bathe and change clothes. When she emerged, Nathan was nowhere in sight. Well, she really couldn't blame him for leaving, she thought, after the waspish way she had behaved. Feeling even more wretched, she sat down on their pallet, then looked up in surprise when Nathan walked back into the tent, followed by four blue-veiled Tuareg carrying items they placed on the carpet.

As the Tuareg walked out, Lorna asked in confusion, "What are they doing here, and why are they putting those things in our tent?"

"They're delivering our wedding gifts," Nathan answered tightly, still nursing his hurt.

"What wedding gifts?"

"When the hawk-faced Arab insisted upon staying for the wedding to make sure we actually went through with it, Chedlya turned the tables on him and invited all the men who had come to the auction to our wedding. That meant they had to give gifts."

The Tuareg walked in with another armful of gifts and silently placed them on the rug. "You didn't tell me anything about that."

"I forgot!" Nathan answered sharply. "Dammit, you can't expect me to remember everything."

"Well, you don't have to get so testy about it!"

"I'm not being any more testy than you were earlier."

Lorna realized his feelings had been hurt. She had attacked him unjustly. It wasn't his fault that she couldn't control her feelings for him. "I wasn't being testy, I was—"

Before Lorna could even offer an explanation of any kind, Nathan cut across her words, saying, "The hell you weren't! You were mad because I made love to you and you weren't in the mood. And you've been snapping at me ever since."

His refusal to listen to her explanation angered Lorna. Well, if he's going to be that unreasonable, I won't even bother to apologize! she thought hotly.

Lorna watched in angry silence as the Tuareg carried in silver and gold platters and candlesticks, jeweled incense burners, statuettes made of the finest ivory, bolts of the richest brocades and silks, a tea service ablaze with jewels. And still, the gifts kept coming.

Then, when the last gift had been set down and the Tuareg had left the tent, Lorna was stunned and said, "We can't accept these gifts. There must be a fortune here. Why, we don't even know those men. Wedding gifts are supposed to come from friends."

"Well, how do you think I feel?" Nathan retorted. "Those men were bidding against me for you. I like it even less. But I thought they'd send doodads, just some little something to fulfill their obligation."

"We'll just send them back," Lorna said in a decisive voice that grated on Nathan's already taut nerves.

"Like hell we will! You never return a gift to a Muslim. That's an insult.

"Then we'll give them away."

"To who?"

"To the emir. You said you felt guilty because he's done so much for you."

"He'd never accept our wedding gifts."

"Well, what are we going to do with them?" Lorna snapped.

"Goddammit, I don't know!" Nathan threw back. "Stop yelling at me!"

"I will when you stop yelling at me!"

The two glared at one another, then realizing

that she was the one who had started it, Lorna said, "I'm sorry. I seem to be a little irritable today." Searching her mind for a plausible excuse, she remembered something and said, "I'm afraid I'm always that way before my monthly."

Is that what's wrong with her? Nathan thought, feeling an immense wave of relief washing over him. And he had to admit that he had been a little overpowering out there in the desert, driven by an intense need to love her right then and there. "Then why didn't you tell me earlier that was what was wrong? I would have understood. After all, I have a mother and two sisters. I'm not ignorant about women and their unstable emotions at that time of the month. I would have understood."

"I didn't even realize it until now myself," Lorna answered.

Knowing she was lying, Lorna couldn't look him in the eye, particularly after she had promised herself she wouldn't lie to him again. True, her monthly was just a few days away, but she had never been one of those women to get shrewish or weepy before her period. Until she met Nathan, she had always had her emotions well in hand—which was what was so unsettling—and his being so understanding only made her feel more guilty. She turned her attention to the wedding gifts lying all around her. Then a golden statuette caught her eye. She rose from the pallet, walked to it, and picked it up. It was a camel with a man on its back, and Lorna knew the man had to be a Tuareg because his face was wrapped. Suddenly she knew who had sent the statuette. "This came from Chedlya."

"Why do you think that?"

"Because only Chedlya would send a statuette of a camel for a wedding gift."

Nathan walked over and removed the card that hung from it, read it, then answered, "Yes, it did come from her."

Lorna ran her hands over the statuette, amazed at how the sculptor had managed to get every little detail in, down to each minute fold in the Tuareg's turban. And the sculptor had caught what Lorna had never been able to see before, the graceful curve of the camel's neck, the long slender legs, the proud tilt of the animal's head. Why, it was beautiful! Tears shimmered in Lorna's eyes as she hugged the statuette to her breast. With this she'd never forget Chedlya or her time with the Tuareg, just as Chedlya had intended. "I want to keep this."

"Yes, and there must be a gift from Ali here too. I want to keep that."

They searched through the gifts until they found the gold tea service from the emir, eloquent in its simplicity and making the jewel-studded items look gaudy and ostentatious. They also found a pair of silver candlesticks, a set of delicate ivory cups and saucers trimmed in gold, and a beautiful Oriental vase from the emir's three sons.

After they had set aside the gifts that they wanted to keep, Lorna said, "Well, that puts us right back where we started. What are we going to do with the rest of it?"

"I think I'll go talk to Ali. Maybe he'll have a suggestion."

After Nathan left, Lorna tiptoed through the gifts and plopped down on the middle of the bed, since it was the only place that wasn't cluttered with gifts. "Damn you, Chedlya," she muttered. "You went and got us into another mess."

As soon as the words were out, Lorna regretted them. She knew Chedlya had meant well. And she

certainly couldn't call her marriage a mess. So far it
had been absolutely wonderful, except for their spat
this morning, and that had been all her fault. But she
had never realized how hard it was going to be, being
married to Nathan and free to love him physically.
And not being able to reveal her love for him was
even harder than trying to play the part of Lady
Hampton. If only she knew how he really felt about
their marriage. Was he just trying to make the best of
a bad situation? The thought depressed her.

It was some time before Nathan came back, and
as soon as he walked into the tent, Lorna asked anxiously, "Did Ali have any suggestions?"

Nathan picked his way through the maze of gifts
on the carpeting and sat down on the pallet beside
her before he answered. "He did better than that. He
figured out a solution. He reminded me that as a Muslim I'm supposed to contribute a tithe of ten percent
of my income to the poor each year. He said he'd sell
the gifts on his trips across Africa—discreetly, so that
the givers will never know—and see that the money
went to the poor in my name. That should take care of
my *zakat* for my entire lifetime."

Lorna was both relieved and touched by the
emir's thoughtful solution to their problem. She wondered what Chedlya would think if she knew what
she and Nathan were doing with the wedding gifts
she had tricked the Arabs into giving them. Undoubtedly, with her strong business sense that had made
her so wealthy, she'd be shocked. No, Lorna amended
with a smile, she'd be furious. Then, remembering
Chedlya's acts of kindness, she wondered.

Nathan and Lorna left the Zenata camp early the
next morning, accompanied by the emir and a force
of a dozen armed Zenatas. As they crested a tall dune,

Lorna looked back over her shoulder for a last glimpse at the place she had spent her honeymoon and the first wonderful week of her marriage, a sadness filling her at knowing she would never see it again.

Over the next three weeks the group made good time on their trip back to the coast, despite the fact that three of the Zenatas were leading pack horses behind them. Nathan was pleased with the way Lorna kept up with the grueling pace and very proud when several of the Zenatas made comments on how well she handled her mount. Coming from men who prided themselves on their horsemanship and rode as if they had been born in the saddle, it was quite a compliment.

A few days later Lorna knew they had entered the Maghrib, that narrow area of land that bordered the Mediterranean all along the North African coast, by the change in the terrain. Instead of the infinite vista of desert, there were rocky hills interspersed with flat stretches of sand.

"Where are we?" she asked Nathan, riding beside her.

"About fifty miles southwest of the city of Tripoli."

"Tripoli? I thought we were going to Tunis."

"We are. We'll swing west tomorrow."

That afternoon they made their camp in a narrow valley between a few scattered rocky hills. Nathan was just finished setting up their tent when one of the sentries Ali had posted on the crest of a hill above them rode his horse down the steep incline at breakneck speed, yelling in his strange Zenata dialect.

"What's he saying?" Lorna asked Nathan in alarm.

"Something about an army coming," Nathan answered with a deep frown. "Wait here. I'll find out what's going on."

Nathan walked rapidly to where the sentry was reporting to the emir, the man gesturing wildly toward the top of the hill he had just descended. Ali turned to Nathan, saying, "He tells me there is an army coming on the plain beyond the hills."

"The Tripolitan Army?"

"No."

"Janissaries?"

"No, he says they are wearing no uniforms, that they are a mixture of Arabs, Moors, and Greeks. But he knows they are an army because there are so many of them and they are well armed. Some are on horseback, some on foot, but they are marching four abreast, as armies do."

"How many?"

"Many hundreds."

"From which direction are they coming?"

"They are coming from the southeast."

To Nathan it didn't make sense. What in the hell was an army of Arabs, Moors, and Greeks doing out here in the middle of nowhere and coming out of the Sahara from the southeast? The only thing in that direction was Egypt. "Let me have a look."

The Zenata stepped back and offered Nathan the reins to his horse. As Nathan swung onto the saddle, Ali said, "Wait. I will go with you."

The emir hurriedly walked to where the horses had already been corraled in a rope enclosure, slipped a bridle over one of the animal's heads, and mounted bareback. Then he and Nathan galloped up the hill, leaving a flurry of dust in their wake. When they came to the crest of the hill, they reined in and looked down on the plain. Just as the sentry had said, there was a motley assortment of men marching toward them. Nathan quickly assessed the force to be around five hundred strong.

He looked at the head of the column and then took a second, closer look, straining his eyes. A man in European dress rode a magnificent white horse, followed by nine men dressed in uniforms behind him. It was the colorful uniforms of seven of those men that caught Nathan's attention. He'd know them anywhere. "Well I'll be damned!" he muttered. "Those are United States marines."

"Marines?" the emir asked, unfamiliar with the term.

"Yes. They're naval soldiers. Wait here, Ali. I'm going down there and find out what's going on."

"And get your head shot off?" the emir snapped.

"You've got a point there. When they see a stranger coming riding down on them out of the hills, they'll shoot first and ask questions later," Nathan answered, looking about him. Spying a stick on the ground, he dismounted, whipped off his white headdress, and tied it around the stick, using his leather headband to secure it. He swung back into the saddle, held the stick over his head, and kneed his horse, saying over his shoulder as he galloped off, "They'll hold their fire when they see this."

But as Nathan came racing down the hill, he had reason to doubt his own words. Seeing him, the ranks broke and several Arabs raised their rifles, pointing them at him, while others yelled in alarm, gestured wildly, and ran helter-skelter, the entire army becoming a mass of milling, excited men. When a bullet flew past him, Nathan cursed under his breath and lay forward with his head next to his mount's neck, riding like hell for the marines at the front of the column. A second bullet whizzed by before the man at the head of the army whirled his white steed around and rode down the ranks, yelling in Arabic, "Cease fire! Cease fire!"

Nathan rode up to the man, both horses rearing and pawing the air as the two men reined in hard. Then, as Nathan's horse came down, he recognized the middle-aged American and said, "Eaton? What in hell are you doing out here in the middle of the desert?"

William Eaton quickly recovered from his own surprise and said dryly, "I might ask you the same thing, Captain Sloan."

As the marines rushed forward with their muskets held before them, Eaton called, "It's all right, men! This man is a fellow American. See if you can calm those Arabs down."

The marines shot Nathan a curious look before they turned and ran back to the broken ranks of Arabs to carry out Eaton's instructions. Nathan glanced back at the milling, ragtag army, then asked, "Who in hell are those men?"

"Mercenaries that I've hired to help us capture Derna and then march on Tripoli to free the American prisoners taken from the *Philadelphia*. I'm acting under orders from Secretary Madison to get together a land expedition for that purpose, since the navy could only spare me an officer, a midshipman, and those seven marines."

"Then the war is still going on?" Nathan asked in surprise.

"Yes. Where have you been?"

"For the past seven months, in the desert."

"Then you've gone back to living with the Zenatas?" Eaton asked.

"No. I went to them to ask for help in locating a young woman who had been captured by the Barbary pirates and sold into slavery. Unfortunately I didn't find the woman I was looking for, but I did find another Englishwoman who was captured from a ship much earlier. She is now my wife. We're on our way back to Tunis with a Zenata escort that's camped beyond that hill I rode down from."

Eaton knew there was more to the story than Nathan had told him. He also knew by the closed expression on Nathan's face that that was all he would ever be told of the matter. Eaton glanced up at the hill where Ali was still waiting, peered closer, then asked, "Is that the emir with you?"

"Yes. Do you know Ali bein Ghaniya?"

"We've met. Once when he was in Tripoli on business while I was still consul there."

Nathan gazed back out at the army, then said, "And that ragtag bunch is what you're going to try to attack Tripoli with? A bunch of Arab and Greek mercenaries?"

"And a few wild Bedouin chieftains and some stray Austrian and Italian adventurers," Eaton added. "But it was the best I could do."

Nathan shook his head in disgust, then said, "Christ, They don't even recognize a white flag."

"They're undisciplined and excitable, particularly the Arabs. I've been trying to drill them into some discipline and order on the march from El Alamein, but they're hungry and thirsty and tired. We ran out of food some time ago. Without the camels to slaughter for meat we would have starved to death. That alone is enough to make any man with their temperament irascible, but to make matters even worse, they haven't been paid yet. Needless to say, they've been threatening mutiny all along. The only way I've managed to get them this far is with promises of sharing in the plunder of Derna when we take it."

"El Alamein?" Nathan asked in shocked disbelief. "You marched this army five hundred miles across the Sahara?"

"Yes. We left El Alamein a little under five weeks ago."

Nathan was amazed. It was an unheard-of feat. Why, not even the Romans, who were superior foot soldiers, could have managed such a grueling march across the desert for that distance and in that short a time. But something puzzled Nathan. "What in hell were you doing in Egypt? Couldn't the navy have landed you closer to your objective than that?"

"The navy didn't land us. I hired this army in Egypt because that's where I finally found Hamet Karamanli."

"Hamet? The pasha of Tripoli's older brother? He's with you?" Nathan asked in surprise.

"Yes." Eaton glanced over his shoulder at the men waiting impatiently, saying, "It's a long story. Too long to go into right now. Why don't you ride up the hill and ask Ali to join us? Then, as soon as we've made camp and set up my tent, I can tell you both over dinner."

Nathan remembered Eaton's telling them that the army had all but starved to death. He certainly didn't want to eat what little food they had left. "No, we'll go back to our camp and eat. They were preparing dinner when we left. We'll come back later tonight."

"If you like. And bring your wife with you. I would like to meet her."

Nathan nodded and rode back up the hill. As he and Ali rode back to the Zenata camp, Nathan told his friend everything he had learned.

The emir frowned, saying, "If Eaton thinks to put pressure on Yusef by holding his older brother captive, he is mistaken. The pasha fears Hamet. It is rumored he has tried to have him killed several times."

"No. I didn't get the impression that Hamet was a prisoner. It sounded to me like he came along of his own free will."

"Ah, I think I see. Your government intends to use Hamet as a figurehead to incite rebellion against Yusef."

"Do you think it will work?"

"There are many in Tripoli who hate Yusef and would welcome the opportunity to rebel against him. By rights, as the oldest son, Hamet should be the pasha, but as you know, Yusef overpowered him and seized the throne many years ago. But first Eaton will have to capture Derna and reinstate Hamet in the governor's palace there. Whether or not Eaton can do that remains to be seen."

While they were eating in their tent, Nathan told Lorna everything he had just finished telling Ali. She was full of questions.

"Who is Hamet?"

"The first of Ali Karamanli's sons and the natural successor to the Karamanli dynasty here in Tripoli. The present pasha, Yusef, was the youngest son and, with the help of some of the desert tribes, seized power while Hamet was out of the country. Yusef has always feared that Hamet would lead a counterrevolution and regain the throne. In fact, Yusef offered Hamet a magnificent bribe in hopes of preventing just that. Yusef offered Hamet half his kingdom in the form of governorship of Derna, the largest city in eastern Tripoli. Hamet was reluctant to accept, but since he had just been turned out of Tunisia, where he had sought refuge, he had no choice. It was that or

starve to death. The situation lasted only a year before
Hamet did attempt a revolution. Hamet was soundly
defeated by Yusef and barely escaped with his life."

"But why did Hamet revolt if his brother offered
him half the kingdom?" Lorna asked. "Half is better
than nothing."

"Hamet doesn't trust Yusef. He was afraid Yusef
only made the offer to get him in his clutches so he
could murder him, just as Yusef did another older
brother in order to claim the throne."

"Yusef killed his own brother?" Lorna asked in a
shocked voice.

"That's not at all unusual in this part of the world.
In fact, it's almost accepted protocol. With multiple
marriages there is always an excess of sons to fight
over the throne. It seems the only way to secure the
throne once and for all is to eliminate the other candi-
dates for it. One Turkish sultan, Mohammed the
Third, killed all nineteen of his brothers for that purpose."

Lorna was horrified. What a bloodthirsty lot these
Muslims were. But then, there had been a few European thrones bought with the price of one's own
family's blood, too. Cain and Abel had been only the
beginning.

"And who is this William Eaton?" she asked.

"He was the American consul at Tripoli for some
time and is considered an authority on North African
politics. Along with James Cathcart, another American who had been a prisoner in Algiers for ten years
and was secretary to the dey during his imprisonment, Eaton was instrumental in obtaining the king
of Naples' aid in this war. It was through the efforts of
these two men that the ports in Naples and Sicily
were opened to our navy and the use of Neapolitan
gunboats was secured."

Nathan glanced out of the tent opening, then said, "It's getting late. We'd better be going."

Lorna rose and said, "I want to change clothes first. These I have on are all dusty."

"Then wear the lavender and violet outfit. That's my favorite."

Lorna wrinkled her nose in distaste. She had wanted to give the ex-consul a good impression of her for Nathan's sake. Now she'd go to meet a representative of his country looking like a wild gypsy.

After Lorna had dressed, she, Nathan, and the emir rode to Eaton's encampment. As they descended the hill that overlooked it, they could see the small campfires dotting the entire plain.

Spying two tents, one to the right and another to the left of the encampment, Ali said, "I wonder which is Eaton's tent."

"The smaller one, I'm sure," Nathan answered, veering his horse to the right. "The big one probably belongs to Hamet."

"Yes, of course. Naturally His Royal Highness would have the bigger tent," Ali replied, his voice heavy with sarcasm. Then, seeing the look on Lorna's face, he said, "Forgive me. I know that sounded hateful. But I am afraid I have no love for any of the royal house of Tripoli."

"Because they're Arabs?"

"Partly. But mainly because of what the Karamanlis have done to this country. When Hamet's father founded the dynasty, everyone in Tripoli was glad to throw off the Ottoman yoke, even the Berbers, for we resented the Turks' presence in our land even more than the hated Arabs. But the Karamanlis encouraged the pirates even more than the Turks before them. Under their rule this country has earned a shameful reputation among the other nations of the world. It is disgraceful enough that they consider us nothing more than a nation of thieves and extortionists, but once the lawless pirates were given a free rein, the Karamanlis could never control them. The corsairs prey on the people of Tripoli as much as on the Christian ships that sail the Mediterranean, and our crime rate has reached such an alarming height that many Tripolitans, Berber and Arab alike, are clamoring for the reinstatement of direct Ottoman rule."

A marine suddenly stepped out of the darkness, calling out sharply, "Halt!" and pointing his long musket at them. Then, seeing who they were, the young soldier said rather sheepishly, "Oh, it's you, Captain Sloan." He stepped aside, saying, "You may proceed, sir. General Eaton is expecting you."

As the three left the young marine behind, the emir said to Nathan, "I never realized Eaton was a general."

"He isn't as far as I know," Nathan answered. "It's true Eaton served in the army many years ago and fought in the Indian Wars, but the highest rank he attained was captain. The last I heard, when he returned to the Mediterranean last spring, he had the title of naval agent." Nathan paused thoughtfully for a moment, then said, "I suspect general is a title he conferred upon himself."

"To impress the mercenaries he's hired?" Lorna asked.

"Or anyone else he can. He's a man who tends to embroider his self-importance."

As they rode up to Eaton's headquarters, the light of the flaming torches that had been stuck into the sand before it sent eerie shadows dancing over the tent and the four marine sentries who were pacing all around it. Reining in, Nathan and Ali dismounted as a young naval officer emerged from the tent and walked to them.

"Captain Sloan?" the officer asked.

"Yes," Nathan replied.

"I'm Lieutenant O'Bannon, sir. I'll take care of your horses. General Eaton is waiting inside."

"Thank you, Lieutenant," Nathan answered, handing the officer his reins.

Nathan walked to where Lorna was still mounted just outside the circle of light cast by the torches and helped her dismount. Leading her toward the tent and into the light, Lorna was very aware of the sentries suddenly coming to a halt and gawking at her. Even the naval officer was staring. She flushed in embarrassment, thinking they were gaping at her outrageously bright clothing, having no idea of how beautiful she looked. But Nathan knew what the Americans were staring at, and his chest swelled with pride.

When they stepped into the tent, William Eaton walked forward with a broad smile on his face. His hand was extended to Nathan, but his eyes were locked on Lorna, the "general" being just as surprised at having this lovely vision suddenly thrown into his midst as the Americans outside the tent.

Nathan gave Eaton a perfunctory handshake, then said, "May I present my wife, Lorna."

"I'm pleased to meet you, Mrs. Sloan," Eaton said with a small bow, his look obviously admiring.

Lorna smiled nervously and replied, "My pleasure, I'm sure."

"You remember Ali bein Ghaniya, don't you, Eaton?"

Eaton turned to the emir, saying, "Yes, we met many years ago." He salaamed and said, "It's a pleasure to see you again, Your Eminence."

Ali returned the Arabic greeting and replied, "And you, too, Mr. Eaton."

Lorna noticed that just the slightest frown came over the "general's" face at the term, "mister," but the ex-consul didn't correct the emir. Instead he said, "Please be seated, gentlemen," then walked to the tent opening and said to another, even younger, naval officer standing at attention there, "Peck, see if you can find something for Mrs. Sloan to sit on."

Out of force of habit Lorna was already in the process of sinking to the floor to sit on the carpet along with Nathan and the emir. She bolted upright, flushing in embarrassment, thinking that she didn't even know how to behave in polite company anymore.

While she waited for the midshipman to bring her something to sit on and the three men passed the time with desultory conversation, Lorna studied the ex-consul, finding the middle-aged man very ordinary looking with his medium height, slight pot belly, and thinning hair. It was the American's self-possession that caught her attention, giving her the impression that he was a very determined man.

Lorna's scrutiny of the ex-consul was interrupted as the midshipman returned with a small barrel of gunpowder, placed it on the rug beside Nathan, and said to Lorna with an beet-red face, "Sorry, ma'am, but this was all I could find."

"Thank you. This will do nicely," Lorna replied graciously, sitting on the small barrel.

As Eaton sat on the rug with Ali and Nathan, Lorna felt very awkward perched up on the barrel, a little surprised to find she actually missed sitting on the ground with the others. Goodness, I have become Muslimized, she thought.

"Now, to answer your earlier questions, Captain

Sloan," Eaton began in a businesslike tone of voice, "for some time James Cathcart and I have been trying to convince the government to land an army in Tripoli. The navy needs the help of a military force to make its presence felt. However, due to the lack of ships to transport men and horses over such a long distance and the danger of disease on such a long voyage, Secretary Madison opted to hire a mercenary army already in the Mediterranean instead. When the king of Naples balked at hiring out part of his army, I returned to the United States and got Madison's permission to seek out Hamet and hire mercenaries on the scene, with the hopes of starting a revolution in Tripoli along with taking Derna and freeing the American prisoners in Tripoli. But when I returned to the Mediterranean last spring, Hamet had disappeared. I finally heard a rumor that he had fled to Egypt after his aborted revolution, but when I reached Alexandria, I found Egypt in complete turmoil. The Turks were trying to retake the country from the Mamelukes, and the whole country was in chaos. With the aid of the British diplomatic corps, I finally succeeded in finding Hamet. He was with the Mameluke army far in the interior."

"Well, I guess that answers my question on what you were doing in Egypt," Nathan remarked.

Eaton let out a long sigh, then said, "Yes, but it turned out finding Hamet was the easy part. I had a devil of a time convincing him that the United States was going to support him if he agreed to start another revolution. He was afraid the whole scheme was another plan by his brother to lure him back into the country so he could murder him, that the Americans would turn him over to Yusef. By the time I found him and finally persuaded him, I had very little money left. Most of it was spent bribing Turkish officials. The rest I spent on weapons and ammunition. That's why I had to hire this army with promises of a share in the plunder of Derna. But even that hasn't kept them from threatening mutiny. To be honest with you, I'm sure I would have been murdered by now if it hadn't been for these marines acting as my bodyguard."

"And how long do you think seven marines can hold five hundred surly, half-starved mercenaries at bay?" Nathan asked in a hard voice. "Christ, Eaton! You've still got the hardest part ahead of you, the taking of Derna."

"I know, and for that reason I thank God that Bomba is just a two-day march from here. That's where Captain Hull and the *Argus* will meet us with supplies and money. Once fed and paid, those mercenaries should be much more manageable."

"Hull? Isaac Hull?"

"Yes, Captain Hull was detailed to help me find Hamet and assist in any land campaign that might follow. Do you know him?

"Yes, I do. As a matter of fact, he's a good friend."

Eaton nodded his head, saying, "Good man, Hull. Steady as a rock and reliable. You have no idea how relieved I was when Commodore Preble assigned him to me and not one of those glory seekers of his. However, I will have to admit Preble did an admirable job of shaping up those young tigers he had in his command."

"Had?" Nathan asked in an alarmed voice. "What happened to Preble? He didn't get killed, did he?"

"No, nothing that drastic. Commodore Samuel Barron was sent to relieve Preble last fall. Preble could have stayed on, but as a subordinate commander, since Barron outranked him. Preble refused to accept that position and went back to the United States."

"Barron?" Nathan asked in a half-shocked, half-angry voice. "The navy sent him to replace a commander of Preble's caliber? Why, Barron is—"

"Yes, I know. Mentally unstable. Nor is he the fighter Preble was. All he has done since his arrival is blockade Tripoli. He hasn't bombarded the port once. He thinks he can starve the Tripolitans into surrendering. My God, Captain Sloan, that could take years! That's why the success of this expedition is of the utmost importance. We've got to pressure Yusef into surrendering."

Nathan was in agreement. Something had to be done. The war had dragged on now for almost four years.

Eaton leaned forward, saying, "Captain, I know you're just as anxious to see those poor prisoners freed and this war come to an end as I am. If anyone can appreciate the hell those men are going through, it's you. Why, six have already died. For that reason I hope you will join my expedition."

"Join your expedition?" Nathan asked in surprise.

"Yes, as a liaison adviser of sorts. Of course, if you want to fight, we'd be more than glad to have you. You see, I'm the only officer in this expedition who speaks Arabic. If something were to happen to me, the entire campaign would fall flat on its face. Lieutenant O'Bannon would take over command, but he'd be totally incapable of communicating with the mercenaries, to say nothing of understanding the way they think. Not only do you speak Arabic and understand them, but you have an advantage over even me. As an experienced merchant captain in the Mediterranean, you speak the lingua franca. You could communicate with the Greeks. And those Greeks are going to be my best fighters, providing I can get them to understand what I want from them."

Lorna had been listening with avid interest to everything Eaton was saying. "What's lingua franca?" she asked, breaking into the conversation, her curiosity getting the best of her.

"It's a mixture of all of the languages spoken around the Mediterranean that the sailors use to communicate with one another," Nathan explained. "A Turk would use it when speaking to a Greek, a Greek to an Italian, an Italian to a Spaniard. There is just enough of the other's language there to be understood."

"Yes, and it's always been a mystery to me," Eaton admitted, directing his words to Lorna. "I speak three foreign languages, but I've never been able to get the hang of lingua franca." He turned his attention back to Nathan, his eyes filled with anticipation as he said, "Well, what do you say, Captain? Will you join me?"

Nathan had always wanted to get into the war, but had not wanted to give up his fierce independence. With what Eaton was suggesting, he could help and yet be his own man, taking orders from no one. An excitement filled him. Then he remembered Lorna and answered, "No, I'm afraid I'll have to decline. My chief concern is getting my wife out of North Africa."

A calculating look came into Eaton's eyes as he said, "Perhaps you'll reconsider when I tell you who is in command at Derna." He leaned forward to give emphasis to his words, saying, "Mustafa Khaldun."

Nathan sucked in his breath sharply, his eyes suddenly burning with interest. "Khaldun?" he asked in surprise. "Where in the hell has that bastard been anyway?"

"Istanbul, but he returned to North Africa a year ago and now commands the Janissaries and Tripolitans at Derna. Just think, Captain Sloan, your old enemy has finally come within your reach. This is not only an opportunity to get your licks in at the Tripolitans and help your country win this war, but a chance to settle a more personal score."

Nathan did want revenge on the Janissary captain, more than anything in the world, not just for himself, but for his shipmates who had died in that stinking hellhole under Khaldun's cruel treatment. His hate boiled up in him and flared in his eyes.

No one had to tell Lorna who Khaldun was. She knew by the murderous look that came into Nathan's eyes that he was the Janissary captain who had beaten him and tortured him with taunts that Nathan would never escape him. She watched as the burning, intense anticipation on Nathan's face was replaced with an inscrutable expression and gasped in disbelief when he said in a steely voice, "No, Eaton. I still have to decline."

Eaton's profound disappointment was obvious to all. He managed a weak smile and answered, "I understand, Captain. Naturally the safety of your wife is your primary concern."

Lorna knew Nathan desperately wanted to join the expedition, and she was determined that she wouldn't let him miss out on getting his long-awaited revenge because of her, even though deep down she feared for *his* safety. Briefly she wondered why he was taking his marriage vows so seriously. He had only married her to save her from slavery. But she would give him no further reason to regret their union. It was enough that he had been forced to marry her. She would not be an encumbrance to him in any way.

She opened her mouth to object, then, realizing this was not the time or the place, held her tongue.

Chapter 15

It was a good half hour before Nathan, Lorna, and the emir left Eaton's tent that night. For Lorna the time passed like an eternity as she became more and more irritated at the ex-consul while he expounded on North African politics. She didn't give a fig about politics, North African or any other. She was anxious to confront Nathan about his decision.

As soon as they topped the hill that separated the two encampments and were out of the hearing of the marine pickets, Lorna turned to Nathan, riding beside her, and said in a firm voice, "I want you to join that expedition."

Nathan reined in, a fleeting expression of surprise crossing his face. He had thought Lorna would be glad he wasn't going to join. Women were notorious for not wanting their husbands to go to war. But those wives cared for their husbands, he reminded himself brutally. Apparently Lorna wasn't that troubled about his safety. Once again he felt hurt at her lack of feelings, but what she was suggesting was out of the question. While she might not be particularly concerned about him, getting her safely out of North Africa and to America was his chief priority. "No. I'm *not* joining," he answered in an equally firm voice. "You heard what I told Eaton."

Lorna whirled her horse and faced Nathan, blocking the emir's path behind her. "Yes, I heard what you said, but I also know how badly you want to go on that expedition." Seeing Nathan open his mouth, she silenced him, saying quickly, "No! Don't try to deny it. I saw the look on your face when Eaton mentioned the Janissary captain."

"All right. So I would have liked to join," Nathan admitted. "But that doesn't change anything."

"It does to me!" Lorna snapped. "I will *not* be the cause of your missing this opportunity. You're joining!"

"Now you're the one who's being ridiculous. What about you? Am I supposed to leave you out here in the desert while I go gallivanting off to war? I surely can't expect Ali to take you to Tunis for me. You're *my* wife, *my* responsibility."

Responsibility or burden? Lorna wondered. The distressing thought made her even more determined. "You won't have to leave me out here, or have someone else take me to Tunis either. I'll go along with you. Many women accompany their husbands to war, particularly in Europe."

"For Christ's sake, don't you realize those men are marching on Derna?" Nathan asked in exasperation. "There'll be a full-fledged battle. It's too dangerous for you."

"I can stay behind at some village during the

fighting," Lorna argued, "just like the European camp followers do."

"And what if the campaign is unsuccessful?" Nathan threw back. "If Eaton's army loses that battle, they'll have to make a run across the desert for the Tunisian border, with the Tripolitan army snapping at their heels all the way. It would be a grueling march, too hard on you."

"Too hard on me?" Lorna gasped in disbelief. She remembered all the things she had gone through over the past eighteen months, and her anger rose. "How dare you say that to me!" she flared out, her eyes flashing. "Treat me like some delicate flower. Have you forgotten what I've gone through? Why, that forced march across the heart of the Sahara I made with the Tuareg would make anything that army out there could do look like a picnic! If I could survive that, I could survive anything."

"Well, you're not going to have to survive it because I'm not joining," Nathan replied in a tightly controlled voice.

"Why are you being so obstinate?" Lorna screamed in frustration.

"I'm not being obstinate," Nathan replied, trying very hard to retain his patience with her. "Has it ever occurred to you that I might get killed? Then how would you get to America?" His hurt over Lorna's apparent indifference to his safety made his next words sound more bitter than he meant. "Or have you forgotten that was your goal in the first place—to get to America?"

Lorna was shocked at his words. Surely he couldn't believe that she'd had an ulterior motive for marrying him? It wounded her that he might think her so self-serving, but even at the risk of making him think she was that calculating, she was determined that he would be free to do what he wanted. "If something should happen to you, I imagine I could find someone among all the Americans to help me, considering the way they were all staring at me."

No, Lorna would have no trouble finding a protector among the Americans, Nathan thought bitterly, feeling a powerful surge of raw jealousy. "Well, that won't be necessary," he answered in a terse voice, "because I'm *not* joining." Then, seeing Lorna about to object, his self-control broke and he thundered, "And that's final!"

Green and violet eyes met in a fierce clash of wills. For a long moment neither wavered. It was Lorna who finally broke the tense silence, saying in a hard, angry voice, "All right! But don't you *ever* blame me for missing your opportunity for revenge. You have only yourself to blame, for being so . . . so damned pig-headed!"

Furious, Lorna whirled her horse and galloped down the hill to the Zenata camp.

Nathan glared at her back. Then, becoming aware of the emir, he turned in his saddle and said, "I'm sorry you had to witness that, Ali."

The emir understood just enough English to follow the argument, but he had been more titillated than embarrassed—after he had recovered from his initial shock, that is. A Muslim woman never questioned her husband's decisions, much less raised her voice to him or called him names, and yet, the young Englishwoman had been magnificent in her anger, and he had found the confrontation between the two stimulating. "There is no need to apologize," he answered graciously, then, with a hint of fascination in his voice, said, "But tell me my friend. Are all your women so outspoken . . . so fiery?"

"No, it's just my misfortune that I got one who's unusually strong-willed," Nathan answered sourly.

The emir smiled, knowing the words were spoken more from irritation than conviction. "But you do want to join the expedition, don't you?"

"Hell, yes! But I can't drag my wife off to war with me, even if she is stronger than most women. It's too damned dangerous."

"And if she were out of danger, would you join?"

"If you're suggesting that you take her on to Tunis, the answer is no."

"I was thinking along other lines. You said Captain Hull was your friend. Would he not take her on his ship?"

"Yes, he'd take her. If he was going back to Syracuse after he supplied Eaton, he could drop her off at Malta. She'd be safe there until this thing is over. But you heard what Eaton said about Hull being assigned to support his land action. The *Argus* will probably take part in the battle for Derna."

"But the ship will be out at sea and out of danger. There are no cannons at Derna with a gun range that long. If it turns out Eaton's army is repulsed, your friend can deliver her to Malta."

"But what if Hull isn't waiting at Bomba?" Nathan countered. "Those plans were made months ago. He might be delayed, and you heard what Eaton said about the men threatening mutiny all the way. If that happens, Eaton will have an uprising on his hands that would make a battle look tame. They'd be out for blood, and Lorna would be in as much danger or more."

"We could travel along with the army as far as Bomba. It's only a few days' ride out of our way. If the ship isn't there when we arrive, we can leave. It will be Eaton they will seek revenge on, not us. And if they should entertain thoughts of attacking us, they will think twice. While the Americans might be helpless to punish them, the Arabs know the other Zenata tribes will not take such an insult lightly. They would pay for their mistake."

Nathan gazed off thoughtfully. The emir gave him a few minutes to consider, then said, "I know more than anyone how much you want revenge on Khaldun. That was all you babbled about those first few days after I found you in the desert. Your wife is correct. If you do not take this opportunity, you will regret it the rest of your life. It will become like a sore, festering inside you, for which there will be no cure."

He *could* take part in the expedition without endangering Lorna, Nathan realized, a tingle of excited anticipation running through him. "All right, Ali," he agreed. "We'll travel along with the army as far as Bomba. But if the *Argus* isn't there when we arrive, we're going to get the hell out of there!"

Lorna was still fuming when Nathan stepped into the tent awhile later. She shot him an angry look, walked to her trunk, yanked out the caftan that she used as her nightgown, slammed the lid down, and walked to the screen, her back rigid with fury.

Nathan couldn't understand her anger. What kind of husband would he be if he put his desire for revenge before her safety? And if anything should happen to her . . . The thought was so distressing that it sent a surge of fear running through him, stunning him, for Nathan was almost a total stranger to the crippling emotion. The only time he had known stark fear was when Lorna was captured by the Tuareg, and then, with supreme will, he suppressed the feeling, telling himself over and over that he would find her. God, if he had known how love for a woman could make a man feel so weak, so utterly helpless, he would never have let himself fall in love with her. Then he reminded himself that he *hadn't* allowed it. It had been something he'd had absolutely no control over, and it irked him. He was a man who prided himself on his strength, his total self-possession. Well, thank God he had kept his feelings to himself, particularly since he had learned that she wasn't all that concerned about his safety.

Lorna walked from behind the screen and gave Nathan another scathing look before she walked to their pallet. She was just about to sink down on it when Nathan announced, "I've decided to join the expedition."

Lorna whirled around, a surprised expression on her face, but before she could open her mouth, Nathan said in a firm voice, "On one condition. That Isaac Hull is at Bomba when we arrive there and agrees to take you on his ship."

Lorna was stunned. Was he sending her away? Would his friend deliver her to some safe port—and she'd never see Nathan again? Oh, why hadn't she kept her big mouth shut? She could have had weeks left with Nathan. And now her time of joy was coming to an abrupt end. And then a more terrifying thought came to her, as her underlying fear for him came rushing to the surface. My God, what had she done? She'd been so busy trying to assure herself that he would never have cause to blame her for not getting his revenge that she hadn't even been thinking clearly. He *could* get killed! And if that happened, she wouldn't want to live. "No!" she cried out with both fear and fierce determination. "I'm staying with you!"

"The hell you are! You're getting on that ship. Even if the *Argus* takes part in the battle for Derna, you'll be safe on it."

An immense wave of relief washed over Lorna. "Then, when the town is taken, I can join you?"

Nathan had really not considered past the battle. But if Derna was secure in American hands, why not? "Yes. But only until we march on Tripoli. Then you'll have to board the *Argus* again. I won't have you around during any of the fighting."

And how long will that be? Lorna wondered. But it didn't matter. She had bought herself some more precious time with Nathan.

Early the next morning Nathan visited Eaton and told him his plans and the conditions on which he would join him. When the army pulled out for Bomba an hour later, Lorna, Nathan, and the Zenatas were with them. The Zenatas kept a distance between themselves and the hated Arabs as the army marched across the rugged terrain, and at Nathan's insistence Lorna was placed in the middle of the Zenata column. Watching the weary, thirsty, half-starved mercenaries struggling along, Lorna thought it an unnecessary precaution. Obviously, the last thing on their minds was a woman.

They certainly don't look like any army I've ever seen, Lorna thought as she studied the mercenaries from where she rode. Besides not holding to their positions in the ranks, they wore no uniforms—the Arabs dressed in their long robes, some with turbans on their heads and others with the three-cornered kaffiyehs, while the Greeks wore the white kiltlike *fustanellas,* white hose, red, tasseled boots, full-sleeved shirts, embroidered vests, and tasseled caps. There were even a few full pantaloons of the Italians and Albanians and at least two or three red felt Turkish fezzes. But regardless of what they wore, their clothes were all grimy and in tatters. Even the ma-

rines' colorful uniforms were stained and wrinkled
from weeks of marching across the Sahara. Lorna had
never seen such a ragged army and fervently hoped
that they could fight better than they looked.

The army was weary, but not so exhausted as not
to be short-tempered. During the day several argu-
ments broke out, sometimes over something as unin-
tentional as accidentally stumbling into the next man,
and inevitably knives were drawn to settle the issue.
It seemed the Arabs had never heard of settling a
disagreement with their mouths, or even their fists.
At these times Eaton and his marines would have to
shove their way through the crush of cheering bystanders and break up the dispute with threats of
shooting both men if they didn't cease their fighting.
As always, when the Americans left the scene, the
Arabs, offenders and bystanders alike, followed them
with sullen eyes. Lorna realized that the Americans
were sitting on a powder keg of seething resentment
that could go off at any minute and she shuddered to
think what would happen to the brave little group if
the *Argus* didn't show up. Why, they'd be slaugh-
tered, cut to ribbons. She was thankful for Nathan's
decision not to join the expedition if the ship wasn't
waiting at Bomba. As another American, he would
share his countrymen's fate, and she refused even to
contemplate what her fate might be.

Toward evening Lorna noticed that one group
kept themselves separated from the rest of the army,
lagging behind at a good distance from the Arabs at
the end of the column. Curious, she asked Nathan
about them.

"They're Bedouins, desert Arabs. Like most of
the Berbers and Tuareg, they're nomadic. Bedouin
means 'people of the tent.' And like all desert tribes,
they're fiercely independent. That's why they keep

themselves apart from the others. As a whole, they're poor, mostly herdsmen. They don't plunder unless they think their territory is being trespassed. The only wealthy you'll find among them are their sheiks, who, unlike the Berber sheiks and emirs, don't share the wealth with the entire tribe."

Lorna turned her attention back to the Bedouins, noting that they all wore coarse-woven robes made from goat hair and that they were smaller in stature than the other Arabs, both testimony to their poverty and their hard life in the desert. And yet there was a certain nobility in their walk, in the way they held themselves, that bespoke their fierce independence. The Tuareg and the Zenatas had that same proud, sure carriage. As did Nathan. Did all men who valued their freedom above all else have this same characteristic? Being reminded of Nathan's fierce independence was not a soothing thought for Lorna. It only served to arouse her own insecurities about her place in his life. If only she knew why he had come after her. If only she had the courage to ask outright. But she didn't, for fear of receiving the wrong answer. She wanted nothing to shatter her beautiful dream world. Realities could wait. At least until they were out of North Africa.

Two days later, around midday, Lorna knew they had almost reached the coast. She could smell the salt in the air and hear the roar of the surf in the distance. But when they reached Bomba, the ragged army literally staggering from hunger and thirst, she couldn't believe her eyes. There was nothing there, no town, no village, not a single, solitary house. Then, seeing even the bay was totally empty, her heart fell in disappointment.

Nathan felt a keen disappointment, too, just before he became aware of the change in the temperament of the army. Before, the men had been excited, despite their weakness and weariness, thinking that their long trek across the desert would finally end and they would have food and water. But now, seeing the empty bay, they began to mutter angrily among themselves. He knew what was coming and regretted that he couldn't stay and help his countrymen out, but his concern for Lorna's safety took precedence over all. He turned to Ali, saying, "Let's get out of here before all hell breaks loose."

"No!" Lorna objected. "Maybe Hull will show up. Let's wait awhile longer."

"It will be too late," Nathan answered in an ominous tone of voice. "That army is about to erupt. No, we're getting out of here. Now!"

Lorna was carried along as Nathan's and the Zenatas' horses tore off, quickly leaving the army behind them in a thick cloud of dust. Hearing the deafening roar of almost five hundred men yelling at the top of their lungs, she looked back over her shoulder and saw the entire army running for the bay, waving their rifles and scimitars over their heads, the metal glittering in the bright sunlight. Seeing them charging down on the small group of Americans standing near the water's edge, she held her breath, wondering why Eaton and the others were making no effort to defend themselves, but were gazing out to sea. She glanced out at the bay and then, seeing the small sail in the distance, reined in and yelled, "No! Wait! A ship is coming!"

Nathan wheeled his horse around and trotted it back to where Lorna sat, looking out to sea. As he squinted against the bright sunlight, Lorna asked, "Is it the *Argus?*"

"Well, I can't be sure from this distance, but it's a

brig all right. It has two masts. And the *Argus* is a brig."

"Who else could it be if not the Americans?" Ali pointed out as he rode up to them. "The Tripolitans have no ships that size, nor do any of the Barbary pirates."

They sat and waited breathlessly until Nathan spied the colors that were fluttering on the ship's flagstaff, the sight of the Stars and Stripes sending a thrill of pride running through him. "It's them! By God, it's the *Argus*. And look." He pointed farther out to sea. "If I'm not mistaken, that schooner with her is the *Hornet*."

"Well, my friend, it looks like you're going to get to join the expedition after all," Ali commented.

Nathan knew the words were a prelude to his and Ali's parting. His excitement at joining the expedition was tempered with a sadness at saying good-bye to his friend. He turned in his saddle, saying, "Yes, it does."

"We will be leaving now," Ali said, his tone of voice reflecting his own sadness at their parting. "I wish you much success on both your country's campaign and your own personal quest."

"Thanks, Ali. For everything you've done for me, for all your help."

"Thanks are not necessary between friends," the emir answered. He reached across and lay his hand on Nathan's broad shoulder, saying, "Allah go with you."

Nathan lay his hand on the emir's shoulder and said, "And with you, my friend."

The emir turned to Lorna. "Good-bye," she muttered, surprised to realize there were tears in her eyes. But if it had not been for this man, Nathan would never have found her.

"No, not good-bye," the emir answered softly.

"Those words have too final a sound to them. We will say farewell until we meet again. *Inshullah.*"

"*Inshullah,*" Lorna repeated, wondering if God would will that they meet again in this lifetime.

Lorna and Nathan watched as the Zenatas wheeled their horses and rode off in the direction of the Sahara. Not until the horsemen had turned into mere specks in the distance did they turn their attention back to the bay.

The beach was a scene of bedlam as the army went wild with excitement, jumping up and down and yelling as the longboats from the two ships with their supplies were rowed to shore. Some of the Arabs couldn't wait for the supplies to be unloaded but splashed into the surf and grabbed barrels from the boats before they had even grounded on the beach, carrying them to the shore and breaking them open on the sand. Soon the boats were surrounded with men, and the sailors were forced to stand back for fear of being crushed under the onslaught.

"We'll wait until they've calmed down a little before we go down there," Nathan remarked.

It was a good half hour before the army, their hunger momentarily appeased, calmed down enough for Eaton to gain some semblance of order. Then the men were kept busy with carrying and rolling barrels of water and supplies up the incline of the beach to where their camp was being set up.

Nathan and Lorna rode down the incline to the beach where Eaton was directing the steady stream of supplies being unloaded on the sand. As they reined in, Eaton turned and said, "Welcome Captain Sloan. I'm glad to have you with me. But I wish the emir and his Zenatas had stayed. God, I could use some disciplined, hard-fighting men like that."

Nathan laughed and replied, "Eaton, you know

damn well no Zenata is going to fight beside a bunch of Arabs to put another Karamanli on the throne."

Eaton grinned, saying, "That's exactly what the emir said when I asked him to join. But still, it would have been reassuring to have had them along."

Nathan was in total agreement. One Zenata was worth ten of this rabble Eaton had.

"But then I suppose I should be grateful that I have you," Eaton continued. "I saw you riding away."

Was Eaton condemning him for deserting him and the other Americans to their fate? Nathan wondered. "I told you in the beginning that I'd leave if the *Argus* wasn't here when we arrived."

"Yes, and I was praying that you would make good your escape. For a moment there I thought it was all over for us. No sense in you getting killed, too. You couldn't have helped us. Not against five hundred angry men."

The "general" glanced over his shoulder and said, "Ah, here comes Hull with the money. Seven thousand in hard cash. That should make these mercenaries happy. As soon as I've paid them off, we can retire to the *Argus*. After the past five weeks I can stand a few hours of relaxation."

While Eaton walked down the beach to greet Hull, Nathan helped Lorna dismount, then untied her trunk from their pack horse. By the time they walked down the beach, Eaton had taken the money and rushed off, leaving Hull surrounded by the marines, all asking questions about how the war was going.

Spying Nathan towering over the marines at the back of the circle of men, a look of astonishment came over the naval officer's face before he said, "By God, Nathan! Is that you?"

Nathan chuckled and stepped forward, the marines clearing a path for him. "It's me, all right."

"What in hell are you doing here?"

"It's a long story. One I would prefer to tell you in private," Nathan answered, shooting the marines a meaningful glance.

Captain Hull gave the marines a look that sent them scurrying away, leaving Lorna standing on the beach alone a few feet away. Hull stared at her in utter disbelief, his expression so incredulous that Nathan had to laugh.

Stepping backward and catching Lorna's hand, Nathan brought her to his side, saying proudly to the portly Hull, "Isaac, I'd like you to meet my wife, Lorna. Lorna, this is one of my oldest friends, Captain Isaac Hull."

"I'm pleased to meet you," Lorna said with a smile.

Nathan laughed and said, "Shut your mouth, Isaac. You can catch flies that way."

Hull snapped his mouth closed, a flush creeping up his neck and turning his apple-cheeked face even redder. Finally recovering from his shock, he bowed and said, "The pleasure is mine, Mrs. Sloan. Forgive me for looking so surprised, but I wasn't even aware that Nathan had married."

Hull shot Nathan a look that asked, What in the hell is going on? Nathan took pity on his friend and said, "About nine months ago I was sent to Tripoli to escort out of the country the wife of a British nobleman who had been captured by the pirates and ransomed." Aware of Lorna's face turning pale and guessing she feared that he was going to give away their secret, Nathan squeezed her hand reassuringly before he continued. "The caravan we were traveling on was attacked by Tuareg, and I was almost killed. After I had recovered, I went looking for the noblewoman, thinking there was a possibility she might be alive. With the help of my old Zenata friends I learned that the noblewoman had been killed during the raid, but in my searching for her I came across Lorna, who had been captured from a British ship a year before all this happened. She's now my wife," Nathan answered, offering no explanation of why he had married Lorna so abruptly.

"What an extraordinary story," Hull answered, not thinking their hasty marriage at all strange. He assumed Nathan had quickly fallen in love with the beautiful creature. With one puzzle solved he was curious about another. "But how did you come to be with Eaton's army?"

"We ran into him a few days back on our way to the coast. He asked me to join the expedition, as an adviser of sorts. It seems he needs some help communicating with those Greeks. I agreed on one condition, and that's where you come in. I have a favor to ask of you. Can you take Lorna on the *Argus?* I won't join Eaton unless I'm assured of her safety."

Nathan knew Isaac wouldn't refuse, and not just because Lorna was the wife of a friend. As captain of an American vessel, it was his duty to remove from the scene any American civilians caught in a war zone, but Nathan felt he owed his friend the courtesy of at least asking.

"Of course I'll take her on the *Argus,*" Hull answered. "But are you aware that I've been assigned to support Eaton? While he is attacking Derna from land, I'll be doing so from the sea."

"Yes, I know. But I also know there are no cannons with a long enough range in Derna to reach you. You might bombard the hell out of them, but I doubt if one shell will reach you."

Hull looked surprised at this bit of information, then remarked dryly, "Well, that's reassuring to know. It's more than I've been able to learn from any naval intelligence." He paused, a thoughtful expression coming over his face, before he said, "It just occurred to me. You probably know the layout of that port better than anyone."

"Well, not better than the Arabs," Nathan admitted, then added, "but almost. When we're aboard ship where we can get to a map, I'll show you where everything's located."

A few moments later Hull excused himself, saying he had some business to attend to on the beach before they could leave for the ship. As he walked away, calling orders to his sailors, Lorna remarked, "He's awfully young to be a naval captain, isn't he?"

"He's only a few years older than I am. All the officers in the American navy are young, because the navy is young itself."

"But he doesn't look like a sea captain," Lorna continued, thinking Isaac Hull didn't have any of the dash or excitement about him that Nathan had, nor anywhere near the good looks. In fact, the captain of the *Argus* looked more like a laborer, with his stout body and commonplace features.

"Oh, Isaac isn't as handsome or dashing as some of the other officers in American navy," Nathan answered, having no idea Lorna was comparing Hull to himself and finding him sadly lacking. "Certainly nothing like Stephen Decatur. That one is as handsome and proud as Lucifer. He has the look of a hero. But don't let Isaac's outward appearance fool you. He has the makings of a hero, too, only he's not a glory seeker like some of the others. He's a man given to deeds, rather than words, modest, reliable, steadfast, and possessing a seamanship that borders on brilliant. Preble recognized Hull's virtues when he took over command. At that time Decatur was captain of the

Argus. Preble took the command away from him and gave it to Hull, as a reward because she's such a sweet sailer. When he did that, he was telling the rest of the squadron that Hull had the characteristics he was looking for in an outstanding officer."

Lorna was impressed because Nathan was obviously impressed. Her eyes drifted to the portly Hull walking heavily down the beach. But still, she thought, while he might outshine his fellow naval officers, he couldn't begin to compare to Nathan. But then, no man could. Her captain was one in a million.

"Stay here on the beach," Nathan said, breaking into Lorna's thoughts, "while I see to the horses. It will be safer down here with Isaac and his sailors than around that wild bunch up there."

Lorna glanced to the rise where the Arabs were now celebrating boisterously. To her it looked as if they were drunk, for more than a few were staggering. "Where did they get the liquor?"

"Apparently there were some casks of spirits in those supplies."

"The navy furnished them with spirits?" Lorna asked with just a tinge of disapproval.

"Yes, their supplies came out of the naval stores. Every sailor is allotted a certain amount of spirits each day. It helps to keep up the morale. It's a standard practice in almost every navy that sails the seas. I guess the navy figured if they could have spirits as part of their daily allowance, so could the army. But from the looks of things, those Arabs are going to drink up their entire allotment at one sitting."

"But I didn't think Muslims drank liquor."

"They're not supposed to. But its a rare Muslim who'll turn it down if given the opportunity."

While Nathan was gone to see to the horses, Lorna walked along the beach, enjoying the stiff, cooling breeze and the tangy smell of salt in the air. She looked out at the Mediterranean, thinking it amazing to see so much water, even if it was salt water and undrinkable.

Captain Hull walked up to her. Lorna smiled at him, then asked, "Why is the water so many different colors?"

"The color depends upon the depth of the water. It's blue where it's the deepest, green where it's shallower, and brown closer to the shore."

Lorna glanced down at the surf where the waves were crashing on the beach, noting that not only was the tumbling water filled with sand particles, but even the foam had taken on a brownish tint.

Nathan walked up to them, carrying Lorna's chest. Captain Hull directed one of his sailors to place it in the longboat. Lorna glanced around, seeing that all the other boats had shoved off and were being rowed to the two ships anchored in the bay.

Eaton hurried down the rise and up to them, saying, "Sorry to have delayed you, Captain Hull. But those men weren't going to be happy until they got paid."

Nathan cast a jaundiced eye at the merrymakers up on the rise and commented, "It seems to me those spirits made them much happier than that money."

Eaton looked back up at the rise, a worried expression on his face. "I hope Lieutenant O'Bannon can handle them. They're getting a little rowdy."

"They're not used to liquor," Nathan commented. "Give them a few more minutes and they'll all be passed out. Then the only thing O'Bannon will have to contend with is their snores. Of course, tomorrow morning will be another matter. Dealing with five hundred men with hangovers will be a little touchy."

"They couldn't be any more difficult to handle than they have the past few days," Eaton responded. "If I can get them five hundred miles across that desert without any food, I can get them the remaining sixty miles to Derna."

While Nathan and Eaton were talking, Hull's attention had been on the bay. "We'd better get going. The wind is picking up and that surf is getting pretty rough."

Hull and Eaton waded into the water where the longboat was waiting, the waves breaking around their ankles, then their calves, and finally their thighs. Lorna started forward, then gasped as Nathan swung her up in his arms, saying, "No sense in both of us getting wet."

He waded into the water, the crashing waves spraying them with spume. "Damn! I wish I had changed into my breeches. These robes are hell to wade in and my pantaloons feel like they have a bucket of sand in them."

The mental picture of Nathan's pantaloons loaded with sand and dragging the thin material down flashed through Lorna's mind. She giggled.

"Think it's funny do you?" Nathan said with a mock growl. "Well, let's see how you like it."

He made to drop her, and Lorna shrieked, hanging onto his strong, tanned neck for dear life. Aware that her shriek had brought curious glances from Eaton and Hull, who were just starting to climb into the boat, Lorna said, "Stop teasing me. Everybody is staring at us."

Nathan chuckled. "They're just jealous. They'd give their eyeteeth to be in my place and have you in their arms."

While Nathan meant the words as a compliment,

Lorna didn't necessarily feel they were. After all, she was the only woman within a good fifty miles.

When they reached the longboat, Nathan lifted her over the side and set her down. Then, with Hull giving him a hand up, he scampered over and sat down on the wooden seat beside her. The boat was shoved off by the two sailors who had been holding its mooring lines. Before the men were even in the boat, the rowers were at work, bending their backs and pulling with all their might to overcome the force of the powerful waves that were determined to push them back onto the beach.

When the longboat reached the *Argus*, Lorna watched as Captain Hull grabbed the Jacob's ladder that was hanging over the ship's side and scrambled up it, surprisingly agile despite his heavy weight. A sailor followed, then another, looking like monkeys as they flew up the rope, hand over hand.

Nathan steadied the rope ladder that hung down to the boat and said to Lorna, "Okay, up you go."

Lorna felt a twinge of fear. The ladder didn't look any too substantial to her. Taking a deep breath, she caught hold and climbed steadily up the ladder, keeping her eyes glued to the railing at the top and not daring to look down at the bobbing boat beneath her, for fear she would get dizzy. Captain Hull lifted her over the rail, and when her feet were planted firmly on the deck, he smiled broadly at her and said, "You did that like a real professional, Mrs. Sloan. You'd be surprised at how many new sailors are terrified of going up and down that ladder and find it one of the hardest things to learn in sailing."

Nathan heard Hull's praise as he came bounding over the railing. He smiled proudly and slipped his arm around Lorna's waist, then said to his friend,

"Yes, it appears I've got the makings of a top-notch sailor here."

As the three walked to Captain Hull's cabin, Lorna wondered at Nathan's remark. What difference did it make if she had the makings of a sailor or not? He was the seaman, not she.

Chapter 16

When she and Nathan entered Captain Hull's cabin a few moments later, Lorna looked around her, noting that it was much larger than the little cubbyhole she'd had on the merchantman. A large desk, bolted to the floor to secure it in heavy seas, sat in the middle of the room, covered with maps, papers, and the strange instruments that sailors use. In one corner of the cabin was a built-in bunk, in another a built-in washstand and wardrobe. Bookshelves and cabinets lined one wall, and through the single porthole in another Lorna could see the sun setting.

Captain Hull and Eaton entered the cabin. Closing the door behind them, Hull said, "Please have a seat and we'll have a glass of wine before dinner."

While everyone seated themselves, Hull walked to one of the cabinets and opened it, revealing a small liquor cabinet. Pouring wine from a crystal decanter into small goblets, he served the others before sitting in the chair behind his desk with his drink.

Since there were only three chairs in the room, Nathan had sat on the captain's bunk. He leaned back against the wall, crossed his long legs before him, and said, "Eaton tells me Commodore Barron has replaced Preble."

"Yes," Hull answered, "and I can't tell you how sorry we all were to see Preble leave. He was tough, but he was fair, and if the navy had given him just a little more time, he might have ended this war."

"How is Barron doing?"

"He isn't doing much of anything," Hull replied with a strong hint of disgust in his voice. "Just blockading."

"That wasn't what I meant," Nathan said in a quiet voice.

Hull shot Nathan a sharp look. Nathan gazed back at him steadily. Hull sighed deeply, saying, "Well, I don't suppose his mental problem is any big secret. I'm afraid his condition is worse. He seems to be suffering under some delusion that we're all against him. Frankly, we're hoping he will be recalled. Trying to win this war is enough of a chore without having a paranoid commander suspiciously watching every move you make."

"Well, maybe now that we have a combined land and sea force, we'll finally get somewhere with this war," Eaton remarked. "I always thought it was ridiculous to try to fight it solely by sea."

A knock sounded on the door, followed by "Dinner is served, Cap'n." Captain Hull rose, saying, "The officers' dining room is just down the companionway. If you'll just follow me."

When they walked into the officers' dining room, several of the ship's officers were already present, looking all spit and polish in their dark blue cutaway coats, white breeches, and newly shined knee-high boots. Against their splendid, meticulous dress, Lorna felt rather shabby and out of place in her dusty Muslim clothing. But from the admiring looks on the officers' faces it was clear they thought her anything but shabby looking and found her strange pantaloons intriguing. They were all goo-goo eyed and Captain Hull had to clear his throat loudly to remind them of their manners. Then there was a mad scramble to see who would have the privilege of seating her. It turned out that Nathan retained the honor, shooting the anxious officers a fierce, possessive look that warned them away.

Once seated, Lorna could hardly believe that she was actually sitting on a chair at a table with china, silverware, and glassware before her, a luxury she had taken for granted before her capture by the pirates. At first the knife and fork felt awkward to her, but as the meal progressed she felt more at ease as the old, familiar hand movements came back to her. And the meal itself was a revelation. There was beef, something unheard of in the Muslim diet, potatoes, carrots, and green peas—vegetables she hadn't seen since she had left England—and wonder of all wonders, fresh apple pie for dessert. When she finished, she blushed, fearing she had made a pig of herself and wondering what the Americans must think of her.

Seeing every eye at the table on her and having no idea they were staring at her beauty and not her ravenous appetite, she said lamely, "That was delicious."

"Yes, it was," Eaton chimed in. "You have to be away from American cooking for a while to really appreciate it."

"I'm glad you both enjoyed it," Captain Hull replied. "And I can well understand. When we've been to sea for a long time, it's the fresh vegetables that I miss the most. Yet when I was a boy, my mother had to force them down me. You don't appreciate things until you don't have them."

You certainly don't, Lorna thought. Things like water and wood and fresh vegetables. And rain. Oh, God, what she wouldn't give to see rain. No, she amended, remembering how the rain she had seen in the desert evaporated before it reached the ground, see and *feel* rain.

Captain Hull pushed his chair back and rose, saying to Nathan, "I don't want you to get away from me before you point out where everything is in that harbor at Derna."

"Yes, and I have some things to discuss with you, too, Captain," Eaton said, rising to his feet. "We have to decide on some prearranged signals and lay out a battle plan."

Captain Hull turned to Lorna, saying, "I'm afraid our business will bore you, Mrs. Sloan. Would you like to take a walk on the deck? I'm sure Lieutenant Simmons here would be more than happy to accompany you."

The lieutenant jumped to his feet, beaming with pride that he had been chosen for the honor.

With the lieutenant grinning down at her, Lorna felt she couldn't refuse, although she hated to be separated from Nathan. This would be their last night together for who knew how long. "That would be nice," she replied graciously.

Lorna thought the lieutenant was going to walk her to death, if he didn't talk her to death first. While they circled the deck of the brig five times, the young man told her his entire life history and then, when he finished that, started pointing out things on the ship that he thought might be of interest to her. By the

time Lorna saw Nathan, Eaton, and Captain Hull
coming from the companionway that led to the captain's cabin, she had a splitting headache.

"Good-bye, Mrs. Sloan," Eaton said, coming to a
standstill beside her. "Hopefully, the next time we
meet will be in Derna."

"Goodbye . . ." Lorna hesitated, not knowing
whether to address the man as mister or general, then
deciding to humor him, answered, ". . . General Eaton. And good luck."

Smiling with satisfaction at her acknowledgment
of his status, Eaton climbed over the rail and started
to descend the Jacob's ladder to the longboat below.

"I'll leave you two to say your good-byes," Captain Hull said to Nathan. He turned to Lorna, saying,
"Your chest, and the box I understand contains your
wedding gifts have been placed in my cabin. I trust
you will be comfortable there."

"But I can't take your cabin, Captain Hull,"
Lorna objected. "Why, you've got all your charts and
everything in there. You'll be needing it. Any little
cabin will do for me."

"Nonsense, Mrs. Sloan. It's customary on naval
ships to give the captain's cabin to honored passengers. As the wife of my good friend, I feel honored to
have you aboard."

As Lorna opened her mouth, Hull said in a firm
voice, "No. No more objections. I've already moved
all my things into my first officer's cabin. He can bunk
in with the second officer. And by the way, my cabin
will be next to yours if you should need me for anything."

Hull turned back to Nathan and offered his hand
to him, saying, "Good luck, and don't worry about
anything. If the need should arise, I'll take care of it
for you."

Nathan accepted his friend's hand and answered, "Thanks, Isaac. I knew I could count on you."

As Captain Hull walked away, Lorna asked, "What were you two talking about? What can you count on him to take care of?"

Nathan had made arrangements with Hull that if the expedition failed and he got captured, or if he got killed, the captain would see Lorna safely to Nathan's first mate at Malta with instructions for him to take Lorna immediately to his parents in America and to deliver two letters to his father. One of the missives explained everything about their marriage, and the second letter was to be given to Jefferson to ask the President's intercession in case any unforeseen problems should arise concerning Lorna's supposed crime in England. Nathan had also made out a will, leaving everything to his wife. But Nathan didn't want Lorna to know of the arrangements, for fear telling her of the lengths he had gone to protect her even after his death would betray his deep feelings for her. "Just some business he's going to handle for me," he answered smoothly.

Lorna wondered how Nathan could think of business when he was going off to war and might be facing death. Again, the full implications of their parting hit her. Fear clawed at her stomach as a wave of sickening regret washed over her. Oh, why hadn't she kept her mouth shut? she thought with self-recrimination. What difference did it make if he blamed her, or even came to hate her, for missing his chance for revenge? At least he would be alive. She had put her stupid pride before his safety. If anything should happen to him, she'd never forgive herself. She longed with all of her heart and soul to tell him she loved him, that she hadn't married him just for his protection. Instead, she stared at him, her misery and apprehension written all over her face.

Lorna wasn't the only one assailed with fear. So was Nathan. But this time his fear was for himself, something that stunned him. He had never been afraid to die. He was a man who had confronted death time and time again and laughed in the dark angel's face. But he had never felt he had so much to live for, either. Lorna had brought a whole new perspective to his life. Then, seeing the worried expression on her face, he realized that she did care, at least enough that she was genuinely concerned about his safety. He should have realized that she wouldn't be so callous as to be that indifferent to him, particularly after her compassion the night he had told her about his imprisonment. No, her indifference had all been a big act to get him to join the expedition, and he had fallen for it. It seemed his wife could be a very convincing actress when it suited her purpose. But now, knowing that she did care to some degree made it all the harder for him to leave her.

He framed her face with his hands, his eyes drifting over each feature as if he were trying to imprint them on his brain. God, how he wished he could make love to her just one last time. With a groan of despair that came from the depths of his soul, he crushed her to him in a fierce embrace, his mouth coming down hard on hers in a desperate, urgent kiss.

Despite the fact that Nathan was about to crush the breath from her, Lorna pressed even closer, hugging him with a ferocity born of stark fear, wishing she could crawl inside him and go with him. To the sailor standing watch farther down the deck, who had tried to keep his eyes away from the scene but not quite succeeded, it looked as if the couple would merge despite their layers of clothing, bringing a furious blush to his face.

With superhuman effort Nathan tore his mouth away from hers, the loss of contact bringing a little sob from Lorna. "If anything should happen to me—"

"No!" Lorna cried out in an agonized voice, cutting across his words. "Don't even mention something like that!"

Do I dare hope that she cares more than I think? Nathan wondered, but his strong urge to protect her came once again to the fore, overriding his own needs. He smiled, a smile he hoped would reassure her, then said, "Then I'll see you in Derna."

Lorna didn't want to let him go. She clung so tightly that Nathan had to pry her arms from him. Then, as he went over the rail, Lorna rushed to it, her nails biting into the wood as she finally managed to get something past the lump in her throat, calling out, "Be careful!"

Nathan didn't answer or look up, nor did he glance back over his shoulder as the boat was rowed away. He didn't dare, for he didn't trust himself not to turn back. But if he had, he would have seen the naked love in Lorna's anguished eyes.

Lorna stood at the railing and watched until the boat was swallowed up by the darkness. Even then she stood on the deck, staring out in the direction the boat had disappeared. Not until she could no longer hear the faint squeaking of the oarlocks and the muted, rhythmic splashes of the oars in the water did she finally turn and walk to the cabin, tears streaming down her face.

Lorna was up with the sun the next morning. She rushed topside, hoping, if nothing else, to get one last glimpse of the army before they marched out. But when she stepped on the sunwashed deck, she discovered that the ship had sailed during the night and all she could see was the blue waters of the Mediterranean.

Captain Hull walked up to her and said with a smile, "Good morning, Mrs. Sloan. You're up early."

"Yes, I was hoping to get a last look at the army," Lorna admitted.

"They just marched out."

"How do you know that?" Lorna asked in surprise.

"My man in the eagle's nest has them in view."

"He can see that far?" Lorna asked in disbelief.

"You can see fifteen miles at sea with the naked eye, and even farther with a spyglass. Since the army is marching up the coastline, we'll be keeping an eye on their progress all the way to Derna and matching their pace as best we can."

Lorna was glad the navy was keeping an eye on things. Surely, with their big cannons, they could cover the army's retreat if they should run into a superior Tripolitan force and be repulsed.

Later that day Lorna heard the lookout in the eagle's nest calling down, "Cap'n! They've stopped!"

Hull stood on the quarterdeck and looked up, calling back, "Have they run into resistance?"

"No, Cap'n. There ain't nothing out there but them."

"Bring me my glass," Hull snapped to one of his officers.

When the officer returned, Hull took the spyglass and peered out toward the faint brownish line that marked the coastline. "Maybe they're taking a rest," the officer who had brought the glass suggested.

"No, they're not sitting down," Hull replied. "In

fact, it looks like pandemonium to me. God, don't tell
me they're going to mutiny this late in the day."

Hull glanced up, seeing the sails filled with wind
in the brisk breeze, the canvas so tight it looked as if it
would burst. "Shorten sail!" he called out.

The sailors scurried up the rigging and rolled up
several of the large sails while Lorna held her breath
for fear they would fall as they swung through the air
from one spar to another. Then they waited, many of
the officers pacing the deck anxiously, while Hull
stood at the rail, looking calm and unperturbed, as
steady as the rock of Gibraltar, although Lorna knew
he must be just as anxious as the others.

It was a good hour before the lookout reported
that the army was on the move again. As the sailors
loosened the sails that had been shortened and the
canvas snapped as it caught the wind, one of the officers asked Hull, "What do you think that was all
about, sir?"

"I can only conclude that the army tried to mutiny again and Eaton managed to talk them out of it.
It's amazing how he's gotten that wild, dangerous
bunch of mercenaries across the desert with just
sheer willpower. Now if he can only hold them together for few more days."

On the morning of the fourth day Lorna noticed
that she could no longer see the faint line of land in
the distance. Curious, she asked one of the officers
about it as he passed.

"No, ma'am," he answered. "You can't see land
anymore. We're sailing farther out at sea. The army
has left the coastline and is swinging in behind Derna
right now."

Lorna was still standing at the rail, being sprayed
with the spume the bow of the ship threw into the air

as it plowed through the water, when she noticed the *Argus* had changed its course. Before her the coastline loomed, coming closer and closer. Then she saw the inlet of the bay, then the bay itself, and finally the faint outline of the buildings in the distance. An excitement filled her as she realized they had reached their destination. Derna, the second largest city in Tripoli, lay before them, dozing in the warm April sun, its inhabitants unaware that they were about to be caught in a nutcracker, attacked by the enemy by both land and sea.

Once they were inside the bay, the sails were reefed and the anchor dropped, the metal cable on the capstan screeching and spitting sparks as it unrolled and the heavy anchor splashed into the water. From where she stood Lorna could see the city in the distance, and she could hardly believe her eyes. Every city, town, and village Lorna had seen in North Africa had had a sunbaked appearance to it, its sand-colored houses blending into the dull, monotonous brown of the land. But Derna looked like a jeweled crown curving around the silvery stretch of beach with its houses painted in a rainbow of pastel colors. She turned her attention to a gleaming white palace that dominated the city and towered above it, thinking that with its graceful lines and high-arched windows, it had none of the ugly fortress appearance that the palace in Tripoli had. And everywhere, scattered among the houses and down the streets, she could see touches of green. Green!

Captain Hull walked up to her, saying, "Well, Mrs. Sloan, what do you think of Derna?"

Lorna turned, saying, "Lorna, remember?"

Over the past days Lorna and the captain had spent many hours in the evenings talking. A friendship had budded, but Lorna still had trouble getting the modest New Englander to call her by her first name.

A flush rose on Hull's face before he smiled sheepishly and said, "I'm sorry, Lorna. I keep forgetting."

Lorna turned her attention back to the city, saying, "To answer your question, frankly, I'm astonished. Derna is the most beautiful city I've yet to see in North Africa."

"Yes, it is. The Italians call it the Pearl of the Mediterranean."

"Will you . . . will you have to level it?" Lorna asked hesitantly, thinking it would be a shame to destroy such a lovely city and yet not wanting Hull to think she was being presumptuous enough to suggest to the navy how to fight their war.

"I certainly hope not. In fact, I'm hoping I won't even have to fire a shot, that once the Tripolitans realize the position they're in, they'll surrender. That's what we're waiting for right now, the answer to Eaton's demand for surrender."

"Then the army is in position?" Lorna asked in surprise.

"Yes."

She looked across the bay to her left, seeing the *Hornet* also anchored there and, like the *Argus,* presenting its broadside to the city. Then, spying a third, much smaller ship sailing into the bay, the American flag above it snapping smartly in the breeze, she asked, "What ship is that?"

"That's the *Nautilus.* She's a handy little twelve-gun schooner that used to be under the command of Dicky Sommers until he volunteered to take command of the ill-fated *Intrepid."* A sadness crept into Hull's voice as he said, "But then, I don't suppose you've heard of that disaster."

No, not heard, Lorna thought. I witnessed what happened to the *Intrepid*. The memory of the flaming spars and debris being thrown into the night sky like an exploding star seemed to be burned into her brain. "Yes, I have heard. Nathan told me about it. They were brave men."

A silence hung in the air, and Lorna knew Hull was remembering his friends who had gone to their fiery deaths that fateful night. Hoping to distract him from his morbid thoughts, she asked, "Will any more ships be coming?"

"No, this is my full complement. Not an impressive sea power, I'm afraid, but hopefully enough to frighten the Tripolitans into surrendering."

It wasn't. An hour later Eaton signaled that the officials in Derna had refused his demand to surrender and requested that Hull land a few field guns.

Lorna watched as the longboat carrying the small cannons was rowed to a deserted part of the beach, then saw the men scurrying down the steep cliff that towered over the beach where the boat was headed. Hull walked up to her and handed her a spyglass, saying, "Would you like to get a closer look at your husband, Lorna?"

"Nathan is with those men?" Lorna asked in surprise.

"Yes. When we made these arrangements, I asked him if he would mind overseeing the landing and setting up of the field artillery. Those Greeks claim to be gunners, but I don't quite trust them. They might know how to fire those cannons, but I don't know how much they know about gun range and elevation and how much powder to use. Nathan agreed to see the guns set up and give them a few instructions, but he made it quite clear he wanted to be in on the taking of the city and not stuck up on some hill miles away from where the action was taking place. And I can't say I blame him. I know one of the main reasons he joined that expedition was to get a crack at that Janissary captain. He's doing this as a personal favor to me."

As Hull walked away, Lorna raised the spyglass and peered through it, amazed at how much closer everything looked. She scanned the men who had surrounded the beached boat and were unloading it. With his height Nathan wasn't hard to find. She noticed he was no longer wearing his Arab dress but had changed into the same tight breeches and white shirt she had seen him in at the consul's home in Tripoli so long ago. Hungrily she drank in the sight of him, watching each movement he made as the cannons were unloaded and dragged up the beach, then holding her breath as he and the Greeks, their short, white skirts flapping in the breeze, struggled to get one of the guns up the steep cliff, slipping and sliding on the loose rocks as they pulled and shoved the small but heavy cannon up the incline that seemed to go straight up in the air.

She breathed a sigh of relief when they finally reached the top, their shirts plastered to their backs with sweat from their exertions. Then she watched while the cannon was dragged to a small hill overlooking the city's fortifications.

"I'm sorry, Lorna," Captain Hull said, coming to stand at her side, "but I'm afraid I'll have to ask you to go belowdecks now."

Lorna tore her eyes away from the sight on the hilltop and looked around her, surprised to see that while she had been watching the scene on land, the sailors had been preparing for the upcoming battle. The deck had been washed down with sea water and strewn with sand, and the entire ship was a beehive of activity as the gunners stripped off their shirts and tossed them aside, tying rags around their foreheads to keep the sweat from getting in their eyes, while powder boys hurriedly weaved their way through the crush of excited men, carrying barrels of black powder and casks of water and setting them down beside the cannons that were being readied.

Lorna handed the spyglass back to Captain Hull and asked, "Can't I stay on deck? I won't be able to see anything down there." Seeing the frown come over Hull's face, she added in a pleading voice, "Please, Isaac. I promise to stay out of the way."

"Well, since we won't be taking any shells," Hull said tentatively after a moment of hesitation that had seemed like an eternity to Lorna, "I suppose so. Come over here."

Hull led her to a place on the quarterdeck away from the frantic activity, then said in a firm voice, "Now, you must promise me you won't move from this spot."

Lorna could hardly believe he was actually allowing her to stay. "I won't," she promised fervently.

Hull turned and walked away. A sudden silence fell over the ship as every eye was anxiously turned on the captain, the sailors standing at ready at their battle stations. As Hull called out, "Load cannons! Two round shot!" the gun crews sprang into action to follow his orders. When the cannons were loaded, Hull called out, "Run out!"

The gun ports slammed open and the heavy cannons were pushed forward, their carriage wheels creaking and rumbling in protest. Again every eye was on the captain as the gun crews anxiously awaited the next order.

"Fire!"

The slow matches went down over the vents,

fuses sputtered; then the eight cannons in the port battery roared, spitting fire and smoke, then slammed back in recoil against the restraining tackles. A split second later, Lorna heard the thunder of the cannons as the guns on the *Hornet* and the *Nautilus* were fired.

Lorna stood on the deck and watched as the gun crews frantically sponged the cannons and reloaded, then shoved the heavy guns back in place. Over and over the cannons roared, making the deck shudder. Lorna squinted her eyes, seeing the puffs of smoke as the balls slammed into the fortifications on the waterfront. For a while the Tripolitans fired back, but the balls from their cannons splashed harmlessly into the bay a good half mile from the American ships, and the Tripolitans finally gave up their futile efforts. She turned her head, taking satisfaction in seeing the little cannon on the hilltop being fired by the Greeks, the white puffs of smoke following each shot drifting in the air, then surrounding the hilltop like a wreath.

The noise on the deck of the *Argus* was deafening, with the roaring of the guns, the rumbling of the gun carriages, the screeching of the pulleys. Powder boys ran back and forth, carrying more shot and barrels to the crews who were now drenched with sweat from the heat of the cannons. Through the rolling smoke on the deck, Lorna could see that the entire waterfront was on fire, the flames leaping into the air and the black smoke billowing in the sky. She glanced up at the hill, seeing the little cannon there was no longer firing. Fear filled her as she wondered why the small gun was silent. Had the entire gun crew been killed? And had Nathan been with them, or had he already left to join the battle in the city?

She strained her eyes, trying to see the battle that was taking place in the city itself, but much to her disappointment, she could see nothing beyond the thick smoke billowing up from the fires on the waterfront. Then, as the acrid smoke from the cannons being fired on the *Argus* enveloped her, surrounding her in a thick cloud, her eyes began to water, and she began to cough.

The next two hours seemed like an eternity of hell to Lorna, the horrendous noises of the roaring cannons giving her a pounding headache, the screech of the pulleys playing on her nerves, the irritating smoke burning her eyes and nostrils. Added to this was the overbearing heat, and Lorna wondered how the gun crews, their faces and bare chests now covered with black soot, could endure much longer.

Then suddenly she heard the order. "Cease fire! Cease fire!"

Exhausted, the gun crews slumped to the deck, their chests heaving from their exertions, their wet hair plastered to their heads, the only sounds the rasping of their breath and the gentle lapping of the water against the ship's sides. She turned and saw Captain Hull standing farther down on the quarterdeck peering out at the city with a spyglass. Then he lowered the glass and turned, announcing proudly, "Derna has surrendered! Good shooting, men!"

The ship suddenly came alive as the gun crews slammed to their feet, yelling and clapping each other on the shoulders. The powder boys joined in the celebration, two dancing a merry jig on the sanded deck as the officers mingled in the crowd, praising the sailors and congratulating one another.

Grinning from ear to ear, Hull turned toward Lorna and motioned for her to join him. When she walked up to him, he handed her the spyglass, saying, "Look at the flagpole on top of the palace."

Lorna took the glass and peered through it, seeing the Stars and Stripes snapping in the breeze.

"It's a beautiful sight, isn't it?" he asked.

"Yes, it is," Lorna answered, but her heart wasn't
in it. The Americans may have won the battle, but she
didn't know if Nathan had survived. Feeling suddenly
dispirited, she handed the glass back to the captain.

"Don't worry, Lorna," Hull said softly, reading
her dark thoughts. "I'm sure he's all right. That tiger
of yours can take care of himself."

The only response Lorna could muster to the
captain's encouraging words was a weak smile.

It was midafternoon when a knock sounded on
the captain's cabin door. When Lorna opened it, she
saw Captain Hull standing there, a broad smile on his
face.

"Derna has been secured," he informed her,
"and I'm going ashore to confer with Eaton. Nathan
sent word for me to bring you ashore too."

The fear Lorna had been living with since the
night Nathan left her flew out the window at Hull's
words. Her eyes lit up with happiness as she asked in
an excited voice, "He's alive?"

"Alive and kicking."

"Oh, Isaac, I'm so relieved," Lorna cried out,
throwing herself at him and hugging him in her happiness.

The captain hugged her back, feeling just a touch
of envy of his friend for having found such a jewel of a
woman. Not only was she lovely and intelligent, but
she had spunk, too. And when she was excited, as she
was now, she was absolutely delightful. He laughed,
saying, "Hurry now. The longboat is waiting."

Lorna shoved her belongings that were lying out
into her chest, not caring how wrinkled they might

get. No sooner had she slammed the lid shut than a husky cabin boy rushed into the room and carried it out. Then she and the captain walked to the deck.

As soon as she and Captain Hull were in the boat, the sailors rowed it toward a point on the beach some distance away from the still-burning harbor fortifications and wharves. Lorna was so excited at the thought of seeing Nathan that she could hardly sit still. She craned her neck to see, finally spying two men standing on the sand at the water's edge. Disappointment filled her when she recognized the two as General Eaton and Lieutenant O'Bannon. Then, as the powerful rollers caught the boat and it went flying toward the shore, she was too frightened to think of anything, seeing the jagged rocks that were protruding from the crashing surf and fearing they would be dashed to their deaths against them. She watched in utter disbelief, her heart in her throat, as the boat skimmed over the waves between two treacherous outcrops and the rocks flew past her, a testimony to the sailors' expert seamanship.

The boat grounded with a dull thud, snapping Lorna's head back. Two sailors sprang from the boat, splashed in the foaming surf, and pulled it farther up on the sand. Then Hull jumped out and swung Lorna down onto the beach.

As Eaton and O'Bannon rushed forward to meet Hull and the sailors alighting from the boat, Lorna bent to the side and peered past Hull's heavyset body at the incline of the beach behind him, looking for Nathan and feeling very hurt that he hadn't even bothered to come and meet her. No, she thought bitterly, instead he had asked his friend to deliver her to his residence, as if she was no more than a piece of baggage.

Aware of her craning her neck and trying to see

around him, Isaac turned and said with a broad smile,
"I believe you have your own welcoming party coming, Lorna. Look up there."

Lorna looked down the beach to where Captain
Hull was pointing to the top of a steep cliff, seeing the
black horse that was rearing and pawing the air at its
sudden stop. But it was the man on the horse's back
who caught her full attention. Nathan had come after
all!

Before Nathan even started guiding his horse
down the narrow path on the cliff, Lorna was tearing
down the beach, not caring what the others might
think. Then, when Nathan reached the beach, he
raced his horse to meet her, hooves spraying sand
behind him and the animal. He flew from the saddle
and the two came together with an impact that
knocked the breath from them. Then Nathan was
kissing her and Lorna heard a roaring in her ears that
had nothing to do with the surf breaking just a short
distance from them.

When he broke the kiss and stepped back,
Lorna's hands skimmed over him as she asked in an
anxious voice, "You're all right? No injuries?"

"I'm fine," Nathan assured her, drinking in her
beauty hungrily. Suddenly he wanted to be alone
with her, away from the curious glances being cast at
them by the sailors farther up the beach.

He waved and called out, "Thanks, Isaac!" Captain Hull smiled broadly and waved back.

At the reminder of the others Lorna blushed,
realizing for the first time how immodestly she had
behaved, running down the beach and throwing herself into Nathan's arms, then kissing him, in broad
daylight, before God and everyone. When Nathan
said, "Let's get out of here," she didn't object, too
embarrassed to face the others.

Nathan mounted and swung her up before him in the saddle. Lorna snuggled against his broad chest, glorying in the feel of his powerful heart thudding against her back, thrilling as his arm brushed her breast as he turned the horse back down the beach.

He took the same steep path he had used to reach the beach, and when they reached the top of the cliff, Lorna could see the entire city before her. As far as she could tell, the only destruction seemed to have been along the waterfront and one or two fortifications that were still burning on the outskirts of the city.

"Was the battle bad?" she asked.

"To be honest, there wasn't much of a battle," Nathan admitted. "Fortunately the Tripolitans were just as undisciplined and untrained as that bunch of mercenaries we had, and there wasn't much of a Janissary force present, or else we would have had a bigger fight on our hands. After the cannon we dragged up to that hill was disabled—one fool Greek gunner got so excited he fired the gun before the ramrod had been removed—Eaton called for a charge. The marines went in, with me and the Greeks behind them and those damned Arabs lagging behind. I guess our sheer numbers panicked the Tripolitans. They deserted their gun batteries and ran for some fortified houses. When we turned their own guns on them, they ran from them, too. The last we saw of the enemy, they were fleeing into the desert."

"Was anyone hurt?"

"Yes, two marines were killed, one marine and and several Greeks wounded, and Eaton took a bullet in his wrist that smashed the bone."

Lorna felt ashamed of herself. In her disappointment that Nathan wasn't on the beach to meet her, she hadn't even noticed that Eaton had been wounded. Then a sudden thought came to her. "Did you confront Captain Khaldun?"

"Hell, I didn't even lay eyes on him," Nathan answered in disgust. "And believe me, I was watching for him. "I had come to the conclusion that Eaton was wrong, that Khaldun wasn't even at Derna, except I talked to some civilians after the battle who confirmed Eaton's story."

Lorna could hear the profound disappointment in Nathan's voice. "But at least the Americans won," she said, hoping to comfort him with that. And thank God you're alive, she added silently.

"Yes," Nathan agreed, "which should be quite a shock to Yusef when he learns of it and that his feared brother has been installed in the governor's palace."

Glancing down, Lorna noticed the long scratch on Nathan's forearm for the first time. Grabbing his arm, she said in alarm, "I thought you said you weren't wounded."

Nathan heard the fear in her voice. Her getting so upset over something so unimportant pleased him. "It's just a scratch."

Lorna saw that what he said was true. She fought her fear down and said, "Well, nonetheless, it needs tending. In this heat even a slight wound can get infected. As soon as we reach our quarters I'll bathe and dress it." She paused, then asked, "Where will we be staying? Did you even find us quarters yet?"

Nathan chuckled, answering, "I didn't even have to bother looking for quarters. Hamet was so elated with the victory and grateful to us that he insisted the Americans reside in the palace during our stay here, as his personal guests. That's why I was delayed in meeting you at the beach. I stopped at the palace to drop off my chest and and stable your mare."

In her anxiety over the upcoming battle and

Nathan's safety, Lorna had completely forgotten about the spirited little horse she had become so fond of. She was glad to know both were safe and sound. And it seemed as if she had come full circle. She had begun her adventures in Tripoli as the "guest" of the pasha in his palace, and now she would be the "guest" of his brother at the palace in Derna. Except for one important difference. This time she would be not a prisoner, but one of the victors.

Chapter 17

As they rode through the streets of Derna on their way to the palace, Lorna became so acutely aware of Nathan's closeness that she didn't notice the beauty of the city with its tall palm trees and its blooming oleander bushes that added splashes of pink and red to the pastel-painted houses. Nathan was just as aware of her. The ride to the palace seemed to take an eternity. He could hardly wait to get to the privacy of their quarters to make love to her.

When they rode up to the dazzling white palace, Nathan reined in and flew from the saddle, then swung Lorna down. While an Arab servant took his horse's reins and led the animal away to the stables at the back of the palace, Nathan rushed Lorna up the wide marble stairs, barely nodding in recognition as the two marines guarding the front door greeted him, then hurried her through the pink-marbled foyer from whose high ceiling a huge brass lamp was hung, and up the wide staircase that split at a landing and then spiraled up both sides.

Lorna didn't object to Nathan rushing her. She, too, was anxious to make love, so much so that she could have cried in frustration when they didn't stop at the second landing with its row of high, narrow-arched windows and go down either of the hallways to each side of it. How much farther is it? she wondered, her heart pounding wildly in anticipation as he hurried up another flight of spiraling stairs.

On the third floor Nathan led her down a wide hallway, his boots beating a tattoo on the marble floor as they all but ran down the corridor in their haste to be alone. Then, stepping into their quarters, he slammed the door shut behind them and took her in a fierce embrace, kissing her wildly with all the pent-up passion he been holding at bay since they had entered the city.

Lorna kissed him back just as hungrily, straining against him and wishing she could absorb him and keep him inside her forever, her hands fumbling impatiently at his clothing as Nathan stripped her of hers. They took another step, then fell into each other's arms in another deep, passionate kiss, and more clothing fell to the floor. Then, on the rug they were standing on, Nathan drew her to the floor and took her with a savage urgency that frightened, thrilled, and excited Lorna beyond her wildest dreams.

Afterward they lay sprawled in a tangle of white and brown limbs on the plush Persian carpet, their rapid breath still rasping in the air, their clothing thrown helter-skelter all around them. The first thing Lorna became aware of was Nathan's chuckle and his saying in a voice still roughened from desire, "I'm sorry. I was trying to make it to the bed, but I was so excited that I couldn't wait."

"Neither could I," Lorna admitted, then looked around her, still feeling dazed. "Where is it?"

Nathan motioned to a large arch that separated the room they were in from the one next door. "In there." Then he rolled from her and stood, pulling her to her feet with him. "What do you think of our quarters?"

Lorna looked about her in amazement. The sitting room they were in was a spacious, airy room furnished with plush, colorful carpets and low divans about which were set pots of shrubbery and small marble statues. In one corner of the room a brazier and a large low table stood, surrounded by silk cushions in every color in the rainbow, obviously the dining area. Glancing to one side of her and through another high, wide arch, she saw that they had their own private balcony overlooking the city and the bay.

Taking her hand, Nathan said, "Come on in here and see the bedroom."

He led her through the arch to a large room in which was the biggest sleeping pallet Lorna had ever seen. It stretched a good six feet in width across the floor and was covered with a canopy of royal blue and gold brocade from which sheer draperies cascaded down the back and half the sides like a light blue waterfall.

Lorna sank to the low bed and ran her fingers over the blue silk sheets, looking about her in wonder. "Are you sure we're supposed to be here?"

"Yes, there are several of these apartments on this floor. Apparently they're used to house visiting dignitaries. Eaton has occupied the one next to us, Lieutenant O'Bannon and Midshipman Peck another, and the remaining marines yet another."

Hearing the strange haunting sound of a *thorbo*

—a lutelike Arab instrument—being played, Lorna asked, "Where is that music coming from?"

"Probably the floor beneath us, since it's being occupied by Hamet and his friends."

"Old friends from the city?"

"No, friends who accompanied Hamet from Egypt—or so they call themselves," Nathan added in a cynical voice.

"Why do you say that?"

"Because they look more like opportunists than real friends to me, men who are hoping they'll be rewarded for sticking by him with a place of importance in the government if this revolution is successful. You know, being a prince isn't all it's cracked up to be. Men like Hamet never know if they're being accepted for themselves or simply used by others. Personally, I'll take my low station in life. At least I know my friends are true to me." He pulled her to her feet, saying, "But you haven't seen the best part of our apartment yet. Come and see what's next door."

Leading her through the arched opening, Nathan stood to the side, watching Lorna's face as she gazed at the room. He wasn't disappointed. Her eyes lit up with delighted surprise.

"Why, it's a bath!" she cried out, seeing the huge sunken marble tub.

"Yes. How's that for luxury? Our own personal bathing pool."

Lorna looked about the room, noting that two walls were mirrored, as, unbelievably, was the entire ceiling. "What are all these mirrors doing in here?"

"I would imagine they serve the same purpose as the thick carpets and cushions placed about. This isn't just a bath, you know, but a place for play, too."

"Play?"

"Yes, it's customary for the governor to loan out

one or two of his concubines to his honored guests for the night. The carpets are here in case the guest wants to extend his entertainment to the bath and the mirrors are so he can watch what's going on from every angle."

"You mean, he watches while he's . . ." Lorna hesitated. She certainly couldn't call *that* making love, borrowing some poor female slave to slake his lust on. ". . . doing it?"

"Yes. It's supposed to add to the eroticism."

Lorna thought it was a little disgusting, just a form of voyeurism, something that she and Nathan didn't need any more than they needed aphrodisiacs to increase their pleasure in one another. Pushing the mirrors from her mind, she bent and picked up one of the many vials sitting beside the tub. She sniffed it, smelling the sweet scent of the perfumed oil, then looked at the inviting water. She hadn't been in a bath like this since she had left the pasha's palace back in Tripoli. "Oh, Nathan this is wonderful! I'm going to take a bath and wash my hair right now!"

She pulled the wooden pins from her chignon and her hair tumbled down all around her. Placing the pins on the rim of the pool, she picked up a bar of soap and hurried down the wide stairs of the pool, wading into the water until she was waist-deep, the sunken tub's greatest depth. She sank down until the water covered her shoulders, luxuriating in the feeling of water all around her.

Hearing a faint splash, Lorna turned and saw Nathan wading into the pool. Seeing her look of surprise, he said, "I decided I'd like a bath too. You don't mind, do you?"

"No, of course not." She laughed and added, "It's certainly big enough for two."

Nathan walked up to her and said, "Stand up and I'll wash your back for you."

Lorna stood and turned her back to him, handing the bar of fragrant soap to him over her shoulder, then allowed herself to enjoy the feel of his strong hands rubbing over her back and shoulders, but when he said, "Now, turn around, and I'll do the other side," she wondered if he had other things in mind.

Lorna shot him a sharp look over her shoulder and replied, "No, just hand me the soap and I'll do it myself."

"I don't mind."

"Nathan, I really want a bath," Lorna answered in a firm voice.

"So do I. When I get through, I expect you to return the favor." Then, seeing the suspicious gleam in her eyes, he laughed and said, "I'm not going to start anything out here in the pool."

Lorna didn't know whether to trust him or not. She turned reluctantly to face him. But even though he kept his word, lathering her skin in a quick, businesslike manner, the feel of his hands rubbing her breasts and brushing across her nipples was sensuous, warming her all over, so much so that she was disappointed when he said, "Now duck down and rinse off."

When she emerged from the water, Nathan handed her the soap and said, "Now it's your turn to do the work."

Lorna found washing her husband a pleasant chore. She loved the feel of the powerful muscles in his shoulders and arms and the crisp dark hair on his chest. As she washed past his waist to where the water hit him at hip level, she was very aware of the black triangle of hair between his long legs and his manhood, its tip brushing her thigh every now and then as it floated in the water. The temptation to reach down and fondle him was almost too much for her. Irritated that it was she, and not he, who was getting other things in mind, she said, "Turn around."

As Nathan turned and Lorna looked at his broad back, she was filled with an entirely different emotion. Seeing the scars on his back, she wished that she could have taken the pain for him. Before she realized what she was doing, she bent and kissed one. Nathan stiffened at the feel of Lorna kissing the length of one scar and jerked his head around. When Lorna glanced up, she saw the hard, warning expression on his face.

"I'm not pitying you if that's what you're afraid of!" she said in a rush of words. "I just . . . just can't stand the thought of anyone hurting you. I just wanted to kiss the hurt away."

"It doesn't hurt anymore."

It does me, Lorna thought. It hurts every time I look at those scars. Then Lorna realized that she was dangerously close to telling him how much she loved him. Fearing she might break down at any second under that penetrating gaze, she snapped, "Now, turn your head around so I can wash the back of your neck."

Nathan wondered at Lorna's quicksilver mood, kissing him one minute, then snapping at him the next. She was a complete puzzle to him. Not only did he not know what she was thinking or feeling, but he never knew what to expect from her.

When Lorna finished washing Nathan's back, she washed his hair; then he washed hers. Then they waded over to the steps and washed their legs, their wet hair hanging in tangles over his forehead and her shoulders. Finished with their baths, they hung on to the rim of the pool, resting their heads back against it and letting their bodies float, feeling lazy and contented.

Watching a cloud float by in the patch of sky she could see through the windows high on the wall of the room, Lorna said dreamily, "I don't know when I ever enjoyed a bath so much."

"Are you hungry?" Nathan asked. "There's a bowl of fruit, some cheese, and some pastries on that low table over there."

Lorna didn't feel hungry until Nathan mentioned it. She had been so anxious about his safety that she had completely forgotten to eat that day. "Yes, I think I am," she answered, then waded from the pool and dropped to her knees on a thick carpet a few yards from the steps, grabbing a towel from a stack piled there and drying herself hastily, her eyes on the food on the table across the room. Hearing a splash, she turned her head and saw Nathan coming from the pool. She sucked in her breath sharply at the magnificent sight he presented, the water slicing down over his powerful, muscled body, the droplets in his thick hair and those caught in the dark hairs on his chest glistening in the light. As he walked toward her with that sensuous, graceful walk that was so much a part of him, the muscles in his legs flexing and relaxing, Lorna's mouth turned dry. The sight he presented as he walked toward her was not only breathtaking, but overpowering. Not only did she see the front of his nude body, but the back in the mirror facing her, too, and behind that a whole procession of naked Nathans striding toward her in all their glory. As much as she hated to admit it, it was the most exciting, titillating sight she had ever seen.

When he stood over her, blocking her vision of the mirror behind him, Lorna glanced up and saw the smoldering look in his eyes, glowing like green coals in his bronzed face; then dropping her eyes, she saw that he was fully aroused, the powerful organ standing proud and full and long and looking as if it would burst the velvety soft skin that enclosed it. Spying a droplet of water on the tip of that proud male flesh, Lorna was seized with the overpowering urge to lick it away. Shocked at herself, Lorna struggled to suppress the urge, but was unable to tear her eyes away.

"Remember what I said?" Nathan asked in a low, husky voice, acutely aware of her avid expression. "We're married. Nothing is forbidden. Do what you feel like doing."

He bent, caught her arms, and brought her to a kneeling position. With the temptation just a fraction of an inch from her, Lorna surrendered to her urge with a little sob, her tongue flicking out like a fiery dart and bringing a gasp of pleasure from Nathan's lips. Spurred on by his response, she continued, kissing and licking his entire length, from crown to base, then back again, an incredible excitement filling her. Nathan trembled at the exquisite sensations of Lorna's lips and tongue on his heated, straining flesh and the palms of her hands sliding up the back of his thighs to squeeze his rock-hard buttocks. Then, as her tongue started dancing wildly around the ultrasensitive tip, her teeth ever so gently raking it, sweat broke out all over him and he heard a roaring in his ears, his loins flooded with molten heat that seemed to make the bones in his legs melt.

Falling to his knees, he pushed her back on the carpet, kissing her everywhere, avidly licking at the drops of water that sat in the recess of her navel and sending Lorna whirling in a shower of fiery sparks.

He sat back on his heels between her sprawled legs, drinking in her beauty, lingering on the full, heaving breasts, then on the dark patch of reddish curls between her creamy thighs, the water drops there glittering like little diamonds. He slipped his fingers into her dewiness there, gently probing, then sliding them back and forth while his thumb massaged the swollen bud, watching her facial expression as he brought her to a shattering release, glorying in his ability to bring her pleasure. While Lorna was still rocking those sweet spasms, he lowered his head, his mouth replacing his hand, his tongue ravishing her hungrily, bringing her to that peak over and over, until Lorna was thrashing her head and writhing, begging him to come into her with ragged sobs.

His entry was slow, an exquisite, almost unbearable torture for them both, then with a little snarl, he twisted his hips and plunged in deeper, feeling as if he was drowning in that sweet, tight, velvety heat. Then he lay perfectly still, savoring their joining.

Lorna could feel his immense hardness filling her completely, feeling like a bolt of lightning inside her. Frantic with need, her hands rushed over the quivering muscles of his back as she dropped feverish kisses over his shoulders, neck, and face, then clasping his buttocks and squeezing, feeling as if she were being consumed in flames and knowing that only he could quench that fire.

"Please . . . please," she sobbed raggedly.

Nathan raised his head and softly taunted, "Please what?"

"Oh, damn you!" Lorna cried out, hitting his shoulder with her fist. Then she wrapped her long legs around him, pulling him even deeper into her pulsating depths.

With her long legs wrapped around him like a burning vise and her loins pressed against his as if she were branding him, Nathan gave in to his own clawing need, every nerve ending in his body screaming for release. He poured himself into her, driving with a wild urgency, reaching for her very soul before he released his passion inside her in a sweet, mind-searing, explosive consummation that left him drifting bodiless in a black empty void.

When Nathan returned to reality, he found he had collapsed over Lorna with his head buried in her damp hair. As he started to lift himself to relieve her of his weight, Lorna clasped him tightly, saying, "No! Stay like you are."

"I'll crush you," Nathan muttered, his head still spinning and his muscles still trembling.

"No, you won't. I don't want you to leave me."

It was then that Nathan realized that he was still lying inside her, his hair-roughened thighs between her soft ones. He slipped his arms beneath her back, resting a part of his weight on his forearms, thinking he really didn't want to move, relishing the scent of her freshly washed hair and the feel of her silky body pressed against his.

Lorna looked up and saw him covering her in the mirrors on the ceiling. She admired his powerful, rippling muscles as her hands ran over his back, touching him and seeing him at the same time, increasing her pleasure twofold. She reached to cup the back of his head, pressing his face to her breasts, her fingers playing in the dark curls at the nape of his neck. Oh, how she loved him, she thought, so much so that it brought tears to her eyes. Framing his face, she lifted his head, her lips anxious to taste his again, and Nathan met her halfway in an agonizingly sweet kiss that kindled embers that had not been quenched, but were merely smoldering.

Feeling him stirring inside her, then hardening, a little sob of gladness escaped Lorna's lips. She gasped as he made his first sweet thrust, feeling the vibrant sensations coursing through her, relishing the feel of her well-endowed, virile lover.

Nathan loved her slowly, leisurely, taking his time in bringing them to fulfillment so that they could savor each thrilling sensation. Then, as he led her up those lofty heights, plunging into her over and over and over, Lorna watched in the mirror above her, finding that seeing as well as feeling the contractions of the powerful muscles in his buttocks and back and shoulders with each breathtaking, spine-tingling, deep thrust did indeed multiply her pleasure. They seemed to be making love amid a kaleidoscope of swirling colors, all of her senses so vitally alive as he filled her with his power that she thought she had gained immortality, until he brought her to a soul-shattering release and a red haze fell over her eyes.

Later they ate, then bathed again. Nathan left the bath first to dress, leaving Lorna sitting on the carpet beside the pool towel-drying her hair. She heard the soft knock on the door of the sitting room and the muted sounds of Nathan talking to someone, then silence.

Wrapping a large towel around her, she walked from the bath, through the bedroom, and into the sitting room, seeing that Nathan had donned a pair of his Arab pantaloons. "Who was that at the door?" she asked.

"Isaac. He stopped by to deliver your chest."

Suddenly Lorna remembered the clothing they had wildly tossed about when they first made love. Horrified that Isaac might have seen the clothing and known they had hastily made love on the rug, she looked frantically about her, then breathed a sigh of relief when she saw that Nathan had picked them up.

Looking at her chest sitting by the door, she asked, "Where's the box with our wedding gifts?"

"Isaac said he didn't see any reason to bring it since we'd just have to take it back to the ship when we left. Besides, they'll be safer there, along with my money."

"Well, that sounds reasonable," Lorna agreed. "Would you mind bringing my chest into the bedroom so I can dress?"

"Do you have to dress right now?" Nathan's voice dropped to a husky timbre. "I had other things in mind."

Seeing the smoldering look in his eyes and his hand reaching for the string that held up his pantaloons, Lorna was amazed as his recuperative powers. A tingle of excitement ran through her at his promise of yet more sensual delights. She dropped the towel and answered in a breathless voice, "No, I don't have to dress. Not yet."

Several days later, while Nathan was busy with Eaton shoring up the city's fortifications, Lorna took a walk in the palace gardens, admiring the statues and the exotic plants there. She stopped and stared in disbelief at a rose bush covered with pink blooms, assuming it had been imported, for she had seen no others in all of her travels across North Africa. The bush brought back memories of England and a wave of nostalgia swept over her. She wondered if they had rose bushes in America. She certainly hoped so. They were her favorite flower.

For a long time she stood admiring the rose bush, then, casting a quick look around to make sure no one was about, bent and plucked a bloom from it. She held it to her nose and breathed in the heavenly scent, then twirling it in her fingers, continued her walk, almost stumbling over a peacock.

The bird ruffled his feathers in agitation, then spread his six-foot tail feathers, showing off the colorful, iridescent eyes in each feather before he turned and proudly strutted away. Lorna had to laugh at his arrogant, conceited manner, thinking that he reminded her of the vain dandies in London who took such pride in their gaudy dress and actually preened before others, thinking themselves much admired.

She turned, finding herself facing a slender middle-aged Arab who was looking at her quizzically. But it wasn't his neatly trimmed beard or the large ruby winking in his elegant silk turban that told her who this man was. Rather it was his royal carriage that told her she had come face to face with Hamet.

Only too aware of the stolen rose in her hand, Lorna flushed guiltily, then stammered in Arabic, "Excuse me, Your . . . Your Eminence. I didn't mean . . . mean to intrude on your solitude."

A look of surprise came over the man's face before he asked, "You're Captain Sloan's wife, aren't you?"

"Yes, I am."

"And where did you learn to speak Arabic? From your husband?"

Lorna wasn't about to tell him she had learned Arabic in his brother's *iyal* in Tripoli. "Yes."

"What were you laughing at when I walked up?"

"The peacock. He's so vain and arrogant that he reminded me of some of the young men I had seen back in London."

Hamet had never paid any attention to the peacocks, but now that Lorna mentioned it, he recalled seeing men who strutted just as much as the vain male birds. A ghost of a smile played on his thin lips before he asked, "Is that where you are from? London?"

"Yes. And now, if you will excuse me."

As Lorna turned, Hamet said, "No! Don't leave! I have more questions to ask."

It was a demand, not a request, and for that reason it brought Lorna's anger to the rise. She turned and looked Hamet straight in the eye, saying in a tightly controlled voice, "I am not a slave, nor am I your subject. I will not be commanded to do something. As a guest in your home, I would be happy to stay and answer your questions—if you request it of me."

Hamet was shocked by her answer, and he had never had a woman look him directly in the eye—or for that matter, few men. The woman intrigued him. "Would you obey my command if I were your sovereign?" he asked curiously.

Lorna remembered her vow that she would never bow to the demands of nobility again. "Frankly, no. I always felt that respect was something that should be earned, not granted by birth. Besides, I'm an American now, and Americans do not recognize any sovereign. We bow to no man."

Hamet was even more intrigued. "Then I will ask, and not demand, that you stay."

Lorna realized that it was quite a concession coming from a man who had been born and bred to having his every wish fulfilled, to say nothing of having his commands obeyed. She smiled and sat on a nearby stone bench, asking, "Now, what would you like to know?"

It turned out that, while Hamet had traveled all over North Africa, he had never been to another continent and was just as curious about her country and Europe as Chedlya had been. She sensed that he asked her questions that he would never ask a European man for fear a European might mock his lack of worldliness or think him stupid. His vulnerability touched a soft spot in Lorna's heart.

When she returned to their apartment much later, Nathan was already present. "Where have you been?" he asked.

"I took a walk in the garden and ran into Hamet. He asked me to stay and talk to him." Lorna sank down on one of the low divans and folded her legs beside her, saying, "You were right, Nathan. I don't think he has many true friends. He seems so lonely, and he's terrified. The whole time we were talking, he kept glancing over his shoulder, as if he expected to see an assassin slipping up on him. It was really pathetic. I feel sorry for him."

Nathan wasn't surprised at Lorna's compassion. But what did surprise him was Hamet. Since when did an Arab man, especially a prince, take the time to talk to a woman, someone considered much beneath him? But then he remembered that Hamet had known the bitterness of defeat, had had more than a taste of poverty in his exile, both humbling experiences, and Lorna was an extraordinarily perceptive woman.

Two nights later Nathan awoke and found Lorna missing from the bed. He sat up and peered in the darkness, then, hearing a loud crash of thunder, looked out on the balcony. In the blinding, split-second flash of a lightning bolt, he saw Lorna standing there.

He threw back the sheet and rose from the bed, walking to the archway between their sitting room and the balcony, then pushed aside the sheer drapes that were being billowed by the wind. It wasn't until he stepped onto the balcony that he realized it was raining. "What are you doing out here?"

Lorna whirled, saying in an excited voice, "Look, Nathan! It's actually raining!"

"I know. And you're getting soaking wet."

"Yes, and it feels wonderful!"

Lorna raised her face to the heavens, the wind whipping her long wet hair around her, saying, "I didn't think I'd ever see rain again. It's so beautiful, so marvelous. Close your eyes, Nathan. Just let yourself feel it."

With the rain pelting down on Lorna's beaming face and the water streaming down her naked body to pool at her feet on the balcony floor, Nathan's love for her came rushing to the surface, so powerful that he feared it would smother him. If only he knew what this beautiful, perplexing woman who was his wife really felt for him. That they shared passion meant nothing. Lorna had a passionate nature he had awakened and then carefully nurtured. Even her concern for his safety didn't mean she loved him. She was a warm, compassionate woman.

His need to tell her he loved her was a physical ache in his throat, and yet he didn't dare, for fear of rejection. Even worse, she might return the words out of simple gratitude for his saving her from slavery and offering her his protection, and that was something his fierce pride would never allow.

Nathan stood on the balcony and watched Lorna until the rain was a fine drizzle. Then he said with a voice choked with emotion, "You're shivering. Come back to bed. Let me warm you."

He swooped her up in his powerful arms and carried her back to bed, then told her with his body what he didn't dare to speak. He loved her tenderly, sweetly, eloquently, and when it was over, Lorna was sobbing in his arms from the sheer beauty of it.

A few days later Lorna returned to their quarters from a tour of the palace with Hamet.

As she walked into the room, Nathan whirled, and shouted, "Where in the hell have you been? We've been looking everywhere for you!"

Acutely aware of Captain Hull standing to the side, Lorna's anger rose. How dare Nathan use that tone of voice to her, particularly in front of others. It was humiliating. "Don't yell at me!"

"I'll yell anytime I goddamn feel like it!" Nathan threw back. "Now, where have you been?"

Lorna glared at him, then replied tightly, "Hamet took me on a tour of the palace."

"Christ! Of all the times for that nincompoop to drag you off someplace—"

"Don't call Hamet a nincompoop! He was only being gracious!"

"Dammit, Lorna, don't you realize the city is about to be attacked? Of all the times for you to disappear—"

"Attacked?" Lorna asked in surprise, cutting across his words.

"Yes, attacked. The Tripolitan Army is marching down on us right now."

"But I thought they had fled into the desert."

Nathan sighed in exasperation, then said, "They did. But they've reformed and received reinforcements from Tripoli. That's why Isaac and I were looking for you, so he could take you back to his ship with him."

He was going to send her away again? Oh, no, Lorna vowed. Over her dead body!

"Well, you could have saved yourself a lot of time

and trouble. I'm not leaving," Lorna said in a firm voice.

Nathan stared at her in disbelief. Lorna stared back, her chin set stubbornly, then said, "You said I didn't have to leave until you marched for Tripoli. I'm staying."

Nathan's fear for her was a living, clawing thing inside him. "The hell you are!" he thundered. "You're going to the *Argus* with Isaac, even if I have to tie you up and put you in that longboat myself."

At the angry, almost wild look on Nathan's face, Lorna didn't doubt his words. She decided to take another approach. She turned to Captain Hull, saying, "Do you really think Derna will fall?"

Hull was only too aware of Nathan glaring at him, but in all honesty he thought his friend was overreacting to the threat. Nathan's fear for his wife's safety had been something of a revelation to him. He had never thought to see the cool, calm, maddeningly composed merchant captain so distraught. "No, with the fortifications having been shored up and Nathan drilling those Greek gunners over the past week, I personally feel that we can repulse them."

"Goddammit, Isaac! You're supposed to be my friend! I want Lorna out of here!"

"She will get out of Derna if the need arises," Hull replied calmly. "My orders are to evacuate Hamet, his friends, and all Americans if Derna is recaptured. Two longboats will be waiting at the end of that half-burned wharf for that reason, the first for the civilians, and the second for combatants, whose retreat the *Argus* will cover. I'm leaving one of my officers here to watch from one of the palace towers. If he sees the fortifications are falling, he will escort Lorna, Hamet, and his friends to the wharf. I give you my personal promise that Lorna will be perfectly safe."

For the love of him, Nathan couldn't fault Hull's carefully laid plans. As usual his friend had everything well in hand. And Hull wasn't a man to make a promise lightly.

Aware of Lorna's expectant look, Nathan turned to her and said, "All right. You can stay. But you do what Hull's officer tells you to, and for the love of God don't disappear again!"

"I didn't disappear!" Lorna snapped back.

Hull grinned, thinking his friend was going to have his work cut out for him with Lorna. That spunky little lady would never bow to any man's authority. Then, afraid the argument would start all over, he stepped forward and said briskly, "I've got to get on my way." He held his hand out to Nathan, saying, "Good luck."

Nathan gave Hull's hand a quick shake and replied, "Thanks. I hope you're right and we repulse them."

As Hull walked from the room, it was Lorna's turn to feel fear as she realized Nathan was going back into battle. Her face drained of all color. She knew the hell she would go through. She had already been through it once. It was a special hell designed for women, waiting for their loved ones to return from war, agonizing over how their men might be faring, or if they would ever be seen again. Compared to it, fighting would be easy.

Nathan turned, hesitant to kiss Lorna good-bye. After their heated words he wasn't sure if she was still angry with him or not.

"You will be careful, won't you?" Lorna asked softly.

To Nathan, Lorna's simple question was a blessing. Feeling a tremendous relief, he stepped forward, saying, "Yes, I'll be careful." He grinned, adding, "If for no other reason than to get back here and make sure you obeyed my orders."

Seeing Lorna's eyes flare, Nathan laughed, caught her to him, and kissed her soundly before she could retort. By the time she recovered from that blazing kiss, Nathan was bounding down the stairs.

Lorna waited anxiously in their apartment for the battle to begin. Then, hearing the muted thunder of cannons being fired, she hurried to the balcony railing and peered out. But all she could see was the city below and the bay beyond it, for their apartment was facing seaward and not toward the desert. For a while, she watched the *Argus* as it sailed back and forth across the bay, firing broadsides, the cannons spitting fire and smoke. Then, hearing sounds of voices, she glanced down and saw Hamet and his friends in the courtyard below. The Arabs were rushing about, their excitement at a feverish pitch, while the prince sat on a stone bench, staring out into space, his face ashen with fear.

Lorna was filled with anger. Not one of Hamet's friends was doing anything to soothe him or to try and distract him from his fears. If anything, they were just frightening him all the more with their wild talk and gestures. Putting her own fear behind her, she turned and walked from the room, determined she would comfort the prince whose kingdom depended on this battle. Like waiting for one's loved ones to return from war, that too was a place designed for women since the beginning of time, the role of soothing away fears and inspiring hope.

Across the city in one of the fortifications, Nathan was directing the firing of the cannons manned by a score of Greeks, taking satisfaction in seeing his drills had paid off. The men worked like a well-oiled machine, swabbing, loading, firing, then repeating the procedure over and over, their shots leaving gaping holes in the Tripolitan ranks. Between their murderous fire and that of the *Argus*, which had caught parties of the enemy a few times in her fire, he knew it wouldn't be long before the Tripolitans, whose attack had been timid to start with, would withdraw.

In a lull in the battle Nathan watched as a Janissary unit of cavalry gathered in the distance to make another charge. Then as the *sphahis* sped their horses toward the barricade, waving their curved scimitars above their heads, his breath caught at the sight of the Janissary captain leading them. He'd know that red-bearded bastard anywhere. It was his old enemy, Khaldun!

His heart racing in anticipation, Nathan turned to one of the Greeks and said in lingua franca, "Take over here!"

Before the surprised Greek could even answer, Nathan had bounded over the walls of the barricade. He tore for his horse, jerked the reins free, leaped on the animal's back, then flew over the barricade, joining the Arab mercenaries who were riding out to meet the Janissaries.

Bringing his horse up beside one of the Arabs' horses, he turned in the saddle and said to the man, "Sorry, but I need that thing more than you do," then yanked the scimitar from the surprised Arab's hand.

Racing away, Nathan heard the Arab's curse, then, from the corner of his eye, saw the disarmed man wheeling his horse back around.

The two groups of mounted men came together with the clashing of steel against steel, and to Nathan's utter frustration, he had to fight his way

through two Janissaries before he could get to his old
enemy. Quickly disposing of them, he called out over
the din of the fight, "Khaldun!"

Hearing his name called, the Janissary captain
wheeled his horse, jerking the scimitar he had just
thrust into an Arab's chest as he turned. His eyes filled
with surprise as he saw Nathan sitting on his horse just
a few feet from him, then narrowed as he spat, "You!"

"Yes, it's me!" Nathan threw back. "And I've
been waiting a long time for this."

Both men charged at the same time, their blood-
stained scimitars meeting with a loud, metallic clatter
that sent sparks flying. Khaldun raised his sword and
swung again, and again Nathan's rose to meet it in
another shoulder-jarring clash of steel. Horses side by
side, so close their legs brushed one another, the two
swung over and over. Once the Janissary's sword,
aimed with deadly intent, came so close to its mark
that it ripped Nathan's shirt and he felt the sting of
the blade before he deflected the blow with a powerful upper cut of his sword.

Unknown to either man, they were alone on the
battlefield, the Janissaries having gone into full retreat, taking the Tripolitan army with them, and the
Arab mercenaries watching the fight from a distance
away, sensing that this confrontation between two
fierce combatants had nothing to do with the war. For
fifteen minutes the two thrust and hacked at one another, sweat from their exertions rolling down their
foreheads and necks, their chests heaving, the dust
kicked up by their horses' hooves forming a thick,
choking cloud around them.

Seeing his enemy was tiring, Nathan taunted,
"You're getting old, Khaldun, and soft."

Khaldun's dark eyes flashed with unadulterated
hatred before he raised his sword high for the killing

blow. As the scimitar came whizzing down, Nathan ducked to the side, feeling the air as the blade passed over his head, then leaned from the saddle and thrust his own sword deep into the Janissary's exposed belly, jerking the blade up in an old swordsman's trick calculated to sever the big artery coming from the heart.

Khaldun dropped his scimitar, his eyes widening in horror as he clasped the sword that was buried deep in his body. Nathan watched as the color drained from the Janissary's face and his blood drained out of his body and stained his white robe. Then with a groan Khaldun toppled off his horse to the ground.

Looking down at the crumpled body of the mortally wounded Janissary, Nathan knew that he was still conscious and could hear his words. "That was for Timothy Jones. Do you remember him? He was the seventeen-year-old you beat to death because he dropped a rock. And it was for me and the rest of my crewmates who died in that stinking hellhole you ran. Now you'll find out what hell is all about."

Chapter 18

When Lorna heard the wonderful news that the Tripolitans had been firmly repulsed and were once again fleeing into the desert, she left a grateful and much-relieved Hamet and retired to her apartment to await Nathan's return. Hearing his firm, sure steps in the hallway, she turned as he walked into the sitting room and then almost fainted when she saw the front of his shirt was covered with blood.

"Now, don't be alarmed," Nathan warned. "It's only a scratch."

Lorna fought a hard battle to keep from feeling just that. It took all of her willpower to remain composed and say in a calm voice, "Then take off your shirt so I can tend it."

While Nathan hadn't wanted Lorna to become alarmed, he savored the attention she was giving him as she bathed the wound on his chest and then dressed it, since the scratch was deep and persisted in oozing blood. Taking a roll of bandage from the medicine kit that Nathan kept in his chest, she rose from where she had been sitting and said, "Hold out your arms." As he complied and she started wrapping the bandage around his broad chest, she asked, "How did you get this?"

"Khaldun gave it to me."

Lorna was so stunned that she dropped the roll of bandage. Nathan caught it in one hand before it fell to the floor. Looking up at him, she asked in surprise, "Then you found him?"

"Yes, I found him," Nathan answered in a voice vibrating with meaningful undertones. "He's dead."

Lorna didn't have to ask who killed him. She knew by both his voice and the metallic glitter of satisfaction in Nathan's green eyes. Nor did she ask any further questions. She didn't want to know any of the gory details. She was just glad that Nathan's quest for revenge was over.

"Will you still stay for Eaton's march on Tripoli?" she asked.

"Yes, when I joined the expedition, I gave Eaton my word I'd stick it out to the end, and after meeting Khaldun today I'm even more determined to see those American prisoners Yusef is holding for ransom freed. For all we know they may be at the mercy of a jailer as cruel and sadistic as Khaldun was."

Lorna had hoped desperately for another answer. While she wanted to see the Americans freed, too, another part of her had secretly hoped that today's confrontation and victory over Nathan's old enemy would have marked the end of his fighting. Now she would have to go through the agony of wondering and waiting all over again, and even worse, another unbearable separation loomed ahead of her, one that might stretch into weeks, or even months.

She wondered, if she asked him to break his word to Eaton, would Nathan consent? Then remembering that she had insisted that he join in order to make him feel free to make his own choices, she held her tongue.

Five weeks later Lorna was standing on their balcony and absently gazing out at the bay, deep in thought. She had seen almost nothing of Nathan during that time, and she wondered if he was really that committed to helping get Eaton's army trained for its march on Tripoli, or if he was only using that as an excuse to avoid her company. Had he already tired of her? What he had said about divorce preyed on her mind almost constantly, a mental torture that fed off her insecurity about her marriage and its future. She had been a fool to think of her time with Nathan as a season of joy. It was turning out to be a time of sheer hell.

Hearing the sound of Nathan's boots on the marble hallway outside their apartment, Lorna started. She hurried into the sitting room, entering it just as Nathan was closing the door behind him. "What are you doing here?" she asked in surprise.

"I live here, remember?" Nathan snapped.

Lorna bristled at his sharp answer. Obviously he wasn't in the best of moods, but then she was feeling a little testy herself. She was tempted to tell him that she had forgotten he lived here, since she so very rarely saw him, but held her anger. "You know what I mean. What are you doing here so early? Did Eaton call off the drilling for today."

"No, I called it off! I told him that I was sick and tired of playing the role of a drill sergeant to a bunch of goddamned lazy Arabs. I joined this expedition in a liaison capacity, nothing more."

"I thought they were doing better," Lorna remarked, still trying to keep the peace. She didn't want to spend what little time she had with Nathan fighting with him.

"Well, they've decided they've had enough training. They'd much rather be out strutting in the streets, playing the role of Derna's saviors. Hell, let Eaton drill them. He hired the bastards."

Nathan threw himself down on one of the low divans and stared at the ceiling, then said in disgust, "God, I'll be glad when this war is over. This waiting is getting on my nerves."

Lorna's patience with his irritability was suddenly at an end. "Getting on *your* nerves?" she threw back. "What about mine? At least you can get out and stir around, while I've been confined to this palace and its grounds. I might as well be back in prison!"

Nathan frowned at her sharp words. Because of the wild, undisciplined and unpredictable mercenaries roaming the streets of Derna, he had strongly cautioned her not to venture outside the walls surrounding the palace, not even to the nearby marketplace, and he had been deliberately avoiding her, fearing he would reveal his feelings for her. But his trying to put distance between them had turned out to be a double-edged sword. He had discovered that he needed Lorna in many ways, not just to relieve his sexual tension. He missed her presence, her laughter, even her irritating stubbornness, and trying to keep away from her kept him tense and irritable. He had to admit that he had been neglecting her sorely, and his treatment of her had been totally unfair. It wasn't her fault that she couldn't love him in return. Those kind of deep feelings couldn't be forced.

"I'm sorry," Nathan said. "I guess I never stopped to think how bored you must be, being cooped up in this place. Would you like to go for a ride? Maybe it would relax us both."

Besides her misery from worrying over Nathan's safety and their marriage, Lorna was feeling restless. "A ride would be nice," she admitted, then said with more enthusiasm, "I'll be with you as soon as I can slip on my boots."

After they had saddled their horses, they rode through the sun-dappled streets of Derna, passing the beautiful mosque with its gleaming domes and towering minarets. Because Lorna had stayed in the palace since their arrival, she caused quite a stir as she and Nathan rode toward the beach, for the Arabs had never seen an unveiled woman riding a horse. After they had left the teeming city behind them and cautiously descended one of the many trails that weaved their way down the steep cliffs to one side of the bay, they gave their horses their heads.

Needing no encouragement, the spirited animals raced down the beach, anxious for a hard, invigorating run, kicking up wet sand and then spraying water as they ran through the waves lapping at the edge of the beach, the water drops that were briefly suspended in the air glistening in the bright sunlight. The wind tore the pins from Lorna's chignon as she raced down the beach, sending her long hair flying out behind her like a streamer. For once Lorna didn't care about her precious pins. It was almost as if the wind tearing past her and whipping her full pantaloons against her legs was sweeping away all of the tension and worries she had been harboring for so long. She gave herself up to the thrill of the race, glorying in the feel of the powerful animal beneath her and letting out a laugh of pure delight. She felt as free as a bird, as if she was soaring into the sky.

She glanced across from her, seeing Nathan was laughing too, his teeth flashing white against his deep tan and the wind whipping his dark hair about his face. As he turned his head and looked across at her and she saw his beautiful green eyes glittering with his own exhilaration from the stimulating ride, another thrill ran through her. She could hardly believe that she was actually here on this deserted beach with the man of her dreams. A sudden thought flashed through her mind. Maybe she wasn't. Maybe she was still back in London and this and all that had happened to her since Nathan came into her life had been nothing but a wonderful dream. If that were true, she hoped she never woke up, that this dream lasted forever.

When the horses tired, they slowed the animals to a trot, still continuing to ride down the silvery stretch of beach, leaving the bay behind them and riding along the Mediterranean until the beach narrowed and finally ended in an upthrust of huge boulders that extended into the sea. Lorna watched as the towering waves crashed into the massive, jagged rocks, throwing salty water a good fifty feet in the air before the water receded, leaving in its wake a swirling froth before the next wave slowly built and then hit with a deafening crash. Lorna felt both awed by the spectacular sight and a little frightened by the awesome power of the sea, wondering how the rocks could withstand the tremendous pounding they were taking over and over and over.

Feeling Nathan's warm hand cupping her elbow, she turned, seeing his lips were moving. "What?" she called over the thundering noise.

"I said let's ride back down the beach," Nathan yelled back.

Lorna nodded her head in agreement, and as

they rode away, she glanced back over her shoulder and her breath caught, seeing the shimmering rainbow in the mist that surrounded the jagged rocks.

Farther down the beach they stopped and dismounted, walking along the edge of the water and beachcombing, both secretly relishing the quiet company of the other and feeling content. They found pieces of wood that had been there so long they had petrified, a glass bottle that had floated from God knows where, a half-smashed sea chest. But it was the seashells that fascinated Lorna, all different sizes and shapes. Picking up a shell whose outer covering was rough and an ugly gray, Lorna turned it over, hardly believing the beautiful iridescent greens, creams, and pinks she found inside it. "What kind of shell is this?" she asked Nathan.

"An oyster shell. Let's look around and see if we can find some that are still whole, so we can pry them open."

"Why? Are you thinking of eating them?" Lorna asked, wrinkling her nose in distaste, for she heard that some people ate them raw.

"No. Maybe we can find a pearl."

"A pearl?" Lorna asked in surprise.

"Yes, this is a pearl oyster. The North Africans dive for them in the bays all up and down the coast, and sometimes you'll find them washed up on the beach. Of course, they don't have the quality of the pearls that are found in the Persian Gulf—those are the best in the world—but they're nothing to be sneezed at."

Excited at the prospect of finding a pearl, Lorna rushed off down the beach. After searching for about thirty minutes, they only managed to find nine intact oysters. Sitting down on the sand, Lorna watched while Nathan pried them open with his knife, feeling more and more disappointed when they found nothing in them but the slimy grayish oysters. By the time Nathan was opening the eighth, Lorna had lost interest and was gazing out to sea.

"Lorna, look!"

Lorna turned her head and looked down at the open shell in Nathan's hand, hardly believing her eyes when she saw the pearl sitting at the side of the oyster. A thrill of excitement rushed through her. "You found one!"

"Yes, and to tell you the truth, I'm a little surprised myself."

Lorna bent and peered closer at the pearl, seeing that it was a soft rosy color. "I thought pearls were supposed to be cream colored."

"There *are* cream-colored pearls. And there are some that are so white that they have a silvery sheen to them. And then there are the pink ones, like this, and a pure black. But the black pearls are very rare and therefore the most prized."

Nathan picked the pearl from the shell, tossed the shell aside, and held the pearl up, examining it before he said, "This isn't bad quality itself. It's perfectly round."

"I thought all pearls were round."

"The pearls you see in most jewelry are. But in their natural state, a great many are oblong or teardrop-shaped, or even pear-shaped."

As Nathan turned his hand and the pearl caught the light, giving it a pink, luminous sheen, Lorna decided she liked the color better than the cream pearls and noticed that it was much larger than any pearl she had ever seen, almost the size of her thumbnail.

Nathan handed her the pearl and picked up the last shell, prying it open. Again there was nothing there but the oyster. But Lorna wasn't even paying any attention to what Nathan was doing. Her eyes were glued on the pearl in her hand, seemingly glowing with a life of its own. "Oh, Nathan," she said softly, "it's beautiful."

"Yes," Nathan agreed, "it's not a bad find for a couple of amateurs. And we didn't even have to dive for it. It was a gift from the sea."

Lorna smiled, liking the thought of the sea giving Nathan and her a gift. She handed it back to Nathan, then, seeing him slipping it in his shirt pocket, said, "Now be careful you don't lose it."

Nathan chuckled and said, "I won't. I'll guard it with my life."

He rose to his feet, saying, "Let's go for a swim."

"I can't swim," Lorna admitted a little shamefully, thinking that as a sailor he would be disgusted with her.

He smiled and answered, "Well, we'll have to remedy that someday. But this isn't the right place to learn how to swim. The surf is too rough. We'll just wade in."

When Nathan removed his shirt and boots, Lorna wasn't alarmed. But when she looked up from removing her own boots and saw him peeling off his breeches, she gasped, "You're going to strip naked?"

"Why not? No one can see us. Besides, clothes would just hamper us, particularly those pantaloons of yours. If you don't remove them, the sand and water that gets caught in them will drag them off."

Lorna could see the wisdom of Nathan's words. Besides, if she wore her clothes swimming, she wouldn't have any dry ones to wear afterward. She rose to her feet and stripped, then accepted Nathan's outstretched hand and walked into the water with him.

Lorna had never been in an ocean, had never so

much as waded in one, for Nathan had carried her to and from the longboat. The feel of the pull of the ocean was a new sensation for her, seeming as if the water that was receding was trying to take both her and the sand beneath her feet back to sea with it. Nathan allowed her to stand and feel the ebb and flow of the water before leading her farther in. When Lorna came face to face with her first breaker, another sensation overcame her, one of pure terror as she watched the water swell, towering over her and looking very threatening. Again she felt the pull, this time much more powerful, before the huge wall of water rolled over and the wave crashed down on her. She screamed as she felt it pulling her under, the sand it was sweeping from the bottom stinging her legs and the powerful, swirling water threatening to engulf her. Had it not been for Nathan holding her hand tightly, she would have been completely submerged and tumbled to the bottom. As it was, she was dunked and came up spitting water, the salt burning her eyes.

Seeing the stark terror on her face, Nathan said, "There's nothing to be afraid of. The next time you see a wave breaking, turn your back to it and lean into it. When it hits, don't fight it. If it pushes you forward, go with it. The water may go over your head for a few seconds, but it won't drown you."

From then on, Lorna did as Nathan directed, but with each wave there was still that tingle of fear when it broke and the water rushed over her head, pushing as if it were determined to dash her to the bottom. And when it had passed, leaving her standing thigh-deep in swirling, foaming water, Lorna would laugh in a mixture of relief and excitement, then turn to await the next wave and the next tingle of fear.

After a while Nathan guided her past the breakers. Here the water came to her breasts, until she was lifted from her feet by the deep swells, then gently set back down, a soothing, lulling motion that seemed at odds with the wild, crashing waves just a few feet away. Then, feeling something brush her bare leg, she gasped.

"What's wrong?" Nathan asked, seeing her eyes wide with fear.

"Something just brushed against my leg."

"Probably a fish. There are fish in the ocean, you know," he said with an amused twinkle in his eyes.

"Maybe it was a shark," Lorna suggested, glancing nervously about her.

"No, sharks don't come this close to the shore. Besides, they're rare in this part of the Mediterranean."

Lorna heard a splash and jumped. She whirled in the direction the noise had come from, but saw nothing but water. "What was that?" she asked apprehensively.

"A fish jumping out of the water. When they land on their sides they make that splashing noise. That's how fishermen can tell they're there in the dark."

A flash of silver caught Lorna's eye as a fish flew through the air, followed by the splash as it dived back in, then another flash of silver. Feeling a little foolish, she laughed, saying, "You'd think they'd stay away with us so close."

"Just standing here, we don't look very threatening. Besides, you'd be surprised how curious fish can be. They can't seem to resist the temptation to investigate something, particularly if that something is still. They'll go right up to a diver and peer in his face, as if they're trying to figure out who that strange-looking creature is."

Nathan took Lorna back to the shore and then went back in for a brief swim. Lorna sat in waste-deep

water, enjoying the gentle pull of the sea, and
watched as he swam in the water past the breakers,
his powerful arms glistening in the sunlight at each
stroke he took. When he dived and disappeared for
what seemed an eternity to Lorna, she watched apprehensively, then laughed with relief when his dark
head bobbed back up.

She leaned back, propping herself on her hands
and lifting her face, seeing the circling seagulls that
were cawing down at her and watching the fluffy
white clouds that were being blown across the sky,
studying their shapes and imagining one looked like a
white horse, another like a sailing ship, and yet another like a castle. Then she closed her eyes, drinking
in the tangy scent of the ocean and relishing the feel
of the warm sun on her face.

Feeling a shadow fall over her, she opened her
eyes and saw Nathan standing over her. With his towering height, his splendid physique revealed to her in
all its magnificent glory, and the sunlight making the
water drops in his dark hair glisten like a crown of
diamonds, she thought he looked like a beautiful god
rising from the sea. And then he smiled, a sensuous
smile that warmed her to the tips of her toes and sent
her heart to doing crazy flip-flaps in her chest.

He fell to his knees beside her, one hand sliding
around her neck to cup the back of her head, saying,
"I've wondered ever since we bathed together what
it would be like to make love to you in the water."

The husky timbre of his voice was still washing
over Lorna as he lowered his head, dropping feather-
like kisses over her face before he kissed away the
water drops that were still clinging to her thick eyelashes and licked the salt from her lips.

He lowered her, lying half over her, the sea tugging at their hips and legs and lapping at her shoul-

ders on the wet sand. When she started to fold her
arms around his broad shoulders, he caught her hands
in his, pinning them down beside her head, his mouth
exploring the length of her neck. The feel of his hard
palms and callused fingers against her soft ones was as
sensuous as that of his warm lips against her throat.
The strong, slender fingers entwined around her as he
captured her mouth in a sweet, lingering kiss; then he
squeezed both hands as he deepened the kiss, his lips
and tongue tasting of salt in a long, hot, drugging kiss
that sent Lorna's senses swimming.

Still holding her hands prisoner against the sand,
Nathan blazed a trail of fire over her shoulders, up her
inner arm, across her temples and eyelids, and then
back down, leaving each inch of her skin sensitized
and tingling. Slowly, ever so slowly, his mouth descended, kissing her breasts, licking the rivulets of salt
water away. Lorna's breath came in shallow, rapid
gasps, her nipples rising and hardening in throbbing
anticipation of his mouth. As his lips closed over one
rosy tip, his teeth gently raking the tender flesh before he took it in his mouth, she arched her back, her
hands clasping and unclasping his hands, telling him
silently and eloquently of the rolling waves of exquisite pleasure she was feeling.

Nathan's head slipped lower, his lips nipping at
her ribs, his hands leaving hers to stroke the wet, silky
skin of her sides. The muscles in Lorna's stomach
contracted as he lapped at the pool of sea water that
lay in the recessed dimple there; then as his thumb
slowly brushed back and forth, back and forth, over
the area between her hip bone and groin, she felt the
skin tingling and burning as new waves of sensation
swamped her, a scalding warmth filling her loins.

Nathan nudged her legs apart with one knee.
Lorna felt the brush of his hot arousal against her

thigh through the warm swirling water as he lifted himself over and knelt between her parted thighs, a brush that promised heaven and more. Lifting his head from where he had been dropping soft kisses on her stomach, Nathan sat back on his heels, gazing down on her.

Slowly his eyes drank in the sight of her wet hair that lay in long tangled strands around her, the thick dark lashes that lay against her passion-flushed cheeks, her parted lips, swollen from his long, torrid kiss, then slipped lower to stare at the soft twin mounds that rose and fell in quick, excited breaths, the wet, creamy skin glistening in the sunlight.

"You're beautiful," he said in a soft, thick voice, his hands stroking the silky skin of her thighs. "A beautiful, seductive sea nymph."

Lorna's eyelids fluttered open, and Nathan felt himself submerged in those dark violet depths. She looked up through dazed eyes to see him kneeling between her legs, the wind ruffling his dark hair around his face, his eyes shimmering green fire in his tanned face, the sun behind him outlining the extraordinary breadth of his shoulders and muscular arms. "You're beautiful, too," she whispered.

A ghost of an amused smile crossed Nathan's sensual lips before his hands slipped beneath her hips, lifting and sliding her buttocks. Lorna sucked in her breath sharply as she felt the moist hot tip of his engorged flesh against her, slowly circling, teasing and taunting as his fingers and tongue had so often done. A wetness slipped from her, bathing him in a scalding heat as a bolt of fire shot through her loins and centered in the core of her womanhood. It was an agony to have him there, so close to the portal that throbbed and burned for him, and yet so far away. She lunged, trying to impale herself on his hot, rigid length, but Nathan held her hips firmly, saying, "No. Not yet."

"Please," Lorna sobbed, "I can't stand it anymore."

But Nathan only smiled and continued his exquisite torture, watching Lorna's eyes widen, then glaze over as her body shuddered, engulfed in the hot waves of sheer sensation that burned her to the soles of her feet.

Only after the convulsive shudders had dwindled to tremors did Nathan let her hips slip back into the water, bending forward on his elbows to capture her lips in a searing kiss that rekindled the smoldering embers of her passion, a kiss that demanded as much as it gave and seemed to go on forever, leaving her weak and spinning dizzily. Finally lifting his head, he smiled down at her, entering her slowly, sinking deeper and deeper into her depths, sheathing himself in her hot wet silk and filling her completely.

Nathan lay perfectly still, savoring the feel of her warm velvet surrounding him, welcoming him, feeling as if he had come home after a long ocean voyage. Lorna, too, savored their joining, glorying in the feel of his muscular thighs and taut belly against hers, the crisp hairs on his chest prickling her swollen, aching nipples, the sea lapping at their sides and gently tugging at their legs. Her hands ran over the wet skin on his back, her fingertips tracing the powerful, corded muscles there before one hand rose to tangle in the wet strands of hair at the nape of his neck. She turned her head into the warm crook of his throat, breathing in his heady male scent before her tongue traced the powerful muscle on his neck to his ear, circling and darting, sending shivers of intense pleasure coursing through Nathan.

Nathan raised his head and kissed her, teeth

gently tugging at her full lower lip. Lorna kissed him back as he began his movements, slow, exquisitely sensual movements, his deep thrusts as powerful as the breakers a few yards from them, then withdrawing, Lorna's hips following him like the grains of the sand following the receding waves, giving and taking away like the sea itself, movements that dated back as far in time as the birth of the salty waters that surrounded them.

He rolled to his side, bringing her with him without even breaking his rhythm. There they lay, embracing and exchanging salty kisses, their smoldering passion soothed by the gentle lapping waters, drawing out their pleasure. Again he rolled, this time to his back, encouraging Lorna to take up the motions, his hands smoothing over her wet, silken thighs and caressing her breasts as he watched the fleeting expressions on her face as the rapturous waves of sensation washed over her.

Lorna felt as if she was riding the edge of a lightning bolt with Nathan's hot, rigid length deep inside her, each downward thrust threatening to melt her spine and sending sparks dancing behind her eyes. She increased the tempo, her passion building to a feverish pitch and her senses expanding, breaths coming in ragged gasps. Seeing her throw her head back and arch her back, her velvety heat feeling as if it would squeeze the life from him, Nathan's own need for release came to a sudden, white-hot peak. He rolled her beneath him, his mouth coming down on hers in a fierce, searing kiss.

With powerful, deep, masterful thrusts he drove them up that wave of mounting rapture, higher and higher, the unbearable tension in both of them building as they strained against each other, then hovered at the crest in intense anticipation. Like the sea around them, the wave broke and crashed down on them, tumbling them into a deep, dark whirlpool, his cry of ecstasy mingling with hers as he released his life-giving seed, a scalding jet deep inside her.

When Nathan emerged from the dark, swirling void, his body still trembling in the aftermath of his explosive release, he felt totally drained and yet strangely filled. He raised his head and looked down at Lorna, seeing the tears trickling down her temples in reaction to her own soul-shattering experience. Feeling his gaze on her, Lorna opened her eyes, the tears in her thick lashes glittering like tiny diamonds around her jewellike eyes.

Nathan felt a lump in his throat and that twisting pain in his chest. The emotion that had nothing to do with his earlier passion—and yet, everything—came rushing to the surface in an overpowering need to tell her of his love. He struggled to fight it down, then buried his face in the silky, soft crook of her neck as the words tumbled out, whispering, *"Je t'aime,"* then repeating it in lingua franca.

"What?" Lorna asked, for the half-strangled words had been muffled against her throat.

As much as Nathan wanted to express his deep love in English, he found he couldn't. He felt much too vulnerable, and saying them in a foreign language had released a part of his tension. "I said that was a beautiful experience."

Lorna stroked the damp curls on the back of his head, saying softly, "Yes, it was," feeling a misery creeping over her, for her tears had come from her need to speak the words as much as in reaction to their lovemaking.

For a long time they lay holding one another, locked in their own brooding thoughts, neither suspecting the other's silence stemmed from the same pain. Finally Nathan lifted his head, tenderly kissed Lorna's lips, and rose, carrying her back in the sea to wash the sand from them. Then they sat on the beach, letting the wind dry them and sharing the water bag that Nathan had brought with him, gazing out at the blue waters of the Mediterranean.

Glancing over and seeing Lorna's nose was beginning to get burned, Nathan rose, saying, "We'd better go. Your nose is getting a little pink. I think you've had enough sun for one day."

Lorna glanced down, seeing more than her nose was pink. With the wind coming off the water, she hadn't realized she was getting sunburned.

They dressed and mounted their horses. As they rode away, Lorna glanced back over her shoulder, reluctant to leave their sandy domain. It had been an afternoon of adventures and new experiences that she would always remember, and she sensed that something very special had happened between her and Nathan during their lovemaking there.

She turned in her saddle and asked Nathan, "Do you still have the pearl?"

"It's here, safe and sound," he replied, patting his shirt pocket.

Lorna smiled. The pearl was precious to her. But not because of its monetary value. It was a gift from the sea to help her remember her wonderful afternoon on the beach with the man she loved with all her heart and soul. And no matter what happened in the future, nothing could ever rob her of that memory.

Chapter 19

When Nathan and Lorna rode down the beach, as it curved into the narrow inlet that formed the bay, Nathan reined in and stared out at the bay in surprise.

Lorna brought her horse to a halt beside his and asked, "What's wrong?"

"The *Argus* is back."

"I wasn't aware the ship had left."

"Yes, three days ago. Isaac took her to Syracuse to buy supplies for our march on Tripoli."

"Well, if he was supposed to come back, why do you act so surprised?"

"Syracuse is a four-day sail from here. He couldn't possibly have made it there and back in three." Nathan stared at the ship that was anchored across the bay thoughtfully, then said, "Something has happened. I can sense it. Come on! Let's get back to the palace."

As soon as the two rode through one of the en-

trances to the palace grounds, they knew Nathan's
suspicions were true. The place was in an uproar, with
people rushing here and there and wagons being
driven madly back and forth, those vehicles being
driven away loaded down with furniture and household items. At the front of the palace a steady stream
of household servants was carrying baggage down the
steps to a wagon parked there, and from the corner of
her eye Lorna thought she got a glimpse of Hamet
and some of his friends riding horseback through the
gate on the opposite side of the grounds, the prince's
face as white as a sheet.

As they tried to thread their horses through the
crowd of people and crush of wagons, Captain Hull
rushed up to them and asked Nathan, "Where in the
hell have you been? I've been looking everywhere for
you."

"We went for a ride along the Mediterranean,"
Nathan answered. "What's going on?"

"We're pulling out of Derna."

Nathan drew his head back in surprise. "Pulling
out? You mean we're marching on Tripoli right now?"

"No, we're pulling out by sea. There isn't going to
be any march on Tripoli. The war is over. The pasha
signed a peace treaty two days ago. I was hailed down
at sea and given the news."

Nathan was momentarily stunned by the sudden
news. "It's over? Just like that?" he asked in disbelief.
"What brought all this on?"

"Yusef. He was impressed by Eaton's marching
his army across the desert and was shocked when we
captured Derna. Then when he heard that Eaton was
planning on marching on the capital and the navy was
preparing to launch a simultaneous attack by sea, he
sued for peace."

"He surrendered?" Nathan asked, still finding it hard to believe.

"If you mean unconditionally, no. Yusef promised to keep the peace and behave himself, and if we were ever at war again, to exchange prisoners of war and never again ask for ransom." An embarrassed flush rose on Hull's face before he admitted, "However, Yusef said he wanted ransom just this last time, and we agreed. We handed over sixty thousand dollars and eighty-nine Arab prisoners of war for our men."

A sudden fury rose in Nathan. "Are you telling me we *still* paid ransom?" he asked angrily. "Goddammit, Isaac, that's what this whole war was about! Our refusing to bow to the Barbary pirates' extortion. And now after four years of fighting, we turned around and did just that!"

"We made our point, and when you stop to consider that it's only about two hundred dollars per man, it wasn't a bad bargain."

"We didn't have to bargain! We had Yusef where we wanted him. We could have forced him to surrender unconditionally, demanded his abdication, even his death. That's what another Arab would have done. That's the only thing these Barbary rulers understand. Destruction!"

"But he promised—"

"Promises mean nothing to these Barbary rulers. They're just words. Yusef will behave himself for a while, then be right back to his same old tricks. We've accomplished nothing with this war. Absolutely nothing! What idiot agreed to this precipitous peace?"

"Tobias Lear."

"Lear?" Nathan asked in surprise. "How in the hell did that stupid diplomat get in on this? Why, you could put what he knows about North Africa and Arabs in the eye of a needle and still have room to thread it. I thought the navy was supposed to handle any negotiations."

"We were, but Commodore Barron's condition got much worse and Lear stepped in and took over the negotiations. Eaton is just as furious about it as you are. He swears Lear did it just to make a name for himself and sold out both us and Hamet. Personally, I feel just as strongly as you two. It's going to make our country look foolish in the eyes of the world." Isaac paused, then said in exasperation, "Dammit, if Preble were still in command, it would never have happened. Lear was always pressing him to make a quick peace at terms Preble thought were ridiculous. Preble came here to fight, to win. All of us in the navy did. But the war is over now regardless of how any of us personally feel about it. I've been ordered to remove all Americans and Hamet and his friends from Derna and transport them to Syracuse."

Nathan realized that he had been unfairly taking his anger and frustration out on Isaac, and that his friend was just as disappointed and disgusted as he. Just short of victory, the navy had been robbed of its goal. He fought his feelings down and looked about him, saying, "So that's what's going on here? You're evacuating?"

"Yes, and thank God Eaton finally agreed to leave. But I had a battle on my hands, believe me. He kept insisting he was going to stay and see this revolution through and put Hamet back on the throne."

"That doesn't surprise me in the least. He's a determined, stubborn cuss. He would never have gotten that army across the desert if he wasn't. What changed his mind?"

"The dangerous conditions here in Derna. Somehow or another the news of the peace treaty and our planned departure leaked out, and the citizens are in an uproar. I can't believe how fast the word spread. They think Yusef is going to punish them for surrendering and that we're abandoning them to his wrath. To make matters worse, Eaton's army is totally out of control. They're just as angry at us and out for blood. We're sitting on a keg of dynamite that's about to explode at any minute. There have already been reports of violence breaking out over the city. That's why I was so desperate to find you and Lorna."

Suddenly Nathan realized what all of the hurry was about. His anger at the hasty peace was completely forgotten as he turned his full attention to the dangerous situation they were in. "As soon as we've packed our things we'll be with you."

Isaac looked about him anxiously. "Can't you just leave your things? The last baggage wagon is ready to leave."

"I can leave *my* things behind—I can always pick up something to wear on your ship—but Lorna is going to need some clothing. You go ahead and leave. We've already held you up long enough and you're needed down at the harbor to oversee things."

"No, I'll wait for you."

"That's not necessary. We'll lash Lorna's chest to her horse and ride double on mine. Hell, we'll probably get there before you do in that slow wagon."

"You've got a point there," Hull admitted. "All right, we'll leave," he said, whirling around and walking to the baggage wagon where two marines were anxiously waiting. "But don't dally," he called over his shoulder.

Nathan didn't. He was already rushing up the stairs to the palace, with Lorna practically having to run to keep up with his long, swift strides. They hurried through deserted halls, his boots beating a tattoo on the marble floor, then bounded up the steps. By the time they reached their apartment on the third floor, Lorna was winded.

As soon as Nathan opened the chest, Lorna was shoving her clothing into it, not even bothering to fold it. As they hastily packed, Lorna was vastly relieved that the war was over and she wouldn't have to worry about Nathan's safety. Then it occurred to her that she didn't know what was in store for her from this point on. Her bitter-sweet season of joy had come to an abrupt end. But before Lorna could even begin to ponder what her future with Nathan might, or might not, be, he was rushing her back out the door and down the hallway.

As they stepped through the front door Nathan saw that the palace grounds were deserted. There wasn't a soul in sight where there had been bedlam less than ten minutes before, and a strange, ominous silence hung in the air. Then he came to a dead halt when he noticed their horses had disappeared. "Dammit, don't tell me that stupid Arab groom took our horses back to the stables," he said in disgust.

Lorna jumped when she heard the sound of gunshots not too far in the distance. "Come on," Nathan said urgently, the sound galvanizing him. "Let's get our horses and get the hell out of here!"

As they rounded the corner of the palace on their way to the stables, Nathan and Lorna again came to an abrupt halt, seeing a crowd of angry Arabs coming toward them and waving clubs over their heads. When the Arabs spied them, they started running toward them, shouting curses and threats, murder in their eyes.

Nathan tossed Lorna's chest down on the ground, grabbed her wrist, whirled around, and took off at a dead run for the front gate, dragging her behind him. Then, seeing another crowd of furious Arabs swarm-

ing through it, he reversed his course and headed
back for the palace.

"Where are we going?" Lorna asked as they tore
up the marble steps.

"To the back door."

They tore through the deserted palace, following
a maze of hallways that ran to the kitchen at the back
of the huge building, the sound of their footsteps
echoing through the empty rooms and sounding inor-
dinately loud to Lorna. When they reached the back
door, Nathan flung it open. What he saw made his
blood run cold. Another angry crowd of Arabs was
rushing toward them from that direction, screaming
for their death, many waving scimitars in the air, the
wicked curved blades glittering in the sunlight. He
slammed the door, shot the bolt to, and leaned against
it, cursing himself for a fool. They should have left
when they had the opportunity, but he'd had no idea
things were going to move that fast, or that their
horses were going to disappear. He glanced at Lorna
and saw her face was ashen with fright. Realizing they
were completely surrounded, a black despair filled
him. They'd be literally torn to pieces by that furious
crowd, beaten with their clubs and ripped apart by
their swords. They were facing a horrible, violent
death, and he had no one but himself to blame. The
thought of Lorna meeting such a death was more
than Nathan could bear. Remembering that there
was a gun in their apartment, he made a split-second
decision. He would kill her before he would let her be
subjected to such a painful, terrifying death. At least
he could make it quick and merciful for her, providing he could whip up the courage to do it. Grim-
lipped, he took her hand in his and hurried from the
kitchen.

"Where are we going now?" Lorna asked.

"To our apartment, where my gun is. We'll make a last stand there," Nathan answered, not wanting Lorna to realize the terrible thing he was contemplating.

Lorna suddenly dug in her heels. "But we can escape!"

Nathan whirled and faced her. "We *can't* escape! We're trapped! Don't you realize that?"

"But we're not trapped! That's what I'm trying to tell you. I just remembered something. When Hamet was taking me on a tour through the palace, he showed me a secret passage that he used to escape when he was forced to flee from Derna when the last revolution failed."

Nathan's terrible despair disappeared like a puff of smoke to be replaced with excitement. "Where is it?"

"In his study." Reversing their roles and pulling on Nathan's arm, she rushed from the kitchen, saying, "Hurry! It's this way."

By the time they reached Hamet's study, they could hear the Arabs running through the hallways and yelling, their bloodcurdling screams bouncing off the marble walls and making their hair stand up on the napes of their necks. Lorna pushed aside a heavy tapestry hanging on one wall and said, "It's behind here."

Nathan frowned, then said, "I don't see any door."

"No, he said one of the bottom blocks of marble is movable, that it can be shoved aside."

From where he was standing Nathan could have sworn the wall was solid marble. He got down on his hands and knees and quickly examined the bottom of the wall, then, finding what looked like a hairline crack in the marble, he shoved on the stone next to it.

Nothing happened. Aware of the noisy Arabs getting closer and closer, he pushed harder. Suddenly, the heavy granite block gave, making a creaking noise as it opened an inch or two. Grabbing hold of the side of the block, Nathan forced it open, seeing a square barely large enough for a person to crawl through. He stuck his head through the hole in the wall and felt around tentatively, then said, "Yes, there's an open space back here." Taking hold of Lorna's hand, he pulled her to her knees and said, "Hurry and crawl through."

Lorna was just a little reluctant to crawl into a dark, unknown space, but the sounds of the berserk Arabs in the next room shrieking and breaking things as they tore the room apart quickly overcame her hesitancy. She crawled through the opening and a short way into the passageway, giving Nathan room to get in. As soon as he had entered behind her, he shoved on the block to close it, and they were engulfed in total blackness and an oppressive silence.

Lorna was aware of Nathan feeling around to determine the size of the opening, although she couldn't see him. Still, she jumped in fright when he whispered, "I think it's big enough for us to stand."

He stood, then helped Lorna to her feet. Holding her hand, he moved down the passageway slowly, groping his way with his other hand and one foot. In the inky blackness, with the musty smell of stale air in her nostrils, and the heavy silence, Lorna felt as if the walls of the passageway were closing in on her and she couldn't breathe. She knew it was just her imagination getting the better of her, but it was still a terrifying experience, so much so that her heart was racing twice as fast as when they had fled the Arabs. To add to her acute discomfort, as they made their way through the passageway, she was plagued with fears that they wouldn't find their way out. Hamet had given her no clue as to what to look for at the other end. If it was another movable block, how in the world would they ever find it in this blackness?

Nathan came to an abrupt halt and Lorna bumped into him. "There's some steps here that go down," he informed her. "Test your footing before you move and be careful. We don't know how far down they go or how narrow they are."

Lorna was glad for the steps. Trying to negotiate them in the dark kept her mind from her claustrophobia and her distressing thoughts. When they reached the bottom, she sensed that they were in a wider passageway and stretched out her free arm, groping in the dark and feeling nothing. "Where do you think we are?"

"I assume this is an underground tunnel. Did Hamet tell you where this thing ends?" Nathan asked, thinking he hoped it didn't end in one of the many caves along the Mediterranean coast. If that were the case, they would be a long way from the harbor when they left the tunnel, and Hull couldn't wait forever for them to show up.

"No, I never even thought to ask him."

As they slowly made their way down the tunnel, Lorna felt something large and furry run across her foot and brush against her leg where her short boots ended. She bit back a terrified scream. Hearing her gasp, Nathan asked, "What's wrong?"

"There are wild animals of some kind down here," she answered fearfully, looking wildly about in the darkness. "One just brushed against my leg."

"It was probably a rat."

"No, it was much larger than that. More the size of a large cat."

"Sewer rats get that big."

His answer did nothing to soothe Lorna's fear. If anything she was even more terrified. "What if they attack us?"

Nathan heard the fear in Lorna's voice. He slipped his arm around her shoulders and brought her side up against his, saying, "They won't bother us as long as we don't bother them."

Walking with her side pressed full length against Nathan's and his strong arm around her shoulders, Lorna felt much easier. But still, she couldn't wait to get out of the tunnel with its frightening darkness and terrifying rats. It seemed an eternity before she saw a small shaft of light ahead of her. Then almost as soon as she had seen it, the tunnel abruptly narrowed and ended, leaving them having to stand with their backs half bent.

It turned out the light was coming through a crack in a trap door above them. Cautiously, Nathan pushed the door open a few inches and peered outside. He couldn't see much. They were surrounded by thick bushes. Lifting himself from the tunnel, he investigated further, then returned and helped Lorna from the tunnel, whispering as he did so, "We're apparently in a remote corner of the courtyard. I didn't see anyone around, but be as quiet as you possibly can and keep your head down."

Using the bushes to screen them, they cautiously made their way to the gate in the back wall of the courtyard, hearing the sounds of gunshots and angry Arab shouts in the distance. When Nathan opened the gate, the rusty hinges squeaked loudly, making Lorna cringe for fear the noise would be heard by an Arab somewhere. Nathan looked about the alley and, seeing it was empty, pushed the door wide open and said, "This is where we make a run for it."

Taking her hand in his, Nathan tore off, again

dragging Lorna behind him. As they rounded the corner and raced into another alley, they came to a skid-
ding halt, finding themselves face to face with an
Arab. As soon as the bearded man recovered from his
surprise, he glared at Nathan furiously and pulled his
scimitar from beneath his robe. Nathan pushed Lorna
aside and pulled his dagger, saying, "Get back, and if
anything happens to me, run like hell!"

Nathan barely had time to jump back from the
Arab's sword as the angry man made a thrust against
him, the blade ripping across his shirt and slicing it
open. Then, poised for battle at a half crouch, the two
men circled one another warily, while Lorna watched
with breathless fear, thinking that Nathan didn't have
a ghost of a chance to defend himself with his short
dagger against the Arab's long, wicked-looking sword.
She screamed as the Arab's curved blade swung
through the air, flashing in the sunlight, then gasped
in disbelief when Nathan deflected the blow with his
blade, the meeting of steel against steel making
sparks fly through the air. When the Arab swung
again, Nathan threw himself into the lunge, his knife
sliding down the Arab's blade until their hilts met
with an impact that jarred his shoulder, then, with a
strength born of fierce determination, held the Arab's
blade in the air in middescent.

For a moment the two men stood, their blades
still locked in a life-and-death struggle above their
heads and their eyes glaring at one another with un-
mitigated fury. Then, in a lightning-quick movement,
Nathan wrapped his leg around the Arab's and
slammed his body into the man, pushing him backward as both men fell to the ground, the Arab grunting in surprise at the sudden turn of events, then
crying out in alarm when he hit the packed sand so
hard that it knocked his sword from his hand. Seeing

Nathan raising his dagger for the killing blow, the Arab quickly caught his wrist, and the two men rolled over and over in the sand, the Arab's robe billowing around them as they wrestled for possession of the knife.

Lorna had watched the fight up until then with a feeling of stunned helplessness, but now she looked frantically around for something to use as a weapon, thinking to hit the Arab over the head if she could find a rock. Seeing none, she caught sight of something else from the corner of her eye and turned around to find another Arab tearing down the alley waving a club in the air. As he came closer, Lorna thought she was looking death in the eye and stood frozen to the spot.

Seeing the new threat running down the alley toward them as he rolled over, Nathan called out to Lorna, "Run! Run for your life! Dammit, Lorna! Get out of here!"

His frantic call shocked Lorna out of the paralyzing fear she had been feeling. Then, as a sudden inspiration came, she crouched on the sand, and turned halfway away from the Arab rushing down on her, pretending to be cowering in fear. The Arab came to a stop and towered over her, his black eyes glittering with immense satisfaction at seeing how terrified she was of him as he raised the club high over his head. Suddenly Lorna jumped to her feet and threw the sand she had been scooping up in her hands right into the Arab's face, catching the man completely by surprise and blinding him. Without even thinking, the Arab dropped his club, his hands flying to his eyes where the gritty particles of sand were stinging fiercely. Seizing her opportunity, Lorna swept up the fallen club and swung it with all her might, then grimaced at the thudding sound it made as it hit the Arab's head.

As the Arab fell to the ground, Lorna turned, intending to use her new weapon against the Arab Nathan was struggling with. She quickly saw that Nathan didn't need her help. While she had been fighting her battle, he had ended his and was rising from the Arab lying limp on the ground still holding the bloody dagger he had just sunk into the man's chest.

His breath still rasping his chest, Nathan looked from Lorna to the man she had felled with something akin to wonder, not having seen her throw sand in the man's eyes and not knowing how she managed to accomplish her remarkable feat. Suddenly he was filled with two conflicting emotions: pride in her courage and anger that she had not obeyed him and had put herself in danger. The two emotions warred until the latter won out and he thundered, "I thought I told you to run!"

Lorna's anger came rushing to the surface. How dare he yell at her after she had just saved his life, for she knew as soon as the Arab had clubbed her senseless, he would have gone for Nathan. "Don't you yell at me that way, you ungrateful bastard! I just saved your life!"

"But *you* could have been killed! You should have run for your life."

"And leave that second Arab to knock your head off while your back was turned! Absolutely not!"

Nathan wondered at the fierce look on her face. Did she care enough to risk her life for him, or had her protectiveness been purely an unmediated reflex? He didn't have long to wonder. Hearing the sounds of Arabs yelling behind them, he looked over his shoulder and saw a crowd of frenzied townspeople running toward them, brandishing every imaginable kind of weapon, from knives to pots and pans and rocks.

He whirled around, caught Lorna's wrist, and took off at a dead run in the opposite direction, almost jerking her arm from its socket in his rapid flight and sheathing his bloody dagger as he ran. They tore down the narrow alley, the sounds of the angry crowd chasing them ringing in their ears and their boots drumming on the packed ground as they twisted and turned down one alley, then another, and another. Just when it looked as if they had lost their pursuers and might have a chance to catch their breath, they came face to face with another crowd of crazed Arabs. Whirling around, they beat a hasty retreat, running as fast as they could and weaving their way through a maze of alleys until Lorna feared they would get hopelessly lost.

Then suddenly they emerged on a wide street just a few blocks from the waterfront and heard the roar of cannons over the yells of the Arabs chasing them. Lorna almost jumped out of her skin when a ball whizzed over them and hit one of the towering palm trees, sending flaming palm leaves and pieces of bark showering down all around them. A split second later, another ball smashed into a nearby house, crumbling it and throwing a cloud of thick dust and smoke in their path.

When they emerged from the cloud, coughing from the choking dust and smoke, Lorna looked wildly about her, seeing the barricade the Greeks had set up in the street. Then spying the muzzle of the cannon facing them over the top of the barricade, she dug in her heels, calling over the din of noises around her, "No, Nathan! Turn back! We've got to find another way to escape."

Nathan jerked her arm, dragging her behind

him, calling over his shoulder, "Those Greeks aren't firing at us. They're covering our escape. Now, dammit, run!"

Lorna glanced over her shoulder and saw the Arabs flowing out of every side street, their long robes billowing as they ran. Many carried clubs, but just as many were wielding swords and carrying muskets, guns that *were* aimed at them. The bullet that whizzed by them gave her the impetus to run even faster, her long hair streaming out behind her as she and Nathan flew past the barricade and down the street, the rough cobblestones tearing at the tender soles of her feet where her soft leather boots had been ripped apart.

By the time they reached the long, partially burned-out wharf, Lorna couldn't run anymore. Her breath came in tortured gasps that seemed to sear her lungs, and there was a painful stitch in her side. She fell to her knees, drinking in deep drafts of air. Nathan bent and scooped her up in his arms, running down the long wharf and cursing under his breath as he passed the sinking Tripolitan fishing boats the American sailors had banged holes into before they left. He wished they hadn't been so damned efficient. If Isaac had given up on him and Lorna and left the wharf, they might have had a chance to make it to the *Argus* in one of the fishing boats. Anxiously he searched the end of the pier as he ran, but could see no sign of the longboat. Then, glancing over his shoulder and seeing that the frenzied, howling Arabs had broken through the Greeks' barricade and were swarming down the wharf behind them, he once again felt a black despair coming over him.

It was Lorna who spied the longboat first, sitting in the water at the very end of the pier where the wood had been blocking their view. She, too, had been afraid the boat had already left. Feeling immensely relieved, she cried out, "There it is! They waited for us!"

Nathan was surprised to see that not only was the boat waiting, but Isaac was in it. He came to a stop at the end of the pier and swung Lorna down to his friend's strong arms, then jumped into the boat as Isaac sat Lorna down on one of the seats. "What are you doing here?" Nathan asked Isaac, his breath coming in short gasps. "I would have thought you would be on the *Argus.*"

"I wanted to be sure my men waited until the last possible minute for you to show up." Hull shook his head, then said, "Christ, Nathan! Don't ever scare me like that again. I thought you two had been killed for sure."

"There were a few times there when I thought we wouldn't make it myself," Nathan admitted, then sat down on the seat by Lorna to catch his breath.

Isaac turned and called out to his men, "For God's sake, hurry up with those mooring lines! That angry crowd is almost upon us."

A second later the lines fell into the water and the sailors set their backs to rowing like mad, their muscles straining against their striped shirts. Hull sat down on the seat in front of Nathan and Lorna, picked up an oar, and began rowing too.

Having recovered somewhat from their wild run through the city, Lorna looked around her, seeing the only other passengers were a few of Hamet's friends sitting behind her, the Arabs looking none too happy at being made to wait for their appearance. Lorna gave them a "go to hell" look and turned back around, catching just a glimpse of the crowd of angry Arabs at the end of the wharf they were rowing away from before bullets splashed into the water all around them, while one hit the boat with a dull thudding noise.

"Get down!" Nathan yelled, catching her around the back of her neck and bending her over double as another wave of bullets whizzed over their heads.

The sailor in front of them and sitting beside Isaac grunted in pain as a bullet hit him. He dropped his oar. Nathan leaned forward and saw the blood streaming between the sailor's fingers where he held the wound on his shoulder. Crawling over the seat, Nathan said, "Climb back to my seat, lad. I'll take your place at the oar."

The sailor shot a glance at Hull, then said bravely, "Thank you, sir, but I can do it."

"Do what Captain Sloan said!" Hull barked.

Having been ordered to relinquish his oar, the sailor obeyed, secretly glad that his captain had insisted. He'd never dreamed a bullet wound could hurt so much. As he seated himself beside Lorna, his freckled face ashen with pain, Lorna rose from where she had been ducking to keep from being hit and pushed his hand away from the wound, saying, "Let me see."

Nathan glanced back from where he was rowing and saw Lorna. "Get down!" he called over his shoulder.

Lorna ignored his call and pushed the sailor's shirt back from his shoulder, revealing the ugly wound. "We need a bandage to stop that bleeding," she muttered, half to herself.

Nathan pulled back on his oar, glanced back, and saw Lorna had not obeyed him. As a fresh wave of bullets spattered the water all around them, his fear for her sent his heart racing in his chest. "Goddammit, Lorna! Get down!" he thundered, his yell so loud it made the other sailors jump and miss a stroke of their oars.

Lorna jerked around in her seat and yelled back, "If you can man an oar with these bullets flying all around, I can help this wounded man. Now you mind your business and I'll mind mine!"

Her retort brought astonished gasps from the Arabs, smiles of admiration from the sailors, and an amused chuckle from Isaac. Nathan's reaction was one of frustrated fury.

Ignoring the glares Nathan sent her over his broad shoulder each time he pulled back on the oar, Lorna looked about her for something to use as a bandage. "Don't worry about me, ma'am," the wounded, pale-faced sailor said, embarrassed at being caught in the middle. "I'll be all right. Maybe, you'd better do like your husband said."

"Now don't you start giving me orders!" Lorna snapped. Then, seeing the startled expression on the youth's face, she said in a gentler tone of voice, "This wound is bleeding badly. It needs attention. Now, not later."

Lorna looked at the shirt on Nathan's back, thinking it would make an excellent bandage, but she hated to interrupt him in his rowing. Besides, he was furious with her for not obeying him. She glanced over her shoulder, then spied the turban on the Arab sitting behind her.

She turned in her seat and held out her hand, demanding in Arabic, "Give me your turban. I need it to make a bandage for this man's wound."

When the Arab drew back, an affronted expression on his swarthy face, Lorna said angrily, "If it wasn't for these men securing your escape, you would have been torn into little pieces by that crowd back there. Now you give me that turban—or I'll personally throw you overboard!"

Seeing the furious look on Lorna's face, the Arab didn't doubt her threat for one minute, even if she was just a lowly woman. Sheepishly he handed over his turban.

Lorna quickly unrolled it and tore it in two, balling up half and placing it over the bleeding wound and using the other half to secure the bandage. By the time she had finished, the sailor's face was totally blanched of all color from loss of blood and beads of perspiration stood out on his forehead from the pain.

Lorna wrapped her arm around him and said, "Lean on my shoulder."

The sailor was too weak to object. He felt if he didn't lean on something he would pass out. He slumped against Lorna, laying his head on her shoulder, the blood seeping from his bandage staining her *entarie*.

By this time they were out of range of the Arabs' guns, even though they were still firing in their rage. Lorna looked back at the waterfront, seeing the clouds of smoke from the Greeks' cannons still floating in the air. She noted that the cannons were silent now. All she could hear was the flat cracks of the muskets. She was left to assume that the brave Greeks had been either killed or taken prisoner.

When they reached the *Argus*, the wounded sailor was the first to ascend the Jacob's ladder, half-unconscious as two crewmates helped him up the rope. As he went over the rail and collapsed on the deck, he was quickly picked up by other crewmates and carried away, the ship's surgeon examining his wound as they went. Lorna scrambled up the rope ladder when it came her turn, bringing a smile of pride to Nathan's lips despite his earlier irritation with her for not obeying him.

As soon as the longboat was pulled from the water, the anchor was raised, the heavy cable shrieking shrilly in the air as two husky sailors strained to turn the revolving capstan where the cable was rolled up. A moment later the sails came tumbling down from where they had been reefed on the masts, the canvas snapping loudly as it caught the wind and then billowing as the sails filled.

"Come on," Nathan said, taking Lorna's arm, "let's go down to Isaac's cabin. These sailors have got enough to contend with with all these Arabs standing around, without us getting in the way too."

Chapter 20

As Nathan rushed Lorna down the companion-way to Isaac's cabin, he was forced to admit to himself that he hadn't been concerned about getting in the way of the sailors on deck. He had only said that as an excuse to get Lorna alone. After their close brush with death he had an urgent need to hold her in his arms, to make love to her, a need that bordered on desperation, as if only by loving her could he confirm the fact that they were truly alive.

Lorna was just as anxious to be alone with Nathan as he hurried her to the cabin, until she remembered that her freedom had finally been secured and that she was facing something she had been dreading all along. She was no closer than she had been in the first place to knowing Nathan's true feelings for her or what her future with him might or might not be; and after their nerve-wracking escape from the Arabs, the uncertainties of their future together and her doubts about his feelings for her suddenly became more than she could bear. She couldn't keep her fears and emotions bottled up inside her any longer. The tension was so intense that she feared her nerves were going to shatter into a million pieces if she didn't find out just where she stood.

As soon as Nathan had shut the door of the cabin behind them, she turned to him and blurted out the thing that had preyed on her mind and tormented her the most. "Are you going to divorce me now?"

Lorna's unexpected and blunt question caught Nathan completely off guard. He felt as if he had been kicked by a mule. Then, as he recovered, he realized that his worst fears had come true. Their marriage had meant nothing to Lorna but a means of escaping her predicament and securing her freedom. Suddenly Nathan felt used and deeply hurt. Then anger came rushing to his defense.

He stepped away from her and stood as rigid as a board. His green eyes glittered with barely suppressed fury as he said in a tight voice, "If divorce is what you want, it can be quickly arranged. All I need is a Muslim witness, and with all these damn Arabs about, that will be no problem."

Before Lorna could open her mouth, Nathan stormed from the cabin, slamming the door behind him. What she wanted? Lorna thought in horror. My God, no! She didn't want a divorce. She thought *he* did. Why, at this minute he might be saying the words that would sever their marriage. No! She had to stop him!

She reached for the doorknob, then jumped back in surprise as the door was flung open with a loud bang. Nathan stood in the doorway, his face looking like a thundercloud.

"I *won't* give you a divorce!" he said in a furious

voice. "Whether you like it or not, we're married, before God and man, and that's the way it's going to stay!"

As Lorna opened her mouth to tell him she didn't want a divorce, Nathan quickly said, "No! No arguing! I won't give you up." He paused, an almost pained expression flicking across his face before he said, "I can't!"

Lorna heard the anguish in his voice and sensed the moment of truth was at hand. Her heart raced wildly in her chest as she asked in a breathless voice, "Why—why can't you give me up?"

"Because I love you, goddammit!" he roared.

Perversely, instead of making her happy, the words angered Lorna. She had gone through all that misery, months of sheer hell, for nothing, while he could have spared her from that pain and anguish just by saying a few words.

"Then why in the devil didn't you tell me that?" she demanded in an enraged voice, her eyes flashing dangerously. "A woman has a right to know when a man loves her."

Nathan shook his head in exasperation, not understanding Lorna's anger. Hell, women were supposed to be pleased when a man told them he loved them. "I did."

A look of surprise came over Lorna's face before she asked in a puzzled voice, "When did you tell me you loved me?"

"This afternoon, on the beach. I told you in French and lingua franca."

Lorna glared at him, saying hotly, "You know damned well I don't understand either language!"

Nathan winced, knowing he had taken the coward's way out when he told her he loved her. "Well, dammit, I shouldn't have to tell you!" he threw back, coming to his own defense. "I came after you when the Tuareg captured you, didn't I? I was prepared to search the whole Sahara for you if necessary. I would have spent a fortune for you if Chedlya hadn't given the money back. I married you. I even killed to protect you, both those Tuareg and that man this afternoon. What more does a man have to do to prove he loves a woman?"

What more, indeed? Lorna thought, a warm smile coming over her face at the many ways Nathan had shown his love. She stepped forward and slipped her arms around Nathan's waist, saying softly, "Just say the words. This time in English, please."

A wary look came into Nathan's eyes. "No. Not until you tell me."

Lorna was surprised when she saw the fear in his eyes, then realized for the first time that he had felt just as vulnerable and insecure as she. What fools we've been, she thought. She wrapped her arms around his neck and cried out in a joyous voice, "Yes, I love you! Yes! Yes! Yes! I love the way you walk, your deep voice, the way your hair curls around your ears. I love your beautiful eyes, the little scar on your cheek, every inch of you. I love your strength, your adventuresome spirit, the excitement I feel when I'm around you, the way you make me come alive—"

Nathan placed his fingers over her mouth, chuckling and saying, "All right! You've convinced me." Then his voice dropped an octave as he said softly, "And I love you."

Lorna closed her eyes, savoring the words she had waited so long to hear, thinking them the most beautiful in the world.

For a moment they stood in the circle of each other's arms, enjoying their happiness at knowing each loved the other, Lorna's head tucked under

Nathan's chin. Then, breaking their embrace, Nathan took Lorna's shoulders in his hands and pushed her back. She opened her eyes to see that a stern expression had come over his face.

"And while we're clearing the air," he said in a firm voice, "let's get a few other things straight between us. If you think I'm going to leave you someplace while I'm at sea and just pop in now and then, you're sadly mistaken. You're sailing with me. I didn't search the Sahara to find you only to turn around and leave you behind. Is that clear?"

She would get to see the world at the side of this exciting man? Why, that would be absolutely wonderful! But she didn't want to tell Nathan how she felt. He seemed to be enjoying playing the role of the domineering husband. Just this once she'd let him think he was getting his way. "If you say so, darling," she replied sweetly.

Nathan cocked his head, a suspicious gleam coming into his eyes. Why is she acting so meek? he wondered. Is it a trick? Then pushing his suspicions aside, he said in an equally firm voice, "And another thing. We're getting remarried as soon as we reach America. I won't have anyone questioning the legality of our marriage because we were married in a Muslim ceremony in a foreign country."

Even though Lorna didn't feel the need, she didn't think it was a bad idea, particularly in view of the fact that most Christians considered Muslims nothing but heathens, and she didn't want anything to mar the perfection of their marriage. And it was going to be perfect, she vowed. She would do everything in her power to make it so. She nodded her head in silent agreement.

Nathan breathed a sigh of relief, then said in a

husky voice, "And now that's all settled, I'm going to do what I had in mind when I brought you here."

Lorna watched as his eyes darkened with desire, feeling a thrill of excitement run through her. When he picked her up and carried her to the bunk in the corner of the room, she snuggled closer, burying her face in the crook of his warm neck and drinking in his intoxicating scent, then sighed in utter bliss.

When he laid her on the bunk, then lowered his body over hers, he whispered against her lips, "Now, I'm going to show you how much I love you. When I'm finished, there will never again be any doubt in your mind."

Lorna framed his face in her hands and answered, "Nor will there be any doubt in yours."

It was a promise that they both fulfilled.

Epilogue

Two months later Lorna stood on the deck of the *Seabird* and watched as Gibraltar disappeared in the distance, the huge, rocky peninsula looking bloodred in the light of the setting sun. The Mediterranean was behind her now as they beat their way westward across the broad Atlantic.

Lorna's mind drifted back over the time that had elapsed since they sailed from Derna. The *Argus* had taken her and Nathan to Malta and dropped them off before continuing to Syracuse, and she had made her sad farewell to Hamet, knowing that she would never see the ill-fated prince again. Then for six weeks after the *Argus*'s departure, she and Nathan waited for the *Seabird* to return to Malta from making a run to Greece, first shopping for new wardrobes for both of them, then spending their time leisurely sightseeing on the small British island, eating at its many fine restaurants and attending its excellent theaters. It was a second honeymoon for them, one much more soul satisfying than their "seven fig days," since their deep feelings for one another were in the open and they could completely relax and enjoy each other's company to the fullest.

When the *Seabird* returned to port, Nathan introduced her to his crew and his first mate, a congenial Scotsman whose burr was so thick Lorna could barely understand a word he said. Because of her nervousness at meeting the men who sailed under Nathan, she hadn't noticed the pride in Nathan's eyes and voice as he introduced her, but the crew had, fascinated with the lovely woman who could bring such a look of warmth to their steely-eyed, fiercely independent captain, a man they had thought never to be smitten by any woman.

In the days that followed, Lorna spent very little time alone with Nathan as he made the hectic preparations for their sailing and then assumed his duties as captain of the ship, for the weather had been stormy since they left Malta, and he had often not come to their cabin at night until she had fallen asleep. But Lorna didn't mind. She knew that she would have to share him with his responsibilities, and just knowing he was near was enough for her.

Hearing Nathan call a command to one of the sailors high up in the rigging brought Lorna back to the present. She turned and saw him standing on the quarterdeck, the wind ruffling his dark hair around his tanned face and molding his shirt to his broad shoulders and chest. He's in his element here, she thought, in the wide open spaces of the ocean, on the deck of the ship that he so ably commands, the crew, who obviously worship the ground he walks on, jumping to obey his orders. He's part of the sea itself, as free as the wind that blows over it, as uncontainable as the waters. And yet, he belongs to me.

She still found that hard to believe, or that they were actually sailing to America, their home when they weren't at sea.

Lorna could hardly wait to get to America, not only because she was anxious to see the country she had dreamed of for so long, but because she was excited at the prospect of meeting Nathan's family. He had told her all about his parents and two sisters who had families of their own and had assured her that they would welcome her into their warm, loving circle with open arms. She still found it hard to believe that she was actually going to belong to a family and would no longer be an orphan. Then, remembering something, she smiled secretively, and her hand slid down to cup her lower abdomen tenderly, thinking that she and Nathan were starting a family of their own.

Lorna had sensed that something special had happened on the beach that last day at Derna when they were riding away. Now she knew what that very special something was. She had conceived that afternoon, but she hadn't told Nathan he was to be a father yet. At first she wanted to be sure, then she hadn't found the right opportunity to tell him with his being so busy and all. Perhaps tonight, she thought, for today's weather had been perfect.

She stood at the rail, savoring her little secret and watching while the light faded from the sky to be replaced with an inky blackness. Then her breath caught as she saw a beautiful full moon rising over the water, the light casting a silver, glittering path that seemed to be dancing across the ocean. She was still gazing out at sea in mute admiration when Nathan stepped up to the rail beside her.

"It's a beautiful sight, isn't it?" he said softly. "Just the night I've been waiting for."

Lorna had been thinking the same thing. That this would be the perfect night to tell him about the baby. She turned from the rail and asked curiously, "What do you mean by that?"

"I've been waiting for a special night to give you this." He slipped his hand into his shirt pocket and brought out a ring. Taking her left hand, he slipped it on her finger, saying, "I know it's a little belated for a wedding ring, but I didn't want just to buy one when we reached Malta."

Lorna looked down at the pearl they had found on the beach at Derna. Tears of happiness came to her eyes. "I thought you lost it that day when you were rolling around in the dirt with that Arab who attacked you."

"No, I didn't lose it. I promised you I wouldn't, didn't I?"

"But I looked everywhere for it."

"I kept it in my shirt pocket until we reached Malta and I went to a jeweler to have it made into a ring. Do you like the setting?"

Lorna had no trouble seeing the ring in the bright moonlight. She turned her hand, thinking the little rubies that surrounded the pearl enhanced its unusual rosy color. "It's beautiful," she answered. But it could have been set in tin and it would still have been beautiful to Lorna for the memories that it represented.

"I could have bought something more expensive, but I thought the pearl would have more meaning since we found it together."

"Yes, our gift from the sea," Lorna agreed wholeheartedly, the memories of that afternoon on the beach washing over her.

Nathan was remembering, too. He slipped his arms around her waist and drew her closer to him. Lorna leaned her head against Nathan's chest and listened to his powerful heart beating against her ear, wondering if she should tell him her secret, then deciding against it. This was their special time together, just the two of them. The other could wait until tomorrow.

She slipped her arms around his broad shoulders and leaned back, looking up at his ruggedly handsome face and seeing his eyes were shimmering with the warmth of his love. An incredible happiness filled her. As it turned out, her time of joy with Nathan had not been just a brief season, as she had feared, but would be a lifetime of unbelievable happiness with the man she loved. She smiled, wondering what fool had said dreams don't come true. Her dream had. The proof was right here in her arms.